Sheila Turner Johnston has written many short stories and articles. She has also won prizes for fiction and non-fiction. She is the author of *Alice: a biography of Alice Milligan* (Colourpoint, 1994).
She has two grown-up sons and lives in Co Down, Northern Ireland, with her husband, two cats and an ancient, indestructible goldfish.
Maker of Footprints is her first published novel.

Maker of Footprints

Maker of Footprints

SHEILA TURNER JOHNSTON

Plover fiction

First published in the UK, 2008, by
Plover
an imprint of
Colourpoint Books
Colourpoint House
Jubilee Business Park
21 Jubilee Road
NEWTOWNARDS
Co Down
N Ireland
BT23 4YH
Tel: (028) 9182 6339
E-mail: editor@ploverfiction.com
Web: www.ploverfiction.com

A CIP catalogue record for this book is available from the British Library.

ISBN: 978-1-906578-18-3

Typeset by Colourpoint Books
Printed by CPI Cox & Wyman, Reading, RG1 8EX

First Edition
First Impression

For the three men in my life, in order of appearance:

Norman, Wesley, Malcolm

CHAPTER ONE

MEETING HIM WAS easy. It was knowing him that burned bone.

There are twists in fate; chances and turns; long straights in the flat lands and winding roads in mountains. In later years, Jenna Warwick traced the beginning of the rest of her life back to this conversation. Here, now, in her own house, in her own living room. If she had known and could have changed her direction, turned this way instead of that way, would she?

No. A hundred times No.

Adam stretched lazily and pushed himself out of her comfortable chair to give her a quick hug. "So you're going to meet my famous photographer brother at last. I'll pick you up about five tomorrow."

She lifted his coat from the sofa and handed it to him. "OK. That should give me time to finish my assignment." She chuckled. "Can't wait to meet his wife. I've never met a real London 'society gal' before."

He wriggled his shoulders into the coat. "I can't imagine why she married him. And she certainly didn't guess that Paul would drag her back to Belfast to live after only a few months of marriage." He pulled up the zip and went into the hall. "But then 'predictable' isn't Paul's middle name."

"I can't stand unpredictable people. They're dangerous." She yawned and pushed a chestnut wave from his forehead. "Now be a good boy and go home."

Adam kissed her. A boyfriend's kiss. Not a lover's kiss. He put a hand on her shoulder. "So when can I stop being a good boy?"

"When I stop being a good girl!"

She watched him walk down the dark row of terraced houses to his car, pulled half onto the pavement of the narrow city street. Solid, dependable Adam, sales rep for a printing company, the young man with the secure future, a man to bring home to meet your parents without a moment's worry that they wouldn't like him. A man who satisfied the exacting standards of a clergyman who was fiercely protective of his student daughter.

She brushed her teeth, slipped into her warm pyjamas, sat up in her narrow bed and read a chapter of a novel, lay down and listened to the midnight news. Then she went to sleep.

She remembered everything she had done that ordinary night; the night she had gone to bed untroubled, like a good girl.

~

Paul Shepherd took his foot off the edge of the sofa and propped his guitar against the wall. He turned back to the window.

"Here they are," he called.

Dianne came up beside him and put her hand round his waist. They watched Adam and Jenna getting out of the car pulled up behind Paul's in the short driveway, looking up at the house, looking round at the overgrown patch of garden. They saw Adam button his jacket and reach for Jenna's hand. Jenna smoothed her hair and they came towards the front door.

"Not as handsome as me, is he?"

Dianne's lip gloss sparkled. "I'd better be careful how I answer that!"

Paul put his fingers playfully round the back of her neck. "Very careful!"

Adam and Jenna had nearly reached the door. Dianne creased her lower lip with one varnished pink nail.

"God, what awful hair!" she said.

"You have exacting standards."

"You wouldn't have to be exacting to improve on that. She's just let it grow and done nothing with it."

Paul was quiet for a moment as Adam reached for the doorbell. Dianne went to answer it. Paul looked again at Jenna. She was only a short distance from him, on the other side of the window, but her attention was on the door. If you were being nice, you could describe her as 'fresh'. If you weren't, Paul thought, you could describe her as ... He watched her adjust the strap of her low slung canvas bag in a nervous gesture. She looked up as the door opened and Paul heard Dianne's words. "Adam, how lovely to see you again! And how lovely to meet you, Jenna. You look wonderful!"

He came into the hall and saw Jenna's smile as his willowy, sophisticated wife bent to kiss the air above her ear. He stopped. 'Plain', he decided.

Dianne's accent was cut as fine as crystal ringing beneath the tap of a spoon. When Jenna could see past the swaying blond hair which temporarily blocked her view, a man was standing in the hall behind her.

She had an impression of subtlety and power, of wariness and curiosity. He was dressed casually in a red sweatshirt and blue jeans, but his manner was anything but casual. His fingers were thrust stiffly into his pockets and, unlike his wife's greeting, Jenna merely received a brief nod before he turned his attention to his brother.

"You're late, little brother. I suppose you accidentally drove into the car park at Shaw's Bridge. Sat there with your girl and couldn't think of a thing to do, so you decided to get on the road again."

Jenna felt herself blushing. She was twenty-three. Time to stop the red face syndrome. Adam's arm tightened round her shoulders.

"England hasn't civilised you, I see," he said.

Dianne showed them into the sitting room. "Come and sit down. Dinner won't be long."

"It smells wonderful," Jenna said.

"Sorry the room's so small," Dianne lifted Paul's guitar and looked around. "Paul, couldn't you put this thing somewhere else? There isn't room to turn round in here!" She tossed her hair and smiled brightly at Jenna. "We'll get a proper house soon, once we've looked round. Not that we'll be staying, of course." She laughed. "Paul's much too much in demand in London."

The room was bigger than Jenna's sitting room, but she decided not to say so. Paul took the guitar from his wife and set it against the wall again.

"It's fine where it is." He turned away from her. "As are we," he added.

"Don't be silly, Paul." Dianne sighed, petulant. "Why, nothing goes on here. Well, not any more anyway."

Ignoring her, Paul settled himself into the chair near the door into the kitchen. The smell of herbs and roasting meat was strong in Jenna's nostrils. "So how's work, Adam?" said Paul.

"Fine. Busy."

Paul raised an eyebrow and leaned back. "Say something different this time." He waved a hand impatiently. "'I've six projects on the go.' 'I visited four clients in the last two days.' 'Have you heard Karen photocopied her bum?' Or do you really just lead a busy, boring life?"

"Don't be so mischievous, Paul!" Dianne turned to Jenna.

"Brothers. Who'd have one?"

"I have," said Jenna.

"Older or younger?"

"Younger. Luke. He's doing his A levels soon."

"Waste of time," said Paul. "He's more likely to become a millionaire with GCSEs and a brain."

"He has those as well," said Jenna.

Paul's eyes swivelled to her. "And so have you, I believe. A brain, I mean. First class honours, I hear, and going back for more. Are you with Adam to counteract the dizzy excitement of the university library?"

It was so ridiculous Jenna couldn't help a grin starting to tug. Before she could reply, Adam said, "Jenna's a bright girl. Stop embarrassing her."

Dianne broke in. "Why don't you take a walk round the back before it gets too dark, while I check the oven? It's a frightfully tiny patch. Just about big enough for rhubarb."

"I hate rhubarb," said Paul.

At the door, Jenna turned.

"I don't think Luke wants to be a millionaire. There are better things to have than money."

Paul had stood up and wandered to the fireplace. His eyebrows rose. "How conventional! I'm sure there are. But money helps you get them."

Jenna put her hand on the door frame. "Or lose them." She looked up at Adam. "What was the song? 'Money can't buy me love.'"

Paul's eyes flicked to the door into the kitchen and back to Jenna. "Oh, I never have to buy that."

I bet you don't, Jenna thought as she followed Adam out to the patch of lawn. Behind the garage, across a mat of buttercup and dandelion, Adam took her hand.

"Sorry about Paul. He's in a mood."

She put her head on his shoulder.

"Seems to be. I'm so used to you. You're so steady and ..." She was going to say 'predictable' but the word stuck, as if it wasn't quite a compliment.

"Paul and I are very different. Always were. He's four years older than me and he hasn't liked me since I was born."

She smiled up at him. "Maybe because you're so much cleverer than him!"

He grinned. "Yes, I am. After all, I've got you."

"And that's very clever!" She kissed him lightly. "Maybe I should try laying on the lipstick like Dianne." She paused. "I must say, her make-up's nicely done."

"Please don't go all lipstick and eye-liner on me."

"Why not?"

"Because I like what I see ..."

"... and what you see is what you get."

"Exactly."

The garden was a neglected riot of overgrown shrubs choked in tussocks of clover and buttercup. The neighbours on one side had kept the top of the hedge within limits, but this side of it was overhanging what must once have been a lawn.

Adam glanced around. "Putting this straight'll keep him busy." They turned back to the house. "But he's more likely to photograph it than dig it."

~

Paul seemed to have changed into the perfect host by the time Dianne served dinner. There was the clatter of cutlery, requests to pass this and that up and down the table, polite offers of more; courteous refusals. Jenna relaxed, talking about herself and her family a little, but mostly listening to Dianne's chatter about her home, her father and how much she missed it all, and how dreadfully bored she was here. Jenna watched her, fascinated to see the formation of the immaculate vowels. There was certainly no way she would blend in here. Paul listened and watched.

They moved back to the comfortable chairs for coffee. As Jenna sat on the sofa beside Adam she looked through the door to the kitchen. Dianne had hooked her arms round her husband's neck and was laughing up at him, her eyes sparkling, her white teeth parted, her blonde hair in thick waves round her face. She was lovely.

That wasn't the word Jenna thought of as she watched Paul. He was built a little lighter than Adam; at about six feet, perhaps an inch taller than his brother. He tilted his dark head towards his wife and his hand rested lightly on her shoulder. The gleam of new gold on his finger caught the light.

Jenna looked away. No, Paul wasn't lovely at all. Paul was perfect.

She slid back in the sofa to touch her body to Adam's and reach for his hand.

"Nice house, isn't it?" he said.

"Great," she said.

Without knowing why, she wanted him to put his arm round her. She moved closer.

"Hey," he said. "you're sitting on my jacket."

"Sorry," she said, and moved away a little.

Paul was back. He was in a mood again.

"So. You grew up in a manse then? Daddy's a preacher man?"

Jenna returned his gaze evenly. "My father's a minister, yes."

Paul's eyes lingered on her shoes, went up to her knees covered in maroon trousers. Back up to her face. Hands clasped loosely on his lap, he said "I can tell."

"It shows, does it?"

Paul spoke in a childish, rhyming voice. "You can't run away from your DNA."

Jenna laughed. "Going into the ministry isn't in the genes."

"Oh, genes are funny things. Precocious. It's amazing what's in genes."

Adam shifted impatiently. "Come on, Paul. Give her a break. She's not used to your obscure babble."

Dianne arrived with the coffee.

~

Jenna wandered out of the bathroom and looked around the tiny landing. She heard the bass sounds of the two brothers. They're catching up on news, she thought, talking about normal things. Occasionally Dianne's lighter tones interjected smoothly, once causing a burst of laughter in the room below.

The door of a tiny box room was ajar. The light from the landing slanted across a picture which hung above a desk. Jenna was enjoying this quiet break from intermittent tensions which she didn't understand. She pushed the door. The picture was in fact a photograph. It was behind glass in a frameless holder, stark in its black and white simplicity. It was a close-up of a carpet of leaves in winter, frosted and crisp. Jenna stood in front of it, fascinated by the lines of the leaves, sycamore and oak tumbled together. At the top right, a tree root lifted the leaves into a small ridge. The wind had blown a leaf onto its edge and below it was the hint of dark soil.

Every line was sharp as if cut by a scalpel. Whoever took the picture must have been frozen also, to hold the camera so steady.

~

"So when are you going to see Mum?" Adam challenged.

Paul set his cup on the small table beside him. "I've been to see her," he said calmly.

"When? She didn't tell me."

"Yesterday."

"At least she's pleased your back. Specially so soon after Dad died."

"Yes, now she'll have a son who calls on her more than once a month."

"Goodness, Paul. Filial feelings? That'll be a first."

"Stop it, you two. More coffee?" said Dianne, bending over Adam's cup.

Paul stood abruptly and swung round to the door. As he left, he looked back at Adam, his brows dark. "What would you know?"

Dianne sat in the chair he had left.

"That was jolly sharp. Are you two like this all the time?"

Adam took a deep breath. "Sorry. Paul and I always sparred. It's a habit."

"There's a bit of a child in Paul still." She put her head on one side. "But then, he's a man. You're all just big children, aren't you?"

Adam threw back his head and laughed. "You're so right, sister-in-law."

~

"Do you see the beetle?"

Jenna jumped. Paul was at the top of the stairs. She felt like a skewered thief.

"I'm sorry. I shouldn't be in here. I saw the photo and ... it's beautiful." She pulled herself together. "Did you take it?"

He came towards her, into the shadowed room. "Yes."

"Where is it?"

"Does it matter? It's just a load of leaves – and a beetle."

"I saw the beetle." She pointed. The small black body shone even in the dim light from the landing, peeping out from beneath the tree root. "What accent would he have, if he could speak?"

"Tyrone. It's a tiny piece of Gortin Glen."

She was surprised. "Really? It's not recent then?"

"No. It was one of the first pictures I took, long before I went to England." He looked at it. "I always liked it."

She looked up at him. His back was to the light and the planes of his face were softened. "Did you use a tripod?" He shook his head. "You must have a very steady hand. Adam told me you were a photographer. I didn't realise you were ..." She stopped.

"You didn't realise I was what?"

She decided to say it. "That good. I didn't realise you were that good."

He shifted slightly and brushed his fingers across the picture. "You're good too."

"What do you mean?"

"Knowing not to turn the light on above it. Knowing that some photographs are best seen in dim light."

They stood for a minute in silence, looking. Then Jenna said, "It's like watching a forest floor in winter twilight. When your breath is coming in clouds and you have gloves on and every step is crisp and crackly."

His head turned towards her slowly. "Yes," he said. "Exactly like that."

Jenna turned away, self-conscious. "Well, I'd better get back downstairs before Adam sends out a search party."

Paul moved aside. Jenna was half way down the stairs when she heard his voice above her: "He's called Fred."

She paused, looking up over her shoulder. "Who's called Fred?"

"The beetle."

~

The rhythmic strokes of the hairbrush finally slowed to a stop. Dianne looked at Paul in the mirror of her dressing table. He had become quieter as the evening had worn on, and now he seemed tired and drawn. She touched his hand as he set down the brush.

"What is it, darling? Tired?"

He kissed the back of her neck, but his lips neither lingered nor wandered. He turned away and pulled back the bed covers.

"Just a bit."

She was disappointed. She could never imagine having enough of Paul Shepherd. He slid between the sheets and turned on his side. She slipped into bed beside him and leaned over his shoulder.

"Sure your tired?" she asked. She waited. She kissed his bare shoulder.

"I've a headache," he said, his eyes staying closed.

Surprised, she said: "Isn't that my line?'

He didn't reply. She rolled onto her back. Hell! How would Paul react if she was as moody as he was; if she threw tantrums, or sulked when he had annoyed her? She looked at the back of his head on the pillow beside her, at his fine, almost black hair curling into the nape of his neck. He was very still.

She answered her own question. He wouldn't care. He would just wait until she got over it and came back to him. So far, she always did, and he knew it very well.

She nestled up to his back, feeling his warmth, his rigid stillness. She sighed. What a tiny room this was. What were they all doing at home now? And what was Luther doing? Did he still miss her? Since Paul had moved over here, Luther hadn't contacted her once. Probably still nursing his broken heart. Absently, she ran her fingers down the ridge of Paul's spine. He didn't move. Creative types were always moody. She closed her eyes, working out how long she would stay here before she insisted on going back to London. Paul would get this notion out of his system and then he'd begin to miss the life, the rich clients. And they would want him back. Already the phone calls were coming. Where are you? We need you for this wedding and that cover shoot. Amanda absolutely *has* to have you for the christening, darling. She sighed again. Good God! Was there anything you could even call 'society' over here?

In the early hours of the morning, just as the very edge of light was nudging past the blinds, sleep left her slowly as she became aware that she was being kissed. Paul was on his elbow behind her, leaning over her, kissing her ear, her cheek, turning her over to kiss her mouth, burrowing down along the line of her throat. His hands began to move across her body. She slipped beneath him, gripped him fiercely.

Afterwards, he held her very close and she lay warm and snug, knowing that if she were a cat she would be purring. She felt his slight intake of breath, the little rise of his ribs, as he spoke again.

"Dianne?"

"Mmhm?"

"I want a child. I really want a child."

CHAPTER TWO

JENNA'S FATHER STROLLED around the crowded church hall speaking to everyone, his infectious laugh spilling into the noise and chatter of the Harvest Supper.

"And how's my girl getting along?"

Jenna balanced the edge of the huge teapot on the trestle table before she turned to smile at him.

"Fine, Dad."

He put a hand round her waist and looked at the three men and three women who sat around the table. "So is she looking after you all right? Milk? Everyone got sugar?"

They all nodded vigorously.

"We're fine, Mr Warwick. We're being looked after very well." said Laura Patterson, a crumb of shortbread caught on her lip. "She's a good girl. You must be very proud of her."

"Indeed I am. We're proud of them both. I'm just sorry Luke didn't come, but he's got a lot of work this year. Needs to get the grades. He has to keep up with his big sister."

He moved on. Jenna continued filling teacups and when she had circled the last table she walked back to the hatch and pushed the empty teapot across to the kitchen.

"So where's Adam?" asked a woman who was refilling milk jugs. "I saw him with you in the service – just below the red hot pokers."

Jenna looked around. "I'm going to look for him. He might

have gone outside for a bit of air."

Where was he indeed? When she had told him that she had promised to help out at the Harvest Supper at her father's church, Adam had said he would come along and give a hand too. People here had met him before, so he wasn't news. But still, she would have liked to be feeling as if he was with her.

Jenna went through the hall, along the passage and into the deserted church by the door next to the pulpit. The flowers and fruit, grain and loaves filled the darkened, silent sanctuary with shapes and scents. Only two lights still burned, high in the roof beams. She picked up an apple that her father had knocked onto the floor in the enthusiasm of making the final point of his address. She climbed the pulpit steps and set the apple carefully back between two oranges.

For a moment, Jenna leaned on the lectern and gazed over the rows of pews. Each pew had a little bunch of greenery attached to the end next the aisle. There was a lot of hard work in this decoration. She could see her mother's hand in it. The mallow in the large display near the porch was probably from the huge bush at the manse gate. Cora Warwick would have directed operations on Saturday afternoon with the precision of a sergeant major. No vase, flower, apple or cabbage was in its place without the express permission of the minister's wife. Any potato found hunched in an unapproved spot was the subject of a detailed investigation.

Jenna smiled as she went down the pulpit steps. The congregation was very loyal to her parents; they loved her father and were in awe of her mother. She both loved and admired them. She just couldn't live with them. Her brother Luke was planning university and independence also. At least Jenna had stayed in Northern Ireland. Luke was getting out.

"Stupid place," he'd said once over tea. "I'm not wasting my time on it."

Her father hadn't let it pass. "But Luke, it's places like this that are in need of people to stay and use their influence for good."

Luke had pushed his chair back. "Well, good luck to them." He stood up, his lanky frame broadening into young manhood. "What's 'good' anyway? Everybody thinks it's something different." He pushed his chair in. "Seems to me, trying to be 'good' is part of the problem."

Jenna remembered how there had been a silence when he left the room. Cora had stirred her tea. "Don't worry, Donald. It's only a phase. He'll come round."

For once Cora was wrong, and for once she could do nothing about it. Luke's first two choices of university were in Scotland. His third was in Wales.

On a high windowsill half way down one aisle, Jenna stopped to study an arrangement of dahlias. Some people didn't like being in an empty silent church. Jenna loved it. She had grown up with churches. Busy, empty, full, sad, happy, tense, bright, dark. Worship-noisy, prayer-silent. She knew them in their every mood. She reached up to touch one of the great dahlia heads. The rich earthy scent of a church at harvest would be in her memory always.

She put her head on one side thoughtfully. The flowers reminded her of the picture of the frozen carpet of leaves. She was looking at these flowers in dim light also. Would Paul say that was right? Or do these need the full blaze of light to display the glory of their woven petals? They were meant to bloom in sunshine after all. A tiny insect crawled from the dark bowl of one crimson petal.

"Hello, Fred," she whispered. She laughed at herself. Realising that the church door onto the street was probably locked now, she turned to go back into the hall and out the other door to see if Adam was outside. A faint noise came from the church porch. Curious but unafraid, she turned back and went on down the aisle to check it out, her footsteps soft on the red carpet.

She recognised Adam's voice and quickened her step. Just before she went through the door, she stopped. He was on the phone. He was saying, "Look, I'd better get back. I'll be missed." Pause. "Yep, see you tomorrow." Pause. "Me too."

He was tucking his mobile back into his pocket when he saw Jenna. He looked startled and spoke quickly.

"Hi, Jen. Did you think I'd vanished?"

"Into thin air. You're supposed to be helping." She took his arm. "Come on. Plenty of dishes await you in the kitchen."

"OK. I'll even brave your mother and do my duty."

When they were near the door beside the pulpit, Jenna said, "Who were you ringing?"

"Oh, just Mum. I like to check in with her now and again. She gets lonely."

"You're a very thoughtful guy," she said.

~

Dianne Shepherd walked briskly along Royal Avenue. It was lunchtime and the main shopping thoroughfare was crowded. She had bought three pairs of shoes and a pashmina in an effort to get over the latest row with Paul.

She went down the stairs in Marks and Spencers and found a free table in the cafe to eat a sandwich. Paul had brought up the subject again. How *could* he? She thought he understood. They hadn't exactly spelt it out to each other. They had married much too fast to have discussed everything they should have discussed beforehand. But, my God! She ripped her sandwich apart. She had explained it the first time, when he had stunned her the night his brother and his girlfriend had visited. He was behaving as if she was just passing her time until the babies came along. She didn't want to be a mother, and she couldn't imagine what it was like to want to be. The thought of being pregnant made her feel sick. She looked at the polish on her long oval nails. How could you change nappies with those? They'd have to go. And she would smell of baby sick and her complexion would go pasty as she lost sleep and walked the floors with a crying baby at night. Paul said he would share all that. She believed he meant it. She didn't believe he would do it.

She had moved to Belfast with him. He had wanted to come back so urgently that she had said yes. She had left her father with his big house in London; she had left all her wealthy friends, partying their way round each others' houses. Her friends had names like Thomasina and Arabella and Rupert. And Luther.

It had been at Arabella's house that she had met Paul. Arabella had arranged a silver wedding portrait for her parents. Paul was a trendy young portrait photographer and Arabella had agreed to his outrageous price without a thought. Whatever the price, she wouldn't notice it missing from her bank account. Besides, Arabella had developed a huge crush on him as soon as she walked into his studio, and what Arabella wanted she got. At least that was always the way it had been. The fact that he wasn't married merely cut out an inconvenient complication.

Dianne was visiting when Paul called at Arabella's for a preliminary chat with her parents and to check out the location. Within the week, Paul and Dianne had their first dinner date and within a fortnight Arabella had to sit with a fixed smile as Dianne raved about this stunning man.

Now, in Marks and Spencers, on a cloudy autumn day, after a fierce row over breakfast, the waters were muddied. And why did he suddenly want children? "What would you want to bring up children here for anyway?" she raged. "They wouldn't meet the right people."

Paul had given her a look of disgust. "You're such a snob." Then he left the house and she had no idea where he was.

She sat back and fiddled with the handle of her coffee cup. Always she gave in. Always it was she who did what he wanted.

His was such a powerful, almost hypnotic personality, that it was exciting to please him. She clenched her fist on the table. But she would not give up this one piece of herself. She would not.

Her mobile phone was on the table. She looked at it, willing him to ring. She picked it up and punched the speed dial for his phone, then immediately cancelled it. He would see her number on his phone. One missed call. What would he do? Where was he? He didn't talk about his work very much, but she knew he was working to re-establish the reputation he had gained in England. He had turned the little box room into a temporary dark room until he could find a suitable studio to rent. She suspected he had bought the house only because it had a basin fitted in that bedroom. He was using film less now. A computer had appeared in the sitting room – as if there was space for it! He had tried to explain digital photography to her one day but she had got bored and he hadn't bothered her with it again. Just get on with earning the money, Paul! I don't care how you do it.

Dianne left the café and pushed her way past all the women's fashions without a look and stopped in front of the racks of men's shirts. A light blue one caught her eye. It had a hint of a white stripe, barely visible. She picked it up and imagined it on Paul. It would bring out the colour of his eyes, those eyes that had sparked like flint this morning; the same eyes that could crinkle with laughter or go smoky with desire. She carried the shirt to the wall of ties and rifled through them. It would have to be a perfect match. Everything had to be perfect for Paul.

~

As Dianne put her key in the door, she could smell cooking. Herbs. A hint of garlic. She set her keys on the tiny table in the narrow hallway and dropped her bag. Paul was in the kitchen. He was humming to himself and chopping something. She came through the sitting room and stopped in the kitchen doorway.

He was wearing an apron with the tapes wound twice round his waist and tied at the front. It was one she had been given as a wedding present. "I hope it'll fit him," her friend had giggled as she handed it over.

Paul looked up at her briefly and then back at the chopping board.

Dianne gestured at the hob where steam was rising from several saucepans. "Is this a peace offering?"

"It's dinner. But it can be a peace offering too if you like."

"I would like that."

There was a single red rose on her plate. A candle shaped like a snooty siamese cat flickered gently in the centre. He was trying, but there was a distance, a harder edge to his glance.

Later they curled up on the sofa. He had rented a video. It was a film he knew she wanted to see but had missed while it was in the cinema.

"That's wonderful, darling. But you should have checked with me. I don't feel like it tonight. She pushed herself away from him a little. "I think I'll have a shower."

He raised an eyebrow. "Can I come too?"

"Could I stop you?"

"Do you want to?"

She stood suddenly and made a dart for the door. "Come and find out!"

Later, wrapped in a towel, she sat on the bed and gave him a parcel. She had even bought gift wrap and a tag. He was standing in a green silk bathrobe towelling his hair.

"What's this? It isn't my birthday."

"So what?"

He ripped the paper and looked down at the shirt in its cellophane wrapper, the tie folded on top. At first she thought he didn't like it. Then he looked round at her with mischief in his eyes. He pulled it from its wrapper and searched for all the pins and cardboard until it was free.

"Don't go away," he said, and left the room.

She lay back on the pillow. She wasn't going anywhere. Soon, the bedroom door was flung open and Paul entered with a proud flourish of his hand, pirouetting to the end of the bed. He was wearing nothing but the shirt, buttoned up to his chin. The tie was wound round his head and dangled over his left ear. In his teeth he held the red rose.

She laughed so hard she gave herself a stitch. He stroked the rose across her stomach and then began to crawl across towards her. She reached for him, anticipation making her flush with ready desire. As her fingers touched his back, she murmured, "Just imagine if we had a baby. It would probably start howling to be fed at this moment!"

He went cold beneath her fingers in an instant, and rolled away from her.

Damn!

~

Paul squinted at the clock on the bedside table. It was nearly three o'clock in the morning. He looked round at Dianne. She was sleeping quietly. He pushed back the duvet and slid out of bed. He felt around the floor. The first thing he put his hand on was the shirt she had bought him. He discarded it and searched again until he found the smooth fabric of the bathrobe. He tied the belt and slipped out of the room. Downstairs he stood at the window of the sitting room and looked out at the night. He had dug half heartedly at one flower bed but the rest was still a mess. A car went by beyond the gate. The street lamps pooled their light in patches along the pavement. He looked up at the night sky and an irresistible urge took a grip of him. He padded barefoot through the kitchen and drew the bolt on the back door. Outside, the overgrown lawn was tussocky under his feet. There were faint city sounds funnelling between the dark shapes around him: a dog barked, a pigeon muttered sleepily somewhere. Across the next garden, a cat froze on a fence, its eyes yellow points in the blacker black of its face. Overhead, tufts of dark cloud drifted across the stars. The more he looked the more stars there seemed to be. Hundreds. Thousands. Millions. The moon was a thin sickle, giving the stars a chance to shine even on the edge of the city.

He looked down at the grass. There was no colour in it in the night. It looked gray. He hunkered down and plucked a daisy, its petals folded tight.

"Hey," he said aloud, "it's getting a bit late for you. There'll be a frost soon." He had startled a small insect. It too seemed gray in the starlight as it scrambled across the daisy leaves.

He stood up. Dropping his arms, he let the bathrobe slip from his shoulders to fold silently onto the grass at his feet. The quiet breeze licked across his skin. The night chilled him to the marrow and told him through every pore that he was alive, he was young, he was strong.

He raised his hands to the throbbing sky. *An insect, a flower, the universe.* He closed his eyes. *And me.*

CHAPTER THREE

DIANNE WOKE SLOWLY and turned her head. Paul was fast asleep, his hair spiked around his head. She ran her fingers through her own hair, remembering the night before. She had managed to lightened his mood again but it wasn't the same somehow. He was changing, subtly yet surely, since they had come here. Something slid from her ear and fell onto the bed beside her. It was a daisy. She picked it up. It was soft and wilted. Odd. Where had that come from? She dropped it and swung her legs to the floor, feeling thirsty.

Paul's mobile phone was on the hall table. Had he noticed that she had dialled his number at lunchtime yesterday? He hadn't mentioned it. Maybe she had hit the wrong number. She picked up the phone. With a quick glance up the stairs, she flicked to the record of missed calls. There were two. Her own name flashed onto the little screen when she checked the first one. The other was a number with no name. She didn't recognise it, although she did know the area code. The caller was from London. Some friend must have been trying to get him, but Paul hadn't answered. She could check the last numbers called from the phone to see if he had returned the call later. She thought she heard a noise and set it down quickly. Another time.

Now what on earth was she going to do today? Maybe Adam's girlfriend – what was her name? The one with the awful hair – would meet her in town. If she was still a student, she probably had no money so she wouldn't be great company, but it might be worth a try.

~

Paul stirred and stretched. His nightmare about fast, swinging pendulums and grandfather clocks had come back in the night, cruel and frightening. With his eyes still shut, he put out a hand and discovered that Dianne had gone. He turned quickly to the clock, immediately pushed back the duvet and sat up. As he tossed the covers back, the daisy tumbled from a fold. He picked it up. It swung limp from his fingers.

He crushed it in his fist and threw it across the room.

~

Jenna was sitting on her kitchen floor. Her back was to the cupboard where the ironing board was kept and her hands, in yellow house gloves, dangled over her drawn-up knees. That'll do it, she thought. It's as clean as I'm going to make it. Any dirt that's left can stay there till the next time. That was one thing about living on your own – there was nobody but you to do the cleaning. Jenna had shared this house with two other students for two years. One got a job in Derry. The other got married. If Jenna's parents hadn't bought the house, she wouldn't still be here herself. Her tutors had persuaded her to stay on for another year to complete an MA. She wasn't sure she wanted to, but it seemed the right thing to do at the time. Everybody said so.

She pushed back her hair, forgetting that she was wearing a wet kitchen glove. That reminded her. She had a meeting with her tutor on Friday; she really had better do some work. She pulled off the gloves with a snap.

Her laptop and notes were spread across the sitting room floor when the phone rang in the hall. It was her mother.

"So what are you up to today?" she asked.

"Trying to get down to some work. Mind you, I've just cleaned the kitchen. You'd be very impressed."

"Did you do the floor? Last time I was there, the floor needed a good wash. I'd have done it for you if Dad hadn't been in such a rush."

"Yes, Mum, I did the floor."

"Did you put disinfectant in the water?"

"Yes, I did. If smells could travel down wires, you'd smell it from there."

"So how's Adam?"

"Fine. He's gone round to his brother's to give him a hand with his garden. It's a bit of a mess and Adam says he needs to dig it over and leave it for the winter frosts."

"Very sensible. He's a great chap, Jenna."

"Yes."

"Did you say Adam's brother – Peter? Patrick? …"

"Paul."

"… took photos?"

"I said he was a photographer."

Cora sounded thoughtful. "Hmm. I wonder would he take a family picture of the four of us? I was thinking. Luke's going to go away to university soon. It'll be harder to get us all together then. Maybe if Paul's trying to set himself up here, he wouldn't charge too much. We'd be giving him one of his first assignments after all."

For some reason, this irritated Jenna. "I don't think he needs to be patronised. He's good."

"Oh, I'm sure he's good, Jenna. He's Adam's brother, after all."

Jenna didn't quite understand that logic, but said patiently, "I'll ask Adam to mention it to him, if you like."

~

Paul threw a stone the size of his fist across to the pile which was growing in a corner of the front garden. Adam straightened his back from his digging at the same moment. He felt the breeze of the stone as it skimmed his ear.

"Hey, you lunatic! That nearly hit me."

"No chance. You were born under a lucky star." Unconcerned, Paul rooted out a dandelion with a deep thrust of his spade. He took it by its leaves and smacked it on the ground, loosening the soil. "Look at that. I got the whole root without breaking it."

"Some lucky star. I got you for a brother."

Paul straightened and grinned at him. "Thought you'd got rid of me, I suppose."

Adam stamped on the fork, pushing it into the ground. As he heaved out a sod of earth and shook it through the prongs, he said, "Absence makes the heart grow fonder, don't they say?"

"Or: out of sight out of mind?"

Adam jabbed the fork into the tossed soil, wiped his brow and leaned on the handle. "More likely."

Paul threw down his spade. "That's enough. Fancy a drink, piglet?"

Adam raised a warning finger. "If you ever call me that in front of Jenna – or Dianne – I'll kill you."

With a quick spring, Paul leapt over a clump of woody heathers onto the path by the front door. With a flick of each foot in turn, he sent his wellington boots flying before pushing open the door.

Adam walked to the drive, cleaned the fork and propped it against the wall. Then he went back, lifted Paul's spade from where it had been flung, knocked the soil off it and propped it beside the fork. He pulled his boots off and followed his brother.

A can of Coke flew towards him as soon as he entered the lounge. It was within an inch of his chin before he caught it.

"Are you still drinking this stuff?" he said.

Paul was half-lying on the couch, already pulling the ring on his own can. He took a long gulp. "So. Is it serious with this one then?"

"Jenna?"

"I believe that's the name of the current one, yes."

Adam sat down opposite him. "I don't know."

Paul's eyes narrowed. "Does she know about Rachel?"

"Why should she?"

"You still see Rachel every day. You work together. Must be hard."

"We've both moved on."

Paul shrugged. "So the engagement ring might get recycled then? If this one doesn't ditch you too."

Adam pulled one foot across his knee. "No sign of it. She's a nice girl."

"Nicer than all the others?"

"Different from all the others."

"How?"

Adam frowned as he tried to explain. "Nice, yes. Good, too. Straightforward." He thought of the phrase Jenna herself had used. "With Jenna, what you see is what you get. She's a bit ..."

He searched for a word.

"Unsophisticated?" said Paul.

"Well. Yes. I suppose so. Wouldn't suit you at all."

Paul sat forward, his drink held loosely between his knees. "Why not?"

"Well, Dianne's a stunner. She could be a model, a movie star."

"Yes, she could, couldn't she?"

"Why on earth did she marry you?"

Paul shrugged. "My charm, my gorgeous ears, great sex ..."

"Or maybe just for your modesty."

"Maybe." Paul set the can at his feet and leaned back, putting his hands behind his head. "Rachel was a stunner, too."

"She still is."

"And you still notice."

Adam pulled at his sock. "As I said. We've moved on."

"And on and on and on. Jenna's just the next attempt at a replacement, isn't she? I'm sorry for her. She's not the end of the line. Admit it."

"I've got time."

Paul's eyes swivelled to his. "All you've got is today, piglet."

"Ha! I'm hearing things. Don't tell me some of that theology's still clinging on by its fingernails? I thought you'd ditched all that."

"You're the one who's going out with a minister's daughter. Anyway, I thought you'd recognise plain common sense when it wandered past you."

"Paul, you never had an ounce of sense in your life. Mum used to say you were behind the door when sense was being given out."

Paul lifted his drink and took a deep draught. "If I was behind the door, you were under the bed, piglet."

"Don't call me that!" Adam snapped. "We're all grown up now, remember?"

Paul's eyes danced. "Speak for yourself, piglet."

Adam aimed a half-hearted kick in his direction, then became thoughtful. "I suppose catching a society girl like Dianne must have taken some talent. She can't be finding it easy, so far from home and family." When Paul didn't reply, he prompted. "How's she settling?"

"Seems OK."

" 'Seems OK'? Haven't you asked her?"

"If she's not, she'll tell me."

"Had any rows yet?"

"No, everything's fine."

Adam stood up and dropped his can into the wastebasket. "You're a lucky bastard. I'm going. Work tomorrow."

As Adam slipped his shoes on at the door, Paul gestured to the patch of garden. "Thanks. You have your uses."

Adam pulled out his car keys. "Count it as penance for breaking your Action Man on your sixth birthday."

"Oh no. For that you have to do the back garden as well."

"Get lost," said Adam, walking down the drive.

Jenna rested her hand on the table in Dianne's house. Dianne had persuaded her to try some of her nail varnish. After a coffee in town they had come back on the bus and Jenna watched as more bottles and potions than she had ever seen in one place outside a shop, appeared on the table.

"Right. A basic hand treatment."

"I have used nail varnish before ..."

"But not properly. I'll show you how to do it properly. Remember, less is more if you don't want to look like something out of one of those ghastly cheap magazines."

Jenna watched Dianne as she moved swiftly and confidently. What must it be like to look like that? Dianne sat with her knees slightly to one side, her blonde hair tucked behind one ear as she bent over Jenna's fingers. Her nose was narrow and straight; her cheekbones were high and fine. Her pink fitted top emphasised the slimmest of waists.

No wonder Paul was attracted to her, Jenna thought. She's classy, just like him. They look good together, well matched.

Jenna looked down at her own trainers, poking out from the ends of her flared denim jeans. She pulled her feet under the chair.

"How's Paul?" she asked.

Dianne glanced up briefly. "Great. He probably won't be back till tonight. Restless as always. Not too fussed about fixing up this house. Or finding a studio."

"Well, what's a house anyway?" said Jenna. "Just a place to keep your stuff so that you can get on with living."

Dianne stopped momentarily and looked up. "Oh, a house is very important. It says so much about you."

The tip of her tongue peeped between her teeth. Jenna shifted a little. "I dread to think what mine says about me. It's a tip."

"I'm sure it says you're a awfully nice person." She crinkled her nose. "Adam must think so anyway."

"Adam tidies up when he's at my house."

Dianne reached for a jar of cream. "He did a great job in our front garden. He was supposed to be helping Paul, but I think he did most of it!"

"Yes, he likes gardening."

"You must have got the domesticated brother. I've got the wild one."

"I haven't got him!"

Dianne finished moisturising one hand and took the other one. She cocked her head.

"Imagine. We might be sisters-in-law some day."

Jenna blushed. "Mum and Dad like him."

Dianne shook a pink bottle, eyebrows raised. "Oh, well. If mummy and daddy like him that's all right then."

Jenna went quiet, trying to reach through Dianne's tone to what she might mean. She wasn't sure she liked it.

After a moment Dianne added: "Just so long as he makes your toes curl."

"What do you mean?"

"You know. That old black magic. Chemistry." Her laughter was like a wind chime as she waved a hand. "Butterflies. Sex. Whatever!"

Jenna let that one float before she asked: "So how long did you know Paul before you got married?"

"Not very long. I was half seeing someone else at the time. We didn't even live together." She paused. "He proposed very suddenly. He can be romantic when he wants to be."

"And is he often?"

She shrugged. "When he wants to be." She massaged Jenna's cuticles and her brow furrowed in thought. "He wanted to move back here just after his car accident. But now he's here, he's finding it hard to settle. It's ..." she shrugged a shoulder again "... changed things a bit."

"Car accident?"

Dianne stopped and her hand flew to her mouth, the brush hovering above Jenna's index finger. "God, I forgot! No-one here knows about that. Paul was absolutely adamant that no-one was to be told about it. He was afraid that his mother would hear. She was still getting over his father's death."

Jenna liked Adam's mother. She couldn't quite think of her as Paul's mother as well. "She still is. Was Paul hurt?"

"Only bruising. He was very lucky. His car was side-swiped by a lorry on the M6. It came across his lane without seeing him. Peeled the whole side off the car, but stopped short of peeling Paul along with it." She made a face. "It really upset me horribly. It was just a new car."

"He must have been very shocked."

The varnish was cold as Dianne started smoothing the brush along Jenna's nail. "The ambulance took him to hospital. He said they scanned everything from his ear lobes to his big toe. But typical Paul, as soon as they said nothing was broken or leaking or whatever, he discharged himself."

Jenna examined her right hand. "I won't say anything."

"Please don't. It's a big secret."

"What about the other guy?"

"What other guy?"

"You said you were half seeing someone else."

Dianne tossed her hair and didn't reply for a moment. Her

smile flashed briefly when she said, "He didn't have a chance. Not after I'd met Paul."

"Didn't you have to think about it?"

Dianne stood up. "With Paul, you don't think about things. You do them. And anyway," she said, "he made my toes curl. He still does." She stood up. "Now mind you don't smudge that." She scooped up the bottles and jars. "I want to show you some new shoes I got. I actually found a shop that had some decent ones."

On the way home, in the real world, in the noise of the newspaper sellers and buses and streams of people, in the damp darkening of an October evening, beneath the lines of muttering pigeons hunched on the high ledges above the city lights, Jenna swung her bag onto her shoulder and looked at her hands. They tingled. Nail varnish felt so cold as the brush stroked along the nail. And her nails were bright pink!

She leaned on the side of the bus shelter, leaving the narrow bench seat for the women with shopping bags and children with hockey sticks and schoolbags. Chemistry. That old black magic. She grinned, remembering Big Spotty McArthur who had dodged into the girls' changing rooms and given her a huge wet kiss. As she recalled, her toes had stayed straight and she had had to wash her face afterwards. And when, in her Fresher year at university, she had decided to let a fellow student practise his fledgling courting skills on her at a party, she had wanted to throw up.

Adam didn't make her want to throw up. But he didn't make her toes curl either. He was comfortable, reassuring. He made her feel secure and safe. She chewed her lip as a bus came into sight through the grey evening. Everything was in shades of grey at the moment.

She swung down the aisle and perched on the edge of a seat which was almost filled by a very wide man in an overcoat. Suddenly she felt depressed. Where is the magic for me? She fiddled with the fringes of her canvas bag and tried to think of one thing which she was enjoying, really enjoying, about life at the moment.

CHAPTER FOUR

JENNA HAD RETREATED upstairs to the broad landing of the manse. Events like this reminded her of why she liked having her own house. Her mother was fussing in a rustle of beige. Her father was calmly reading in his study. Luke was shut in his room. But he had put on his jacket and navy trousers as requested. A tie had even been dragged from the back of a drawer. There was nothing to be done about the blond streaks in his hair – or the earring.

The view from the landing window was of a long driveway down to the country road on which the manse stood, solid and grey. The village was out of sight to the left, across a river bridge.

Jenna perched on the window ledge beside the geranium. It was a wonder from childhood that her mother's geraniums never seemed to stop flowering. The red cap of flowers and the sharp scent of the leaves were two lasting evocations of the spirit of her home. The lawns – the bane of her father's life – were fringed with shrubs and flower beds, now dormant in readiness for the coming winter. The pillars matched the stone of the house itself and supported iron gates which Jenna had never seen closed.

Cora Warwick called up the stairs. "Are you sure you want to wear that dress, Jenna? This photo is the way future generations will see you, remember."

Jenna turned away from the window and spoke over the banisters. "Future generations won't know me, Mum. It doesn't matter what I wear. Anyway, this is the best outfit I have."

Cora came half way up the stairs. "No, it isn't. And red doesn't go with pink nails either."

Jenna glanced at her hands. "I forgot about those."

"It was very nice of Peter's wife to do them for you but a colourless varnish might have been more practical."

"Paul, Mum. He's called Paul."

Cora went downstairs again and Jenna heard the door to her father's study being opened. She stopped listening. Paul was late. But then Adam was driving. Although it was a weekday, Adam had managed to get some time off that was due to him, to bring Paul to the village. The manse was difficult to find, coming from Belfast. Besides, as he had whispered into her ear on Saturday, it would give him a bonus opportunity to see her.

Jenna hugged the memory, watching the road from the village, waiting to see the green Volvo turn into the gate. A car was coming. Jenna tensed and then relaxed. It was black. Below her, she saw her tortoiseshell cat stroll across the driveway and wander onto the edge of the lawn. The cat sat down and began to wash her face. She must be taking a break from her kittens. They were two weeks old now, dependent and exhausting.

The cat stopped licking, paw crooked in the air, ears forward as she turned her head to the gate. The black car had slowed and was turning in. Jenna frowned. Not a visitor just now surely; some pastoral crisis to take her father away? She looked down on the roof of the car as it swung round to stop at the front door. There was a pause and then the driver's door opened. It was Paul.

Jenna watched the passenger door, but it didn't open. Disappointment bit into her. Adam mustn't have come after all. Paul was alone.

He took his time. He leaned his elbow on the roof of the car and looked around. Then he walked a little way down the drive and seemed to scan the countryside around. Jenna watched her cat walk to him with a languid swish of her tail. She rubbed around his legs as he looked down. He bent and tickled her ears and Jenna saw his lips move as he spoke to her. Then he lifted her and put her onto his shoulder and Jenna saw him rub his cheek on the fur of her mottled side. The gesture brought his gaze to the house and he looked up at the window where Jenna stood, right into her eyes.

She should go down the stairs; she should hurry to open the door; she should ask why Adam wasn't with him. Instead, she watched Dianne's husband watching her and felt the look from his eyes as tangible as fingers on her skin.

Her mother's voice called. "Here's Patrick now, Jenna. Tell Luke."

~

"Adam couldn't come. Something came up at work." Paul was sitting in the lounge ignoring the cup of tea which Cora had put on a table beside him. "Something about the price of paper and having to do re-quotes." He waited a heartbeat then added, "He says."

Donald Warwick stood in front of the fireplace where flames crackled around the log he had just thrown into the grate. He was dressed as Jenna would always remember him best – a still slim figure in a dark grey suit with a black stock and clerical collar. People said he had kind eyes.

"Too bad," he said. "We like Adam."

Jenna had perched on the arm of the sofa. This was only the second time she had met Paul and yet he was exactly as she remembered. Perfect. She tried to sense what it was that made him unique in her eyes. He was paying no attention to her. Of the four of them, he was watching Luke who was picking absently at the arm of his chair.

Suddenly Paul said, "Luke."

Luke jumped and stopped picking. "What?"

"Why am I here?"

Luke's eyebrows shot up. "Don't you know?"

"I want you to tell me. It's not a hard question."

Jenna glanced at her mother and father. They looked as puzzled as she was.

Luke rolled his eyes and sighed. "To take a picture."

Paul sat back. "And you're going to be the star of it." Cora took a breath and opened her mouth. Paul continued before she could make a sound. "Your sister says you're going to go away to university. What's your first choice?"

"Dundee."

"Nice place."

Luke showed a flicker of interest. "Do you know it?"

"Not well. I had an assignment there a few years ago."

Cora said, "Jenna says you've been away for a few years, Peter, and have come back to live here."

"Paul, Mum." said Jenna.

"We keep trying to persuade Luke not to go away," her mother went on, straightening her skirt. "Home's best, isn't it? Even a troubled place like this."

Paul was still watching Luke. "What do you think?" he asked him.

Luke said seriously, "There's got to be a better place than this. I'm tired of it. It's so narrow, so …" he shrugged "… pathetic."

His father looked towards Paul. "Perhaps we should set up the portrait …"

Paul was nodding agreement with Luke. "It is, isn't it? Pathetic."

"Then why did you come back?" asked Luke.

Jenna watched as Paul took his time to answer. He sat forward and put his elbows on his knees. He examined the carpet. Then he looked up.

"You know those game shows where they show you something photographed so close up that you only see a tiny bit of it? You have to guess what it is. Only you can't guess because you're seeing too little too close. Ever seen those?" Luke nodded. Paul looked down again. He reached between his knees and drew his finger around a pattern in the pile. "When you leave your home place, you look back and you see the whole shape of it for the first time: the hollow here, the mountain there, the badness, the blackness." He opened his hands. "But after a while you see the shining bits too. The bits that are coloured and glowing. The bits that are good and that you never knew were there. Because you were too close before."

Nobody spoke, not even Cora. Paul wasn't finished. "And then you think you might come back. Because of the good bits, the shining bits. And because you've discovered that there's blackness everywhere anyway. You can never run away from it. So you come back to your own God and your own Devil, because they're the two beings who know you best in all the world." He shrugged. "But you have to go away to discover that."

Jenna hadn't realised she was holding her breath. Luke's expression of utter concentration broke in a broad smile.

"You're the first person who's ever said anything sensible about it," he said.

"So will you be a star for me?"

"OK," said Luke.

~

They sat as they were told to sit. They smiled. And yet it was all done with great ease, great good humour. Paul moved smoothly to adjust a shoulder here, an arm there. A chair was at the wrong angle. Luke moved it. Paul managed his cameras and lenses with quick economical movements. He took many shots, talking as he did so, making them relax. Donald asked him if he had the same church connections as Adam.

"I used to have," Paul replied, his fingers working deftly.

"Used to?" said Donald.

Paul glanced up briefly. "I had a great Bible class teacher many moons ago."

"Ah. Are you still in touch?"

Paul raised the camera. "Not since he ran off with the organist."

To Jenna's great surprise, her father roared with laughter. "Off-putting, I agree!"

She wondered if any of the others noticed the two quick shots which Paul took as her father's face creased in amusement.

When his bag was packed up again, Paul seemed restless, as if he wasn't quite finished to his own satisfaction. The lounge window looked out onto the narrow strip of lawn at the back. Paul went round the sofa and gazed out. It was mid-afternoon and the November light was already losing its edge. Beyond a wire fence, the field rolled away from the house, its uneven surface bounded by thorn hedges.

"In the summer there are often cattle in that field," said Jenna, coming to stand beside him. "Luke and I used to pull buttercups and long grass and the cows would come up and their huge tongues would curl them out of our hands."

"What are those?" Paul was looking to the right where the ruins of some buildings still remained.

"They're old huts from the war. We're near the airfield used during the war. There are quite a few bits and pieces of old huts around here."

"I want to see them," said Paul.

As the front door slammed behind him, Jenna took only a moment to run up the stairs, drop the red dress on the floor and pull on a jumper and jeans. From her bedroom window she saw Paul put one hand on a fence post and spin himself over the top wire, supple as a cat. Then he was kicking through the grass. His hands were deep in the pockets of a long black coat which he must have pulled from the car.

She followed him, clambering over the fence with much less grace. One remaining hut still had part of its corrugated roof in place. Jenna picked her way carefully into it, stepping over pieces of brick and chunks of concrete hidden in grass which had long ago reclaimed ownership of this patch of earth.

Paul was sitting on an old piece of a bench which lay lopsidedly to one side. Rubbish was piled in one corner – a rusting bedstead, several old cans and buckets, a chest of drawers with one drawer missing and the others sagging like slack lips. The place smelled of damp earth and autumn leaves.

She walked past him without speaking. It seemed right. The frame of one wooden window was still in place. She stopped beside it and waited. His back was to her. Somehow the ordinary everyday rules of social chatter didn't apply when she looked at the silent figure on the broken bench.

"Where are they, Jenna?" he asked softly.

"Who?"

"The airmen who were sent here. Are they dead?"

She turned towards him, her back to the light. "Probably."

He looked around. "Who were they? Did they have families, children?" He stopped. "Or did they give up their immortality to the war?"

Jenna kicked aside some shards of concrete as she took a few steps away from the window. "You know Rupert Brooke?"

"No."

"I can't remember it all, but he said something like that." She stopped, trying to remember. "Something like 'These laid the world away, poured out the red sweet wine of youth.' " She tested a few words in her head before speaking again. "I think it ends 'those who would have been their sons, they gave their immortality'."

He turned his head slightly. "I must get some of his stuff."

"I might have some. Left over from school. Or you'd get it on the internet." She lightened her voice, trying to bring him out of this mood. "But come over here. I can introduce you to one of them."

She pointed at the wooden window frame. He read aloud, "S. L. C. 1944." Jenna traced the weathered initials with her finger, the nail incongruously pink against the darkened grain. To her surprise he covered her hand and guided her finger over the letters again.

"S. L. C." he repeated slowly as he did so. "Stephen? Shaun? Spencer? Sam? He let go of her hand. "You've touched someone else. You've connected with the past. You've made yourself more than just you." He looked at her, questioning. "Do you know what I mean?"

"Yes," she said simply. "I've come here many times." She shifted a little, wondering whether to go on. He was waiting. "I think … we're only moments from this man." He was listening. "We're only moments from the past. It's only moments since you spoke. Just then. Before that, it was only moments since you were walking over the grass with your hands in your pockets. Before that it was only moments since you jumped the fence." She held out an open palm. "You see? So we're only moments from William the Conqueror, Brian Boru. The only difference is the number of moments."

Paul covered the carved initials with his palm. "So this airman is very close to us."

"I've always felt that." She walked away, embarrassed now. "Sounds silly, doesn't it?"

"It sounds about right."

She turned and smiled, her arms folded against the cold. The light was fading rapidly and the air was damp on her face.

"I think you took some good pictures in there," she said.

"You weren't the worst group I've had to deal with."

"You managed to get even Luke to cooperate."

He walked past her to examine the bedstead. He gave it a push with his foot. "When you're taking family portraits, there's always one person who's the key. If you can identify that person and make a connection, you've got a great portrait."

"And Luke was the key?" said Jenna. "Mum and Dad think he's the problem."

He turned and raised a finger playfully. "Ah! But the problem is often the key."

"You're talking in riddles."

"Then think in riddles!"

"Why?"

"Because it's the way to the answers. Riddles make the world go round."

"I thought love did that."

"The biggest riddle of all." Suddenly he kicked the bedstead, sending it crashing onto its side. "Why is there always a bloody iron bedstead? Can't people leave anything to rot without putting a bloody bedstead in it?"

"Anyway," said Jenna calmly, watching the rusty springs shudder to rest, "you weren't just making a connection with Luke. You were talking about something you've experienced yourself. Something true."

He said, almost carelessly, "The truth is the only connection worth making." His feet scuffed the loose floor as he turned again. "Did you go away to university?"

"No, I stayed here."

"Why?"

She shrugged. "I don't know. It was easier, I suppose."

He folded his arms and put his head on one side. "And unlike Luke, you always do what your told."

She bristled. There was mockery in his tone. “No, I don’t!”

“Yes, you do.” He nodded towards the house. “I didn’t even have to look at you in there. Within minutes of seeing the four of you together, I knew who would be the hardest subject and who would be no trouble at all, because she’s a good girl and she always does what she’s told, sometimes even before she’s told it.”

A faint scrabbling of raindrops on the tin roof turned into a deafening batter as the rain began in earnest.

Jenna raised her voice, annoyance pawing at her. “You don’t know me at all. How can you say that?”

He cocked his head. “No, I don’t know you. Who are you? Apart from my brother’s girlfriend?”

This was ridiculous. “I’m Jenna!”

He was relentless, his eyes intense. “Who’s Jenna?”

“Me,” she said, the sound of the rain drumming into her skull.

“Who’s ‘me’?”

She stopped. Truth is the only connection worth making, he had said. She looked up at the rust and cobwebs of the tin roof above. The rain pounded the roof as she turned her eyes back to him, her own words surprising her. “I don’t know. I don’t know who I am.”

He planted his feet apart, stood immovably in front of her. “Are you good? Are you bad?”

“I’m not bad.” The rain was beating louder, a breeze wrapping damp and cold around them, weaving through the gaping holes in the building .

“Are you good?”

She raised her voice again and made a fist, low at her side. “I don’t know!”

He kept going. “Am I good?”

“I don’t know.”

“Am I bad?”

"Only you know that."

"But, Jenna, I don't know that."

"Then how can I know?"

He stopped. Then his shoulders dropped and he spread his hands. "Well, well. It's an uncertain world we live in. Isn't it?"

He walked back to the window and leaned his shoulder against the worn wood. Raindrops flew through the opening, dappling his coat. Jenna felt as if she had been rolled across thorns. Who the hell was he, anyway? Apart from her boyfriend's brother? She took a deep breath.

"It's an uncertain world all right." She looked at the back of his head, stilled as he watched the waves of rain sweep the field outside. "But that's OK, Paul," she said suddenly, unsure why the sight of his hair ruffling in the wind should make her want to say this to him. "It's OK not to know."

He turned slowly and faced her. Even against the light, she could see the sadness in his shadowed eyes. "No it's not," he said. "It's not OK at all."

Jenna turned away and sat heavily on the broken bench. She put her elbows on her knees and her chin on her knuckles. She felt depressed. He was messing with her head. She thought with longing of the uncomplicated solidity of Adam.

Something tiny moved near her foot. It was a woodlouse, its legs fussing along the floor.

"Hallo, Fred," she said aloud.

She didn't know Paul was close until he dropped to his heels in front of her to look at the woodlouse. He touched it lightly with his finger. It changed course.

"That's not Fred," he said. "That's his Uncle George."

Jenna looked closer. "So it is," she said. "His nose is a different shape."

Paul made it change direction again. "And his legs are shorter."

Jenna nodded. "Right enough. Specially the second from the back on the left."

Paul looked up at her, balancing easily on the balls of his feet. "But the real giveaway is the socks. Fred doesn't have any socks that colour."

She caught his eye. His smile was lopsided and mischievous. That was when she noticed his mouth. It was a wonderful mouth, unique, mobile, all his own. As he relaxed into seriousness again, his upper lip curved high into the two arcs of a tightly strung bow. The centre was deep and expressive, his lower lip full beneath, rising to deep corners which tucked into the curve of his pale cheek.

It wasn't until he rose suddenly to his feet that she realised she had been staring.

"There's only one way back" he said. "We'll have to run."

He hunched against the drenching rain and darted from the cover of the old hut. Reluctant to move out onto the sodden grass, Jenna watched him running like a hunted hare across the field. When he reached the fence he did not alter his stride. With the lightest of touches on a post, his knees flexed, his legs swung high and he landed with a small splash on the other side.

An extraordinary feeling surged through Jenna, unidentified but no less real for that. Paul turned and spread his arms wide. His voice came back across the green distance, broken by the incessant staccato of the rain. "Come on! I'll help you over!"

She rose onto her toes and down again. Then she ran. She had no coat and the rain streamed through her hair, soaked her face like tears, chilled her skin through the wool of her jumper, darkened her jeans to the knees. When she reached the fence, she placed a hand on the fence post and flung herself high into the air.

Paul skipped backwards a few steps as she landed lightly beside him.

"Hey!" he shouted, clapping. "That's doing it!"

Jenna straightened, caught her breath, spat a dripping strand of hair from her mouth, raised her chin and looked him in the eye. She didn't need to say a word.

As they came through the kitchen, her mother was aghast. "Take off those wet things straight away, Jenna. What possessed you?"

Luke turned back to the small television in the corner. "I didn't know you could jump that fence, Jay."

Paul went into the hall to collect his camera bag. "Neither did she," he said over his shoulder.

They gathered politely at the door. Paul and Luke exchanged a high five, their palms meeting close to the ceiling.

"When you get to Outer Mongolia," Paul said, "send me a postcard."

Luke grinned. "I don't know your address."

Paul slung the strap over his head and swung his bag round his hip. "Just send it 'care of home' ".

Cora closed the door as the black car turned the corner by the river bridge. Jenna turned to go up the stairs to change. Dianne's husband had not addressed another word to her. Her mother shook her head.

"What an odd man. Normally the elder brother's the more sensible one. But Adam's a good chap."

"What's sensible?" said Jenna.

"What's good?" said Luke.

"Any more tea in the pot?" said their father, opening his study door.

CHAPTER FIVE

IT WAS TEN o'clock that night and Adam still had not phoned. He knew she was at her parent's house because she had told him she would stay overnight. Her father had a meeting in Belfast the next day and she planned to go back with him.

Luke was watching a film about an asteroid which was hurtling towards the earth. He was sprawled on the sofa, legs spread across the floor, his knees pointing in different directions. Jenna flicked over the pages of the TV magazine. There was an archaeology programme on another channel. At least the science on it would make sense. She left her chair restlessly. She wouldn't have a hope of getting the channel changed. Luke would cheerfully tell her that she didn't live here any more. He glanced round as she reached for the door handle.

"If you marry Adam, that guy would be related to us, wouldn't he?"

"If," she said. "Why?"

Luke tore open a packet of crisps. "No reason." He splintered a crisp between his teeth. "He's OK."

In the hall, Jenna looked at the phone on the table. Beside it was a picture of herself at her graduation. She glanced across at her father's study. There was a phone in there also. She could hear her parents sharing a cup of tea in the kitchen, talking over the day. They had always done that. No matter how busy or how distracted he was, her father had always had supper with her mother.

Undecided, Jenna drummed the table with her fingertips. She shouldn't ring him. He was the one who hadn't come. He should ring her. But she really wanted to hear his voice, talk to him.

Quietly, she shut the door of the study behind her and turned on a reading lamp which stood beside the broad desk. The phone nestled between a pile of her father's papers and a huge open commentary on the Gospel of John.

She dialled the number of Adam's flat. One of his flatmates answered.

"Sorry, he's not in. Probably out with his girlfriend."

"No, he's not," said Jenna.

There was a silence. Then "Well, try his mobile."

"Yes. Thanks."

She replaced the receiver. She wouldn't chase him. He would get in touch tomorrow. A thought struck her. His mother. That's where he was probably. He would have worked late and then gone to his mother's. He seemed to be good to his mother. They would have got talking and maybe he was doing the odd thing for her in her house. He would have forgotten all about what Jenna was doing today.

Her old room didn't feel quite the same as she lay down in bed and pulled the duvet over her. All the things that had made it her room were gone, now scattered round her own house. She lay and looked at the ceiling. The rain had stopped but the wind still tossed the trees outside. Her eyes closed slowly.

It seemed as if her feet flew across a wet green field. She was light and free, the wind snatching at her hair, the grass whipping her ankles. A smile touched her mouth as she felt herself lift into the air, her arms spread like wings, her face to the wind. Way below her, someone was clapping, cheering, willing her on.

A weak sun had begun to dry the ground as Donald Warwick pulled the car round a three point turn and drove out through the manse gates. Jenna snapped on her seatbelt.

"So what's on today, Dad?"

Her father slowed to cross the river bridge and turn up the village street. "Just a church committee. Exciting stuff." He smiled across at her briefly. "And there's someone I must visit in the City Hospital. Nothing too serious, but I need to check he's OK."

He waved to an elderly woman who had just come out of the village shop. Jenna watched her shift her carrier bags and free a hand to wave back. Her father turned out of the main street and onto the road to Belfast. "Mrs McCormick was asking about you the other day. A lot of people do."

"So what do you say to them?"

"I say you're fine. Studying away. Doing well."

Jenna looked away from him, out of the side window. The trees were almost bare now. Some leaves still clung to branches, rippling like russet bunting in the fresh morning breeze.

"You should have that on tape," she said.

"What?" Her father leaned his ear towards her.

She turned her head back and spoke more lightly. "You should have that on tape. It's what you always say."

"Well, it's always true."

"What if it isn't?"

Her father slowed to pass a car parked at a bend in the road; indicated, worked down the gears.

"Some people have no imagination when they pick their parking spot," he said. He gathered speed again. "Of course it's true. The whole village is proud of you."

Jenna didn't reply immediately. Then she shifted round in her seat. "Dad, I'm not too far into this year yet. Sometimes I wonder if I'm doing the right thing. Maybe I'm wasting a year. I'm costing you a lot of money."

Donald's eyebrows rose. "We're glad to support you, Jenna. Goodness, don't chicken out now. The sky's the limit for you with your brains. You're getting the educational chances I never had. Or your mum."

"I suppose it depends what you want brains for," said Jenna.

Her father drove for a while in silence. Then he said, "I know what's wrong with you. You're still down because Adam didn't come yesterday."

No, and he hadn't rung either. She didn't want to talk about it.

"He had a good reason," she said.

"Of course he did." He put on what Jenna called his pastoral voice. "You've been very fortunate. You've always been a hard worker. Your mum and I want the best for you. A good man and a good job. You've got the first ..." he flashed a quick smile "... we hope. And this extra year at university will give you a great advantage in getting the second." He took one hand off the steering wheel to pat her knee. "It'll be worth it, Missy."

Missy. When would he stop calling her that? The sound of it was like the pull of reins on a horse's bit. Years ago, he had used it when she had been naughty or needed something explained which he thought she should have known. The sound of 'Missy' pulled her back, set her on the straight and narrow again, enclosed her in a paddock with high fences.

On her seventh birthday, she was told she could go to bed an hour later every night from now on. She had skipped with delight. She was really grown-up. Not like baby Luke who fretted on her mother's knee after his bath. She had been sent to the kitchen to fetch Luke's bottle. She felt tall with importance as she brought it through the hall. Her father came out of his study.

"Missy! Time to go to bed. It might be an hour later, but it's still bedtime. Up you go."

He had taken the bottle from her and steered her to the stairs. She had tried not to cry. After all, it was her birthday.

The outline of the city was coming into view. She hated Missy. She didn't want to be Missy ever again. She closed her eyes, a unexpected refrain starting in her head. *Who are you? Are you good? Are you bad? Who are you? Who are you?*

Paul was still using the small bedroom upstairs as a darkroom, much to Dianne's annoyance, even though he used film less and less. Spread on the table in front of him were four black and white portraits, still damp. The Warwicks would get their family portrait, but he had also got four character studies.

He loved photographing people, particularly when they were unaware. He was tired of formal portraiture. There was a falsity about it, a manipulation of the truth. He picked up the picture of Cora and played his word game. Proud. Fussy. Hard-working. He paused and then added the word 'loyal'. Donald was next. His head was thrown back and he was laughing. Intelligent. Strict. Paul set down the portrait. But kind. A good pastor.

He had caught Luke in a rare smile. He was looking to his left, the gelled tips of blond highlights outlined against the velvet curtain. Restless. Intelligent. Shy. Angry. Paul set the photograph beside the others. Luke had more in him than anyone knew, maybe even more than Luke himself knew. He was sure of that. Anger and restlessness were giants that could nurture or destroy. What would Luke do with those giants?

And Jenna. He didn't pick up the portrait of Jenna. He left it on the table and leaned over it, a hand on each side. Jenna was simply looking straight at the camera, almost expressionless. Only a slight narrowing of her eyes betrayed that she was listening to instructions he was giving from behind the lens. When he said "Raise your head a little, Jenna," she had raised her head thinking he was composing the group. When the light was striking her cheek just where he wanted it, he had snapped the shutter.

Fresh and plain. Those had been the first two words he had assigned to her the night she and Adam had called. Now he wasn't so sure. He joined his thumbs and index fingers into an oval and held them over her face so that her hair was hidden. Then he angled his hands to reveal only her eyes. She was more her father's daughter than her mother's.

His word game was failing this time. Of the whole family, she was the only one who had startled him. How could someone be plain who could trace the carved initials of a dead man as if she cared about him? How could someone be plain who could talk sensibly of being only moments from William the Conqueror? He remembered the flushed cheeks, the dripping hair, the defiant tilt of the chin as she had landed in front of him in the rain. He lifted a hand to the portrait and put a finger on her mouth, the mouth his brother kissed. But that was all Adam did, because he remembered something else, a fact he had absorbed effortlessly as they had agreed the identity of the woodlouse. She had stared at him for a moment and the knowledge had slipped into his mind. This girl wasn't sleeping with Adam. There was an unawakened innocence about her, a way of looking at things which was unencumbered by complexity. He gave a low laugh. She still thought love made the world go round! She had never slept with anyone. He knew it as if she had told him.

At the back of the table, his mobile warbled. He reached for it, read the number. His thumb hovered for a moment and then he cancelled the call. He was turning away to go downstairs when it sang again with the rising notes of a text message. He picked it up.

"Talk to me Paul."

He stood looking at the tiny screen. Then he jabbed delete. He opened a drawer and threw the phone to the back of it and slammed it shut again. He put his hand out to the door handle. Then suddenly he leaned back against the wall, slid down onto his heels and lowered his head onto his crossed arms.

~

Dianne put her key in the door. She had been visiting an exhibition at an art gallery and had got into conversation with the owner. It was a wonderful, interesting conversation. She had even told him about Luther's gallery in London. Now she was even more homesick and lonely for familiar people and places. She was so absorbed in her thoughts, her head buzzing with ideas which she would love to talk over with Luther that she boarded a bus which took a different route from the one she had become familiar with. She spent the journey worrying that she was on the wrong road, that she would find herself in some strange part of this strange city and have no idea how to get back. When she lived with her father, she had travelled everywhere by car, or occasionally by train. She didn't drive; there had always been somebody, even a taxi, to take her wherever she wanted to go.

By the time the bus lurched round a set of traffic lights and into the road she knew, she was feeling nauseous. Her head throbbed. She was longing for a quiet evening curled up in front of the television or listening to Paul strumming quietly, as he often did.

She set her keys down on the hall table and called hallo. Silence. His car was in the drive. She hung up her coat on one of the pegs on the wall and went into the lounge. He wasn't there. Through the door into the kitchen, she saw dishes piled on the ledge, all of them dirty, not a single one washed.

She wasn't up for this tonight. She really wasn't. Irritation rising, she mounted the stairs. As she had walked up to the front door, she had seen that the blackout curtains were tightly closed at the window of the little room upstairs. It didn't necessarily mean anything. Paul didn't bother to open them sometimes. She thought it looked terrible from the outside, but he just ignored her if she said anything.

He had fitted a warning light to indicate when the door of the darkroom must not be opened. It wasn't lit. Nevertheless, Dianne paused outside.

"Paul?" she called.

The door handle turned and there he was. "Hi," he said. "You're early."

"No, Paul. I'm late. Didn't you notice?"

His eyes flicked to his watch. "I was busy."

Irritation was turning into rage. "What the hell at? It certainly wasn't at washing dishes. And it certainly wasn't at cooking!"

He came out of the room and tried to put an arm round her. She pushed his arm away. He raised his hands, let them drop.

"Dishes can be washed any time. Dishes can wait. Life can't."

Dianne turned and stormed down the stairs. "What do you think life is, Paul? A free ride?" At the bottom of the stairs she spun round to look up at him as he followed her. "There's no-one else to do the dishes in this house, is there? Just us! On our own." He reached the bottom step, his hand on the bannister. Her voice rose. "I'm tired, I had a horrible journey home, I'm homesick, I've a headache, and I don't want to come home to another one of your moods."

Paul stepped off the last step and went past her without a word. In the kitchen, he began to run water into a basin in the sink. She followed, flinging out a hand.

"What's the point of doing them now? By the time we've cooked dinner it'll be midnight."

He turned off the tap, reached for a towel. He dried his hands, watching her steadily as he did so. He dropped the towel on the ledge. She lifted it.

"The towel has a rail to hang on."

She hung it on the rail. Paul's eyes were beginning to narrow, his expression to harden.

He spoke carefully. "A towel's mission in life is to be there when it's needed. It doesn't matter where it stays. And the point of eating is to avoid being hungry. It doesn't have to be any more than scrambled eggs in front of the fire."

"Scrambled eggs! Maybe you were brought up on scrambled eggs, but I wasn't!"

His eyes snapped, his voice rising to match hers. "So what were you brought up on? Sautéed silver spoons in a champagne sauce?"

He was never like this before. She put her hands over her face. After a silence, she felt him come closer, put a hand under her chin. She stayed rigid.

"Would you like to go out for dinner?"

She hadn't foreseen that life with Paul would be quite so exasperating. Her voice was muffled by her fingers. "We wouldn't be having to live like this if it wasn't for you."

His eyes narrowed. "Explain that."

"My father would have bought us a house. He told you that." She was shouting again. "But you would rather we lived in a city side street!"

He held up a hand, raised his own voice again. "We've done nothing that you didn't agree to."

She whirled round to the other end of the kitchen. "Paul, I want a proper house. I want it now!"

His eyebrows shot up. "What exactly do you mean – 'a proper house'?"

Something in his tone enraged her. He just didn't understand. He didn't understand and he didn't care. Before he could see it coming, she grabbed a white pottery mug from the sink and hurled it at him. He ducked and it missed, flew through the door into the lounge and knocked a porcelain penguin from a bookcase onto the floor, its fragments mixed with the white shards of the mug. Her grandmother had given her that penguin years ago, after her mother died when she was three years old. She loved it.

"I mean a house that doesn't have black curtains draped on the front window and a jungle for a back garden!" she yelled, wrenching open the back door. "Just look at it! My father's grounds are always beautiful."

"But then, 'Daddy' doesn't have to look after his 'grounds' himself, does he?" He leaned back against the ledge above the fridge and folded his arms. "Anyway, I can't look at it. It's dark outside. Hadn't you noticed?"

She slammed the door shut. "I'm the one who's just been jolting around in a bus, remember? I did notice it was dark. It's cold too." She wrapped her arms around herself. "I'm cold."

Paul examined the floor for a moment. Then he looked up at her from under his brows. "What happened to agreeing to live in my world rather than live without me in yours, Dianne?" he asked softly.

She stared at him. "That's the way it has to be, isn't it? Here, on your terms." She hadn't asked this before. She took a deep breath. "You wouldn't have stayed with me in my world. Would you? You didn't love me enough to do that." She swallowed. "Did you?" He met her eyes but didn't speak. "I said ..." her tongue flicked across her lips "... you didn't love me enough to do that."

He lifted a spoon and examined it, tapped it on the back of his hand. Then he said, "But that cuts two ways, Dianne."

"What do you mean?"

He dropped the spoon into the sink with a clatter. "I mean – why shouldn't I use the room upstairs?" She didn't understand. He pushed himself upright and took her by the shoulders with strong fingers. He had never been anything other than gentle with her. He shook her a little and brought his face down, close to hers, glaring. "After all, we're not going to need it as ..." his fingers tightened "... a nursery, are we?"

She was trembling. "That's not fair, Paul."

"It seems perfectly fair to me. You don't get what you want. I don't get what I want. That's what I call quits. What do you call it?"

They stood like that, locked, silent. Then abruptly, he seemed to tire. He let her go and walked into the lounge. She followed. At the door into the hall, he put a hand on the door frame and half turned back towards her.

"If the garden bothers you, you know where the spade is." He went into the hall and lifted his car keys. "Just watch you don't break a nail."

The door slammed. After the noise of the car engine receded, Dianne bent to the pieces of her porcelain penguin. Cold fingers of resentment gripped her skin within a silence that descended like a cage.

CHAPTER SIX

HE WANTED TO see his mother.

Forty-five minutes after walking out on Dianne, Paul strode from a cold foggy night into the seaside house where his father had died in the frozen hours of a January dawn. A smell of baking filled his nostrils. Across the beige and gold swirls on the carpet, past the china cabinet that he remembered as long as he remembered anything, the light was on in the kitchen. He heard classical music on the radio and realised his mother hadn't heard him arrive.

He peeped round the kitchen door. Her back was to him and she was making pastry, turning it, rolling it, turning it, dusting flour on the board and rolling the pastry again. The small radio was in the corner where the jar with the sweets used to be kept. Adam and he were allowed six each when they came in from school. Small sweets counted as a half.

He watched her for a moment. Hazel Shepherd was fifty. A widow at fifty. Her movements were those of a vigorous woman in her prime. Only her sons detected the slight slump which had curved her shoulders the night her husband died, and had never lifted from that time.

If he spoke, he would alarm her. He walked softly back to the front door, opened it and shut it again loudly.

"Mum?" he called.

She appeared round the corner of the door where he had been

standing, wiping flour from her hands on a damp cloth.

"Paul! What are you doing here at this time of night?"

"Why are you baking at this time of night?"

"I'm just stocking up the freezer."

He gave her a peck on the cheek.

She stood back and examined him. "What's the matter, Paul?"

He went through the kitchen into the small den. A black cat lay in a perfect circle on his favourite chair. He picked it up and sat down. "Hi Widget," he said, feeling the warm fur slipping beneath his fingers as he settled it onto his knee. The cat yawned, stretched one white paw into the air, turned round once and curled again into a soft circle on his lap.

"Do I look that bad?" he said.

"Worse." He didn't say anything. She went back to the pastry. "I've one more to put in the oven and then I'll make coffee."

He listened to the sounds of her moving around: the rolling pin, the knife trimming the edges of the pastry, the knife being set down, a cloth being lifted. The oven door opened. The warm smell of baking pastry transported him back to the edge of memory, back to a time of uncomplicated, uncompromised love; a time before everything changed. Two pies, one apple and one rhubarb, were already turning from pale cream to the colour of nutmeg.

"Seen Adam lately?" he asked as she shut the oven.

"Not for ages. He doesn't really call that often." She reached for the kettle. "He doesn't even ring that often."

Paul heard the hint of complaint in her voice. "It's a tough time for printing companies and he's on the road a lot."

She propped herself beside the kettle while it boiled. "I know. But it's nice to see you more often. You're only fifteen miles away now, instead of across the water."

He smiled briefly. "Getting through the city's the hard bit."

There was a brief silence. Then she said, "I suppose Dianne wanted to be on the south side. It's a bit more ... her sort of place."

"I picked the house, Mum. Dianne doesn't know the Falls from the Shankill. And it's small, compared to what she's used to," he added.

He willed her not to say anything more about Dianne. It didn't work.

"How is she, anyway?"

"She's fine."

His mother picked two mugs from the rack and spooned coffee. She lifted the kettle. "I'm not an idiot, Paul. She was with you last time you were here. She's not happy."

He took the steaming mug from her as she sat on the worn green sofa opposite him. He felt her studying him over the top of her mug. "But you've married her now," she said. "You'll have to work at it."

He blew on his coffee and took a sip. "Let's not go into all that again. She's fine."

They sat in silence. He ran his hand down the cat's fur. He noticed that Widget still had his three white whiskers: two on the right and one on the left. Gradually he relaxed, emotional exhaustion drifting through him.

"Mum?"

"What?

"Did you ever regret having me?"

"Good heavens! What an odd question!"

"You know what I mean. Did you?"

She settled back with her mug between her hands and became serious. He wanted the truth. "No. Never. Never once. Once you have a child, that's a new person in your life, a new little person to get to know." She smiled at him, her eyes twinkling. "You were fascinating."

"I could have arrived a few years later, when you felt ready."

She shook her head. "No, you couldn't. That wouldn't have been you. It would have been somebody else. It wouldn't have been the same recipe." She became thoughtful. "I think there's a time for someone to be born. If you miss that time, then you won't ever know who they could have been."

The cat's ears were like silk between his fingers.

His mother got up to take the first pie out of the oven. Paul rested his head back. His eyes fell on a photograph on the wooden surround above the electric fire. It was of Adam and Jenna smiling at the camera, their arms loosely round each others' waists. It had been taken on a day out to a park. He nodded at it.

"I see you've banished Rachel."

"Rachel banished herself," said his mother briskly.

"I don't think Adam's over her yet."

She dusted sugar over the pie with some force. "Well, I hope he's found who he needs in Jenna. She's a nice girl." She sat down again. "She's a good girl." She sniffed. "So different to Rachel."

"But has Jenna found who she needs in Adam?"

She sounded surprised. "Of course she has. He's a lovely guy."

"And of course you're not biased."

"I know his dad would have approved, even though he never met her."

Paul cocked his head. "Why exactly is Jenna a good girl?"

She thought for a minute. "She's got standards. She doesn't swear. She's thoughtful. She doesn't ..." she rocked an open hand from side to side "... make waves."

He nodded slowly. "Standards. No swearing. Thoughtful. No waves." He tickled the cat's chin. "Sounds like a thrill a minute."

"And her father's a clergyman," she finished.

"Ah!" said Paul, "that must be where the adrenaline rush is."

She jerked her mug towards him. "You're making fun, aren't you?"

"How did you guess?"

They sat in silence again.

"You should get a cat," she said.

His head was back, his eyes closed. "Maybe."

"Jenna's cat has kittens."

"I know. I met the mother." Another silence. He lifted his head to look at her. "Mum?"

"What?"

"How are you?"

She knew what he meant. "Better some days than others." She gave a brittle laugh and brushed flour from her blouse. "I didn't expect to be alone just yet."

"I'm sorry I wasn't here more often when Dad was ... suffering."

Her chin puckered. "It was awful. Watching him." She shrugged her shoulders. "But that was all I could do. Watch."

The last word slid out on the cusp of a sob. Paul saw her struggle with a pain that was still raw after eleven months. What was it like to watch someone you love die slowly in front of your eyes and be powerless? His father had only a few days to live when Paul returned to see him for the last time. A tall, proud man reduced to a living, yellowing skeleton by a cancer that raced through his every tissue and bone faster than any doctor had predicted. Medical pain management had done all it could, but it couldn't do everything.

A need of his own made Paul push the cat to the ground, move over to the sofa and sit beside his mother. His arm went round her, she buried her head in his shoulder before the storm broke. He held her tightly. Above her shaking, greying head, his own eyes were wide, sightless, filled with the memory of the horror of it all; some that he shared with her and some that were his alone.

She gave him one of the apple pies, knowing better than to give him a rhubarb one. It was still hot and he balanced it on a tray on one palm as she hugged him again in the hallway. "Take care. I couldn't bear it if anything happened to either of you. It's after midnight and that's a bad road back to Belfast."

As he opened his car door, she called after him. "You never told me what was the matter."

He looked at her figure silhouetted in the doorway. "Neither I did," he said, and slammed the door.

~

Dawn was beginning to filter down the city streets as Paul closed the front door quietly behind him. In the lounge, there was no sign of the broken pottery on the carpet. He checked the kitchen bin. The bits were in there, topped by a used teabag.

In the doorway of the bedroom he stopped. In the dim light from the landing he saw Dianne in their bed, lying on her side, facing away from him. Her blonde hair was spread like a fan on the pillow. One arm was above the clothes, the other under her cheek. Her breathing was regular and shallow.

He looked round the room. Her pink dressing gown was draped over the stool by the dressing table. How could one woman use so many bottles, jars, powders and tubes? Beside a clump of nail varnish bottles lay her hairbrush. He picked it up. A few of her hairs tickled his hand as he turned it over. He motioned with it in the air, imitating the many times he had drawn it through the waves on her head. He hadn't done that quite so often lately. He wondered if she noticed. But she would ask if she wanted him to do it for her.

He set the brush down and moved soundlessly round the bed. He crouched down beside her and put his head on one side. Even in the shadows, he could see that her eyes were swollen in the delicate features of her face. The fingers of one hand still clutched a crumpled tissue.

Elbows on his knees, he joined his hands and rested his chin on them. "How long will you stay, Dianne?" he whispered, very low. He crouched there for several minutes, motionless, listening to her breathing. Then his brow creased as if in pain and he lowered his head abruptly, his brow on the thumbs of his linked hands. There was a rustle as she stirred and he looked up quickly.

"Paul?"

"Hi."

She sat up on one elbow. "Where have you been?" She looked at the clock. "It's nearly morning!"

"My mother's. And then I went walking."

"Walking? In the middle of the night? Paul, that's not safe!"

His smile was small and tired. "A lot safer than in here."

"When you didn't come back, I tried to ring you. But your phone rang in the darkroom. You forgot it."

He had gone very still. "Did it ring any other time?"

"No. Not that I heard. But it seemed a bit faint. I only heard it because I was up here." She hesitated. "Paul ..."

There was nothing left in him to say. She would want to talk about it, analyse it. Sometimes it was better not to do that, whatever the agony aunts said. It would mean analysing himself and that frightened him. What he wanted most was to sleep.

"Am I allowed in the bed?" he asked.

She didn't reply for a moment, studying him. He knew he was disappointing her. Finally, unsmiling, she said "OK."

He undressed, left all his clothes on the floor and crawled in behind her. She didn't turn round so he put an arm across her waist. As his eyes closed, he heard her say, "You stink of night air and fog."

Sleepily he replied into her hair. "That's not a stink. That's a scent."

CHAPTER SEVEN

JENNA SAT IN a coffee bar at the university. There was too much onion in her egg and onion sandwich. Her breath was going to empty the library in sixty seconds. She stuffed the sandwich back in its wrapper and looked around. There wasn't a single student that she knew, really knew. Everything had changed this year. All but one of her friends from the past four years had left after graduation. The one who remained was pursuing a different discipline and in any spare time she had, she seemed to be stapled to her boyfriend.

Jenna had spilt a puddle of coffee. Her chin in her hand, she pulled it into figures of eight with one finger. She wondered what Adam was doing and whether she should tell him what her tutor had said this morning. He had gestured at her assignment on the desk in front of him.

"You should be producing better than this, Jenna." He had leaned across his desk, hands clasped in front of him. "You've always been a great student. Conscientious. What's happened to you?"

She sighed at the memory. Doing better was going to have to be a priority or this whole year was going to be a disaster. She pushed back her chair and reached for her folder. Her phone rang; it was Adam.

"Hello, brainbox," he said. "I'm just outside."

"Hey! I was just thinking about you."

"Where are you?"

She told him. A few minutes later he walked into the coffee bar. His dark blue business suit marked him out as a visitor as he made his way to her.

"What are you doing here?" she asked as she raised her face for a quick kiss.

He screwed up his nose. "You've been eating onions." He pulled out a chair. "I was on my way back from a call up the motorway and thought you just might be around. So you were thinking about me, were you?"

"Don't get a big head. Coffee?"

"Yes, please. And a biscuit or something."

She joined the queue at the counter. She should be back in the library by now. She had some research papers reserved and needed to look at them before the week was over. She set his coffee down and handed him a chocolate biscuit.

"I can't talk long, I'm afraid," she said. "I've already had a very long lunch."

"You seem a bit tense. What's wrong?"

She decided to tell him. "My last assignment was crap."

"Of course it wasn't. You only think it was. You're too hard on yourself."

"My tutor said it was crap. Well, not in so many words but that's what he meant."

"The next one'll be better." He patted her hand. "Not long to Christmas. You'll get a break then. We'll have some fun. Don't go all gloomy on me."

She was quiet. She wasn't exactly depressed. There was a discontent grubbing about in her head. Suddenly she said in a rush, "Adam, I'm not sure I should be here."

He looked puzzled. "You mean in the coffee bar?"

"No, I mean in the university."

He sat back and laughed. "Hey, get a grip! I'd love to be back here lounging about drinking coffee instead of driving miles every day to crabby clients."

Jenna looked down at the puddle of coffee on the table. When she looked up again, Adam had tipped his chair back, put his hands behind his head and was looking around. She studied him. Well dressed, confident, earning good money. Everything that she was not.

"This is as good a place as any to spend a year," Adam was saying. "What else would you do anyway?"

"Something useful, maybe."

"Like what?"

"I don't know. Build houses in Africa maybe."

He was incredulous. "You're not serious? You're not a muck and dust kind of person. Your parents would have a pink fit. And so would you. All those spiders and huge bugs. And Aids and malaria." He sat forward again. "Besides, I'd miss you."

"Would you really?"

"I would, Miss Warwick."

"Well then," she said, "I suppose I'd miss you too."

"So you'll just have to stay here."

She took a breath to speak. Stopped. Looked at the tables around them. Looked back at Adam. "Adam, what do you see in me?" She laughed a little. "I mean, I really want to know."

"What a question! I thought you didn't have long."

"Give me the short version."

"OK." He checked off on his fingers. "You've a gentle personality. You're honest and kind. You're very unselfish. There isn't an ounce of guile in you." He reached his thumb. "And I love your nose."

"My nose?"

"Yep. Specially that bit ..." he touched the very tip of it "... just there."

She made to bite his finger and he pulled it away, laughing.

"Well, OK," she said. "I suppose that'll have to do." She relaxed. "So what have you been doing with yourself?"

"I beat Paul at squash last night."

"Congratulations. I didn't know he played."

He made a face. "Usually wins too. Losing puts him in a foul temper. He likes to think he's invincible. Paul the wonder boy! Always was, always wants to be."

"Go easy! You won, didn't you? Did you see Dianne?"

"I did. We went back to their place afterwards." He fiddled with his cuff. "She was a bit quiet. I don't think she likes it here."

"She seemed OK when she did my nails." She looked at them. They were their natural colour again.

"Why don't you meet her for lunch or something? I think she could do with a friend. Make her feel at home."

"I have met her a couple of times. Anyway, hasn't she got a husband to be a friend?"

He snorted. "Paul? Paul's an idiot."

"He didn't seem like an idiot to me."

"You don't know him. He's even more self-centred since he came back home."

"That doesn't make him an idiot."

He laughed suddenly. "You're so logical!"

She pushed back her chair and stood up. "I'd better apply my logic to some work. How's your mother?"

He put an arm round her as they walked out. "Great. She doesn't say much but she seems fine."

They walked towards the main entrance, through the noise and bustle of the corridor, past the notice boards pinned with society announcements, and torn pieces of paper posted by students still trying to find accommodation they could afford.

"Back to work for you, I suppose?" she said.

"No way! I finished early at the last place. The office thinks I'm away for the day. I'm going to head home."

She stopped. "But it's only just after lunch."

"So?"

"You mean you're going to take a half day?"

"But one the boss won't know about."

Her brow creased. "You devious brat!"

He put his hand on her shoulder. "Maybe you should grow just a little bit of guile! You're too straight to survive. This is the real world."

"Don't be daft," she said with scorn. "I know people do things like that." She looked up at him. "You should see what goes on in a university! I just didn't think you would do it somehow."

He chuckled. "What? Do you think I'm perfect? Nobody's perfect, honey."

Adam let go of her and turned to work his way through the crowds of students round the door. When he had gone a few yards, Jenna called, "You could always come with me."

He looked back. "Where to?"

"Africa."

He laughed. "Sure!"

She went to a window and watched him striding towards the car park. He was still laughing.

Dianne was curled on the sofa, a cushion hugged to her stomach. The television was on with the sound low, but she was looking at the flowers which almost overwhelmed the small table under the window. The curtains were drawn against the frosty night and the mock coals of the fire flickered in the grate. The room was cosy with warmth and music and the scent of the flowers. The bouquet had been delivered yesterday. It was a very expensive one, specially at this time of the year. She had propped the small card beside it. "To beautiful Dianne. Paul."

She looked across the room to the chair beside the kitchen

door. Paul was sitting forward, his guitar on his knees, strumming softly. By the look of his fingers, he was practising, testing chords, trying a few bars. He was concentrating, looking down, his face hidden.

There was nothing on the card, or in his words, to give away any of his feelings. That horrible row was two days ago now. He had gone to the Sports Centre with Adam in the evening, even though she had thought they might stay in. Then Adam had come back with him. The flowers were the end of it as far as Paul was concerned. He hadn't said sorry, he hadn't asked her to forgive him. She wasn't used to men who behaved like that. Paul's lack of slavish adoration had been an intriguing novelty at first. In fact, it had been part of his attraction, his difference. Now she was beginning to feel nudges of a starvation, a denial which were becoming impossible to ignore. She was also bored.

She looked at the card. Even his message was conventional, bland, without warmth. Anybody could have written that card. "To beautiful Elizabeth. Darcy." It could be on a computer somewhere, ready to be churned out on demand.

The television still muttered in the corner. The signature tune of a late-night repeat of an east end soap opera played over the opening credits. Lazily, she half-watched it. On the screen, a pub brawl broke out. Two men were flinging each other across tables, glasses were smashing, women were screaming. After a moment she jumped as Paul rasped a loud discord from the strings. As it jangled into silence, he said,

"Slumming it tonight, are we?"

She sat without speaking, not looking at him. Then she reached across and the flowers shook as she felt for the remote control. The television snapped into blackness.

Even a week ago, she would have just laughed.

A week ago, maybe, he wouldn't have said it.

Her phone rang. It was Arabella. Her voice could be heard

across the room.

"Hello darling! How's our little emigrant?"

Arabella's familiar English voice seeped into Dianne like soothing ointment. Paul glanced at her and swung his guitar from his knee to set it against the wall. He went into the kitchen and she heard him putting on the kettle.

Everything was super with Arabella. In fact everything was a hoot. But they all so missed Dianne. There was a party last night ("Justin's twenty-fifth. You remember Justin? He has a Ferrari.") and someone said that it just wasn't the same without her.

"And," said Arabella, who had not encountered a full stop since Dianne answered the phone, "Luther was there. He's still devastated, the poor thing. Moping about like a baby that's dropped its rattle. I swear he's lost weight."

Dianne chuckled, Luther's slightly tubby features vivid in her mind. "That'll do him no harm."

"Has he phoned you?"

"No."

"He's still huffing. But we all miss you, you spoilt brat."

"I'm not a spoilt brat."

"Yes, you are. Your father spoiled you, darling. He even went along with you wanting that gorgeous Irishman. But none of us thought you'd actually go and live out there in that awful place."

" 'Out there'? Bella, how far away do you think I am? I could be with you in the time it takes you to pick a frock in Harvey Nick's."

"Well, I want to see you at Christmas. You *are* coming back for Christmas, aren't you? There's loads of stuff planned."

Dianne glanced towards the kitchen. Paul was still in there. "It's hard to pin Paul down."

Bella's voice rose an octave. "Just tell him you're coming, for goodness sake! And he has to come too." Her voice lowered huskily, "I want to see him again. I want to be in shooting range when you get tired of him."

"Bella, I won't get tired of him. I'm going to make this work. I love him."

Arabella laughed lightly. "Oh, I believe you think you do! The way you loved your pony until it threw you one day. Then you hated it. You always get tired of your toys."

"Shut up, Bella."

Bella sighed. "Well, you wanted Paul and you got him. I could even say," she giggled, "you've made your bed and you have to lie in it. A lot of us are very envious of your bed, Di!" She giggled again.

It was so good to hear Bella's giggle. It was a giggle that could go through walls.

When Dianne hung up she felt a physical ache inside. She missed Bella and the way she talked in paragraphs. She missed Luther. But she had married the man who made her toes curl, the man who could make her fizz inside simply by the way the light flashed from his dark eyes. In looks, he was the opposite of Luther's slick and golden elegance.

He came back into the room carrying two mugs of coffee.

"How's Hell's Bells?" he said, setting a mug beside her.

"Great," she said. She looked up at him and flicked her hair. Bella wasn't going to be right this time. So many of her friends back home were waiting to see how long it would take her to regret her impulsive marriage. Some of them probably had bets on it. She would not be humiliated like that. She was going to keep this man; and she wasn't going to stay here. She was going back to London and she would make sure he went back with her. It was inconceivable to her that he wouldn't go back. He was very nearly famous, for God's sake. In the last week, he had been contacted by a gallery offering to host an exhibition of his wildlife photography. He had turned it down without discussion.

She put a hand on his arm and pulled him down to sit beside

her. She took his mug from him and set it beside her own. He studied her, making no move. She leaned forward and kissed him with unmistakable intent.

"I want you, Paul," she whispered.

"I know you do," he said.

Still he didn't move. He was going to make her work for it. She raised herself and turned to straddle his knees, facing him, pressing her body against him. She kissed him again, deeply. He broke away and took her by the shoulders. He seemed to search in her eyes for something. Then he tilted his brow to meet hers and sat still. She was holding her breath. Surely he wouldn't snub her? She had made herself as plain as she could without words. She was coming back to him, as she always did.

His hands came up to the sides of her head and he kissed her lightly, almost thoughtlessly. Supporting her with his arms, he slid to the floor and laid her there. He left her briefly to turn down the lights. Then, dizzy with her victory, she forgot Arabella, she forgot parties, she forgot London, to revel in feeling his strength, his power, his passion centred on her again. As her hair spread across the carpet she swore to herself that she would make him follow her back home when she could bear this God-forsaken place no longer.

~

She lay on the floor, alone. He had left her very quickly. She heard his guitar. He was already back in the chair, guitar on his knee, strumming quietly.

She rolled over onto her stomach and pulled some of her clothes over herself. She leaned on her elbows, looking at him, feasting on him. He had pulled on his jeans again, but the brown curves of the guitar crossed his bare chest and shoulders. He smiled across at her and winked, then turned back to his guitar. Already he was leaving her again, receding, back where she could not follow. The warmth of loving seeped away and light fingers of desolation crept across her flesh. She didn't really know him at all. She was looking at a beautiful stranger who gave nothing of himself to her. The top of his head turned as he cocked his ear to the strings. As his fingers danced across the frets, the firelight struck sparks from the plain gold ring on his finger.

She put her hands flat on the carpet and rested her cheek on them as she listened.

I was wrong. I can't keep you. Nobody will ever keep you.

CHAPTER EIGHT

WHOSE IDEA WAS it anyway, to take Dianne Christmas shopping? Jenna adjusted her canvas bag as she waited at yet another shop window. It was handbags again. Dianne could pass no tinsel-strewn, cotton-wool clad, Santa-infested window if there was a handbag anywhere in it. She could talk about Gucci, Prada and Louis Vuitton as if they were as important as schools and poverty. Jenna leaned from her right foot to her left. Some people go on pub crawls. Dianne would get drunk on a handbag crawl.

In a long cream leather coat with a wide fur collar which touched her chin and mingled with the waves of her hair, Dianne looked like a model for Vogue. Her cream trousers were tucked into brown suede boots. Jenna buttoned her denim jacket against the cold and pulled her red scarf higher on her chin.

Christmas had taken over the city. In Corn Market, the Salvation Army was playing in the misty Saturday morning, the colours of the city's Christmas lights all around. Jenna loved the strong mellow notes of their instruments, the way the music soared on smokey air above the shoppers, twined round the excited children and enveloped even the pigeons in its warmth. Music with muscle, she thought.

She stopped to listen. The players shuffled their music sheets. Then the first bars of 'Hark the Herald Angels Sing' filled the streets. Everyone started to sing, even a Santa Claus who happened to turn the corner at that moment. Jenna's voice was insignificant in the crowd, her enjoyment rooted in the years when Christian music beat the tempo of her life.

There has been so much bad, she thought. But I've never blown anybody up. I've never shot anyone. I've never really hated anyone. Disliked maybe. Even strongly disliked. But not hated. Is that enough? I really hope I'm good. Beside her, a mother had crouched down between her children and had an arm round each one. The little girl was holding a knitted doll. She was waving the doll's arms around and jiggling it as if it sang too.

Two pigeons bobbed around the conductor's feet as the band began the crescendo for the final chorus. There was a joint intake of breath. Jenna had her mouth open for the first note when she heard a voice close to her ear.

"When you've had enough, I'll be over there."

When Jenna found Dianne, she was gazing into a window, at a handbag which, she said, her friend Bella would just die for. Jenna looked for a price tag. There wasn't one; that was a danger sign.

"My feet are killing me," she said.

It wasn't easy getting a seat in the small restaurant, but they managed it by strategy, Dianne keeping watch for an empty table while Jenna queued. With a trailing garland of holly behind their heads and the thin strains of Bing Crosby dreaming yet again of a white Christmas, Jenna eased off her shoes. Dianne was quiet.

"Have you much more to do?" Jenna asked eventually, fingers crossed under the table.

"I haven't got anything for Paul yet."

"Has he asked for anything?"

"No. He says he can't think of anything."

"Men are like that," said Jenna. "If they can't have a Ferrari then they can't think of anything else."

Dianne open her mouth to speak and shut it again. The men

Dianne knew probably had Ferraris already.

"Are you going back to London for Christmas?"

Dianne hooked a stray strand of hair from under her fur collar. "Well ... yes, I think so."

Jenna was startled. "You'll not get booked on a flight now if you haven't decided."

"Oh, I've booked two tickets." Dianne arched her brows. "I've never been away from home before at Christmas."

Jenna was puzzled. "Why wouldn't you go?"

"Paul doesn't want to go. He says he wants to be with his mother this Christmas."

Jenna nodded. It was the first Christmas since Adam and Paul's father died. "It'll be a tough Christmas for them all."

"But I'm his wife," said Dianne.

Jenna looked at her, her cup paused half-way to her mouth. "So?"

Dianne tossed her hair. "Well, he can see his mother any time. I haven't seen my father in months. And this is our first Christmas together. We should stay together."

"Hazel will have a bad Christmas. Paul and Adam both know that. And it'll be hard for them too," she added. "It was late January he died, so the first anniversary isn't too far away either."

"Well, Paul lives here now. He can see her any time," Dianne repeated.

Jenna studied her. She hadn't realised that Dianne could be quite so single minded. She decided to say one thing and then keep quiet. It wasn't any of her business.

"I think it's not that he can see his mother any time. It's that she needs to see him. He knows his mother will need him particularly this Christmas."

"When a man gets married," said Dianne stubbornly, "his wife should come before his mother."

"I don't envy him his choice."

Dianne's eyes widened. "But Paul should come with me. He doesn't need to choose."

"Did you ever meet his father?"

"Once. He was already very ill when Paul and I met." She sat back. "Did you meet him?"

"He died before I met Adam."

"So you only met Adam this year?"

Jenna smiled. "About six months ago. At a friend's barbecue."

"Adam suits you."

Jenna put her chin on her hand. "Why do you think so?"

Dianne waved a hand dismissively. "Oh, he's ... solid, straightforward." She took a sip of her coffee. "And he has a good job with a regular income." She laughed. "Bella says if you can't marry old money, then marry someone making new money!"

Jenna rattled her spoon on the table. "Is that what you did?"

Dianne examined her manicured nails. "I thought so. Paul was making money then. And I wanted him." She touched the golden pine cones surrounding the red candle in the middle of the table.

"He's a brilliant photographer. The family portrait he took for us is stunning. Mum's very pleased with it. She says anyone who can make Luke smile in a photograph must be a genius."

Dianne lifted a pine cone and turned it over in her hand. Her voice was wistful. "Paul was good enough to photograph royalty. If he'd stayed."

Her tone made Jenna pause. Then she asked, "So why did he give it all up?"

Dianne shook her head. "He said he wasn't giving it all up. He just wanted to come back home."

Jenna smiled a little and said, "Back to his own God and his own devil."

Dianne frowned. "What?"

"Nothing. It must have been an upheaval for you?"

"Well, I couldn't make him change his mind so here I am." Dianne placed the pine cone back, carefully arranging it amongst the others, draping the tinsel just so. "And I'm not ready to leave him here yet."

Jenna looked down. The table covering was white with the green and red of holly twigs scattered across it. The word 'yet' bounced around inside her head, refusing to settle in any corner that would render it harmless. But the relationship between a married couple was no-one else's business. Then she felt Dianne's fingers on her hair, where it hung from her bent head.

"You need a good haircut, Jenna!"

"Do I?"

"Yes, you do. I've found a salon that's not too bad. I'll give you the name of it." Jenna leaned away from her fidgeting fingers but Dianne pulled her hair across her cheeks, held it up a little, brushed down a mock fringe. "Tell them to cut it shorter and feather it down the sides and across your cheeks." She cocked her head to one side, considering. "And get highlights."

She let go and Jenna shook her hair back the way it had been. "Right," she said.

"I could take you to a brilliant place in Knightsbridge. Pierre used to look after my hair all the time. He's a sweetie. He was so desolate when I said I was going away." She sighed. "Perhaps I'll visit him when I'm home at Christmas." She shrugged. "But you're stuck with Belfast, I'm afraid."

"Pity," said Jenna.

At the table beside them, a toddler suddenly screamed. It was a little girl. Her harassed mother was trying to get a break. Whatever had provoked it, the child was giving a master class in tantrums. Her fist held a crushed piece of cake and she hurled it across the table.

Dianne got up. "Let's go. I can't *stand* children."

Jenna squeezed her shoes on again, regretting taking them off.

As they passed the next table, she put her face down to the child's. "Boo!" she said. The child jumped, surprised into silence. Jenna grinned at the mother. "Happy Christmas," she said.

~

The bus was crowded, it was cold, everyone was tired and Dianne was still talking.

"Thank goodness you were with me. I'd never have found half of those places without you."

Jenna shifted slightly to restore feeling in her left foot. "Belfast's a good place to shop now."

Dianne wrinkled her nose. "But it's not London."

Thank God, thought Jenna.

They gripped their bags tightly as they alighted and dodged across the main road, the pace frantic, the lights fast and the noise making conversation impossible. Past the row of shops, they turned down the quieter street where Dianne and Paul lived, past the flickering lights of the Christmas trees in every front window. Up the drive past Paul's car, Dianne put her key in the door.

She said over her shoulder, "You go on into the lounge. I want to put these bags upstairs."

Jenna dropped her own shopping bags in the hallway. An arrangement of holly and candles garnished the hall table; a bell of tinsel hung from the ceiling. The lounge felt cold as she entered. To her left the Christmas tree stood in the window. It was one of those elegant ones with only gold and white decorations, and white lights.

She turned round and stopped. Paul was sitting on the floor by the open window at the other end of the room. His feet were bare, one leg crooked under him and the other drawn up as he leaned his camera on the sill. Jenna heard the soft click of the shutter. Beyond Paul's head, in the garden, she could see a bird table. Around it there was a little storm of birds.

Silently, she dropped to her hands and knees and crawled over to the window. Paul must have felt her presence but he didn't acknowledge it. He was totally still, his only movement the slightest tilt of the camera, the faint whirr as he shot another frame.

Nets of peanuts swung from the rim of the bird table. Two bluetits hung upside down, busy and alert. Several sparrows had possession of the top of the table, pecking, hopping, pecking. The shutter clicked again. A magpie swooped down with an arrogant swagger – click – and the sparrows jumped into the air and fluttered to the bushes nearby. As the magpie snatched at the crumbs, it knocked more onto the ground. The sparrows regrouped on the winter grass which still showed the white of frost in the shaded hollows. Click.

On a bare branch of the bush where the sparrows had retreated, Jenna saw a robin. Its body was fluffed out into a round ball against the cold and stood proudly on two stiff little legs. It cocked its head from right to left, left to right, in anxious jerks. Come on, little guy, said Jenna silently. Come and get some before it's all gone.

Slowly she brought her mouth close to Paul's ear. "On your left. The bush. A robin," she whispered.

His eye never left the viewfinder. The camera moved left silently. Click. He took several frames before the robin flew away. A rook dropped from the sky. All the other birds scattered, some to the bush, some to the wire of the clothes line next door. Keeping the camera braced on the window sill, Paul aimed at the rook. Jenna had never really studied a rook before. They were just big birds who walked busily around the manse garden and who played games with her cat, flying off just as she crouched to leap. Now Jenna looked at this rook as though through Paul's viewfinder, seeing what he was seeing. The sheen of the feathers, the thickness of the beak with its grey base, the line of the tail against the thrust of the strong legs. The shutter fired. It flew away.

The robin was coming back. It landed on the edge of the table.

Its head bobbed, up and down, side to side, checking, watching, alert to life and death. Behind it, the bush gave a barren backdrop to the flame red of the bird's breast. Momentarily it was alone. Jenna knew Paul had a clean shot. She stopped breathing, waiting for the click.

The door slammed. "It's freezing in here! Paul! What are you doing? Shut that window."

Outside, the garden emptied of life in a clatter of panic and feathers. Paul swore.

Dianne stopped and put a hand over her mouth. "Oh, I didn't realise ..."

"Did you get it?" Jenna asked.

"No," he said, unfolding himself. He pulled the window shut.

"But you got it earlier? On the twig?"

He twisted the lens and removed it. "Yes." He looked at her for the first time since she had entered the room. "Thanks."

"No problem." She searched in her pocket for her phone. "I'll just ring Adam. He's going to take me to the bus station."

"I could have done that."

"So you could." She held the phone to her ear. "Thanks anyway."

Paul followed Dianne into the kitchen. Jenna frowned; although Adam's phone was ringing, there was no reply. Strange, he should have been waiting for her call. She hung up. She'd try later, but if she was to catch the bus to her parent's in time for tea, he'd need to get here soon.

The room was still cold. She slipped to the floor in front of the fire and sat cross-legged, leaning back against the sofa. When Adam and she had dinner here in October, she had seen Paul and Dianne sharing a secret hug, Dianne looking up at her husband, Paul with his hand on her shoulder.

Something had changed. She could hear them talking in the kitchen. Paul was asking about their morning. But it was different, formal, a polite request for information. She opened her bag and pulled out a small packet. Inside was an embossed jewellery case. She had bought her mother a pendant. The delicate cross lay golden across her palm as she examined it, the chain trailing to her knee.

She heard a click.

Paul was by the kitchen door, a different lens on his camera, pointing it at her. She opened her mouth to protest and he shot again. Before she could move, he had sprung onto the sofa and crouched on the arm, slightly behind her. A quick turn of the focus. Click.

Dianne appeared with a plate of sandwiches. "Paul! Leave the poor girl alone."

Paul put the camera down. "She doesn't mind. Do you, Jenna?"

"If you'd warned me, I could have combed my hair."

"But I didn't want you to do that."

Dianne produced napkins from a drawer. "All women need to comb their hair before they get their picture taken," she said and went back to the kitchen.

He had come to stand over her. Jenna looked up the length of him. "Why didn't you want me to do that?"

"Because it wouldn't have been you. It would have been Jenna with her hair combed for a photograph."

He sat on the sofa, his feet only a few inches from her side. "But that's me as well," she said, her eyes on his long toes, so close she could touch them.

"But you don't know who you are. You said so."

Jenna turned her head sharply to look up at him over her shoulder. Dianne came in with a cake and set it on the table beside the sandwiches.

"Paul, pass Jenna a sandwich. I'll make some tea. It'll warm us up."

She left again.

"That conversation doesn't count," Jenna said.

"It counted for me."

She held up the golden cross, still in her hand. As it swung sparkling in the glow from the lights on the Christmas tree, she said, "I heard the Salvation Army Band today." She glanced round at him and gave a half smile before she looked away. "I listened to them singing 'Hark the Herald Angels Sing'. And I hoped I was good."

"Why? Being bad's more exciting."

"And more dangerous."

"You're not a coward."

"Are you?"

He grinned. "Depends."

"On what?"

"What I'm afraid of."

He was like a flint, striking sparks from her brain.

"What are you afraid of?"

"Lots of things." He slumped back against the cushion. After a moment he relaxed. "Not getting any presents at Christmas. Now that scares me."

She drew her knees up to her chin and hugged them. "Me too! What do you want for Christmas?"

She didn't see his smile, but she heard it in his words. "World peace! That'll do as the stocking filler."

She turned her face sideways to look at him again. She felt his humour touch her gently, a gossamer strand of connection.

"Some stocking." Without thinking, she brushed her fingertips along the arch of his foot. "Your feet don't look big enough."

Dianne came back with the teapot. "Paul, move those sandwiches a bit so I can put the teapot stand down. I'm just going up to change and get out of these boots."

She went into the hall and Jenna heard her running up the

stairs. There was a silence. Beside her, the foot vanished as Paul pulled it up and across his knee.

"I looked up that poem."

She was hugging her knees again, not looking at him. "Did you? And?"

He spoke quietly, deliberately. " 'These laid the world away; poured out the red sweet wine of youth; gave up the years to be of work and joy, and that unhoped serene, that men call age; and those who would have been their sons, they gave their immortality.' "

She got to her knees and turned round to lean her elbows on the cushion beside him.

"They were fighting for peace."

"Can you fight for peace?" he said. "Peace is the absence of fighting."

"No, it isn't," she said. "Peace is a way of living. Even in the middle of a war, you can be at peace deep inside, because you feel right with yourself." She shrugged. "And with God."

He was looking at her intently. She returned his gaze, the gossamer thread tugging at her. His eyes were very blue, his mouth still as unique and mesmerising as she remembered.

Suddenly he leaned away from her and reached over the arm of the sofa to pull his guitar onto his knee. He settled it on his lap and strummed a chord.

" 'Hark the Herald Angels Sing', was it?"

She smiled and settled back on the floor at his feet. His voice was a full rich tenor and yet in the lilt of it there was an untrained ease. After the first two lines he took his eyes from the strings and turned to her, one eyebrow raised in invitation. She began to sing along with him.

"Peace on earth and mercy mild,
God and sinners reconciled."

He knew the words. All of them, better than she did. After the first verse, she put her cheek down onto her hands, closed her eyes and listened. Total relaxation wrapped her like a blanket of wool and she felt the moment slipping softly, deeply into her memory.

"Mild he lays his glory by,
Born that man no more may die,
Born to raise the sons of earth,
Born to give them second birth."

He slowed the rhythm slightly as he came to the last chorus. She raised her head. He was looking at her. She sang it with him until his fingers trailed down the strings, across the last chord.

There was a silence. Neither of them moved. It seemed to Jenna that she heard his thought, picked it up along the gossamer thread. Her voice came out as a whisper. "This Christmas will be hard. Hard to sing words like that."

He swung the guitar to the ground and held it by the neck between his knees.

"Words aren't hard to sing. Or say."

He was looking down. She touched his arm timidly. "Paul." He looked sideways at her. "Don't stop singing. Even if you don't mean it."

Dianne was coming down the stairs. Just as she came through the door, Jenna's phone rang. She got to her feet and turned away to answer it.

"Hi," said Adam. "Sorry I missed your call. I was in a shop and you know what the noise is like. I never want to hear Rudolph the Red-nosed Reindeer again. I'll be there in fifteen, honey."

Dianne dropped onto the seat beside Paul, pulling her legs up under her. She leaned across and put her face up for a kiss. He touched her cheek with his lips. Over her shoulder, his eyes met Jenna's. He got up, propped the guitar against the wall beside the sofa and lifted his camera.

"I'm going to see if I can get some more shots before I lose the light."

The room seemed smaller without him.

Dianne reached for a sandwich. "I heard you singing. He's a nice voice, hasn't he?"

"He's a great voice."

Dianne took a small bite of the sandwich. "Multi-talented, my Paul. He's wasted here."

Jenna sat in front of the fire. She wasn't hungry.

CHAPTER NINE

JENNA HAD ARRIVED at the manse that evening to find her mother banging saucepans.

"Who does that man think he is anyway? Coming in here and planting such ideas. I wish I'd never thought of the portrait in the first place."

Cora was supposed to be making the tea, but the noise seemed to be an equal, if not more important goal. Jenna sliced some bread and set it on the kitchen table. It was set for three. Luke had made a tactical retreat to spend the weekend with a friend.

"But you like the portrait! It's good of all of us."

Cora stirred a pan of meat vigorously. Loud and plaintive meowing assailed the back door. "Let those kittens in, will you, before they drive me mad."

Four kittens tumbled over each other into the kitchen, followed at a more dignified pace by their mother. Jenna hunkered down to play with them. One was tortoiseshell like its mother, two were an even mix of black and white and one was pure black, except for a single white front paw.

Jenna detached one of the black and white ones from her leg. "Have you got homes for them yet?"

The lid of the potato saucepan banged. "Two are going to a farm. We'll probably keep one, but one might have to be put down. Can't find anyone to take it."

"You can't do that! You could keep two."

"No. we couldn't." The oven door slammed.

Jenna stood up, leaving the kittens leaping on their mother's twitching tail, trying to kill it.

"Mum, it's Luke's life. He's old enough to make his own decisions."

Cora spun round, a wooden spoon held aloft. "He never would have thought of it if it wasn't for that man! He's a bad influence. I thought he was odd at the time."

One kitten, the one with the single white paw, had ascended as far as Jenna's knee. She bent to unhook its tiny claws from her jeans and held it to her chin, tickling its ears.

"Just because you think he's odd, it doesn't mean he's bad." Even if he thinks bad's more exciting, she didn't add. "And Luke's not saying he won't go to university, for goodness' sake. He's just saying he won't go this year. He just wants to travel a bit first. And he probably did think of it for himself anyway. Everybody thinks of it these days."

"You didn't. And your Dad's devastated. He won't say very much, but he's devastated." Cora bent to pull a tray of roasted vegetables from the oven. "Thank God for you, Jenna. That's all I can say." Her mother set down the vegetables, dropped the cloth she was holding and gave Jenna a quick hug. "You've always been a great girl. Never gave us a moment's worry. Boys are always harder to rear." She put her hands on her hips and looked at the table. "Call Dad. I think we're ready."

Jenna found her father bent over his papers in his study. He looked up as she put her head round the door.

"Tea's ready, Dad."

His smile was strained and tired. "Thanks, Jenna." He stretched out a hand and she came into the room and took it. "It's good to see you this weekend. Your mum's very upset."

Jenna put her head on one side. "And you? What do you think?"

Donald set down his pen and slumped back. "I'm worried. The world's not a safe place any more. It's not Brighton Luke wants to go to. It's much, much further than that."

"But lots of people take gap years, Dad. He'll be back."

"Will he?" His kind eyes were sad as he looked up at his daughter. "Will he? So many people never come back once they leave here." He sighed. "That would kill your mother."

"He was going to go to university in Scotland anyway. Not here."

"Scotland's not that far away." Donald swivelled his chair and stood. "Outer Mongolia's a different matter."

Jenna stayed only one night. It was the candlelight carol service in her father's church on Sunday evening but she decided to go back to Belfast on the afternoon bus. He ran her to the bus stop in the village. As they waited in the car in the darkening afternoon, he asked, "Are things still good between you and Adam?"

Jenna grinned happily. "Great. We've a dinner date tomorrow."

Her father's anxiety seemed to lift a little. "It's great to see you happy." A look of concern crossed his face. "Don't rush things, will you?" He shifted uncomfortably. "He ... Adam doesn't ... make demands ..."

Jenna laughed. "No, Dad. He doesn't 'make demands'!"

Donald looked relieved. "Anyone who lays a finger on my daughter will answer to me!"

"You'll thump him with your commentary on Revelation!"

"And that would hurt!"

The bus arrived and the doors hissed apart. Jenna opened the car door and leaned over to peck her father on the cheek.

"Next time I come, it'll be Christmas."

"Be good till then, Missy," he said.

It was dark when Jenna walked through the patches of lamplight to her own door. Every house she passed had a Christmas tree; some were more flamboyant with reindeers flying across the glass and coloured lights framing the windows. As she skipped up the two steps to her door, she could see the tinsel on her own unlit tree glistening faintly from the reflected light through her living room window.

The dim silence of the hall embraced her like a welcome. She dumped her bag and, without putting any lights on, sank into her favourite chair in the front room. Adam said this chair was Jenna-shaped. There was a headache trying to break into her head. She couldn't imagine life without the refuge of her own house, her own patch of this earth. It was like a wedge from a sliced loaf, in the centre of a long unbroken terrace, in a mass of identical streets.

Since the others had left, Jenna had made it entirely her own. Clean but chaotic. Dimly, she saw her slippers near the tree, under the window where she had last discarded them. One was upside down. And on the floor at the side of the sofa was the pink polo-neck she hadn't been able to find yesterday when she was rushing out to meet Dianne. Luke said that everywhere collapsed into bedlam as soon as she set foot in it. She had this house until the summer, until this extra year at university was over. Her parents couldn't pay for it any longer than that. She closed her eyes and leaned back.

If she gave up her studies, she'd have to move back to the manse, to her parents, until she had a job and enough to pay rent somewhere. No way. Even if she bored herself stupid over tutorials and assignments, no way. She sighed. She would have to start looking for a job in the New Year. That way, she might have something to go to as soon as she got her MA. A stab of anxiety jabbed her. *If* she got her MA.

She decided to try Luke's mobile. Her phone nestled beside the jewellery case where it still lay at the bottom of her bag. She stood behind the dark tree, looking out onto the street, quiet now on a Sunday evening. She liked the dark, the feeling of looking out and knowing that no-one could see her watching. There was both stealth and security in it. Luke answered almost immediately.

"Hi, LW. It's me."

His voice was deep and wary. "So you've been home then."

"I have. I'm just back."

There was a slight pause before Luke said, "How's Mum?"

"Not pleased."

"I know that. Shit."

She walked round the room and back to the window. "You might have told me. Maybe I could have ... worked them round to the idea."

"Yeah. Well. They know now." His tone became exasperated. "What's wrong with them anyway? There's three of us going. We're going to work our way around a few places for a year. That's all."

"How long have you been thinking about doing this?"

"A few of us have been talking about it since the summer. I suppose you're mad at me as well."

She imagined him, probably sitting with his legs straggled across a room, hair spikier than ever, defensive and stubborn. She loved him.

"No, I'm not. I think I'm a bit envious."

His voice rose. "Envious?"

She leaned against the wall by the window. "Yes, envious. What's so wrong with that?"

"Can't imagine you canoeing across a swamp."

"Maybe not a swamp." Outside, three children ran past giggling. She put a hand to her head. The headache was making progress. "But I don't suppose you'd take your big sister along too, would you?"

"Shit!"

She held a hand up to the empty room. "OK, OK. I'm joking." She did a circuit of the room again. "Mum thinks Adam's brother put it into your head."

"No, he didn't. But he did ..." his voice tailed off.

"He did what?"

"I suppose it was him made me finally decide to go for it. Before I talked to him, I hadn't ... it hadn't ..." He stopped and took a deep breath. "Been real. It hadn't been real. That I could do what I wanted and that doing what I wanted wasn't stupid."

A man and girl walked past. The girl had her head on the man's shoulder and he held a lead which ended in a small terrier.

"It'll be OK. They'll get used to it. You're not going for a while yet anyway."

"Shit, no. I'm going to get good results this year." He paused. "You're not the only one with brains, you know."

"I know that."

"I wish they did."

"There's a lot they don't know about you, Luke. Like the fact that you say 'shit' when you're not at home."

She heard the grin. "Yeah, well."

"But you wouldn't embarrass Dad."

"Shit, no. He's OK. In his own way."

"You're going back home tomorrow, are you?"

"I'm going to stay here for a bit. But I will, yeah. I'll go back in a couple of days. I need some socks. And stuff."

"Right. They'll have calmed down by then. But ring Mum and let her know you're OK."

"If you see Paul, tell him I said hi."

"If I do, I will. See you at Christmas then."

"Oh, shit, yeah. Cheers."

Jenna set down her phone and bent to the plug under the

window to switch on her tree lights. Before her finger touched it, she stopped. Someone was standing outside her front door. She peered round the branches of the tree, knocking a silver ball to the floor.

It was Paul. He was wearing a knee length coat and a wool hat pulled down over his ears. She saw him checking the number on her door. Then he took an envelope from his pocket and pushed it through her letter box. The noise of it falling into her hallway broke her surprise and made her move.

The pendant she had bought for her mother was inside the envelope. She pulled open the door. He was several doors away, walking back the way he had come. He heard the door and turned. The street lamp lit his features from above, gilding the woollen hat and throwing shadows below his throat. He walked back.

"I didn't expect you to be here. You got the bus home yesterday."

Jenna held up the envelope. "Does this mean I have an empty box in my bag?"

She was above him, in her own doorway, two steps up.

"Unless there were two, I suppose it does."

"Where did you find it?"

"A little piece of the chain peeped at me from down the side of the cushion."

"How did you know where I lived?"

"Dianne's added you to her Christmas card list."

"Ah." He stood with his hands in his coat pockets. She moved back a little. "Come in."

He walked past her and turned into her front room as if he knew the way. He was standing beside her Christmas tree as she flicked on the coloured lights. It wasn't nearly as sophisticated as Dianne's tree. The colours were all over the place, the tinsel tangled this way and that. She reached for the main light switch on the wall.

"Leave it," he said suddenly, startling her. "There's enough light from the tree. Don't spoil it."

Her hand hovered, then dropped. Like a child, she thought, he wants to watch the bright lights. His fingers touched a branch, then another.

"Yes, it's real," she said.

He looked over his shoulder, his hand still on the branch. "Don't you mind the pine needles all over the carpet?"

"No. In fact I love pine needles. They smell good."

He sat down in her chair. Her chair. She went to the sofa and pulled her knees up to curl into a corner of it.

"Thanks for returning the pendant. Adam could have given it to me tomorrow night. I'm seeing him then."

Red, green and blue light smudged across his face as the colours danced on the tree.

"Lucky old you," he said. "I tried him, but he's not about."

He pulled off the woollen hat and ran a hand through his hair. It stood up in short spikes. Instantly, she was reminded of Luke.

"Luke says 'hi'."

He twirled the hat on one finger. "Say 'hi' back. How's he doing?"

She didn't feel like being polite and tactful. She was too tired for that. "He's going to Outer Mongolia."

"Seriously?"

"Somewhere like that."

He laughed in delight. "Well, way to go, Luke!"

"And my mother never wants to see you again."

He looked puzzled. "She probably won't. Unless you marry my brother and I have to be polite to all your relatives at some fancy hotel. But why the particular desire?"

"She's blaming you for putting ideas into his head."

He went quiet, absently smoothing the wool of the hat on his knee. Then he said, "If it helps her, I don't mind."

"What do you mean: 'If it helps her'?" She mimed quote marks.

"She'll worry about him. He's her son. She needs to be angry."

Jenna looked at him in amazement. "She doesn't need to be angry at all. She needs to talk to Luke like she can hear what he's saying."

Red, green, blue in his eyes. Red, green, blue across his wonderful mouth. "You don't know how your mother feels," he said. "And you'll not know until you have children of your own."

The headache was chiselling the back of her eye. "Yes, well. You'll know about that sooner than me."

He put his elbow on the arm of the chair and dropped his chin into his hand. His look was teasing. "Maybe you haven't noticed, but I'll never be a mother."

"I noticed."

The silence lengthened. Then he straightened back in the chair. Her chair.

"I'll talk to him again if you like," he said.

"I'll pass on the kind offer. As long as you don't convince him he should be the first man on Mars."

He ignored that, his thoughts already moving on. The hat was on the arm of the chair now. "Will you all be together at Christmas?" he asked.

"Yes, as always. Where will you be?"

"As always. At my mother's."

"And where will Dianne be?"

He looked at her in surprise. "Has she been talking to you?"

"It's hard to shop together for a morning without talking."

He looked away. "She wants to go back to London."

"I know."

He moved the hat to the other arm. He folded it in two, unfolded it, folded it again. His eyes flicked to her and away. Red, green, blue. He wasn't going to ask. And it was none of her business. But she'd tell him anyway. That's the sort of night it was.

"You should go with her."

"I want to stay here."

"I know. But you should go with Dianne."

Words flashed like bullets in a gunfight.

"She should stay here with me."

"You should stay together."

"Yes," he said. "Here."

"No. Do what she wants in this."

"Why?"

"She's homesick. You're stronger than she is."

He snorted derisively. "You think?"

"Your mother will understand."

"Maybe."

"And Adam'll be here."

"Ha! Some company!" The hat became a ball in his fist.

"What about relatives?"

"An aunt and uncle up in Coleraine."

"Then she could go there."

He flicked the hat across his knee. "I don't want to go back to London."

Jenna put her hand to her right temple. "Paul, put that hat down."

Ostentatiously, he held it in his finger and thumb and dropped it over the side of the chair onto the floor. Jenna gave up and stretched her legs out along the sofa.

"Suit yourself," she said. "What do I know? It's not a problem I have. I'm nobody's wife."

Red, green, blue in his eyes. Shadows chasing through the waves of his tousled hair. "I noticed."

The bells from the church at the top of the street began to ring. She had been thinking of going to their carol service. Not now.

In one smooth movement he stood and turned to go. "I'd better go before I get caught up in all the traffic. More people going to sing about 'mercy mild'."

His tone annoyed her. It was only yesterday that he had sung about it himself. She swung her feet to the floor.

"Don't knock it. It goes along with the 'peace on earth' you want in your stocking."

He had reached the hall but he put his head back round the door of the room again as she stood up.

"Not that sort of mercy. The mercy that's worth having is tough stuff."

She sighed. "Paul, go home."

He grinned, his lips curving over white teeth. She stood looking up at him in the dark hallway, reluctant to put on the light and hurt her head any more. She touched his arm.

"Wait a minute."

She went back to the room, the red, green, blue room, and picked up his hat. Holding it in both hands, she reached up and pulled it down over his head, over his ears, tugged it over his brow. Then she raised his collar and folded the lapels across his throat. He stood still, letting her work at him. Her hands dropped to her sides.

"Now go home."

He turned the latch on the front door. "Yes, ma'am. And you take two aspirins, a mug of cocoa and a hot water bottle. Your headache'll be gone in the morning."

"You think?"

"I know. It's worked for me so far."

"You know everything."

A cold wind cut into the gap as he opened the door onto the street. At the bottom of the steps he turned to look up as she stood with her hand on the door. Then abruptly he strode away. The peal of Christmas bells chased him to the corner; a flurry of snow zig-zagged through the air. Jenna watched him until he disappeared into the night like a fugitive, leaving the street empty, yet full of noise.

In the kitchen she put on the kettle, reached into a cupboard and pulled out the cocoa tin. She looked round. She'd seen the packet of aspirin somewhere. Thank goodness the bells had stopped. The service must have started.

She couldn't read. Instead, she lay down in her bed and curled round the hot water bottle. Her eyes closed over the pain in her head and at first she couldn't sleep. The aspirin began to take effect. She rolled onto her back. Red, green, blue; red, green, blue, strobed within her eyelids.

Restlessly, she threw one arm across the pillow above her head. Tonight there had been a shifting; one small move on a game board. She and Paul had accepted each other. He wasn't just Adam's brother any more. He was Paul.

Mad, bad and dangerous to know.

CHAPTER TEN

THE KEY TURNED in the front door, followed by a slam. Upstairs, Dianne had just switched off the hairdryer and tossed her hair back over her head where it hung in thick, tangled strands. She heard the drop of Paul's keys on the hall table. After a moment of silence, she heard him coming upstairs on light feet. She could visualise him. Two stairs at a time, sometimes three. He appeared at the bedroom door.

"Hi," he said.

"Hi. Did you find the house?"

"Yep." He sat on the edge of the bed and pulled off his shoes and socks.

"What's it like?"

"A bit smaller that this one and opens straight onto the street. No garden."

"How ghastly!"

"It suits her."

Dianne turned back to the mirror. She saw Paul's eyes taking in the towel which was wrapped round her, her bare shoulders peeping through her tangle of hair. She opened a jar of face cream. He lifted his feet and lay back on the bed, his hands behind his head. In the mirror, she saw him watching her lazily. She tossed her hair over one shoulder and began to smooth cream into her neck slowly.

"She seems to really like Adam," she said.

"Weird."

"She really lit up like a beacon when I asked her about him yesterday."

"They've only known each other for a few months."

She smiled into the mirror, teasing. "That worked for us."

"Yes," he said. "The whole of England's still getting over it."

"Well, she'll be glad to get the pendant back. It's only nine carat, but I suppose her mother wouldn't notice the difference. They're only a clergy family after all. I didn't say anything when she picked it."

"That was very restrained of you."

"He's not even a bishop. Do they have bishops over here?" Curiosity paused her fingers.

Paul wiggled his toes. "Yes," he said. "But not all denominations are enlightened enough to have them, I'm afraid. I don't think Jenna's father would ever be a bishop."

Dianne made a face. "No career ladder then."

Paul crossed his ankles and rubbed his eyes. "Just Jacob's ladder. Poor man."

"Jacob who?"

He rolled onto his side. "A guy in the Bible. He saw a ladder. The bottom of it was on the ground and the top of it reached heaven. There were angels climbing all over it." He yawned. "No bishops, though."

"Oh, that Jacob." She dipped her fingers into the jar of cream again. "I wonder did she notice the pendant missing. I suppose she would have rung if she did. Anyway, she'll find it on the mat when she gets back. I wonder when she's coming back?"

"Who knows?"

"I suppose she might stay in the country until after Christmas now." She put one finger on her chin, considering. "She's a homely little thing. A study-bug."

"A study-bug? What on earth's that?"

Dianne turned round and faced him. "You know. A book person. Someone who'd rather stay in and read than go out for the night." She turned back to the mirror. "I've met one or two before."

"Goodness, have you?" he said.

She stopped and looked back over her shoulder. Sometimes she didn't know when he was making fun of her. He returned her gaze blandly, giving her no clue. He removed one hand from under his cheek and rubbed his nose, then settled back again, his head cocked towards her.

"So what do you think of her?" she said. "Do you think she and Adam will stay together?"

He didn't reply at once. Then he said, "I've no idea. That's their business."

She gathered her hair and pulled it across and over the other shoulder. She began to move her fingers slowly over the other side of her neck, down across her arched throat. Through half-closed eyes, she watched him in the mirror. She put the lid back on the jar of cream, lifted the hairbrush and looked round, her shoulder hunched up to her chin.

"Would you like to brush my hair tonight?"

He sat up and swung his feet to the floor. "OK."

She closed her eyes as she felt his hands in her hair, straightening each strand as he brushed. His movements were smooth, rhythmic, the brush stroking through her hair right to the ends. Back to the top; smooth, gentle, down to the nape of her neck. She leaned against him. She felt him parting the hair at her neck; felt the brush strokes slow to a stop as he bent; felt his lips on her skin. One hand moved over her shoulder, across her collar bone and slipped under the towel at her breast. She sighed.

"Merry Christmas, darling," she whispered.

He set the brush down. "By the way," he said, backing away, "I'll go to London with you for Christmas."

She jumped up and whirled round, the towel falling from her. "Paul! That's super!" She flung her arms round him. "What changed your mind?"

He unwound her arms from his neck. "I changed it, that's all."

He was moving away from her, towards the door. Stepping over the towel on the floor, she put her arms round his waist and tried to kiss him. He shook her away impatiently.

"Leave me alone, Dianne! I'm tired."

Hurt skewered her. She stood back, her eyes wide. She lifted a hand.

"Don't go, Paul. I need you tonight. I'm lonely."

He bent his head for a moment and then looked up at her. "I'm not very good at being needed."

Dianne stood still. Then she bent and lifted the towel. Covered again, she turned her back. He left the room.

~

The tree lights were still on in the chilly room downstairs. They didn't flicker as Jenna's had. Their steady glow burnished Paul in silver as he dropped to the carpet by the sofa, where Jenna had sat the previous day. He sat crossed legged, as she had, and put his elbows on his knees.

Dianne was irritating him more every day. *But I didn't have to hurt her like that. I didn't.*

He reached up to tug a golden bauble from the tree and fiddle with it. Memory heaved in him like a rush of sickness. It was the Christmas just before his ninth birthday. His mother was getting the dinner ready. He and Adam were crawling round the floor of their lounge, racing the cars that they had been given in the morning. It wasn't the floor any more. It was a race track, better than any race track anywhere else in the whole world. The pits were behind the rubber plant; the spectator stands were the coffee table; the chicane was round the Christmas tree. There were baubles on it just like this one.

His car was running out of fuel. He would have to make a pit stop! It would have to be quick – Adam's car was closing on him! He dived behind the rubber plant. Adam crashed into his legs and jolted him onto his side. The rubber plant shook, then tilted. It seemed to happen in slow motion. His father came into the room at that moment. The rubber plant keeled over and landed with a crash at his father's feet. Soil and pebbles flew across the carpet and the carefully polished leaves and branches twisted and snapped.

It was twenty years ago and yet the memory was still jagged. The golden bauble broke in Paul's hand and a drop of blood stained the mound of his thumb. His father had roared at him. He didn't hit him. Christopher Shepherd had never hit either of his sons, but he had a quick temper. It flared and died, but burned to cinders while it lived. Paul remembered three things about that Christmas. One was being sent upstairs, banished from the family table, the turkey, the plum pudding. One was knowing Adam was there at the table, eating, laughing, asking for more.

The third thing was Christopher's roar following him up the stairs. "You're a bad bastard! A waste of space!"

It was confirmation of what he already knew. He sucked his palm as he realised there was a fourth memory. His mother coming into his room before tea, hugging him, telling him no-one was angry any more, she'd always hated that plant anyway; bringing him downstairs, cutting him a large piece of Christmas cake. Christopher had put an arm on his shoulder, awkward.

"It's OK, lad. I didn't mean it. I'm just a bad tempered old man."

Adam wagged a red cracker at him. He pulled it. Bang! When you feel, you get hurt. Bang! It's better to shut down part of yourself than try to reason things out.

Paul looked up at the tree above him. He hated Christmas. He didn't belong. He really was a bad bastard. The wire from the plug snaked across the carpet beside him. His hand darted out and gripped, yanked hard. The room blackened in an instant, leaving him cold, blind and alone.

~

Several hours later, Dianne woke to find Paul still had not come to bed. Usually, he would be sprawled on his stomach, legs poaching space across the sheets, arms thrown across the pillows, black lashes feathering his pale cheeks, twitching slightly to the tune of his dreams.

She snapped on the bedside light and reached for her robe. The landing light spilled down the stairs into the darkness of the hall. There didn't seem to be a light on down there. Dianne hesitated on the bottom step, feeling the loneliness of the night in the silent house. A shiny garland was woven through the bars of the bannister. She jumped as it brushed her hand like a running spider.

The lights of the Christmas tree were out. She snapped on the wall light and saw his figure on the floor, slumped against the sofa near the window. His head was bent to his chest, his legs straight out in front of him and his arms limp by his sides. She dropped to her knees beside him.

"Paul?" Her voice was edged with fright. She took his hand. It was like ice. Pieces of a broken bauble fell from his fingers. "Paul? Are you all right?" He stirred. "What on earth are you doing? You're freezing!"

His eyes opened slowly, looked around beneath drooped lids, finally rested on her. "Sleepy," he muttered.

"Come up to bed, you idiot," Dianne scolded, relief making her sharp. She helped him to his feet. He was stiff with cold.

She pulled one of his arms across her shoulders, and the two of them made slow, awkward progress side by side on the narrow stairs. He still seemed slow and sleepy. She turned on the electric blanket and helped him undress.

When she slid in beside him, he was still cold. Cold now herself, but still not as cold as he was, she rubbed his sides and back briskly. Gradually heat began to spread across him and he nuzzled up to her, seeming more content.

"Go to sleep." She kissed his forehead. "You're the one who needs me, I think."

She was surprised by the strength of his reply. "I don't need anyone," he said firmly.

Dianne lay still, holding him as he seemed to become drowsy again. The darkness circled her, touched her open eyes as she lay wondering again about this man she had married so proudly, how she seemed to know him less and less instead of more and more. What have I done? she thought. How long can I live with him? Frightening was the insidious knowledge that he did not really love her now. He had never denied it. He did not love her in the way she needed and craved, the way that was her due, her right. He was hurting her now more often than he was delighting her.

His voice was low and muffled again, coming from the cleft of her breasts where his head rested. "A baby would love this feeling." She stiffened. Even in sleep! Why wouldn't he let it go? Finally he muttered, "Hot water bottle." His last word was indistinct. It sounded like "aspirin."

Then she felt his muscles relax as sleep caught him and pulled him under.

~

Jenna grinned as the first bars of 'Rudolph the Red-nosed Reindeer' wafted from the speakers in the ceiling. Adam put his head in his hands and groaned. The waitresses were wearing tinsel hairbands and a reindeer and sleigh occupied a raised stand in front of the entrance.

"Poor old Rudolph," said Jenna. "It's not his fault."

Adam picked up his knife and fork again. "That song's suffering from severe over-exposure."

Jenna studied him as he ate. His chestnut hair was like his mother's, before the gray was sprinkled through it.

"What colour was your father's hair?"

Adam chewed and swallowed before he replied. "Brown. A bit like mum's; a bit more gingery maybe."

She was about to comment on Paul's black hair when Adam spoke again.

"I'm afraid I'm not going to be around for Christmas after all." He lifted his napkin and wiped his mouth. "It's Paul. He's going to go to England, to Dianne's folk." He waved a hand in annoyance. "He said he wasn't, but typical! He phoned me at lunch time and said he'd changed his mind."

Jenna's fork paused only momentarily on its way to her mouth. "Oh? So it'll be just you and your mum?"

"I'm going to take her up to Coleraine for the few days."

"To your mum's sister?"

"Paul's so unreliable. You think you've got everything planned and then he throws a googly. Typical of him. It's very short notice for Sally and Bob."

"I'm sure they understand. What did your mum say about it?"

He sighed. "She seems OK with it. She said Paul had been to see her this morning and that it's important that he and Dianne stay together for their first Christmas." His mouth took a bitter twist. "He's worked his old black magic. He can make anybody do anything if he wants it hard enough. And then make them thank him."

Jenna let the waitress lift her plate. Then she said, "Adam, why

sudden burst of frustration, she kicked them. Adam was the one person who was making this year endurable. He was around, able to call and see her, lift her mind. If he wasn't there, how boring life would be. What would be left?

She saw the silver ball on the floor, the one she had knocked from the tree last night when she had seen Paul at her door. She picked it up and tossed it from hand to hand. Without Adam, she would just be ... her mouth twisted ... a nice girl. Maybe she should throw herself at him in low cut dresses and boob tape. She held the ornament in her finger and thumb thoughtfully, watching the light dance in curves around it. *But that's not me.* She hooked the ball back onto a branch carefully. A shower of pine needles fell to the carpet. She stood back and the red, green, blue flashed across her still figure. She was back in the ruined hut. Who are you? Who are you?

She had part of the answer. *I know what I'm not.*

CHAPTER ELEVEN

JENNA HAD NEVER met any of Adam's work colleagues before. Nerves prickled her stomach as she held his hand and walked down the carpeted passage to the large room which had been booked for his firm's Christmas party.

He glanced round and squeezed her hand.

"Relax!"

"I hate entrances."

She had made a special effort. Her hair was shining, her sandals were just high enough to be elegant, low enough to be comfortable, her dress was pink and graceful. Trying to remember exactly how Dianne had done it, she sat on her bed, tongue between her teeth in concentration, and carefully painted every nail on her fingers and toes. She stood in front of the mirror in her bathroom and applied her eye shadow and mascara with extreme care. She did a twirl for Adam. Then he said they had to go; he didn't want to be late.

"You could at least tell me I look nice."

"You look lovely. Now come on."

It didn't help her mood. The band was already playing and the first few couples were dancing in the centre. Was it her imagination, or did people pause and look round when she and Adam joined them? Pause more than they needed to, more than her nerves expected? Paranoid, she scolded herself.

Glitter was everywhere. Strands twined up the microphone stand, holly climbed the walls, tinsel edged the tables. Balls of coloured light spun above their heads as Adam moved through the crowd. With an easy familiarity, he joked and chatted to everyone he passed. He stopped at a table half way up and introduced her to the group who shuffled over and made room for two more chairs.

She looked around. So these are the people Adam works with, the people who see him more than I do. It was hard to make conversation above the noise of the band. A small blonde girl in a cream trouser suit was beside her, her scarlet nails clutching a wine glass. Jenna put her hand to her own chin briefly, just to show off her own nails.

"Hi, Lucy," she said, glad she remembered the name. "What department do you work in?"

"I'm in reception. You don't get into the factory without passing me. What do you do?"

"I'm a student."

Lucy sipped her drink. "You don't look like one."

Jenna smiled as Adam returned and handed her a drink. "I'll take that as a compliment," she replied.

Adam sat down and Lucy said with a mischievous twitch of her brow, "So you're into students now, Adam."

Adam's smile was thin. "Just one. Shut up, Lucy."

Lucy feigned a huff and twirled a small foot. "Oh! Touchy!"

An older woman in green and wearing huge earrings, leaned round Lucy and said, "I'm Agnes. I'm the one who has to try to keep Lucy under control. I don't always succeed."

Lucy grinned. "Come on, Agnes. I brighten up your dreary days."

Jenna began to relax. The band finished one song and the lead singer called for more couples on the floor. Then the drums began again and the floor thrummed with the vibrations.

Lucy jerked her chair a few inches to bring her ear closer to Jenna's. "So how did you and Adam meet?"

"At a friend's house."

"How long have you been going out?"

"About six months."

Lucy nodded and sipped her drink. "That figures."

"Oh?"

She smiled brightly. "Well, Adam's back to being one of the eligible bachelors around here."

Jenna studied the crowd while her mind turned over the precise words Lucy had used. They sat without speaking for some minutes. Adam had left her side. Jenna looked around for him. He was at the far side of the room, amongst a group of men of his own age. They were laughing, gesturing, joking. She willed him to look round, to smile across at her. It was early for him to have left her alone and she felt the breeze of his absence.

There was a nudge at her elbow.

"Who's that?" asked Lucy, pointing. "She seems to know you."

Jenna looked. It was Dianne. She was weaving her way gracefully though the crowd, waving at Jenna, her blond head a few inches above most of the women and her progress tracked by most of the men.

Jenna was surprised. "What on earth are you doing here?"

She sat in the chair Adam had left. "Darling! I'm so glad to see you. I don't know anyone, except you and Adam. But at least there are people – lots of people!"

Lucy said, "You're English?"

Dianne's laugh tinkled. "I just have to open my mouth, don't I?"

"Is Paul here?" asked Jenna.

She nodded. "He allowed himself to be dragged along after I pestered him for two days. He bought me a drink and then went to sulk in a corner."

"So ... you knew this party was on?"

Dianne's lip gloss shone in the spinning lights and her cheeks glowed with pleasure. "Adam mentioned it one night he was at our house. I was just dying to get out." She sipped her drink and gestured around the room with the glass. "There are parties all over the place at home and I'm missing out on them all. So Adam said we could come to this one. He said no-one would notice another couple."

People have already noticed you, Jenna thought, looking round. Her eyes kept searching, moving, checking. She could see Adam; where was Paul?

"You'll get to a few when you go over for Christmas, I'm sure."

The lead singer was calling for volunteers to have a go at the microphone. Dianne raised her voice as 'The Rose of Tralee' belted from the throat of a middle-aged man in cords and a shirt with a pattern of holly and berries. "Yes, we fly over tomorrow afternoon. Arabella has things planned for every night." She held up a hand theatrically. "Wonderful! I can't wait."

"Paul must be looking forward to meeting up with a few old friends."

Dianne made a face. "He says I should be grateful he's agreed to get on the plane."

The evening became layer upon layer of music, lights, chatter and tinsel. Adam appeared. "Come on, Jenna. Let's give the dance floor a whirl."

She took his hand and felt wonderful, carefree. She put an arm round his waist as he introduced her to more people around the room. She found herself at ease, happy, chatting, secure. A plump woman in a dress which was sprayed on over every bulge, was singing 'Hey, Big Spender'. Adam found a cracker on the floor and held it out to Jenna. He caught the paper hat as it flew from the centre and unfolded it.

"It's a good fit," he said, arranging it on her head.

"Hey, don't muss my hair!" she laughed.

They were standing at a pillar. A shiny red bell swayed slowly beside her head. She looked around. "There's got to be mistletoe somewhere."

"Will you be all right for a minute?" He was looking round the room, his attention straying from her again.

"Sure, but ..."

He gave her a peck on the cheek. "I'll be back for the slow one. Keep it for me?"

"Who else?" she said to his back. Now he was irritating her. She deserved better. She leaned against the pillar, watching, listening.

"You must be Adam's friend." A girl in a bright red top and silk trousers had appeared in front of her. Her head was heavy with loose black curls. She stood with her feet apart, a hand on one hip.

Jenna smiled at her. "Yes, I'm Jenna."

The girl held out her hand. It was a formal, surprising gesture. "Rachel," she said. Her handshake was firm, almost masculine. "I've heard of you."

Rachel's eyes were not smiling. Jenna felt a faint unease; there was something in this girl's body language that was alert, feline. Rachel looked down to Jenna's feet and back up to her head, where the paper hat still perched.

"Nice dress," she said.

"Thank you," said Jenna.

"I used to have one just like it ..." she took a sip of her drink "... about five years ago. You're a student, I believe." She said it as if it were faintly amusing.

"Yes. How did you know?"

Rachel waved a hand vaguely and her curls swayed. "Oh, Adam

must have mentioned it one night."

Suddenly Lucy appeared from nowhere. "Hey Rachel!" she said brightly. "Come over here. There's someone wants to meet you."

Rachel allowed herself to be pulled away. Her eyes stayed on Jenna as she turned. "Check out the nail bars sometime. You might be able to get varnish that actually matches the dress."

Jenna watched her go. Meow, who let the cat in?

"Are you OK?"

She knew the voice before she turned round. Paul was leaning against the pillar, the shiny red bell obscuring his eyes.

"What could be wrong?" she said to his mouth.

"Stay away from her. She's got claws."

Jenna's brows rose. "So have I."

He pushed himself upright. "Not nearly sharp enough."

The room was very warm. Jenna walked away from him and found a bench seat against the wall. She was beginning to feel tired. Luke said he always knew when his sister had tuned out because she went to a corner and just watched. Rachel was on the dance floor now, her hips moving, her red sandals tapping, her arms swaying in rhythm. She was attractive rather than beautiful, an effortless sexiness about her which gave her an aura of power. How did Paul know Rachel? And know her well enough to know about the claws?

Lucy flopped down beside her. "Are you all right?" she asked.

"You're the second person who's asked me that."

Lucy wrinkled her nose. "Well, it's a pity you had to meet Rachel. She'd want to meet you, of course."

"Why would she want to meet me?"

Lucy looked at her curiously. "Well," she said slowly, "I think she's regretting what she did."

Jenna spread a hand, baffled. "What did she do?"

Lucy put a hand over her face. "Oh, God!" When she looked

again, Jenna saw pity in her eyes. "You don't know, do you? Adam hasn't told you."

Jenna frowned. "Told me what?"

Lucy blew out her cheeks and looked down. Jenna saw her come to a decision. "Rachel and Adam were engaged. She jilted him a week before the wedding." She looked away, up at a glittering ball on the ceiling. "I don't think ... he's ever got over it." She turned back to Jenna. "I also think she wants him back."

The heat, the music, the lights, all receded, became the stage scenery of shock. After a moment, Jenna whispered, "Engaged to her?"

Lucy had leaned in to hear her. She nodded. "They were supposed to be married last year," she replied.

Jenna closed her eyes. Waves of realisation broke in her. Everybody in the room knew this. Including Paul. Everyone except her. Adam had been about to get married. He had never told her. Never mentioned it.

Lucy touched her arm. "She mightn't get her way, you know. You're a much nicer person than Rachel."

Jenna's hands balled into fists on her lap. *Does the whole world think I'm 'nice'? Next she'll tell me I'm 'good'.*

The room began to come into focus again. She would ask him about it. Plenty of people have relationships that don't work out. They move on. He didn't want to hurt her feelings. That's probably it. She'd talk it over with him.

The band was breaking for a drink. The chatter and laughter were thrown into relief in a room empty of music. Near her, strands from party poppers were shooting between tables amidst roars of laughter and sliding chairs. One landed on Jenna's head. She pulled it off, crushing the paper hat as she did so. She threw it on the ground.

A single guitar chord cut above the noise. She looked up. Paul was on the raised platform where the band had been, holding a borrowed guitar. Curious, everyone watched him. She could hear whispers: Who's that? Don't know. I think he's Adam's brother. Does he have a brother? Never mentioned one.

Colours from the spotlights slid across Paul's white shirt. She was reminded of him sitting in her chair, colour from her tree lights flicking across his cheeks. He plucked a few chords, checked the tuning. Then he looked up, his gaze travelling the room.

"I've been shoved up here by my brother. He's never liked me, so I shouldn't be surprised." Laughter. "But I'm a gate-crasher, so I'll sing for my supper."

His fingers ran down the strings slowly. Then he set up an easy lazy rhythm, caressing the strings. A solitary figure, head bent, he held the room in the hollow of his hand. Jenna looked around. People were quiet, hardly a movement stirred the shadows. Even the lights stopped spinning and Paul was left in a pool of white, his fingers plucking a faultless riff.

Suddenly he jerked his head up and sprang to the front of the platform. Everyone jumped amid squeals of surprise. He scraped the strings raucously and placed his feet apart. In amazement, Jenna watched him launch himself across the stage in a wicked send-up of Elvis' 'Hound Dog'. The room erupted, yells and whoops accompanied the beat, stamping, clapping. Jenna hunched back in her seat, too surprised to join in. He was torturing the strings, strutting, spinning. Lucy was on her feet, bouncing and clapping.

Jenna's eyes followed Paul across the stage, watched his mouth curve in mischief, his eyes wink at the girls around him, his feet tap in time to his flying fingers.

And you asked me who I am! Who are you? A shape-shifter? I thought you were sulking in a corner.

It took some minutes for the room to calm down. Jenna caught the faint glint of sweat on his temple as he set down the borrowed guitar and Dianne threw her arms round him in delight, owning him. She didn't see where he went after that.

Jenna wanted Adam and wanted to go home. She got to her feet and looked around for him. The slow dance, sleepy in his arms, was a pleasure in store. Except Adam was on the other side of the room and Rachel was close to him, closer than she should have been, laughing up into his face. A coloured strand of some decoration had landed on his shoulder. Rachel reached up and pulled it off. There was something in the way she did it, something intimate about the gesture. Adam wasn't smiling, his concentration on her totally.

Rachel's black curls tumbled round her neck as she pointed to the ceiling. Jenna stopped breathing. Something very like mistletoe peeped from a cross beam. Very deliberately, Rachel put her hands on Adam's shoulders and kissed him full on the mouth. He stood with his hands rigid by his sides as she pulled away. Jenna was aware of people looking, nudging. Adam said something. Rachel replied. Adam looked up, cast a brief glance round the room. The loose, red silk rippled on Rachel's back as she kissed him again. His arms came up and he pulled her to him, lingered, then kissed her deeply. The slow dance was starting, the last dance. Keep the last dance for me. He had totally forgotten. Rachel pulled him onto the dance floor.

Jenna put a hand to the wall to steady herself. People were looking at her. Suddenly Lucy was beside her, pulling her away, saying she felt faint and would Jenna come outside with her for a minute or two? Jenna shook her arm away. Adam had been flirting, bantering all evening. He had not been paying her enough attention. She had been trying to keep the thought at bay. After all, she was just Jenna, but Adam was Somebody here. Now the first flicker of real anger lit in her head. Now she had found out he had been about to marry another woman only a year before. Now he was kissing that woman in front of her. This wasn't flirting. This girl knew exactly where her head would reach on Adam's shoulder, knew the length of his arms, the way of his walk, the turn of his step. Adam's palm knew the small of her back, the angle of her neck, the twine of her fingers, the scent of her hair.

Jenna raised a finger to Lucy who was still trying to pull her towards the door. She bit out the words. "Don't follow me." She turned to leave. Lucy came with her. Jenna swung round. "Just don't!"

~

The hotel foyer was cooler but still not cold enough. Jenna strode through, round chairs, coffee tables and knots of late drinkers. Her pink dress billowed in the breeze as she flung herself through the swing doors and out into the freezing night. She didn't stop until she was under a tree at the far side of the car park. Halfway across, brakes squealed and the radiator grill of a Mercedes halted two feet from her legs. She scarcely heard it.

Hidden from the lights of the car park, she wrapped her arms round herself. Everything she had felt had turned to vapour. Everyone brought history with them. It was part of the baggage people collected as they lived and loved. She could accept that. It wasn't right that Adam had not told her about Rachel, but she could have got over it, understood, sympathised even. But she had just witnessed a relationship that was far from over. It was very much alive. And the bastard had humiliated her in front of the whole room. Her fist thudded into her palm.

After a moment of silence, a calm voice said, "That's good."

She spun round. Paul lounged on the bonnet of the nearest car, his arms folded and his ankles crossed.

Jenna exploded. "Why do you have to be so bloody *quiet*?"

He looked up at the stars. "Nice night. Cold."

"Go away."

He looked down, uncrossed his ankles and kicked a pebble. "No."

She turned her back. The skirt of her dress caught on a thorn twig. She pulled it and heard the thin material tear. It was enough. She put her arm on the trunk of the tree, dropped her head onto it and wept into the black, cold wood.

When her sobs shuddered down to jerky breaths, she turned round slowly, wiping her nose on the back of her hand. Paul was still there, arms folded, still calmly surveying the car park, the lights of the hotel, the moon. Finally he turned his head to her.

"No tissue. Sorry." He stood up and tore some grass from the verge. He handed it to her. "That might work."

She took it and blew her nose. It did work. She had left her bag back in the hotel. She pulled another clump of grass and wiped her eyes. She tried a small laugh. "And I took such care with my mascara!"

He had come onto the grass beside her. "Don't do that again."

She sniffed. "Do what?"

"Cry. Not over this. Not over Adam."

Another tear spilled down her cheek. "Why the hell not?" She raised her voice. "It hurts."

His voice came, low and urgent beneath the bare winter branches. "Jenna, what hurts – your heart? Or your pride?"

She looked up at him. His back was to the lights of the car park, his face just shadows on shadows. Some guests spilled from the hotel entrance, their tipsy laughter carrying across the cold distance to where they stood. She opened her mouth to speak, then stopped. She began to shiver, put her arms round herself again and turned away from him. He stayed where he was and spoke to her back, flicked his question like a dagger.

"Is he your lover or your brother?"

She felt the damp on her bare toes where her sandals sank into the rough grass. She said over her shoulder, "He doesn't have to be either."

He came closer. "Yes, he does. Yes, he does, Jenna. If he's not your lover – and he's not, is he?" He waited. She said nothing. "If he's not your lover, then what is he? A brother? Luke in a suit? Your father, taking care of you?"

She flung round, her dress catching again. "Mind your own business! What do you know anyway?"

The shadows of his face shifted in a smile. "That's it! Bring back the anger. Thump me if you like." He held out a hand but didn't touch her. His expression was so intense that a point of light found his eyes even in the darkness. "Don't waste your life on buddies. Go for the passion. Want the moon and the stars and the sun. Find things that are worth tears." He turned to go. "Demand more for yourself, Jenna. It's there. And you'll be dead a long time." He backed away, then turned and strolled off across the car park. Half way across, he turned and, walking backwards, called out, "You're a big girl now. You can find your own way home."

Jenna watched him reach the entrance, push through the revolving door into the light and warmth. He didn't look back. He's just left me here, she thought, incredulous. Adam would have called me a taxi. She kicked the tree. She had never before stubbed all her toes at once.

"Shit!" she said.

CHAPTER TWELVE

WHEN SHE GOT back to her house, the lights were on and Luke was lying on her sofa watching television. He had turned on the tree lights. Adam had made her turn them off before they left. She paid the taxi driver who stood distrustfully at the door until she returned with the fare.

Luke waited expectantly, his eyes on the door of the room.

"Where's Adam?"

"Not here. I see you haven't lost my house keys."

Luke grinned. "Can I crash here tonight? I missed the last bus."

"Sure. Where were you?"

"At a party." He shifted a little. "They started to ... do stuff, so I left."

"Joints and stuff?"

"Yeah. And stuff."

She sat down on the edge of the sofa, exhaustion toppling her. Luke stared.

"Why have you got a piece of grass stuck to your cheek?" He sat up. "Hey, you've been crying."

Jenna rubbed her face and the piece of grass stuck to her finger. She flicked it off, not caring where it went.

"You've had a row with Adam, haven't you?"

Her shoulders drooped and she fished in her bag for her phone. "Sort of."

His hand brushed her skirt as it fell over the arm of the sofa. "Hey, your dress is torn." He looked up sharply. "Did he ...?"

She gave a short laugh. "I should be so lucky!"

"Jay!" He was shocked.

"No, he didn't do anything like that, so you needn't punch him."

There were three missed calls on her mobile, all of them from Adam, all of them while she was in the taxi, all of them ignored.

"It can't be your first row. And he's a man." He shrugged. "What do you expect? They've no sense."

"Not one of them." She mussed his hair affectionately. "Except maybe you."

Still, she wasn't going to cry again. Not over this. Not over Adam.

"I rang Dad," said Luke. "He says he'll come in and pick both of us up tomorrow."

"Good old Dad. That'll be great." She got up and went to the door. "Want a coffee?"

"Had one." He put his long legs to the floor and stood, fiddling with his gold earring. "Don't you want to talk about it? I mean, you'll fix it with him, I suppose?"

The answer to his question came out without thought. "I don't know."

"You will," he said confidently. "People have barneys all the time. Even Mum and Dad. Wait till you see. He'll be begging forgiveness by tomorrow." His brow furrowed. "What happened anyway?"

"He was about to get married last spring. She called it off. She was there tonight."

"Shit!" he said and was silent for a moment. He scratched his head. "But, so what? If it's over ..."

"It's not over. She wants him back." Her mouth twisted. "He wasn't exactly resisting."

Luke gave a small shrug. "So it's serious then?"

She turned to go. "No-one's been in the bed since you were last in it. You know where the towels and stuff are."

Fifteen minutes later, she was just coming out of the bathroom when the doorbell chimed. Luke called up the stairs. "Want me to get it?"

She wrapped her towelling robe tightly round herself. "If it's Adam, I don't want to see him."

It was Adam, his voice agitated.

"I need to see Jenna. Is she here?"

On the landing, Jenna held her breath.

"Yeah, mate. But it's late."

"Let me in. I need to see her."

Luke's voice took on a firm edge. "She doesn't want to see you."

To Jenna's surprise, Adam became aggressive. "This is none of your business. Get out of my way!"

Jenna gasped and Luke's surge of disgust rose on the cold air from the hall.

"You're drunk, you bastard! And my sister's very much my business."

"I'm not drunk. Maybe I've ..."

"Are you driving?" asked Luke sharply.

Jenna sank to the floor beneath the banisters. Adam's tone became more conciliatory. "No, I'm not. Paul called me a taxi." With a slight slur, he added, "Told me to go home."

"Yeah. Well, you do that." There was a thump as if Adam had put his hand on the door forcefully.

"I'm not going till I see her."

Jenna could hear that Luke was beginning to grit his teeth. "Well, you'll have a cold night because you'll have to wait outside."

Adam raised his voice. "Jenna, I know you can hear me! I didn't know you were in the room. I didn't know you were there. Rachel said she'd seen you go out."

Jenna put her head down on her bent knees. Bitch! she thought. Luke slammed the door. To her relief, Adam seemed to leave without causing a scene in the street.

Luke came up the stairs and peered round the banisters. "You all right?"

Jenna pulled herself to her feet. "I'm OK. Do you think he'll get home all right?"

Luke sat on the top stair. "Yeah. There was a taxi waiting up the street a bit. Probably his." He was quiet for a moment. "So her name's Rachel?" She nodded. When he spoke again, the disgust was back in his voice. "He was drunk. Adam was drunk." He looked round. "Have you ever seen him drunk before?"

"Never."

Luke shook his head. "Asshole," he said. Jenna started to laugh. "What's so funny?" he asked.

There was nothing at all funny about this evening, but Jenna laughed until her face began to crumple and she felt the tears close again. Then she stopped. That bit was over. Adam was neither the moon, the stars nor the sun, and so he wasn't worth her tears.

She wiped her nose – she still hadn't a tissue. "Oh, Luke," she said, "I'm so glad you were here. But you're a nutcase. You can swear for Ulster, but if you've the slightest suspicion that someone's had one too many, you can be as shocked as a Puritan."

He grinned sheepishly. "Yeah, well. Swearing doesn't kill anybody."

She pulled him to his feet and gave him a hug even though he hated it. "Dad would be proud of you," she said.

He disentangled himself. "Go to bed," he said, grumpy.

Paul tugged off his shirt and yawned. Dianne dropped a suitcase on the bed and flung open the lid.

"I still can't believe you never told me, Paul."

"It was past history and nothing to do with me."

"It must have been. Weren't you going to be best man or something?"

He sat on the bed and pulled off his shoes. "I was. But I didn't have much to do in the end."

Dianne gazed into her wardrobe and rattled hangers. "I can't wait to tell Bella." She pulled out a dress and held it in front of herself. "What do you think of this one? Should I bring it?"

He glanced round. "Sure. Looks good."

She hung it back in the wardrobe and flicked along the rail again. "Mmmm. I don't know. I still have lots of clothes at home. I mightn't need ..."

"This is home."

She stopped and turned. "Well, yes, of course, darling."

He walked round the bed and took her by the shoulders. "This is home," he repeated firmly.

She put her hands up to his bare chest and spread her fingers. "Yes, Paul. This is home. I just meant ..."

"I know what you meant."

He dropped his hands and left the room. She heard the bathroom door shut and lock.

Later, she lay with her head on his shoulder, unsure of his mood.

"Poor Jenna," she said tentatively. "I was so sorry for her." He didn't reply. "She'll tear Adam into little pieces."

"She won't," he said, surprising her.

"Goodness, I would, if it was me."

"But she's not you. Definitely not you."

"No, but ..."

"She'll be very quiet about it."

He was lying on his back, speaking to the dark ceiling, almost speaking to himself. Dianne raised her head from his shoulder to look into his face. She could just see the outline of his open eyes, the ruffle of hair at his brow.

She could still picture what had happened – Paul sending the revolving door spinning as he came back into the hotel foyer; Rachel turning a dazzling smile on him; Paul not breaking his stride as he passed her, his words slicing the air: "Slither back up your tree, Rachel." A small girl in a ghastly trouser suit wandered about with Jenna's bag. Paul sent her outside to return it. Then he had cornered Adam. She was too far away to hear the exchange, but Adam was white by the time Paul shoved him into a taxi. Bella was going to love this!

She lay down beside him again. "Thanks for going tonight."

He turned his head towards her. "Enjoy yourself?"

"Enormously."

"If Jenna's a study-bug, what are you?" He thought for a minute. "A party pixie!"

She giggled in delight. "I like that!" She curled a leg round his, relaxing now that he was talking this way. "I can't wait." She sighed and added, "There'll be so many people to see and proper parties to go to."

He stayed very still and she began to feel drowsy, his arm still round her and his hand relaxed on her side. Through the first mist of sleep, a thought surfaced.

"Paul?"

"Mhm?"

"What else haven't you told me?"

He turned onto his side, tumbling her off his shoulder.

"I used to be a bank robber. Now go to sleep."

She woke briefly in the small hours of the morning and felt that he wasn't beside her. When she woke again, he was back, lying on his stomach with his head turned away from her, his breathing rhythmic and deep. She moved her head slightly and something small fell from her hair and landed on the pillow by her nose. She flicked it away, afraid it was a spider.

In the morning, she saw the cream and green of an ivy leaf on the floor. It was firm and waxy in her fingers. She dropped it in the bin and checked to see if any more had been walked in on their shoes last night. But there were no more.

It was the Saturday before Christmas and the manse looked beautiful. Usually, Jenna loved coming home to see the tree and the decorations which her mother erected every year. Cora placed every golden twig, every silver ball, every holly wreath, with great care.

Luke and she were home in time for lunch and now, dishes done, Jenna stood in front of the family portrait which Paul had taken in the autumn. It hung on the wall below the stairs, where visitors would see it when they took off their coats, but where it couldn't be accused of being ostentatiously displayed. Cora had fixed silver tinsel around the frame. Seated at the front, Donald and Cora looked out proudly, leaning slightly towards each other as they smiled at the camera. Jenna and Luke stood behind them.

Jenna looked into her own eyes which looked steadily back at her. She remembered that day. Truth is the only connection worth making, he had said. Which is hurt, your heart or your pride? he had asked last night. She was trying to give herself an honest answer to that.

Luke had been made to promise to say nothing about the previous night. When Adam rang that evening, Jenna took the call in her father's study.

"Jay, I'm sorry, I'm so sorry. Did you hear what I said last night?

I didn't know you were there. Rachel ... I was told you'd gone out ... to the loo or something."

She didn't bother sitting down. "Sobered up, have you?"

"Look, it was a staff party. I'm not an angel ..."

"I never thought you were."

"It's not your sort of thing. You're just not used to what goes on."

"So what goes on, Adam?"

"Things that don't mean anything. Things you'd never do any other time of the year."

"Like kissing your ex-fiancée? A quick one under the mistletoe, just for old time's sake?"

"Well ..."

"And the slow dance? Was that for old time's sake too? I was looking forward to that. I was really looking forward to that. I thought I might have your attention for longer than a minute."

He tried a laugh. "Oh, well, what could I do? Rachel's very strong minded."

"I could see that. You really put up a fight, didn't you?"

He was silent for a moment and she waited, looking at a hymn-book, open at 'O Come all ye Faithful'. Her father's notes for the order of service the next morning lay beside it.

"I would have told you about Rachel."

"Well," she said thoughtfully, "why would you? What's it to do with me? We all have history, don't we? Specially these days. Serial monogamy's all the rage."

"So we're OK then?"

She twisted the cord of the receiver round her finger. "I'm not OK with a man who would humiliate me like that."

"Oh, come on, Jenna!"

"You hurt me very much. I liked you, Adam."

"Well, I'm still me. And I like you too."

"But it's not enough, is it?"

"What do you mean?"

"It's just ..." she bit her lip. Is he your lover or your brother? She tired of the conversation suddenly. "I'll see you in the New Year some time. Let's just have a break."

He coughed and tried to sound normal. "I'm taking Mum up to Coleraine on Monday. Maybe I'll ring you from there?"

"Whatever."

"Paul's gone off to the London scene this afternoon." He paused. "He gave me an earful last night."

"Oh?"

He laughed. "Yeah. He told me I should realise what I've got."

"What did he mean – what you've got?"

"He said you were worth ten of Rachel and that I was a – well, I'll not tell you what he said I was. You're a well brought up girl!"

"And all my goodness might melt into a puddle of shock if you repeated naughty words."

"Don't be like that, Jay."

A kitten suddenly jumped onto the desk and started to play with the telephone lead. She jiggled it and the kitten leapt on it, ears cocked over its head, paws soft and agile.

"Have a good Christmas. Give my love to your Mum." She hung up.

She picked up the kitten and went to the lounge. The television was on and Luke was in possession of the sofa as usual. He looked up. "Made it up?" he asked.

She just shrugged. A listlessness was coming over her. She pulled a chair nearer to the fire and sat. The kitten curled into a tiny ball and novice purrs rattled out on a sigh as it went instantly to sleep, one white paw curled over its nose.

Aunt Susan came to stay. Susan was Donald's only sister and Christmas hadn't really arrived until Aunt Susan was collected at the airport. Jenna couldn't remember a Christmas without her. Before Jenna was born, Susan had moved to the south of England and taken a teaching post in a private girls' school. Prim, proper and incredibly skinny, her accent was refined English, laced in moments of carelessness with the vowels of east Ulster. Jenna went for a walk with her one cold frosty afternoon.

"Did you ever think of coming back to live here?" she asked as they dropped sticks over the river bridge.

"My goodness, no. All my friends are over there now." She sniffed. "I only come back to see Donald and the family. It would be too hard readjust now."

The water bubbled along the ragged edges of the grass and stones below them. Frost still hung in the hollows of the bank.

"I know someone," said Jenna, "who's moved back here. But his wife's English. She'd only ever seen Northern Ireland on the News before."

Susan tut-tutted, her breath puffing in staccato clouds. "That will be very difficult for her, poor girl. Has she any friends here?"

"Just me, I think. And her husband, of course."

Susan waved a dismissive hand. "Husbands aren't friends."

Jenna looked at her curiously. "What are they then?"

"A nuisance!"

"Aunt Susan! Have you a dark secret?"

Susan pushed herself upright and they turned to go back along the road. "No secrets, only mercies, the chiefest of which is that I never had a husband."

They walked some distance together in silence, then Jenna linked her arm in Susan's. "I think you're right. I've decided I don't want one either."

The Sunday School went carol singing in the old people's home in the next village and Jenna went along as usual. She stood at the back with the Sunday School teachers and sang 'Hark the Herald

Angels Sing'.

At the Christmas morning service, there wasn't much she could do, so she sat and watched her father talking to the children, bending over to admire the toys they had brought. He never left a child out, no matter how long it took. He spoke to each one as if their toy was the most wonderful in the whole church. Luke had got up in time to come to the service and Jenna and her mother and brother sat in a row, the minister's family, celebrating the Nativity once again, just as they should.

Aunt Susan went back to England the following Monday morning. She wanted to visit a few more friends before school started again. Christmas was over. After lunch, Jenna took a walk in the garden. Her cat followed her at a distance, but the two remaining kittens bounced round her in delight, loving the company. She picked up the little black one, the one with one white paw which had slept on her lap every night. There was moisture clinging to its eyebrows where it had snuffled into the flower bed, chasing leaves.

With her finger and thumb round its stomach, Jenna held it up. "Well, little chap. I hope you get a home soon." She tickled its ear. "But I don't think Mum and Dad will do anything nasty to you. You're far too cute." The kitten blinked and then put out its white paw to touch her nose. It felt like the touch of a feather. She set it down carefully on the grass. Its sister jumped on it and the two kittens rolled into the long grass next the fence which bordered the field.

Jenna stood with her hands in the pockets of her coat, looking across at the humps of stones and corrugated iron of the old huts. Her hand touched the top of the fence. Slowly, she clambered over and dropped to the other side.

Patches of frost were here too, on the rumpled, faded grass and in the shade of the bigger stones. She put her hand on the wall of the hut she and Paul had entered weeks before. The old bedstead was still there. It was on its side, just as it had landed when Paul had kicked it in a sudden burst of annoyance.

She sat on the broken bench and looked at the floor. Although she searched for a long time, she could not catch sight of a single insect. At the window, the wind lifted her hair as it rose through the gap. She put her hand on the initials carved in the wooden frame: S.L.C. 1944. Her fingernails still bore traces of the varnish which she had applied so carefully over a week ago.

We are only moments away from the past. But it only takes a moment for everything to change, for the world to wobble on its axis and make the familiar strange. She looked back across the field to the fence. Her cat was sitting on one of the fence posts, perfectly balanced.

If the past is only moments gone, then the future is only moments from us too. It's OK not to know. She dropped her head. No, it's not. It's not OK at all.

She trudged back across the field, shoulders hunched. There was no one there to clap. She clambered back over the fence again, almost tripping as she pulled her foot over the top wire.

Disappointed, her father agreed to drive her back to Belfast the next day. Cora was worried. "What is it, Jenna? You've been quiet all the holidays." She felt her daughter's forehead. "You're not ill, are you?"

"No, Mum, I'm fine. I've work to do. I have stuff to hand in in January and I haven't finished it yet."

Luke came to her room later that night and sat on the edge of her bed. "Have you and Adam talked?"

"A bit."

"So ... ?"

"So nothing. I don't want to talk about it, Luke."

He stood up, huffing. "OK, OK." He stopped at the door, and swung it between his hands in a way that never failed to annoy her. "There's something about Adam."

She punched her pillow. "What do you mean?"

"I'm not sure. As if he wasn't always saying what he meant." He frowned. "It's hard to explain. It's as if he has to pretend all the time."

"You never said this before."

"I don't think I thought it before." Finally he opened the door. "Pity you didn't meet his brother first."

"He's married," she said.

Luke shrugged. "Doesn't seem to matter these days."

"Luke!" She threw her slipper at him. "I'm not a saint, but I'm not that much of a sinner either."

Next afternoon, after a drive in which neither of them said very much, her father came into her house and checked the boiler for her, turned up her radiators and went out to inspect the oil tank.

"You seem to have plenty of oil." He looked worried. "It's New Year's Eve, Jenna. We've always been together as a family for New Year. You always come to the Watch Night service."

"I'm sorry about the service, Dad. Maybe I'll go to the church at the top of the road."

He was wearing an ordinary collar and tie and looked uneasy as he went to the front door. He gave her a hug.

"You know you can talk to me, don't you? About anything?"

"Yes, Dad. I do. Stop worrying. I just want a bit of time to myself. There's nothing wrong with that."

"When will Adam be back?"

"Not for a few days yet, I think."

Finally he left her. As he opened his car door, he called, "Be good, Missy."

She had been waiting for it.

She took down the Christmas tree. Bare of decoration, its branches held very few needles. What ones remained were shed as she pulled it through the kitchen and out into her back yard. She dug out the vacuum cleaner from under the stairs and swept the carpet until all traces of the tree had vanished. She went round the house taking down every sign of Christmas which she could find.

Then she sat in her chair and watched the room darken into evening, into night, until she could hardly see. She wasn't going to go to the service. She got up slowly. She was going to bed.

People see in the New Year because they want to celebrate a new beginning. They are looking forward, hoping, dreaming, planning, wondering. She wanted to sleep through the turn of this year. She didn't want to know about its dawning. She wanted it to sneak in past her, leave her alone. She wanted to wake up and carry on and know no difference in the time because time has nerve endings.

She slipped into bed. Her novel lay on the bedside table. Always, she read before going to sleep. Tonight she lay down and curled into a ball, the house silent around her. The logical side of her brain was very strong and she was well aware that a deep and dangerous depression had begun to drag its heavy folds across her shoulders. She should fight it; she could fight it. But there was another part of her that didn't care, that wanted to go to sleep and told her that there was no particular reason to get up in the morning.

CHAPTER THIRTEEN

LIKE A SMOTHERING hug from an old friend, the red leather sofa moulded itself round Dianne. It was deep and soft, just as she remembered it, right back to the time when Luther, the child next door, had been allowed to visit. She and Luther had played pirates on this sofa, ignoring the scolding of her nanny for turning the cushions into desert islands and the back into the gunnel of the privateer.

Her father stood with his back to the blazing log fire, its flames making a golden fuzz of his full head of grey hair. He held up a cigar, caressed it between his fingers and waved its length beneath his nose.

"It's been wonderful to have you back, Dianne," he said, his eyes resting on her with pleasure. "You've no idea how much I've missed you."

She smiled up at him. "If it's anything like how much I've missed home, then I do, Daddy."

This was the library, its carpet deep red, its drapes red and cream brocade. It was a place where Charles Butler had stamped his style and not since his wife died had anyone interfered. It was a room where his only child felt safe and secure. She laid her hand along the broad arm of the leather and felt the happy thoughtlessness of childhood rise in her. This was who she was. For the past few days of Christmas, she had shed the person she had become – the married woman whose husband had made her cross water

– and reverted to the girl she had been.

Charles sat in the chair to one side of the fire and examined the cap of his cigar carefully before he clipped it. It seemed such a long time since Dianne had seen him perform this familiar ritual.

"You've been flitting about so much since you arrived, we've hardly had a chance to talk," he said.

"But I've had so much to catch up on, and so little time to do it." She pouted. "You do want me to enjoy myself, don't you?"

He took a spill from a narrow vase on the fender and held it in the fire. "That's my dearest wish and always has been." The lighting of the cigar was not to be interrupted. Charles turned the end above the flame, charring it lovingly. Finally, satisfied with the burn, he threw the taper into the fire and curls of smoke wreathed his head. He sighed. "When you announced that Paul wanted to go back to Ireland and that you were going too ... Well, it was all so rushed and frantic." He held up the cigar and examined the end of it. "After you'd gone, there was such a low."

"It'll only be for a while. It seems like something he has to get out of his system."

He shifted in the chair so that he was facing her. "Are you happy, my dear?"

Her breath of hesitation was loud even to herself. "Of course I am! He's gorgeous and ... "

Charles' eyes narrowed. "Is he kind?"

"He buys me flowers and ..." she trailed to a stop, finishing her sentence with a slight shrug.

Her father snorted. "Hah! Flowers! My girl's worth diamonds. Where is he anyway?"

"I don't know. I think he went out with his camera. You know Paul."

"No, I don't know him at all. Does anyone?"

"He's been really trying, Daddy. He was quite chatty last night. He even talked to Bella. She went quite pink. She was flirting with him."

He smiled. "She was. I saw the minx." He became serious. "Quite a few of your friends have been flirting with him. He's been welcomed back like a renegade film star. Must be going to his head." He chewed the cigar. "Do you trust him?"

"Of course I do. He loves me."

"Who could fail to?" Her father was quiet for a minute or two, smoke drifting lazily around his chair and gliding along the deep green leaves of the tall palm in the corner behind him. Dianne inhaled the familiar scent and the little girl in her flowered and grew. A log fell in the fire in a whoosh of flame and a spark cracked out across the fender. Charles pushed it back with his foot. There was a moment of silence and then he asked, "Have you seen Luther Chevalier yet?"

"Not yet."

"He's still pining, you know." He checked the ash forming on the tip of the cigar. "Nice lad." He looked across at her. "I wonder if you understand how much you hurt him?"

She felt colour heat the tips of her ears. She didn't want to talk about Luther. His family had not spent Christmas at home, but he was back and amongst those invited to the house this evening. She laughed lightly.

"But he's poor, Daddy! All the Chevaliers have left is a house, a grand name and an art gallery no-one's heard of. Anyway, when Paul wants something, nobody gets in his way. Specially not Luther," she added.

Charles mouthed a few more clouds from his cigar, regarded her with narrowed eyes. "Not too many people get in your way either." He pointed at her, smoke rising between his fingers. "When you want something, you stamp your foot until you get it."

A smile took some of the sting from his words, but she pouted again. It was easy to pout when her father spoke to her. With

Paul, pouting wasn't any good at all.

"Well, I get that from you, Daddy," she said.

"Oh no," he said, "you get that from your mother." He stood and crossed to the window, the window where she used to kneel to watch for Luther and his mother coming to visit. Lawns swept down to the private road which led to the four other residences in this exclusive enclave. The Chevalier house was on a raised site almost opposite. The light was fading now into late afternoon. He spoke quietly as he always did when memories like these stirred. "Luther remembers your mother, you know. He's a bit older than you and he remembers." He turned back to her. "You've been away, so you wouldn't know. The gallery's becoming quite a success. Luther's got flair and good judgement. He took me to see it a few weeks ago. He has an exhibition of West African art. Stunning, some of it. In fact I've reserved a piece – a wood carving. I think you'd like it."

Charles became brisk again and paced across the room. Dianne suspected he was about to bring up some topic which slightly embarrassed him. Surely he wouldn't ask her anything intimate? She felt a stab of pleasure as she remembered Paul's passion of last night. It had been the first time for a while and he had surprised and delighted her. She thought that he would fall asleep quickly after the party but he closed the bedroom door and looked at her in the way that made her toes curl.

To have his full attention after sharing him all evening, to have him wrap himself round her, in her, over her; hear him say her name, feel him in her body, taste him on her skin, was still an intoxication better than wine. Some hours before, she had taken his arm in the room full of people and the jut of her chin said, "Look what I've got!", the arch of her neck said, "Don't touch, he's mine!"

Charles stopped in front of her, took the cigar from his mouth and pushed out a smoke ring.

"What about money?"

She blinked. "What do you mean?"

The cigar left smoke trails in the air as he waved his hand. "If Paul had stayed here he'd have been a celebrity in a year or two. And your name would have been a great asset to his career. Now what's he got? You didn't expect this, did you?" He cocked his head sideways. "You know what people are saying?"

She did. Bella had told her. Her father told her again. "They asking: What's he running from? Or who?"

She stood up. The warmth of her memories ignited a rare spark of loyalty to her husband. "You can run *to* something as well as away from it. Remember, his Dad died a year ago. His mother's alone now."

He spread his hands to encompass the room. "And what am I? She has another son, hasn't she?"

She put an arm round his waist. "I'll be back. Be patient."

His lip curled. "Damned fellow wouldn't let me buy you a house so you're living in a cupboard off some city road."

"You've never even seen it, Daddy."

He sighed in annoyance. "No, I haven't. I'm sorry about that. What with all the war talk, the City's been humming." He walked back to the window and she heard him muttering, "Bloody Americans." He turned round again. "But I'll visit you soon. I promise."

That wasn't what she wanted. "Oh, it's not worth it. We'll be back soon anyway."

"When?"

She sat down again and fiddled with her wedding ring. "I'm working on it," she said eventually.

Her father sat beside her. His hand came across and took hers. Firelight sparked on the huge gold signet ring on his wedding finger, his initials carved in majestic swashes on its vast surface. On the little finger of his right hand, a polished black gem was set in the thickness of a gold band.

"You must get him to come back, Dianne," he said. It was a statement. "Otherwise, why didn't you marry Luther?"

The loyalty still flickered. "Because I wanted Paul! He'll do well. He will. He's getting royalties from previous work. And he had oodles saved from his work here. He's getting commissions again."

Charles let out a heavy breath of derision. After a silence, he squeezed her hands. "You're all I've got, Dianne. And you'll have all I've got. Most of it, anyway." He paused. "Even if he's a creative genius, Paul's stubborn and proud and I don't like him. He took you away from me and I can't forgive his selfishness. There's something about him that ... But you fell for his black eyes so I have to accept it." His voice took on a greater strength. "I don't have to accept my little girl living on fresh air and artistry!"

"His eyes are blue," she said defiantly. "And living away from London's quite a novelty, actually."

Charles released her hands and got to his feet, growling. "He's a novelty too." He swung round. "Novelties have a habit of wearing off."

Annoyance tinged her voice. "Why does everyone say that? It's as if everyone thinks I made a mistake. Even you." She hung her head, pouting.

He leaned on the mantle and looked into the flames as he said, "I have a suggestion." When she said nothing, he continued. "I want to set up a bank account for you. Just you. You may not need to use the money, but it will be there..." he paused to push out another smoke ring "... if ever you do need it." He raised a warning finger. "But you mustn't tell Paul about it. I don't want him knowing and causing a fuss."

Dianne drew patterns on the leather arm. Arabella had pointed out that the Harrod's sale started on Monday. She looked around the room, felt the memories in every corner, both here and in the rest of the huge house. She wondered if Paul would mind her coming over to her father's more often, maybe a week here, a fortnight there. Eventually he would follow her back. He would. The thought ran through her with the sweetness of syrup.

She looked across at the window where a light rain was beginning to mist the glass. Already marriage wasn't as she planned. She had thought that they could share everything, but reality was blowing cold and insistent across her fantasies. Paul didn't talk. Paul didn't share. Did Paul have secrets?

She stood up and went to her father. She put her arms round his neck and kissed his cheek, warm from the fire, mellow with the scent of cigar smoke.

"Thank you, Daddy. That would be wonderful." She smiled. "And I won't breathe a word to Paul."

"And you'll talk him into coming back?"

"Oh, yes," she said.

This was a smaller affair, just twenty or so friends and neighbours in to chat over drinks and supper. Bella was there of course. Bella's cleavage was even fuller this evening, her lips shinier, her dress shapely and short. She had fixed on Paul like a guided missile. Dianne intercepted her trajectory.

"Stop chasing my husband, Bella."

"Darling! What are you talking about?" She dropped her voice. "Anyway, I saw him first."

Dianne threaded her arm through hers and pulled her towards a side table where plates of food were laid out. "Yes, but *I* got him," she hissed. She glanced back to the corner by the marble fireplace where Paul appeared to be listening intently to a woman of about forty. She was talking rapidly, gesturing, flashing quick smiles up into his eyes. "Hey, look at Vicky Spencer. That outfit looks as if it's been dragged from the back of a charity shop."

"So does she!" said Arabella. The two girls giggled and wove round some more groups in the middle of the room. Then Dianne tugged her arm again.

"Seriously. Stop drooling over Paul. I know you're just fooling about but you're making an idiot of yourself. I'll get frightfully annoyed." She pinched Bella's arm. "You're my best friend and enough's enough."

Arabella picked up a tiny cracker topped with a piece of cheese in the shape of a swan. "But best friends share, darling!" She swallowed and licked her fingers with sulky lips. "So you haven't made any best Irish friends then?"

"None at all. Belfast's hopeless." She waved her glass and added as an afterthought, "Well, I suppose I'm sort of friends with that student I told you about – the one Paul's brother treated so dreadfully." The gold bracelet on her wrist slid gracefully to her hand as she reached for a stick of celery and twirled it in a dip. "But really, she's not my type. Her father's in the church." The celery snapped between her teeth. "But she's useful sometimes."

"Who else is coming that might at least be interesting? Luther, of course. What about Justin?"

"Skiing."

"Harry?"

"Checking out his vineyard in Italy apparently."

Arabella sighed. "And Toby?"

"Still married to his patients." Dianne glanced at her watch. "Probably doing a late surgery or something."

Arabella tapped her glass thoughtfully and gazed round the room. "There was a time when I'd have considered Toby. But he's getting frightfully old and much too dedicated to his work to have time for a wife." She turned to Dianne. "Did you ever wonder ...?"

"Wonder what?"

"If Toby's gay?"

"Of course I did! Didn't everyone?" Over Bella's shoulder, someone caught her eye. "Hello, Luther," she said.

Bella backed away. "I'll leave you two to chat."

Luther Chevalier had lost weight. Not a lot, but Dianne noticed his jawbone was a little more angular, his jacket slightly looser. He was only a little taller than she was, his hair the dark blond of cut wheat lapped in a field. He used to tell her that their hair colours were different swatches from the same shade card. He nodded, his smile slight and tense.

"Welcome back, Dianne."

"It's good to be back." She hid behind a sip from her glass.

"You look beautiful."

"Thank you."

Luther looked around the room and then back at her. "Is the library being used tonight?"

"Why?"

"I want to talk to you. Alone."

She tossed her head. "There's nothing to say."

"Between you and me? There was always plenty to say."

He stood aside and motioned for her to pass him. After a moment, she did. The library was through an archway and further down the hall. He closed the door behind them, the sounds of chatter, laughter and the chink of glasses smothered to a distant murmur. Three lamps diffused a soft light across the room. She set her glass on the ledge which ran along the wall of bookcases with their carved wood and glass fronts, and turned to face him, leaning back on her hands. Beside her, the heavy curtains had been drawn across the bay window. He stayed by the door.

"I've been watching you for a while."

"Oh? I didn't see you."

He picked up a porcelain figurine from beneath a lamp on a small table; turned it round; set it down again. "So how's it working out, Dianne?" he asked.

She walked round the sofa and sat down, crossed her slender ankles. "It's working out just great. Really. You should be happy for me."

"I am really happy for you. If you're telling the truth."

"You think I'm not?"

He came and sat where her father had sat earlier that day. A guard was across the whitened remnants of the log fire. "I've known you since you were born. I'm the one person here who can read you like a book."

"And what do you see?"

He sighed and pressed his finger and thumb into his eyes. After a moment he looked up. "Why did you do it, Dianne? Why him and not me?"

She laughed merrily at him. "I think we've had this conversation before."

"Let's have it again."

"Oh, don't be so boring!" She stood up. "Let's go back ..."

She staggered a little as he jumped from the chair and confronted her. "Paul isn't who you thought he'd be, is he? He's lost his money-making power. He's lost his fans. He's jumped off the ladder. You thought you were marrying the Next Big Thing but he's buried himself in the Irish bog he came from and he's burying you with him!"

She felt the scarlet rising on her face to match the flush on his own pale skin.

"And what would you have done for me, Luther?" Her voice became icy. "You'll never be anything. Your father hadn't enough brains to keep his money or his job." She stepped away from him, flinging her words like stinging hail. "You know how families go. They branch off. Some do well, some don't. You get the successful ones and the failures." She jabbed her finger at him. "You're just average, Luther. Mr Average. You'll never be anything else." She took a breath and added, "It was OK being my 'chevalier' when we were children. A Huguenot family tree and big spaniel eyes don't do it for me now."

His face bleached to the colour of his lashes and he said quietly, "I was a lot more than your chevalier. Have you forgotten?"

She went to the book case, picked up her glass and fingered its stem for a moment. Then she turned. "No, I haven't forgotten."

There was a silence. Then she pushed her hair from her eyes and walked past him. His hand flashed like a cobra and bit her wrist. Her glass smashed to the floor. Gasping, shocked, she jerked to a stop. His grip covered her gold bracelet and made it cut into her skin. She pulled away but his fingers bit harder. He brought his face close to hers, his voice hoarse.

"Does he make love to you like I did?"

She squeezed her eyes shut and turned her head away. They stood like that for a moment, frozen. Then shock and anger made her vicious. She turned her mouth to drip each whispered word into his ear like acid.

"No, he doesn't make love to me like you did. He's much, ..." she licked her lips slowly and nudged her mouth closer "...much, much better than that." Her lips touched the flesh of his lobe. "He sends me to the stars. You never even reached lift-off." She felt his muscles bunching and hissed, "You never did it for me, Luther. Never."

It was fortunate that the sofa was behind her, for he threw her away from him with force. She rubbed her wrist where the pattern of her bracelet was incised in a red welt. He spoke with rigid control.

"You're still a lying bitch." He looked at her for a long moment and then he dropped to his heels and began to pick up pieces of glass from the carpet. He brought them to the fender and set them in a heap. He turned back to her. "When that man breaks your heart ..." he gestured at the glass fragments on the fender "... don't wait for me to gather up the pieces. And when he gets you pregnant and you're lying in his bed beside him, terrified and thinking about your mother ..." he sliced his hand sideways "... don't even tell me."

He walked to the door and touched the handle, let it go again and turned back. His voice shook a little. He wasn't as calm as he was trying to appear. "Just tell me one thing. I need to know." Her mouth was dry. Luther took a deep breath and the lick of hair at his brow trembled. "If he hadn't appeared, we'd have made it. You and me. Wouldn't we?"

She didn't reply at once and he came to stand in front of her. She put her hand to her collar bone in a gesture of defence, but he bent and there was unlikely tenderness in his touch as he lifted her hand and pulled her back to her feet.

"We nearly made it, didn't we?" he repeated. "Until he came, there wasn't anyone else." His tongue flicked across his lips. "Was there?"

She shook her head and found her voice, small and strained. "No, Luther, there was no-one else."

"You're a spoilt brat." He smoothed the hair over her ear. "I know you inside out, and I have no idea why I still love every hair on your selfish head." His eyes travelled to her mouth. She held her breath. He dropped her hand and stepped back. "You made a big mistake."

He left the door open when he walked out.

Her legs gave way and she sat abruptly. She put both hands over her face and started to shake. She'd been all right until he mentioned her mother. And being pregnant. She had no idea that she had hurt him so much.

"There you are, Princess! I've been looking for you." Her father stood in the doorway. "Have you and Luther been catching up on old times?"

CHAPTER FOURTEEN

HOW MANY MORE evenings like this could he stand? Paul backed into a corner, held his glass like a shield. Next week they would go back, go home. Five more days. He pressed each finger in turn into the cold glass in his hand, counting up to five as he did so.

He coiled his body tight behind the chimney breast. He was doing this because he really did want to try, doing this because Dianne was homesick, doing this because they should stay together, because he was stronger than she was.

He looked at his feet. That last one was wrong. Jenna was wrong there.

He escaped from the Butler house when he could. He had files full of images of grand facades, massive columns, stone lions and fussing pigeons. He had experimented with winter lighting, contra-jour, shadows, filters. Today, he had concentrated on shapes, close-ups, juxtapositions. He'd stayed away as late as he could to capture the tricks of evening shade.

Arabella was crossing the carpet towards him, business in her eye. Dianne ambushed her. A woman in rumpled green appeared beside him. He'd forgotten that corners weren't a good idea. No back door.

"What a treat to see you again, Paul!" she declared. "You really must come back to us."

"Why must I?"

Chevalier had arrived in the room.

"So many of my friends ask for you. They say 'We want that marvellous young man who did the christening for you.' You've abandoned us!"

"I just went home."

Chevalier was talking to Dianne.

"But poor Dianne! She must be so lonely. It's such a shame!" He watched her sherry glass wave in agitation. She was going to spill it. "The photos you took of Oliver have been so admired."

Chevalier and Dianne were leaving the room.

Civility left him. "Who the hell's Oliver?"

She blinked. Her chin tucked in. "My son! He's four now, you know." She leaned towards him. "You must remember. He was sick on your bag and you were so patient with him."

He remembered. The brat.

She threw a smile up at him and dropped her voice. "But I'm sure you'll be photographing your own soon."

"Are you?"

He pushed his way past her, out of the corner and into a pool of space. Bella was on the loose again. Through the archway he could see the stairs and an oasis at the top where the landing bowed out from the mouth of the passageway which led to the bedrooms. It formed a veranda overlooking the hall. He didn't make it to the first step.

"Well, Paul. What have you been up to today?"

"My own business, Bella."

She gave a deep chuckle and moved her cleavage into his line of sight. "But I find your business absolutely fascinating."

He tried to move past her but her neat side-step kept her in front of him. He stood perfectly still for a moment, looking at her. Her eyes darted up, a glance crooked from the corner of her lids. Then he put his hand on her bare shoulder and returned her gaze with deep concentration.

"Tell me something, Bella," he said, his brow furrowed.

Surprised, she glanced round at his hand. "Certainly."

"Would you sleep with me?"

Startled, she backed away and his hand dropped from her shoulder. Her laugh was awkward. "A lady would never answer a question like that!"

"Maybe a lady wouldn't." He raised an eyebrow. "But I'm asking you."

She ran her finger slowly round the rim of her wine glass. "I could be offended at that."

Chevalier and Dianne had not returned.

"Suit yourself. I thought it was what you wanted me to ask."

He tried to move past her again. She touched her fingers to his arm. He looked down at them, scarlet nails against the dark navy of his jacket. Nails that had probably never touched the grain of old wood in wonder or felt hot tears of humiliation run over them and onto ragged grass at midnight. Disgust boiled up in him. She was speaking again.

"Well, maybe I like a man who says what he means." He felt a slight pressure from her fingers. "Don't get me wrong. I'm very choosy."

He lifted her hand from his arm. "But then, Bella ..." he dropped her hand with a flick of distaste "... so am I."

This time she let him pass. He almost felt the venom hit the back of his neck. Inside, part of him smiled. She'd be back for more tomorrow.

Careful not to catch anyone's eye, he hooked his fingers round the wooden sphere on top of the newel post and swung himself up the curved and carpeted staircase. At the top he turned and looked down with the relief of a squirrel in a tree. It was a broad landing consisting of two deep armchairs arranged at an angle to a low table. Against the wall were a grandfather clock and a semi-circular table on which there was an elaborate arrangement of large white lilies and broad green leaves. Its twin was in the hall below. The calm of sanctuary creamed over him.

He sat down, patted his pocket and took out his phone. His Uncle Bob answered on the third ring. His mother was in another room. He listened to her name being called through the house in Coleraine. Opposite him, beyond the rail around the landing, a large chandelier hung from the ceiling, lighting the hall below. He counted the bulbs on it while he waited.

Hazel's voice was bright, eager.

"Paul?"

He smiled at the chandelier. "Hello, Mum. Just checking in. How are you?"

"Great. I've never eaten so many chocolates! Bob and Sally have been wonderful."

"Well, it's about time you had a break from making the dinner."

She wanted to know all about his Christmas, where he'd been, what he'd been doing. How was Dianne? And Charles? She had met him only once, at the wedding, but had liked him.

"What about you, Mum?" he asked eventually.

"Well, I've already told you about the chocolates. But I miss you. That's been really strange. Not having either you or Christopher."

"It's different this year all right."

"And how!" she said. There was a silence. Then he heard her voice become slow, tentative, as if she wasn't sure she should say this. "I remember ... when there was only you and me. You were too young to remember."

"I remember some things. Feelings mostly," he said. "But things changed for the better for you."

"For me, maybe, but sometimes ..."

"Stop it, Mum," he said sharply. "How's Adam?"

He heard her take a steadying breath. "He's eaten even more than me," she said brightly. "But he's anxious to get back to Belfast. Probably misses Jenna."

Paul put his foot up on the edge of the coffee table.

"Has he spoken to her?"

"I think so."

He could think of nothing else to say.

"Well, I'll see you next week."

"You will call in as soon as you get back?"

"Of course."

"Maybe next Christmas," she said, and he heard the spirit in her coming back, "you and Dianne will stay here. Turn-about with the in-laws. Lots of people do that. At least until the children come along."

"We'll see," he said.

"Yes, do that," she replied. "Don't forget I need you too. And any children you have will have only one granny. Me."

He snapped the phone shut and dropped it back into his pocket. For a long moment, he was motionless, his eyes wide and unfocused. Below him, someone was telling a funny story. The last line was punched out and an explosion of laughter stampeded the stairwell, swirling him into a vortex of noise. Suddenly, as if an invisible rampart had been stormed, he raised both his arms high above his head, stretched his fingers to the roof.

"Please God!" he cried.

The laughter subsided, trickled back down the walls, left him marooned as if he had never uttered a sound.

He stood and went to the rail, bent to lean his forearms on the wood. Some people had seen him, but not being family, they would not go up the stairs of their host's house without an invitation. His eyes swept the room below him and he began to play his game. 'Rich' was an obvious word. A group of three men was standing near the front door. One man was talking, his hand resting on his chin; the other two had their heads tilted slightly, listening. 'Friends'. Somewhere out of sight, Arabella's laughter rose and fell, joined by a deeper guffaw. 'Slut'. Maybe that was unfair. He tried 'pest'. That was better.

He was tiring of this very quickly. There wasn't much scope. A woman in a pink dress squeezed between the three men and a bay tree in a pot. 'Jenna'.

He mulled that one over. It must have been the dress which popped the name into his mind. That and his mother mentioning her. She had looked well that night at the hotel, despite how it ended for her. He didn't know why he called her plain when he had first seen her. She wasn't. He had also called her 'fresh'. He rolled that one round his mind. It still fitted.

He wondered where he would photograph her if she were here tonight. Probably down there, sitting on the bottom stair and leaning against the bannister. Would she wear that dress and would it still have the tear in its hem? Like a sculpture through drifting mist, her figure surfaced in his mind. She was in her combat trousers and denim jacket, incongruous in this clot of opulence. A scarf lay tangled beside her. She was turning, looking up at him with those bright, inquisitive eyes. From her open palm hung the chain of a gold cross.

Why had that image fixed in his mind? Of course! He had a photograph of her preserved in that pose for ever.

He stiffened. From beneath where he stood, Chevalier appeared. Paul recognised the fair hair and the broad shoulders. He was walking quickly, looking to right and left. He checked the room through the archway and then swung on his heel and looked up, directly at Paul. Paul didn't move as Chevalier locked eyes with him. He watched as hate and pain struggled on the face of the man below. Chevalier took three steps towards the stairs. Then he turned, pushed his way to the front door, and left the house.

Paul straightened. He should go and find Dianne now. A lethargy came over him. He found he didn't care. If she wanted to see him, she could come and find him. He rubbed his brow. He really was a bad bastard.

He looked down again. Now Charles was crossing the hall. His arm loosely on her waist, he was leading Dianne back into the company. Paul couldn't see her expression, just the blonde hair on the bare shoulders where he had laid his head last night. But her posture was tense, her head turning quickly from side to side.

He saw her begin to play the social game again. Only occasionally did she glance round, searching, checking. When she did so, he ducked backwards briefly. He didn't want her just now. Still, he reached for his glass and raised it to her. "Here's to you, Dianne," he said silently. "With or without me."

Slowly, she relaxed and he leaned on the rail again, his eyes latched on her. He saw her laughing, tilting her head to listen, refusing another drink with a smile and a shake of the head, sitting on the arm of a chair, touching a friend on the hand, whispering in her ear, sharing a giggle.

Even as he watched, he felt himself leaving her. She was losing the little blaze that made her stand out in his universe. She was blending in, fading into the colourful, shifting pattern of the room. She was losing the edges of her difference, becoming ordinary in his eyes. Last night he had caressed her silky skin and loved her with the desperation of hope, a craving to belong. Now, he felt his attachment to her sifting away like the whisper of sand falling through a sieve. He could try to catch the sand, but it would trickle through his fingers, inexorably departing.

He could say it now, so he did, whispered low and sorrowful. "I'm sorry, Luther."

Unleashed by the words, fear leapt at his throat. His hands came up as if against attack; he turned and sank into the chair, fixed his eyes on the long bulbs dripping from the chandelier. *I'm on my own. I'm really on my own. It isn't going to work.* He leaned back and closed his eyes. The lights ghosted into black dots on the inside of his lids. People think loneliness is absence. It isn't. It's a filling up, a rising, spilling tide that crashes into every gully and chasm of your mind and soul until you're choked with emptiness, awash with desolation, thrashing in the foam of it, reaching for a hand to hold and yet finding no hand, no refuge, no comfort. He had been here before.

He kept his eyes shut and breathed himself slowly back to land.

"Hello, Paul."

His eyes snapped open. A man of about his own height but perhaps twenty years older, stood beside the grandfather clock at the top of the stairs. Speckles of white hair swept from his temples and sprinkled the neat, pointed beard. In one hand he held a brandy glass. The other hand rested loosely in his pocket as his clear, steady gaze rested on Paul.

Slowly, Paul got to his feet.

"Hello Toby," he said. "When did you get here?"

"A few minutes ago." His voice was mellow, cultured. "Arabella told me you'd gone upstairs to be mean and moody." The man extended a finger from his glass and pointed at the passage which led from the landing. "I'm sure there's somewhere here we can talk."

Paul's hands came up again, palms out in self-defence. Then they dropped to his sides and he flashed a brief, forced smile. "Sure," he said and walked ahead, past the deep trumpets of the white lilies, down the long, lamp lit way, past the pictures in their grand frames, the linen cupboard, the table at the corner with the Chinese urn which he had always detested, the door of the bedroom where he and Dianne would lie later, the cream curtains pulled over the window which overlooked the back gardens.

Back here, there wasn't a sound.

The brush tore through her hair in fast, angry sweeps.

"Where were you, Paul?" Dianne stopped and swivelled round to glare at him. "I was looking for you. You just disappeared."

He was already in bed, lying on his side. He seemed distant, as if he were hardly aware that she was talking. That annoyed her more.

"A lot of the visitors tonight had come to see you. Poor old Vicky Spencer's too nice to say you were rude to her, but that's what she meant."

He stirred. "You disappeared too."

She turned back to the mirror and resumed brushing her hair. "That was different. I came back. You went to bed!" She glared at his reflection and jabbed the brush at it irritably. "Two nights ago you were being wonderful and funny. People were hanging on your every word."

He watched her for a moment. Then he asked, "How's Luther?"

"Fine."

"Just fine?"

"Busy. The gallery's doing well for him at last."

"Good."

She set down the brush and came to sit on the edge of the bed. "You agreed to come. The least you can do is be sociable. A lot of these people were your clients and will be again when you come back. And they're all contacts you need. They have friends."

He rolled onto his back. "I'm not coming back."

"Oh Paul! You'll never get anywhere if you desert the reputation you've built up here."

"I don't want that any more."

She laughed a little, brittle and strained. "Don't be silly. What on earth *do* you want?"

He sat up and the covers fell from his bare shoulders leaving his body tense and naked in front of her. He put his hand up to the back of her neck and held her head so that she felt pinioned by his eyes. Tonight they did look almost black.

"I want," he said, the words slow and deliberate, "a child."

She recoiled, twisted from his grasp and stood up, backing away from him. "We've been over this so many times! It's not the right time."

There was a long silence. She wished he would reply, get angry, fight with her as he used to do. Instead, he seemed to give up. He fell back on the pillow. Short locks of black hair nudged round his head and fringed his brow. Muscles rippled across his shoulders and round his collar bone, then became still.

He swallowed once, seemed to be thinking. Then he said, "You don't need me here."

She frowned. "Of course I do."

"You don't," he repeated. He turned on his side again and pulled the cover over his shoulders. "I'm going home tomorrow."

Alarm spread through her body. "You can't! We're staying till next week."

"I'm going home tomorrow," he repeated.

She stood up straighter. "How? You haven't even got a standby ticket. And tomorrow's New Year's Eve."

"I'll get there," he said, closing his eyes. "You could come with me."

She went round to her side of the bed and slid in behind him, anxious, disturbed. She put her hand across his body. "I can't, Paul. Daddy would be so disappointed. And Bella and I have plans ..."

He interrupted her. "Fine. I'll see you after the weekend then."

She felt the long firm muscles of his back, the maleness of him. Where had he gone? He had always been difficult, but yet hypnotically delightful. Tonight, she sensed a greater change.

Something more than moodiness was tugging him away from her.

He stirred and turned to face her. Face to face with her on the pillow, his hand came up to cup her cheek.

"You're right," he said softly. "Now's not the right time. I won't mention it again."

He put his arm under her neck and pulled her close. She settled her head into the hollow of his shoulder. Of course he wouldn't leave tomorrow!

She slept.

When she awoke in the morning, she was already alone.

CHAPTER FIFTEEN

HE WOULD HAVE got home if he had had to swim. As it was, patience, persistence and liberal charm lavished on the check-in staff had located a seat on a plane to Belfast by mid-afternoon. It was dark when finally Paul put his key in the door of his own house.

He dropped his bag, set his keys on the hall table and stood listening to the silence, smelled the scent of emptiness. He ran up the stairs, running his hand over the fuzz of tinsel which Dianne had threaded through the banisters. A quick check round satisfied him that all was well.

He spent the evening at his computer, watching his new pictures open into life before his eyes. It was a process which fascinated him endlessly. Some pictures he discarded because they dissatisfied his standards of perfection.

Many were devoted to pigeons – walking, pecking, squabbling. The birds made him smile and reminded him of the batch of shots he had captured the day he had staked out the bird table in the back garden. Jenna had arrived and located the robin in the bush for him, unerring and calm in her instinct for what he was trying to do.

The thought of food hadn't crossed his mind since he had boarded the plane. Late in the night, his stomach reminded him that he was hungry. He made himself a cup of coffee and some toast from frozen bread. Restless, he paced round the kitchen and sitting room eating and drinking as he moved. When he had finished and left the dishes lying in the sink, he forced himself to sit down. His eyes caught on the clock on the side table. He got up again and put on his coat.

He didn't want to sleep through the turn of this year. He wanted to know about its dawning, watch its birth. He wanted to catch it slipping into time, gathering him with it, pulling him on down the tunnel of days as if the journey had no end.

The bolt on the back door was stiff and cold to his fingers. Outside, he crouched on a stone at the edge of the untidy path and breathed in the air of his home place. The stars wheeled into the new year and, across the city, fireworks shot into the sky, bursting above his head in cascades of light. With a whoosh, several more scored the darkness – up, up, until his head was back and his neck ached with looking. Light splashed across the blackness, tossed above the rooftops and fell in a tracery of fire. Transfixed, he watched the sparkles as they whirled and fell and dimmed and vanished. When all was done, the darkness hunched itself over him again, the cold breeze brushed his face, the black dart of a bat cut above the tiny rustle of unseen things.

He pushed himself to his feet and went back inside. The bedroom was strange without Dianne. There was no smell of her cream, no rhythm of her brush.

He didn't believe in prayer so he closed his eyes tight and wished. He knew what he was going to do in the morning, and he knew who he wanted at his side.

He wished again and then he slept.

Dianne didn't have to tell her father that Paul had gone back without her until they met over a light snack at lunch time.

"It was a New Year assignment that came up. Some major VIP dinner." She broke her soup roll delicately. "Someone rang him last night and said the photographer they'd booked had gone down with flu. It's a Press thing, so it had to be covered." She gave a small laugh. "Paul can't turn anything down."

Her father looked up from under his brows as he bent over his soup. "Isn't it strange that there wasn't anyone on the same island who could fill in?"

She shrugged. "Well, sometimes people want Paul and no-one else will do."

He didn't say another word about it.

She tried the same story on Arabella who was more direct in her response when she phoned.

"Don't tell porkies, Di darling. He was smouldering with boredom last night. I could tell. More likely, you've had a frightful row over your little tête-à-tête with Luther."

"No, we didn't have a row. He trusts me. That's over."

Bella's throaty chuckle sounded in her ear. "And Buckingham Palace is made of green cheese! It's not over for Luther, darling. What's a wedding ring these days? Besides," she added, "I wouldn't trust you the length of my little finger – and I'm your friend."

It was afternoon when Dianne walked slowly up the long drive of the Chevalier house. Here was the slope where she and Luther had raced snails. There was the patch of lawn beside the beech trees where the swings used to be. His much older brother and sister would play with them for a while and then get bored and leave them to their own devices.

And over there – Dianne stopped – was the garden seat where Luther had first kissed her. He was sixteen and she was only thirteen. It hadn't happened again for years, but that one kiss had loosened the promise of womanhood in her. She was becoming an attractive girl and a rich one. There was fun to be had. After the parties and clubs, the taxis and chauffeurs would take them all home and Luther and she would talk on the phone, analysing the evening, gossiping. She would tease him about his girlfriends and he would insult her men friends with caustic wit.

Then came the day when he had kissed her for the second time. They came together that day, two plants from the same hothouse. There was no-one else for either of them – until that day she had visited Bella. A talented young photographer had bounded into the house. Energy sparked from his eyes, humour danced round his mouth and strength flexed his body as he checked lighting, angles, moved furniture and told Bella's mother that the colour of her outfit wouldn't do, wouldn't do at all. Bella's parents were ensnared into effortless obedience and the portrait which he took was priceless. Never before had Dianne called a man perfect, but it was the only word for this one.

Three days later, she rang Luther. "Sorry, darling. I think I'm coming down with something. I don't think I'm up to going out tonight. I'm going to have an early night."

Three hours later, she was having her first dinner with Paul Shepherd and Luther was totally eclipsed by his shadow. When she heard of the Chevalier's ill-advised investments and the devastating loss of money which the family suffered, she remarked to Bella, "Heavens, to think I might have married him! I might have been a pauper. Ugh!"

She walked the last few yards of the drive and saw Luther standing at the front door, arms folded. When she reached him, he greeted her tersely. "What do you want?"

She pulled her collar up against the cold wind. "It's chilly. Can I come in?"

"Why?"

"Well, I thought maybe last night wasn't a good way for old friends to part."

He unfolded his arms and leaned an elbow against the door frame. "Are you apologising?"

Her chin jutted. "No. You provoked me. Are you apologising?"

"No. I said you were a lying bitch and you are."

She looked at his sturdy figure, the slightly chubby fingers stroking his chin, the sandy hair just a little too long at his ears. He was so different to the lean darkness of Paul, and yet ... She turned away and walked in a small circle. And yet he was part of something which she missed so much. Paul was magical and sensuous and still perfect. But he was hard, tiring work. It was his own fault that she was here, now, standing at the door of an old lover.

She faced Luther again, holding with one hand the strands of her hair as they blew across her face.

"Well, this is true. Paul's gone back early. I don't know why." She blew a blonde curl from her mouth. "So I've no-one to see in the New Year with," she added.

There was a moment while they just looked at each other, seeing through each other as through plain glass. Simultaneously, they began to grin, slowly at first and then with the wide delight of reprieved thieves.

Luther backed into the house. "I'll pick you up at nine," he said, and closed the door.

Dianne stared at the door as it slammed. Then she spun on her heels and walked briskly down the driveway. At the huge metal gate, which was rusty and neglected, she gave a little hop and skip. Her chin was up, her mind was already rattling through the dresses in her wardrobe. She had absolutely *nothing* to wear.

⁓

The phone was shrilling through the house. Jenna pulled the bedclothes over her head, unwilling to waken, unwilling to face this day. Who would be ringing her house, her land line? Her mother or father, wanting to wish her a happy New Year? She squinted at the clock on the bedside table. Ten past seven! She came alive on the thought that at this hour, it could be that something was wrong. Luke! What scrape had he got into last night?

She stumbled down the stairs expecting the ringing to stop any moment. The phone perched in a corner behind the front door, on a built-in wooden unit which housed the fuse box. She grabbed the receiver.

"Hello?" There wasn't a sound in reply. "Hello? Who's that?"

There was a click and the dialling tone burred in her ear. She slammed the phone down. "If you got a wrong number, at least have the grace to apologise!" she bawled at it. She sank down onto the bottom stair and dropped her head into her hands, scrunching her hair into tufts and tangled strands. What a way to wake up. *Hallo, New Year.*

She decided to go back to sleep. She looked at her rumpled bed and then decided she was thirsty. A towelling robe was tossed over a chair. She pulled it on and yanked the belt tight. Hmm. She'd got thinner. A glass of orange was joined by a bowl of cereal and became breakfast in front of the television. Outside her window, a cold, damp, night still hung over the street, the first creep of dawn still an hour away. Not too many people were about at this hour, especially as most people were sleeping off the night before. Had Adam been with Rachel last night? She set the bowl of rice crispies on the floor. She didn't feel like it after all. She drew her knees up to her chin and huddled in her chair. She didn't feel like anything. Adam would probably ring later. He said he would last time they had had a brief, stilted conversation. He might even call in once he found out she was here. She folded her arms tightly. They were going to have to have it out. Whenever she tried to work out what she wanted to say, what she wanted to happen, her feelings still hurt too much and she put the thoughts away again.

After half an hour gazing sightlessly at cartoons, she decided to get a cup of tea and go back to bed. The kettle was coming to the boil when her doorbell rang. Startled, she tugged at the belt of her robe and looked down at her pink slippers, a present from Aunt Susan. There was a cat woven on each toe. It wasn't even eight o'clock.

She opened the door on the chain and put her eye to the chink. Paul Shepherd stood on the footpath, woollen hat pulled over his ears and his hands in the pockets of his long coat. A brown envelope was tucked under one arm. He was looking up, his eyes bright and restless in the street light.

"Is something wrong?" she asked sharply.

"Not a thing," he said. "Can I come in?"

"It's eight o'clock in the morning!"

He looked at his watch. "Well, what do you know? So it is. Can I come in?"

She took the chain off and went back to the kitchen, leaving him to close the door himself. He didn't follow her, instead turning left into her sitting room. She poured two mugs of tea. He was sitting in her chair, looking round, flicking the woollen hat between his hands, his hair ruffled. When he set the hat down to take a mug from her, she picked it up and set it on the sofa out of his reach.

"You've taken your tree down," he said.

She stood by the window. "It was crap anyway." She sipped her tea and wrapped her fingers round the mug. "I thought you were in London."

"I was. I came back."

"So you're not a ghost then."

He felt down the length of his arm thoughtfully, then declared, "Not yet."

She stood in front of him, curious. "How did you know I was here?"

"I wished you here." He grinned. "And you answered your phone earlier."

"That was you? How did you get my number?"

"You've been here long enough to be in the phone book. And Dianne had put you in ours anyway."

She sat down on the sofa and leaned forward, elbows on knees, propping the mug below her chin. "What do you mean – you wished me here?"

"I wanted to see you, so I wished."

She sat back. "Well, I seem to have popped out of the lamp for you."

They were silent for a minute. She was puzzled. There was something odd about this. "Is Dianne back too?"

He set the mug on the floor and saw her cereal bowl. "No, she isn't. Did I interrupt your breakfast?"

"I didn't feel like any."

He looked her up and down. "Love the gear. Not quite as nice as the dress you wore for the party." He looked at her feet. "The slippers would match though. As for the hair style," he winked, "pure Knightsbridge."

"Funny man," she said, scowling.

He seemed to tire of this and sprang to his feet. He paced the room, seeming to Jenna to fill it, to expand its walls, to make the air crackle with electric energy.

"I want to go to Rossnowlagh." He stopped in front of her. "And I want you to come with me."

"Rossnowlagh? Don't be an idiot. That's the other side of the country. That's the Atlantic side, Paul."

"I know where it is. If we don't stop, and we go now, we'll be there before lunch."

She stood up. "I don't want to go anywhere. I'm off people, particularly men."

He held his arms wide, his enthusiasm engulfing her in a tide. "Pretend I'm a Martian."

"Called Fred, I suppose."

"If you like."

"A Martian called Fred? Nope, can't do it."

"I'll paint myself green."

She shook her head. He put his hands up to his temples, one finger extended above each ear. "Antennae?"

"You really want company, don't you?"

"I really want yours."

Her temper snapped. "You want! You don't always get what you want."

He dropped his hands and she saw temper begin to ignite in him also. "God, you are grumpy this morning."

She waved a hand and turned away. "Well, look who's arrived in my living room at the crack of dawn – a married man demanding that I accompany him across the country just because he wants it."

He raised his voice, impatience in every syllable. "Oh, be a devil for once in your life! Dig a hole and bury your halo."

She spun round. "Well, that's not a hole you have to dig, is it?" she shot back.

"No, it's not! What's the point of a halo? It's just another damn thing that needs polished. Stop sounding like a granny. What are you – twenty-four going on eighty?"

She stabbed a finger at him. "So what are you? Twenty-nine going on three?"

There was a sudden silence as they faced each other in the middle of the room.

He raised an eyebrow. "I bet you never had a row like that with Adam."

She noticed his mouth again, noticed how it tilted naturally upwards ever so slightly on the right. "No, I never did."

The smile tilted further to crease his cheek and crinkle tiny lines round his eyes. "That's a bad sign. No sparks."

Now she was following the line of his nose, up to the wide bridge between his eyes. His black lashes fringed his lids as he looked down at her. In a sudden rush, she realised what she must look like. She pulled the robe across her body and tugged the belt tight again.

"I can't take off with you, Paul. It wouldn't be right."

He was silent for a moment, then he reached down to the far side of the chair and lifted the envelope he had been carrying when he arrived.

"I brought you a present."

She took it and opened the flap. It was a photograph. She pulled it all the way out, speechless. It was a close-up shot of a robin, its eye touched by a point of light as it looked straight at her from its perch on a twig. Its feet curled round the twig, its toes clenched in little bunches at the end of firm, sturdy legs. The red of its breast fluffed and bled into the creamy white feathers of its stomach and brown wings were folded straight and strong, down to the proud slant of the jaunty tail. Paul had set the focus to bring the bird into sharp relief against the softly blurred branches of the barren shrub.

She sat down, cradling it, studying every detail. She looked up. "That's the robin...?"

"The very same. I got that picture because of you."

"He's beautiful."

He hunkered down in front of her. "So much of this world is beautiful. We just have to see it."

It was the shapeshifter who was before her now, morphed into thoughtfulness, his humour and his anger both melted away. She was silent for some minutes, slipping into his mood, feeling that deeper parts of herself could rise and be safe.

"But betrayal is ugly," she said quietly. "Hurting is ugly. Realising you aren't loved is ugly."

"That's the ugliest of all," he said, soft. He pushed himself upright and paced to the window, thrust his hands in his pockets. Finally, with his back still to her, he said almost to himself, "You must get out of here today."

"There's no point."

He swung round and came back to her. He took her arm and pulled her up and out into the hall. "Go upstairs. Have a shower, wash your hair, put on your warmest clothes and then come with me to Rossnowlagh."

Startled, she shook her arm free. "Don't give me orders."

He turned back into the sitting room. "And leave the halo on the bedpost."

Jenna stood alone at the bottom of the stairs. Somewhere at the core of her there was a tingle of life, a touch of interest, a tiny thrum of excitement.

She stuck her head round the door. "It'll take more than three hours to get there."

He was fiddling with the TV remote. "So hurry up," he said, still fiddling.

She swung round again and scampered up the stairs, losing a slipper on the way.

CHAPTER SIXTEEN

JENNA FOUND IT inexpressibly strange to be beside Adam's brother, in an unfamiliar car, on the long road west. There was more traffic on the road than she expected but, unlike Adam, Paul made no impatient remarks, no sudden moves.

A tetchiness still clung around her.

"You'll not get petrol today. You won't have enough to get there and back."

"I've a full tank."

"Why didn't you say anything when I answered the phone? You got me out of bed."

He glanced round at her. "Because I didn't want you to say no. It's easier to say no on the telephone."

"So you came round and bingo! I'm here."

"It wasn't quite as easy as that. I've changed my mind. You don't always do what you're told."

She folded her arms across her seat belt and looked out her side window. "Not any more, anyway."

A few miles further on, she said suddenly, "I don't know why I'm doing this."

It annoyed her that he merely carried on driving and didn't reply.

"Adam'll be looking for me," she said.

They reached a long straight and he moved up a gear. "Do you care?"

Five minutes later, she replied, "He'll ring my mobile."

"Turn it off," he said instantly.

Five minutes after that, she did. He smiled slightly. That annoyed her too.

By the time they reached Fermanagh, the day had brightened into windy, crisp sunshine. They passed a roadside cafe and noticed it was open. Paul swung into the car park.

"Coffee break? There won't be many chances."

She sat opposite him. "Why Rossnowlagh? Why do you want to go to a freezing beach in the middle of winter?"

He was sitting forward, stirring his coffee. He flicked a glance at her and away again. After a moment he said, "Something happened to me there. I need to revisit it."

"So where do I come in?"

She thought he would never stop stirring, round and round and round. A frown gathered and then he answered slowly, "I don't know, but you do, somehow."

"But you said you wished me here? You must have a reason."

He lifted his cup and sat back, stretched his arm across the back of the seat beside him. Now, his eyes danced with mischief. "But Jenna, it's OK not to know. Isn't that what you said?"

They had crossed the border into Donegal when she asked, "You will tell Dianne about today, won't you?"

He slowed behind a tractor. Bales of hay were on a scoop behind it, winter fodder for animals still outdoors. "Maybe."

They wound down the narrow road between the sand dunes, past the shop closed and shuttered for the winter. Caravans squatted in lonely parks, cream and green and curtained, beneath the dull gorse hills behind. A large hotel fronted the sea, tall and grand, with a long glass lounge edging the narrow car park on the land-ward side.

Jenna sensed a tension in Paul as they neared the coast. She couldn't have explained how she knew; it just circled him. He pulled up at the side of the road beyond the hotel, and switched off the engine. As the sudden quiet snapped round them, neither of them spoke. Paul lowered his window and the incessant sound of the sea spilled into the car, the air salty on the tongue. He turned round.

"By the way," he said, "I'm not twenty-nine."

"What are you then?"

"Twenty-eight and three hundred and fifty-one days."

She did a quick calculation. "So your birthday's the fourteenth of January." She frowned, searching her memory of conversations with his mother. "But that's the day your father died last year."

He patted the steering wheel. "Considerate of him, wasn't it?"

"Correction then. I should have said this morning that you're twenty-eight-and-three-hundred-and-fifty-one-days, going on three."

He raised a hand in acceptance. "That's better!" He opened the car door. "Now let's go walking."

The wind had blown sand into every crevice of the land, piling it in small drifts in the corners of the road, little pieces of seaweed peeping through the surface of it. She was wearing a new coat, cream with fur round the hem and cuffs and at the edge of the hood. It was a Christmas present from her mother and she hugged it round herself as they walked along the narrow roadway towards the ramp down to the beach. When she had appeared in it this morning, her hair shining from the shower, Paul had said only, "You've spoiled my picture. I always think of you in denim."

They walked down onto the beach and Jenna felt as if the bickering on the journey down had purified murky air, deposited them both on this golden arc of sand, clear-headed. It was all right now. The day was packaged by the sounds of the sea. As they set foot on the sand, she looked up at Paul, happy. He caught the look and said, "I thought you were grumpy."

"Not any more," she said.

"Why not?"

"I don't know."

"And that's OK!"

She laughed aloud and began to run. "Race you to the water!"

It was wonderful. He passed her easily and stood, feet apart and hands on hips, just out of reach of the nearest wave, waiting for her, teasing. Even as she ran, the sight of him, long coat battered by the wind, face alive and dancing in the cold sea air, the foam of the breakers crashing behind him, burned itself effortlessly on her mind. If this were Adam, he would probably catch her now, swing her round. But then Adam wouldn't dream of crossing Ireland to spend New Year's Day racing along a freezing beach beside the Atlantic.

Paul took to his heels again just as she reached him. "Snail!" he called over his shoulder, running, running along the rippling lace of the edge of the incoming wave. She trotted after him, imbibing his delight like a sweet tonic, the delight of the child who must still lie deep inside him. His footprints in the wet sand faded in front of her as she followed them, the water rising to make his passage vanish, as if he had never run that way at all.

Eventually he stopped and waited for her. Beyond him, on the damp surface near the edge of the sea, seagulls and oyster catchers mingled, searching the sand for food left at the tide's edge, their reflections keeping pace, wrinkling along the sand beneath their feet. Birds squabbled in the air above the breakers, wheeling and diving, dropping to ride the waves, to rise and fall on the turbulent swell.

It was impossible for Jenna to keep her hood up against the wind and her hair streamed behind her. This close to the sea, she had to shout as the wind whipped her voice away.

"This is beautiful!"

"Look." He pointed along the sand and brought his mouth close to her ear. "See the patterns the water makes."

Over every inch of the sand, lines curved and met, crossed and arched, branched along the beach as far as they could see. She nodded and bent to pick up a shell, shook the sand from it. It was a complete razor shell, open and empty but perfect. She held it up. He took it from her and turned it over. Finally he handed it back.

She put it in her pocket. Around their feet were mussels and scallops, and random bunches of brown seaweed. She felt his touch on her back.

"Look, surfers," he called in her ear, pointing further along and out to sea.

Indeed there were surfers far out where the swell broke into mighty white froth, line after line of it, racing in to land, bearing with it the men riding their boards, knees flexing, bodies turning to skim across the faces of the waves.

It was cold! She pulled her hood up and held it tight beneath her chin, fur fringing her cheeks and fluttering at the edges of her vision. She looked round to see where Paul was and caught him looking at her some yards away, half smiling. The wind billowed into her hood and pulled it back, leaving her hair flying again and her nose running. Today she had a tissue, a whole packet of them.

Paul pulled off his woollen hat and walked back to her.

"Here," he shouted, and pulled the hat down onto her head, tucked in her ears and tugged it over her brow. "That hood's hopeless!"

"But now you've nothing. You'll freeze!" she protested.

He walked away, calling something over his shoulder. It was something about not caring. She scuffed along behind him, the hat like hands upon her head, the warmth of Paul's own flesh within it fading only slowly.

Suddenly she had to stop. She turned to face the sea. At the horizon, beyond the nearer foam, the steel of the winter ocean touched cream at the sky's end, rising to the golden edges of clouds backlit by the sun.

She wished she'd brought her halo. It might be helping now, helping fight the quick twist of mind which said "I could like this man." That she could even start along such a route within the privacy of her own thoughts was a revelation to her. She bent her head and pushed at a scallop shell with her toe. She glanced sidelong to where he still walked away from her, hands thrust deep in his pockets. He broke into a trot and aimed a kick at a lump of seaweed, slowed again, stopped.

Parallel, but too far apart even to shout to each other, they stood still, watching the running waves. The tide was flowing and a wave washed further in than the last, making them both take a few steps backwards. Then Jenna turned slowly on the ball of her foot and went towards him. He turned his head and watched her coming. His skin, naturally pale, was rosy in the stinging wind.

She reached him and he smiled. For the very first time, she hoped he wouldn't tell Dianne about today. That was bad.

They turned together and walked in step, away towards the southern arm of the bay, where the hill rose more steeply and some buildings perched beside the road along the cliff top.

Eventually Jenna said loudly, up towards his ear, "What happened to you here, Paul? You said something happened." He kept walking, head down. His step lengthened and she had to speed up to stay beside him. "Don't you want to tell me?" she asked.

"Not really, no."

"That's not fair."

He glanced round briefly. "Why's it not fair?"

She put a hand into the crook of his arm and pulled him to a stop. "I came here with you because you wanted me to. I'm entitled to know why."

"You wouldn't understand."

He walked away again, the wind flapping his coat and tossing his hair. She ran after him and pulled at his arm again, angry this time.

"Don't you dare make assumptions about me!"

That stopped him. They stood facing each other for a long moment. She couldn't read his expression but it was bent on her, concentrated, thinking. Then he looked up and around. He put his hand in the small of her back and guided her towards the tumble of rocks and boulders that had been piled between the grass bank and the beach to fight the constant erosion of the strong sea. He walked along until he found one which formed a fairly flat surface. He sat on one side of it and patted the space beside him. She sat down.

Neither spoke as the breakers raked the beach, flowed closer by centimetres with every wave. A sand martin darted past them, its bobbing flight taking it across the sandy bank and along the beach. Two of the surfers ran from the sea, boards under their arms, their wet suits glistening in the low sun. Several were still far out, jumping and waving, surfing and falling, exhilaration in every line of their bodies. Jenna shivered just to watch them.

She had asked Paul a question and he still hadn't answered it. She glanced at him but he was looking out to sea, quiet. She looked back to the surfers.

"You remind me of a king's palace," she said.

"How come?"

"Because you're behind so many closed and guarded doors."

He looked round at that. "So who's this then, sitting on this boulder beside you? Winnie the Pooh?"

"Peter Pan, maybe."

He scoffed. "You're talking in riddles."

"Then think in riddles!" she flashed, "they're the way to the answers. Isn't that what you said?"

He shifted on the rock to face her slightly. "So solve the riddle then."

She hesitated and then put her hand up to touch his shoulder and left it there as she spoke slowly. "I think Paul Shepherd lives in the farthest room, at the farthest end of the longest corridor in the palace. I think he controls every room, every key, every door in that corridor. He lives in the inner chamber and no-one gets in there. Because he won't let them. Not even his wife." He was holding her gaze, still and intense. She smoothed her palm gently across his shoulder, lifting it only when her fingers felt the merest touch of his neck. "I wonder why."

He took a deep breath, opened his mouth as if to speak, stopped, looked at the sea. Short locks of black hair blew back and forth across his brow. Her own head was still circled by his woollen hat, close and warm. She waited.

Finally he said, "Once, when I was a child, I was helping my father clear out our roof space. I found an old suitcase. It was really old, brown and stitched, with those silver coloured clasps that opened with a snap when you pulled a slider back. You know the type I mean?" She nodded. "It was quite small, just an overnight case." His eyes became bright as he remembered. "But the really magical thing about it was that there was a key inside it. It could really lock."

She smiled, imagining the delight of a child at this discovery. Why was he telling her this?

"I loved that little suitcase. It became my secret place, the place where I hid things just for the sake of knowing they were hidden. A book, a pebble, a notebook. There was even a shell from here. Only I knew they were there. You know?" She nodded. "One night Adam said I must have stolen one of his toy cars. We used to race them round the living room floor and play 'garages'." He stopped for a moment. Then, "Anyway, I said I hadn't taken it. I'd enough of my own. But Adam said I had. He even said ..." he gave a short, bitter laugh "... he'd seen me. My father didn't believe me. Adam told him about my hiding place, the suitcase.

I kept it under my bed. My father marched me upstairs and ..." she sensed him tremble a little "... he made me open the case and let him and Adam look inside. Of course there was no car in it. I was too young to put a word to what I felt. But now I know I felt violated. Someone had power over me to make me show my secrets, to expose me, to show things which I'd hidden."

Jenna looked down at her lap. Paul's fingers were entwined with her own, gripping, moving, meshing. He had reached out for her hand at the moment he said "You know?" as if to check she really understood what he was saying. She was sure he didn't know what he had done.

"That feeling's been with you ever since, hasn't it?" she said simply. You've vowed that no-one will ever do that to you again."

There was still a slight tremble in his fingers. Well, there would be. He had allowed her through a door and let her place a foot upon that long corridor. She left his hand where it was, quieter now within her own, his wedding ring somewhere in the tangle of fingers.

"I suppose," she said, "your father was just trying to solve a quarrel. He loved you both."

"No, he didn't," he said. "He loved Adam. I was a nuisance, a cuckoo."

Jenna frowned. "What do you mean?"

He stood up suddenly. In doing so his hand left hers and he felt it go. For a second he paused, looked at her, startled. Then he straightened.

"I was building sand castles over there when he told me I wasn't his son."

Shock froze her. Then she got to her feet slowly and stood beside him, looking across to where he pointed, as if she could go back through the years and see the scene he spoke of. Neither of them spoke until Jenna took his arm and asked, "So you and

Adam ...?"

"Half-brothers," he said and his mouth twitched a little. "Mother's my mother all right."

Another silence. "That's another thing Adam didn't tell me," she said.

"Don't blame him for that one. We don't talk about it. For Mum's sake."

"Does Dianne know this?"

"No."

She stood in front of him, hands in her pockets. How long until the door slammed shut again?

"Do you know who your father is?"

"I know who he was."

"Was?"

"He was killed just before I was born. His Land Rover was blown up on a routine patrol."

Her head came up, her eyes wide. "Was he in the police?"

"He was an English soldier."

The gulls were gone now, the short day fading. The sea was close, but not yet close enough to make them move. Loose sand coloured the edges of the water as it rippled into turning arcs, swirled in retreat, ducked beneath the white fringe of the next wave.

There were so many questions in her head she couldn't catch hold of them in any order.

"Adam," she said. "When did he find out? Who told him?"

Paul sat on the rock again. "Adam was beside me, knocking down the castles I built. He was four years old. He ran up to my mother and asked her what a bastard was."

Jenna dropped to her heels and dug a mussel shell out of the sand. She brushed it clean and turned it over in her palm. *I know what happened. I know why he's here.* That tug of connection, that gossamer strand was blowing in this salty wind as surely as it spun between them that day before Christmas. She looked up. His face above her was pale again, despite the cold.

"You haven't been here since that day," she said. "Have you?"

"No."

She balanced the shell on her open palm and raised her hand towards him. "The shell in the suitcase. It was from that day, wasn't it?"

"Yes."

His expression was calm, steady, as if for now, he was content to watch her unpick his mind.

"And when you were made to open the case and they saw the shell, I think you threw it away. Did you?"

"Yes."

"You've come back today to face it again. To deal with it."

This time he just nodded. She pushed herself to her feet. The sea lapped closer, reeling across the nearer sand. Far out to sea, a tissue of cloud had ripped and sunlight made a butter yellow tent upon the water.

"Jenna, do you miss Adam?"

She blinked at the unexpectedness of it. She took a few steps away from him. What was the truthful answer to that? She turned back, thoughtful.

"Not at the moment," she said.

His mouth curved into that wonderful smile, a smile that slipped into every part of his face, changing it the way sunshine changes the sea. He raised his hand and reached for hers. His fingers wrapped around her own, deliberately this time.

She pulled her hand away sharply, bantering. "No need to shake my hand! All I did was read your mind."

He looked down at his feet then, solemn again, as if somehow she had made him sad.

After that, he went for a walk alone and she let him go. Her head was full of questions, but none of this was any of her business. She pulled her coat around her, hunched into it and watched a mist descending on the Donegal hills. Still she couldn't understand why he wanted her here. Indeed it seemed as if he was unsure himself.

When she turned again to look, Jenna saw his footprints in the dryer sand, firm and even, the line of them leaving her as he strode off. Now, he was a far away figure, stopped, as if abandoned on the beach like a lost toy.

Slightly anxious, she could see that the waves were getting closer. He would have to return soon, for the sea came up to meet the shore at high tide. She sighed. The door which he had opened reluctantly had not slammed, but it had shut nevertheless, firmly and ever so gently. Her brow creased a little as she tried to decide which of them had closed it.

CHAPTER SEVENTEEN

FEELING DANGEROUSLY HAPPY while having dinner with someone else's husband wasn't the way Jenna had imagined she would finish New Year's Day. It was only twenty-four hours ago that she had cleared away every vestige of Christmas from her house and crawled into a lump of misery in her bed.

When Paul returned from his solitary walk, she had been sitting on the bonnet of the car. She grumbled that he might have left her the car key. He told her to stop complaining – she was the one wearing his woollen hat. She said he was an unfeeling prat. He said it was great to find a woman who knew that without having to be told.

A contentment had rested between them as they left Rossnowlagh on the long journey home. They said very little and Jenna's thoughts whirled in the silent car, reluctant to let go of a day which must end in a few hours. The cold air of the sea had sapped her energy, and eventually she began to feel sleepy. When Paul turned into the car park of a hotel just outside Omagh and said he was starving, Jenna had stretched her arms in front of her, yawned and lazily agreed.

It wasn't until she got out of the car and the late evening air sharpened her senses that misgivings leapt from the corners of her mind. She stopped by an island flower bed where spears of yellow mahonia were floodlit from the path to the hotel steps.

"Paul, this mightn't be a good idea."

He locked the car and came to her side. "Since when was eating a bad idea?"

"That's not what I mean," she said, "and you know it."

He held up the car key, dangled it from his finger and thumb. "Here's the key. Stay here if you like. I'm going to eat." He grasped her hand and dropped the key into it. As he walked up the steps he called back, "Steak, I think. Well done. See you later."

She had to laugh.

So here they were. Paul was chasing a prawn round his plate, and she was trying to eat her melon without dropping any raspberry coulis on her pink jumper.

She discovered that when he was relaxed he could be very funny. Between mouthfuls of steak, onions and potatoes, he told her stories of the people he had met during his years in London. With wicked impersonations and mobile expressions, he conjured up for her the self-important stockbroker, the paranoid mother, the grumpy granny. There was even a baby who had crawled to his camera bag and been sick in it. He could laugh about it now. At the time, he said, he nearly committed murder. He held up his knife and fork, close together. "It was this close to being an ex-baby!"

He wanted a dessert and, reckless, she took one too. When it came, he admired the artistry of it: the square plate, the dusting of sugar, the cream swirled just so, the cape gooseberry splayed in the centre.

Yet again he had changed, shapeshifted before her. Jenna put her chin on her hand and watched him, just watched and didn't mind that he knew it. He caught her eye as a forkful of cream passed his lips. He smiled. A trace of cream tipped the point of his upper lip. His tongue flicked it away.

Once again, the thought overwhelmed Jenna. He is perfect, absolutely perfect.

Today had explained something. Since the day she had met

Paul, she had known with her head that he was Adam's brother. But at a deeper level, she had felt them to be different. They did not have that unconscious shared identity, that common way of walking, that angle of the head, that use of the same phrases, all those little common things by which brothers betray a shared parentage. It explained the hair colour. And that matchless mouth.

"I wonder," she said suddenly, "if you look like your father, your real father."

He didn't reply and the silence changed the mood.

Jenna crumpled her napkin. "We should go. This has been quite a self-indulgence. I'm not used to it."

"I don't want to go yet."

"It's late."

"I want coffee."

"You don't need my permission."

"OK then."

They took their coffee at an open fire in the hotel lounge. Only one other group of diners remained. Two deep soft chairs sat side by side and Jenna sank into the one next the fire, acquiescent again, warm and lazy, chin tucked into her pink polo, somnolent with the meal and the day's end. After some minutes, Paul's voice came from her right.

"You like pink, don't you? You've a pink dress and your slippers are pink."

Propped against the back of the chair, she turned her head towards him, aware that sleepiness must show in her eyelids.

"I suppose I can't deny it then. But I don't have the pink dress any more."

"Oh? Where is it?"

"In the bin. I tore it, remember."

"Was it that bad?"

She shrugged. "I wouldn't have worn it again."

"No, you probably wouldn't. Bad memories."

"You understand?"

"Of course. Smells, places, tastes, sounds. They all gain baggage depending on what was happening when we met them."

"Like Rossnowlagh?"

He nodded. "And rhubarb."

"Rhubarb?"

It was some moments before he said, "The day I discovered I wasn't who I thought I was, we had rhubarb for tea. I haven't been able to stand the stuff since. So I know how you feel about the dress." He studied her. "So do you feel better?"

"Better than what?"

"Than this morning. This morning you were a sad case."

She pulled a face, embarrassed to remember how she looked when he had called. "Much better. But today was about you, not me. Has it been worth it?"

He spread his hands wide. "It beats a day of being polite in London. And ..." he leaned towards her a little, across the arm of his own chair "... today was about you as well."

Light was dancing on him again, firelight this time. He attracted light, she thought, her lashes heavy. But it doesn't illuminate him. It makes shadows.

"I want to talk about you now," he said.

She gave a short laugh and turned her head away. "Ha! That'll be a short conversation. I've a better idea. Tell me about your Christmas. I suppose Dianne's family has a big house?"

He picked at the arm of the chair. "Huge."

"I suppose you met some old friends."

"A few."

"Will you go back there to live some day?"

"Never." He had replied almost before she had finished the question.

"When Dianne talks about it she seems homesick. I think she wants to go back."

He sat back and stared at the ornate sideboard on the other side of the lounge. "It'll be without me."

"What a weird thing to say."

"That's the unfeeling prat talking."

It was becoming important to Jenna that they talk about Dianne. Dianne wasn't here and she was his wife. Her presence should be invoked. "When's she coming back?"

"After the weekend some time."

"It must have been nice for her father to see her again. Her mother's dead, isn't she?"

He was still staring ahead. "She is."

Jenna studied his profile, the fine nose, the little darkness beneath the jut of his lower lip, a spiral of hair curling neat behind his ear. Dianne ran her fingers through that hair. When was the last time she had done so? When was the last time he had made love to her?

She spoke again, quickly. "So did she get to all those parties she talked about?"

He said nothing, a frown beginning to nudge between his brows. Then he looked up, petulant. "I said I want to talk about you."

"So how is she? Have you wished her a happy New Year yet?" She laughed. "That's funny, wishing your wife a Happy New Year by phone."

His left hand reached across and fell on her own where it lay along the arm of her chair. She blinked in surprise. "Jenna," he said, "shut up. I said I want to talk about you."

She looked down at his hand. "And I said you don't always get what you want."

"Not always. Just most of the time."

She pulled her hand away. "I think we should make for home as soon as we can," she said.

His head tilted in question. "Jenna, what's wrong?"

"This is a mistake. I shouldn't have come with you." She wanted to be home, away from here, away from him.

He asked again, "What's wrong?"

She looked at the light shade on the wall; she looked at the leaves of a fern on a table in the window embrasure; she looked at the people in a group across the room. Then she looked back at his face, at the line of his jaw where it smoothed down beneath his chin, down the pale cream of his neck to the swell of his throat. Truth burrowed its way through all the lies she could have told. She lifted her hand and, one finger extended, brought it down slowly to touch the ring on his finger where it still lay beside her.

"That's what's wrong," she said.

He held up his fingers and studied the ring. It was broad, with fine bevels on each side. He didn't ask her what she meant and she didn't expect him to. He gripped the ring with the fingers of his other hand and held them there. Then she saw him come to a decision. He slid the ring from his finger and held it up between his finger and thumb.

"Will you talk to me if I take it off?"

The fire was crackling, chatter rose in the other corner of the room, a clock ticked. Yet to Jenna it seemed as if they were stopped in a cavern of silence as the ring hung aloft between them, halo-shaped.

Then she whispered, "Put that back." A shiver of anger trembled across her words. "How could you?"

He tossed it in the air and caught it in his fist. He sat forward on the edge of his chair. Elbows on his knees, he cupped his hands and dropped the ring from one palm to the other and back again, back and forth, over and over, watching the gold spilling through the firelight.

Finally he looked round. "You told me I was like a king hiding in a palace. I don't think you're hiding." He held the ring up and looked through it. "I think you're in prison."

Amazed, she said, "Now we're back to riddles!"

He ignored that. "You're afraid of what's in you, Jenna. You're afraid of what you could be and what you could do. There are bars around you." He jabbed a finger at her. "So don't talk to me about hiding."

"Bars aren't just for trapping. Bars are for protecting."

He lounged back in the chair and threw the ring high. "I'll take my chances outside the cage!"

She considered him for a moment. "That's a lonely place to be."

He held out a hand towards her. "Lonelier than I hope you'll ever know."

He pulled his hand back. He must know she would not take it.

"So why stay there then," she challenged. "if it's so lonely?"

He looked down at his hand where he was jiggling the ring between his closed fingers. She thought that he wasn't going to answer her, then he swung round.

"Because, Jenna, I haven't time to rattle bars."

She was reminded of something he had said to her before. She said, "You mean you're chasing the moon and the stars and the sun. Your wings are spread." He was listening, as if waiting to see how far she would go in reading him this time. "Rules are to be broken." Still he did not speak. "Paul, that's dangerous. Very dangerous."

He exploded in frustration. "Oh, don't be so bland!"

"Don't be so childish!" she shot back, loud.

Two men across the room glanced over their shoulders. Paul and Jenna sat in silence. She could swear he was sulking. She began to gather up her things, feel for her bag. It was time this day was over. They were both tired.

"Jenna?"

She looked up at him under bad-tempered brows. "What?"

"Look." He held up his hand. His wedding ring was back in place, snug on his finger. He spoke slowly. "The last time I saw you, you were crying under a tree because Adam had hurt you so badly." He paused, watching her. "And yet for all of today, you've said not one word about it. You've listened to me. You've walked with me. You've read my mind. I told you something I've never told anyone else. Not anyone."

She nodded, sombre. "I know."

"Payback time," he said.

She folded her arms against him. "I don't like talking about myself."

He grinned. "That's a pout Dianne would be proud of!" When she didn't relent, he spoke again. "All right. Then I'll dissect your mind. I think five people lived in your house. Your mother, your father, Luke, you – and Duty. Everyone was more important than you. You didn't rock the boat because that would have been selfish. If someone needed your father, he went to them, even if you needed him too. And that was all right. And that's the way your world is still." He stopped. Then he added, "Adam's part of this. Adam seemed like a station on the right railway. The train was calling at all the right stops." He raised an eyebrow. "Am I right?"

She kept her arms folded and didn't look at him. So he went on.

"I said I wanted to talk about you. Now you tell me how you feel about betrayal. Tell me how you cope with the hurt. Tell me how the world seems to you, now the train's come off the rails." His head tilted and a slight smile brushed his lips. "Don't stay in the cage, because that's dangerous too. Very dangerous."

For a moment, she said nothing, unsettled. Then, "Why would you care?"

"Beats me," he replied.

She sat back and closed her eyes. Paul was tiring, so tiring. Adam never made her feel like this, as if her mind were alight, crackling with life and thought, challenging, restless. For the first time it dawned on her. Dianne couldn't possibly be a life companion for this man. She couldn't come close. Was he realising that too? Did that explain what he did with his ring?

She opened her lids just enough to see him through a sliver of sight. He had pulled one ankle across his knee and was studying her while he waited. His eyes roved across her hair, down to her hands, her legs, even to the ankle boots on her feet. She shut her eyes again before he returned to her face. No-one had ever reeled her in like this. No-one had ever focused on her like this, spirit, mind and body, like a shaft of light piercing through crystal.

She opened her eyes and sat forward. "All right," she said. "I'll tell you how I feel." She stopped to gather her words. It was an effort. "We're all defined by other people. I mean, who are you really? Who am I? I'm my mother's daughter, my aunt's niece, my brother's sister. You're a husband, a son, a ..." she hesitated "... brother, even if only a half one." The firelight was fading a little, the light not so bright as its flame dappled them both. "But when all things end, we won't be any of those things. When you left me to walk away by yourself today, I saw your footprints in the sand." She dropped her head in thought. This was really how she felt and she hadn't said it before, even within her own soul. "I thought I meant something to somebody. And that made sense of everything else. Now, I think maybe I'm nobody at all. I'm alone in the world, a maker of footprints." She raised her eyes to his. "That's all. Just a maker of footprints. And even they disappear when the water comes." She swallowed. "I think I'm scared."

He was quiet, his restlessness stilled by her words. Then he said slowly, "It's a great thing to be loved. It's not the same as loving, though. Is it?"

She smiled a little, sad. "A little bit of both would go down well."

Moments passed. Then he held out his hand to her. "Let's go home," he said softly.

He did not withdraw his hand this time, held it steady beneath her bowed head. Finally her own crept into it and their fingers curled together.

"Yes, let's go home," she said.

CHAPTER EIGHTEEN

IT WAS AFTER one o'clock in the morning when Paul found a space by the kerb round the corner from Jenna's door. Most houses were in darkness, and lamplight patched the street. A dog trotted by, busy.

They had been very quiet on the way home, as if there were nothing more either of them had the energy to say. Paul turned the engine off. Jenna reached for her bag at her feet. "I hope I wasn't boring company."

Paul's teeth showed in the low light as he smiled. "That comment is just typical of you."

She looked down with a little laugh. "Sorry."

"So's that one."

"I'd better stop talking then. I can't say anything right."

He shifted round in his seat to face her. "Yes, you can. Quite a lot."

She turned her head away, looked out the side window. A Santa Claus still stood on a window sill across the footpath. Still not looking at him, she said, "Paul, I'm not sorry about today." She turned her head back and sought his eyes. "But we can't do it again. A day like today can't ever happen again."

His voice was low, almost wistful. "No. It never could. There never could be another day like today."

"OK." She reached for the door handle.

"Wait," he said. She did. "You and Adam. What will you do?"

"Talk. I'm not sure."

She felt the brush of his finger on her hand. "He doesn't deserve you."

She smiled. "You're good for my ego."

A slant of lamplight crossed the road and cast a haze on the back of his head as he faced her. "Remember this morning?" he said. "No sparks, no life?"

She nodded, wrapped by his voice in the stillness of the car in the silence of the street. Still she stayed. Then she rummaged in her pocket. She held out her hand and in her fingers she held the razor shell. "Would you like this?" She looked down at it, embarrassed a little. "To replace the shell you threw away."

He took it. Some grains of sand still clung to her fingers. He reached over to the back seat.

"Here, keep this." He held out his woollen hat. "It looked far better on you." She folded the softness of it in her fingers. There was a silence. Then she pulled the handle.

"Goodbye, Paul. Give my love to Dianne."

She got out of the car and began to walk. Behind her, the car door slammed and he appeared beside her. "I'll come to the door with you."

They walked round the corner and a short distance up the street.

Jenna exclaimed, "There's a light on in my house! It must be Luke. Missed the last bus again, I suppose. He has a mad social life."

As she searched for her key, the door was flung open from inside. She looked up, a smile ready on her lips.

"Luke ..."

It was Adam. His hair was finger-tossed, his expression a mixture of relief and fury. He jumped down the two steps and took her by the shoulders.

"Where have you been, Jenna? We've all been frantic. Your

mother's up the walls with worry."

Jenna was confused and alarmed. "Adam! How did you get into my house?"

Luke appeared in the doorway. "Shit, Jay. Why didn't you say you'd be away?" He turned back into the hall and kicked the door, the blond tips of his hair brushing the lampshade. "So now can we all go to bed?"

A calm voice behind Jenna said, "Adam. Let her go. No need to be melodramatic."

Only then did Adam realise that Paul was there. "Paul! I thought you were in London."

"I was. I came back. Shall we take this little scene off the street?"

Jenna rang her mother. She told her she had been away with a few friends for the day and they had only just got back. She didn't think anyone would be trying to contact her. She had turned her phone off for some reason and had forgotten to turn it back on. Her father came on the line. Relief was only just easing out the grip of worry in his voice.

"So long as you're all right. I was worried about you and rang you this morning. We wanted to wish you a Happy New Year. Seeing you weren't here with us last night."

There was reproach in that last comment.

When she went back to her sitting room, Paul was in her chair and Adam was on the sofa, eyeing him with some puzzlement. The photograph of the robin was propped on the mantelpiece where she had put it so long ago, yet just this morning. She could hear Luke in the kitchen.

"All of a sudden this place is like Royal Avenue at lunch time." She sat down beside Adam, weary to her bones.

"It's even more crowded than you think," Paul said.

He reached under his coat and pulled out a kitten. Luke came in and the kitten, cupped in Paul's hands, miaowed at him. Luke caught the expression on Jenna's face.

"Well, what was I supposed to do?" he demanded. "Mum was getting fed up with him. She was going to put an ad in the shop. Some loony might have taken him. That was totally not going to happen."

"So you brought him here? That's supposed to be a better idea?" She spotted the small litter tray on the floor beside her television. It had been used. "Oh, Luke!".

"It's all right," he said confidently. "I brought half a dozen tins of cat food too. They're in the cupboard under the sink. Along with a ping pong ball and a toy mouse," he added helpfully. "Maybe some of your student mates might take him."

The kitten had climbed onto Paul's shoulder and was exploring his ear.

"So when's Dianne coming back?" Adam asked him, taking up a conversation which must have been going on while Jenna was on the phone.

"Next week some time," said Paul. His finger was caressing the kitten as it clung to his shoulder. It began to tap at his nose with its small white paw.

"So where did you meet Jenna?" Adam asked, frowning.

Jenna stood up. "Let's call it a day, shall we?"

Paul hooked the kitten from his shoulder. "I'll take him if you like."

Luke punched the air. "Way to go, Paul!"

The cat food, toy mouse and ping pong ball were put in a plastic bag, the litter tray – emptied – was put in another. Luke produced a pet carrier and, with a last scratch of the black ears, Paul put the kitten into it.

"Are you sure about this?" Jenna asked Paul.

"No," he said. "But I can always boil him for supper if we don't get on."

Luke left with him to help carry everything to his car. There was a cold wind funnelling down between the close-packed sleeping houses. The kitten started to miaow in alarm, the sound loud in the night as it was carried away.

Jenna went into the kitchen and filled the kettle. Adam came up behind her. "Were you and Paul away somewhere? Did he give you a lift home?"

She plugged in the kettle and stood with her back to him, studying the dishes dumped in the sink. Luke must have had lunch here as well as his tea. He had probably drunk all the milk in the house. She swung round.

"Yes. He gave me a lift home."

He looked puzzled. "Where were you?"

"Actually," she said, "that's none of your business."

"Jenna!" The kettle began to sing, the noise rasped into the air behind her. "You disappeared. No-one knew where you were. We were all worried out of our skulls"

"Why should I tell you where I was? Specially now?"

He was wearing his blue jumper. She had always liked it on him. The collar of a checked shirt peeped above the round neck.

He spread his hands. "Because you always do!"

"Well, maybe I don't any more." She sighed and her shoulders slumped. "We do have to have a conversation, Adam." She walked past him, out into the hall, up to the front door which was lying ajar. She opened it. "But not now."

He stayed in the kitchen, looking after her with a bewildered expression. "But ... it's so late. I thought I could stay here tonight. On the sofa of course," he added quickly.

"Not even on the sofa. "

He looked at her for a moment, decided she was serious. His anorak was on a hook in the hall beside her own coat. He pulled it on and stood, awkward, in front of her.

"Jenna, I know you're still angry with me." He put a hand on her shoulder and tried to kiss her. She turned her head away and felt the brush of his auburn hair on her cheek. "I'm sorry I was such a prat." He cupped her chin in his fingers. "And I was very, very worried about you today."

She pulled her chin away. "Maybe I should have disappeared before."

His laugh was unsure, forced. "Maybe!"

Luke sprang up the steps from the street, shivering. "It's baltic out there!" He shouldered sideways between them, called good night and took the stairs three at a time. Adam went down into the street and looked back.

"I'll ring you."

"OK." She shut the door in his face.

Luke had captured her bathroom. She heard him brushing his teeth loudly. Luke was the only person she knew whose tooth brushing could be heard through a wall and two closed doors. He was seventeen and had never had a filling. The whole village knew that the minister's son had beautiful teeth. Jenna knew that her mother hoped the information would distract from the blond highlights and the earring.

He came out of the bathroom and called, "Paul says he'll call the kitten Jack." He put his head round her bedroom door. "And he says he'll take me on a few shoots. Some Saturdays. Cool, eh?" His head disappeared and then reappeared. "He took that pic of the robin, he said. I want a camera for my birthday."

He went off to the spare room, tired and happy. The towel that Jenna had used for her shower in the morning was still on the floor of the bathroom. She held it to her face before dropping it into the laundry basket. She had just climbed into bed when Luke appeared again. By his face, she knew his thoughts had moved on in a new direction. That usually meant trouble. He sat down on her bed. He was holding something in his hand.

"I'm glad you're back. You haven't said where you were. I noticed that." He waited for her to say something, but she was too tired and wished he would leave her in peace. "So his wife's still in London?"

"She is."

Luke shuffled his feet and kicked up the edges of the mock sheepskin rug on the floor. "You know how you said that I swear a lot, but that I wouldn't do it anywhere it would let Dad down?"

She wriggled down on her pillow. "Yes."

Luke held out his hand and seemed to change the subject. "Paul said to give you this."

It was an elegant white business card. Paul's name and the address of his studio in London were written in deep green letters. A strong X was crossed through the address in black ink. In the same ink, a circle had been drawn round a mobile phone number. Jenna held the card for a moment and then looked up.

Luke frowned down at the rumpled mat. "Why would he give you his business card?" She didn't reply. "I heard you on the phone. You told Mum a lie. That's really, really weird." He looked up, directly at her. "If I wouldn't let Dad and Mum down, you wouldn't either. Would you?"

Jenna held the card carefully, turned it over, turned it back, set it on her bedside table on top of her neglected novel. She spoke slowly, her eyes unfocused.

"Maybe I don't know what I could do." Her attention came back to him. "I'm sorry if people were worried. But I checked out for a day. One day. You're going off round the world for a year. We won't know where you are every day."

"That's different."

She turned onto her elbow, switched off the light, thumped her pillow and lay down on her side facing the wall. "Fix that mat before you go. And you'll have to go out for milk before we can have breakfast."

She felt him get up from the bed and heard the mat being flattened. He muttered something about "bloody women."

"Go to bed. Your hair could do with a lie down."

She lay still for five minutes. Then she turned on the bedside light again and slipped out of bed. Her mobile was in her bag on the floor. With Paul's card beside her, she punched the number into it and stored it. She turned off the light again and lay down. She closed her eyes. She sat up again. It couldn't hurt, could it? Just a quick message to check the kitten was all right. She was fond of it, after all. By the light of the tiny screen, she sent two words. "How's Jack?"

With her arms round her drawn up knees, she waited in the dark. Even so, the chime of an incoming message made her jump. It was just one word, "Miaow!"

She chuckled, not too loud. She lay down again and closed her eyes. Through the twilight of half sleep, a thought floated into her unwary head. She had told a lie since she had come home today. Her eyes opened on the dark as she realised how easy it had been.

~

The melodious notes of her mobile on the bedside table made Dianne stir under the warm covers of the bed. She turned over and squinted at her watch. Half past seven. The middle of the night! Surely civilisation didn't surface until lunchtime, specially at the New Year? She fumbled for her phone and checked the number calling. Immediately she swung herself upright at the edge of the bed and flipped the phone open.

"Hello, Paul. Nice to hear from you. At last."

"Hi. How's things?"

The timbre of his voice was so clear, so memorable even now.

"As well as they can be." Frost was all he deserved. She waited a moment then asked, "You got home all right then? I had to assume so."

"You could have checked."

"You could have let me know."

"What day do you want picked up at the airport?"

"Tuesday. The day we were both supposed to be going back, remember."

"Ok. See you then. Have fun."

"You don't mind if I do?" she said, half mocking.

"Dianne, I really want you to have a good time."

"Then I will."

She snapped the phone shut and put her hands over her face. Oh, God, it wasn't supposed to be like this. His voice, his lovely voice in her ear and she was being a shrew. But he drove her to it. He had asked nothing about what she was doing, who she was seeing. He hadn't said "I miss you." All he seemed to need were his camera and his guitar. There was a rustle in the bed behind her. A hand on her shoulder pulled her backwards.

"Come here," said Luther, "and I'll make you forget him all over again."

~

Luther extricated an arm and phoned room service. Dianne arranged her silk robe in graceful folds as she sat at the table by the window and peeled a peach slowly. There was triumph on Luther's face as he lounged against the window, only a towel round his waist.

"So do you take it all back?"

She waved her knife. "I never take anything back."

He came up behind her and gripped her head, pulling it back against him. "But I do. I take back what's mine."

Her smile was confident. She was back in a game she knew. Luther let her go, lifted the lid of the platter on the trolley and inhaled the smell of bacon.

"So what did you think of the gallery? Really?" he asked.

He had brought her to see it yesterday, New Year's day, opening it up specially to give her an exclusive tour. She licked her fingers, flicking her tongue out slowly, teasing.

"I think you've got something. Can you invite the right people? Ambassadors, the aristocracy, a few big literary names?"

"I've got them already. It's all about contacts. Your father has helped."

"He always liked you."

Luther loaded his plate and brought it to the table. "I've a proposition."

She arched her eyebrows. "Another one?"

His pale lashes swept across his eyes as he grinned. "A different one. I need someone with class and experience to run the gallery with me." He chewed a mushroom slowly. "Someone like you."

Her knife hovered over the remaining piece of peach. "Are you offering me a job?"

He set down his fork and leaned back. "I'm offering you a partnership."

The peach was cold in her hand, slippery. A minute passed. "Luther, I don't live here at the moment."

He regarded her steadily and then picked up his knife again. "Pity." He cut a sausage and paused, fork hovering at his mouth. "What time's your plane on Tuesday? I'll run you to the airport."

Delicately, she set the peach slice on her plate and stood up. She went to the bathroom and took a long, slow shower. When she emerged, her hair was damp-darkened to deep honey and the silk robe clung to her scented body. Luther was dressed and sitting at the window. His legs were crossed and he was flicking through the pages of a magazine. He didn't look up. Dianne came to the table beside him and lifted the peach slice. She walked to the window and looked out.

"How long," she asked casually, her back to him, "would the offer be open?"

He turned a page and scanned it idly. "I'll give you till Easter." He turned a few more pages then threw the magazine aside. "Now get dressed. It's time we left."

"Are you ordering me about?"

"I always did." He glanced round and she saw the pain flicker behind his eyes again as he asked, "Does he?"

Dianne came and bent over him. She popped the peach into his mouth.

"Mind your own business."

CHAPTER NINETEEN

THE NEW YEAR sputtered into life like a badly driven car. To Jenna, everything seemed out of joint. None of the pieces were where they should be. She tried to work, answered e-mails from friends. Mostly they were doing interesting things, earning money, even getting married. One had moved out of her boyfriend's flat and swore to Jenna that all men are cheats and liars. Jenna thought for a bit before answering. "Maybe not all of them," she typed. An answer came back within minutes. "Yes, all of them. Get out of that library, Professor. What planet are you on?"

That was a good question. Jenna slumped back in her chair. After that long day with Paul, depression and pointlessness still hung over her, but now a discontent ruffled its edges. She was scared, scared of being nobody, scared of wasting her life the way so often she wasted a day. The knowledge of it had been prised out of hiding by Paul, his mind dissecting her like a scalpel, exploring parts which she did not know were within her.

On the first Saturday of the year, she closed her computer, shut her books and agreed to go for a walk with Adam in the Botanic Gardens in the south of the city. The paths were thick with leaves and a groundsman rattled his cart to a stop and pulled off his brush to scrape the crisp brown heaps onto his shovel. There were very few people on the paths between the grass and trees; only students trudging through on their way to and from the Sports

Centre, bags hefted on their backs.

Jenna was aware that this conversation had to take place yet she felt an inability to raise herself to the emotional challenge which it presented. Almost, she would rather have been struggling with the complexities of her latest assignment. She watched a magpie on a flower bed, tossing twigs and leaves aside as it walked amongst the dormant undergrowth.

This walk was totally unlike any other which she had taken with Adam. She did not touch him and he did not try to touch her. They walked like two chance acquaintances, apart and alone, though side by side. Adam kept his hands deep in the pockets of his blue anorak. There was a broad white stripe running the length of the outside of each sleeve. She had been with him when he bought it. It was one of the first things they had bought together.

Jenna pushed her hair from her eyes. There was just a little wind, nothing like the boisterous exhilaration of an Atlantic beach in winter. She glanced round. Adam was a little, just a little, shorter than Paul, and he was stockier. With the eyes of new knowledge she noted the differences. They had been through the formalities. *How are you? Fine. How's Luke? Fine. He was worried too, you know. I know; I don't want to talk about it.*

The Palm House came into view, huge and white, the glass glinting in the low sun.

"Let's sit down for a bit," Adam said. Lines of benches edged the paths beside the flower beds, which were neat with stumps, pledges of new growth. In places, some plants were protected by straw and polythene sheets. The claws of a loping red setter clicked rapidly on the path, the loose-limbed prance of the dog followed by the bobbing strides of a man in a raincoat. The light dimmed as a dark cloud loomed across the sky and all the colours seemed to flatten into a palette of grey.

Jenna sighed. "Adam, I really don't think I've anything much to say."

He looked relieved. "I haven't either. Nothing more than what I've said already."

She looked at him for a moment. Then she stood up. "So this is a bit of a waste of an afternoon then." She began to walk back towards the park gate.

"Jenna!" He ran after her and caught her arm. She stopped. His hair reminded her of the red setter, except his was a little darker, more of a deep copper. OK then, she would ask him.

"How long have you been seeing her again?"

"I don't know." He waved a hand carelessly. "A couple of months maybe."

He didn't know!

"You've been sleeping with her, haven't you?"

He stepped back, his eyes dropping momentarily. She knew she was right.

"She's been very ... persistent."

"And very successful," she said. Irritation was scratching her nerves.

"Well, Rachel and I ..."

"Were going to get married. I know that. How many types of a fool do you take me for, Adam? Do you think I'm just the goody-goody, the wonderful contrast to the scarlet woman who dumped you so hard you're still licking the wounds?"

"Jenna ..."

Suddenly she was on a rush, letting out all the anger, the hurt, the humiliation, the conclusion of two weeks of swimming round at the bottom of a pit of worthlessness. "Shut up, Adam. I'm not going to be the plaster on your broken heart." She had to walk in little circles, waving her hands in the air. "You had the nerve to tell me you only kissed her because I wasn't looking. Everyone else would have known, but as long as I didn't ..." she spread her arms wide "... well, that's OK then."

"Look, Jay ..."

"He was right. You never wanted me as a lover because you already had one. And I certainly don't want another brother. The one I've got's enough." Freckles splashed across Adam's cheeks, japs of sepia on his flushed skin. A few large drops of rain began to speckle the path. "He was right about another thing. You didn't hurt me, not the real me. You just hurt my pride."

"Who's 'he'?"

"Your brother." She stopped, then said it. "Your half-brother."

Rain made a noise like the white water of river rapids, rushing through the barren trees, smacking into the soil, striking the path and turning it from pale to deep shiny gray. In seconds, leaves mulched into soggy pulp. Birds bickered loudly in a bush behind them, sharp squawks cutting above the rain.

Adam had to raise his voice, surprised. "Did Mum tell you?"

Jenna's hair was plastered to her head. A calmness descended on her. There was something very private about that day with Paul. It was not a day to be described, betrayed. It was almost as if to speak of it would be to betray Paul himself. He had spoken secrets. She would keep them.

"You never thought to mention it."

"Are you annoyed that I didn't tell you my brother started life as a bastard?"

She had turned away. She whirled round. "Oh, grow up!" she yelled above the storm of rain. "Half the children in the country are bastards." She took a deep breath and hurled a strand of dripping hair over her shoulder. "And some others become bastards rather later in life." She pointed at him. "Like the one I'm looking at."

He looked utterly amazed. "Jenna, I've never seen you like this."

"Maybe it's time you did."

He held out his hands. "I don't know what to do for the best ..."

"Oh, please! Don't agonise on my account." The rain was slowing to a patter again, the scent of pine and soil and wet leaves began to drift from the sodden ground. "You made your decision that night." She started to walk again. "I could never trust you, and what's a life without trust?"

He walked after her, his voice becoming tetchy. "I think you're over-reacting a bit, you know."

She stopped and faced him. "Do you know when I knew we were finished? It wasn't at the party. It wasn't when I was outside curling up with mortification. I might still have forgiven you, talked it through. For so long, I thought I needed you." Her voice faltered a little. "You lit up my days, Adam. You really did. I was bored. I was looking for something. Someone. The future. I don't know. I thought it was you."

"Maybe ..."

"But I knew I could never stay with you the moment I realised you were drunk at my front door."

"What?"

"I could never be with a man who got drunk. Not even once."

Adam's eyebrows rose to his saturated hairline and he began to laugh. "Jenna, you innocent idiot. Where are you ever going to find a man like that? Come on, get real!"

"No, you get real. I don't need you. I don't need anyone." As she said it she knew it was true. At last it was true. "And don't dare question my values. At least I have some."

He made an exasperated noise. "This really is over the top, you know. I've apologised. What more do you want? Blood?"

The red sweet wine? She tilted her head. "Life's very simple for you, isn't it? Screw up. Say sorry. Trundle along to the next screw up. From what I saw of her, I'd say you and Rachel are made for each other."

A flush of anger rushed into his cheeks. "OK! That's enough.

Leave her out of this."

She laughed in amazement. "But Adam, she's right in the middle of it. Maybe she's standing behind that tree there. She might as well be."

Two girls in tracksuit bottoms and fleece tops walked by, sports bags over their shoulders. They caught the angry tones and exchanged glances, grinning.

"This isn't like you, Jenna. Not the Jenna I know."

"Maybe there are other Jennas inside here." She pointed at her chest. "I don't think any of us knows who we are or what we can do." She paused, thinking this through. "There's a part of us that can't speak until something speaks to it. Wakes it up and speaks its language."

He laughed in scorn. "That's the daftest thing I ever heard."

She regarded him. She was neither loved nor loving here and she would not stay any longer.

"Go back to Plan A, Adam." She turned away. "Plan B is going to get her hair cut."

This time she kept walking.

~

The squirrel flashed along the branch like a dart. Its tail was an undulating broom, whisking the bare wood a second after the skittering feet had gripped and fled.

A red one! Yes! Paul stopped breathing. The muscles of his back rippled as he braced himself more firmly against the tree trunk, checked the firmness of his foot against the knot of a root. He had waited, motionless, for almost two hours for this. With a slow touch, he adjusted the focus, picked out a spot where the tangle of branches bisected a shaft of light from the afternoon sun.

Come on, Tufty! You're an endangered species. Let me make you live for ever. The squirrel scampered and then froze, as if by forest sorcery, in the shower of cool beams. One paw was stopped in the air like suspended stone, the red bush of its tail dropped below the branch. The gleam from its eye, almond oval beneath the tufted ears, turned towards the man-shape. The tawny nose quivered.

Paul's finger tensed on the shutter release. Perfect! In his back pocket, the vibrations of his phone, switched to silent mode, barely registered on the outskirts of his mind. The sliding click of the shutter sent the squirrel hurtling vertically up the cobbled bark of the spruce, tail bouncing, tiny claws grasping at escape.

Got you! Paul smiled and turned his head up to follow the trajectory of the leaping creature through the forest canopy. He pulled a notebook and pencil from his coat pocket and noted the time and the exposure.

He put his notebook and pencil back in his pocket and stretched his tense muscles. That was probably enough for today. He looked around. Fingers of bright silver sunlight tipped the needles of spruce and pine, streamed on to paint a ribbon of crumpled light the length of the tree trunk in front of him. Around his feet was the soft brown shade of pine needles and old cones.

He let the camera settle on the front of his coat as he picked his way back to the forest path. He kept it in easy reach, ready for the quick shot, the chance encounter. As he had many times before, he marvelled at light, how today it was silver, cool and graceful. Yet sometimes, as at Rossnowlagh, it was a golden warmth, amber honey in the air. Sometimes he had seen a sheen of blue cascading from a summer evening. And thunder was grey, throwing a pewter stain across land and space.

On the carpet of needles, his feet were silent in the almost silent forest. The path wound through tall tree trunks, pillars rising from the hollows and hummocks of grass which was moulded by mossy boulders and the indiscipline of wandering roots.

He breathed deeply, scenting the air like the squirrel. There was the tang of recent almost-frost on soil, the brown scent of gnarled wood, the green flavour of saplings, the sharp taste of pine. And that other silver hint on the breeze, water.

Yes, he could hear it now. The path split into two, one going further up the hillside to the shallower soil, the more barren parts. Paul turned down the other path, downhill towards the water sound. Dry on top, the matted surface of the path was slippery beneath, where moisture still clung in the mesh of needles.

The path turned and in front of him was a wooden bridge across a stream. It was a low plain stretch of planks, edged by simple wooden rails. The water bustled beneath the wood, tugging at straggles of grass which swayed into the ripples, dipping downstream in the jaunty current.

Paul slung his camera across his body to hang safely at his side. He walked to the middle of the bridge and leaned his forearms on the rail. Like cream sinking through coffee, sensation spread through him. Light and beauty, green on nut brown, waving grass, fussing water, now black, now green, now tossed silver. He loved the winter. He loved summer too. And autumn. And spring. He loved this country wherever and whenever he was in it.

He swung himself down to sit on the edge of the bridge, his feet hanging above the water. He was exquisitely alone, alive to the end of every nerve. He swung his legs. Yet he was restless, uneasy at that deep point where solitude slips into loneliness.

In a hollow of the steeper bank, some leaves stirred. A flash of black nose, a scuffing of paw, a flick of fur and all was still again. His hand flew to his camera; relaxed again. What was that? A mink? A stoat?

He ran his fingers through his hair. His ears were cold. No hat. Was she wearing it? Absently, he turned his wedding ring round and round, his sight blurring as the pictures in his mind took over. Jenna came towards him on the beach, her hair flying from the rim of the hat which he had just pulled onto her head. Her nose was pink, her cheeks glowing in the salt air. He liked the cream coat. It suited her, the way the fur skimmed her knees and circled her wrists. Her hair was the colour of the moist dark sugar which his mother used when she was making coffee cakes.

Jenna was gentle, peaceful company. His eyes focused again on the straight trunks of the trees rising around him, the slice of the stream through the forest floor. She would not disturb this. She would love it as he did and, loving it, she would blur the line where solitude became loneliness and all of him would be content. He wanted her here now and the impossibility of it became a small ache. Even if he was a bad bastard who made up the rules as he went along, she would play by her own rules, not his. She was a woman of her time and yet above it also. She was vulnerable in her security and innocence; stronger than she yet knew in the untested boundaries of her mind.

Luke was like her. Paul smiled. Luke was Jenna with testosterone. Bright, underestimated, determined to mark his difference. He liked Luke.

He felt something drop onto his hand. He put the back of his hand to his nose and sighed. Not again. Blood trickled across his hand and dripped onto his coat. He rummaged in his pocket and found a tissue. He unhooked his camera from his neck and set it carefully beside him. Then he lay back until he was flat on the wooden planks, his eyes on the swaying canopy of trees above him. The breeze made patches of light wink through the branches like tilted diamonds. He held the tissue to his nose and felt it grow warm with blood. The red sweet wine. Drops began to seep down his throat. He recrumpled the tissue and coughed.

After some minutes he sat up again. He should head for home. Jack would be hungry. He and the kitten had decided they could get along and Jack followed him everywhere, sitting on his shoulder, sleeping on his bed, playing with the strap of his camera. Most of all, Jack loved to sit on the arm of the chair while Paul strummed his guitar. Its ears turned in the sounds, perking forward for the higher notes and dropping back for the lower ones. Eventually, the kitten's mouth would stretch into a wide pink yawn and the soft body would drop into a small circle on his master's knee, the purr of pleasure slowly fading into sleep. Paul loved the blue-black of the fur, the miniature perfection of the single white paw curled over the nose.

He lifted his camera and stood up. He hooked the strap over his head, patted his pocket – notebook, pencil, phone in the back pocket. Vaguely he remembered his phone vibrating earlier. He dug it out and checked it. One missed call. It was Dianne's number. What day is this? He stabbed the phone with his thumb. Tuesday. He was eighty miles from the airport.

CHAPTER TWENTY

THE TAIL LIGHTS of the taxi accelerated away and left Dianne at her gateway in the soft mizzle of rain. She pulled up the handle of her suitcase and hauled it up the drive. There was no car and the house looked empty. Where was he? How could he do this?

Her father had come with Luther to the airport. His last words stayed in her mind.

"You belong here, Dianne. Come back soon."

She waved to him from the departure gate. He looked forlorn, smaller than Luther who stood, unsmiling, beside him.

Now here she was, back at an empty house, in a city she did not like, in the rain, and the person who was the only reason for her being here had let her down – again. It was almost as cold inside the house as outside. She left her suitcase at the bottom of the stairs. Paul could take it up for her. That was what he was supposed to do: look after her, carry things for her. Pick her up at the airport, damn it!

The Christmas decorations were still up. The tree still stood in the window, dull. Dianne looked around, temper flaring higher. This should all have been put away by yesterday at the latest. It probably never occurred to him. She yanked a piece of tinsel from the tree and threw it on the floor. A mug with dregs of coffee in it sat on the small table. She snatched it up and went into the kitchen.

Unwashed dishes were piled beside the sink. She counted. The mug she had in her hand was number five. Toast crumbs littered the ledge. She stopped. There was something curled up in the sink. It was black and had eyes. It was looking at her. She stared at it, transfixed. The green eyes blinked. "Miaow," it said, and stretched a white paw lazily towards the tap.

Dianne's hand flew to her mouth. A cat! There was a cat in the sink. She set down the mug carefully and backed out of the kitchen, shutting the door firmly.

Arabella wasn't sympathetic. "Well, what do you expect if you leave him alone for days? He's a man. And a kitten might be fun."

"But the place is a tip, Bella! And he left me alone."

Bella's deep chuckle came down the line. "Well, darling, you weren't exactly alone now, were you?"

Dianne pouted. "Whatever happened was Paul's fault."

"He mightn't see it that way. Some old fogeys might say you and Luther getting jiggy again is adultery, you know."

"Oh, Bella! That wasn't adultery. That was just Luther. Jason or Alex or Toby would be adultery ..."

Bella's giggle interrupted her. "Toby wouldn't be adultery. Toby would be a big disappointment, darling. Considering."

"OK. Maybe not Toby. But Luther and I ... "

"... go back a long way. I know." Bella paused. "You never should have left him, Di."

Dianne's voice was brittle. "He's still there, isn't he?"

"But for how long?" Bella's tone was serious. "Luther's like you, ruthless when he wants something. If he doesn't get it, he doesn't give up. He just stops wanting it." Dianne fiddled with her hair. Bella's next question slipped into her ear, quiet. "How long has he given you?"

"Till Easter." It was almost a whisper.

There was a silence on the line. Then Bella said, "Say you get

Paul to come back to London. Then what?" She paused. "Then what, Di?"

"I don't know, Bella. I don't know."

"You shouldn't have given in to Luther. You should have let it die. You're getting yourself into a ghastly pickle."

Dianne put her hand to her head. "It was Paul's fault."

"It was your choice."

"It'll not happen again."

Bella snorted. "Tell that to Luther! You can't keep doing that to a man, you know. Loving him and leaving him." She sighed. "Paul was probably right, darling. You shouldn't have come back for Christmas. He knew what would happen."

"But he's supposed to love me." That sounded pathetic.

Bella chuckled again. "The only person Paul Shepherd loves is Paul Shepherd."

When Dianne hung up, the sudden absence of Bella's husky tones was like a door slamming. In the kitchen, a spoon fell on the floor with a clatter. She looked at the Christmas tree, out of place and out of time. It seemed to mock her. Bella was right. Luther and she were alike. When he doesn't get what he wants, he just stops wanting it. Dianne's chin set firmly. *I can do that too.*

She decided not to be sorry about the fit of pique and self-indulgence which had sent her back into Luther's bed. Her last few days in London had been unsettled by an undertow of guilt. This home-coming washed guilt from her and left her back on the high ground, the victim.

She hugged her arms around herself in the cold sitting room.

~

Jenna was watching a film on television. She had just taken the first bite from an apple when her doorbell rang. It couldn't be Luke. He would just barge in using his own key. Wary, she turned off the television and went to the window to peep through the curtain.

It was Paul who stood on the footpath, gazing up at her door as if willing it to open. He must have seen her slight movement because he turned his head quickly. He put out his hand to the wall as if to steady himself as he met her eyes. He didn't smile, didn't frown, didn't speak. He stood, hand on the wall, looking at her.

When she opened the front door, he walked past her, into her house, into her sitting room, without a word. She walked after him. In the middle of the room he swung round. He looked pale.

"What on earth are you doing here?" she asked.

He was studying her. After a moment he bent and threw the red and black cushion onto the floor and sat in her chair as if he owned it.

"Why do you keep spoiling my pictures?" he grumbled.

She walked round in front of him. "What pictures?"

"My pictures of you." He threw a hand up to indicate her hair. "You've done something. Changed."

She put a hand up to her face, swept her hair back. It was shorter now, cut and shaped round her cheeks.

"I can't help it if you think in stills," she said. "I'm a movie."

He laid his head back against the chair. "It's OK. But I liked you anyway."

So much for the change of image. She sat on the sofa and curled her legs up.

"Is something wrong?"

He took so long to answer she thought he was ignoring her. He stared straight ahead at the curtains. Finally he looked round, focused on her.

"I got a great shot of a squirrel today. A red one. I waited ages."

"Where were you?"

"Gortin Forest." He wasn't restless, she noticed. His arms were relaxed along the arms of the chair. "When I was getting into the car to leave, I looked up and there was a hawk ..." he pointed upwards "... hovering high up. The sky was blue, a sharp, clear blue and the hawk was still, watching, waiting." His eyes stayed fixed on Jenna. "And I thought of the squirrel. My squirrel. I knew that there were thousands and thousands of creatures below that hawk. But it seemed to me that it was watching my squirrel." He stopped, but Jenna waited. He had more to say. "I thought: God! don't let it see that squirrel. Silly, isn't it? I wondered what your father would say. And then I thought: it'll make no difference. It isn't God who'll decide whether that squirrel lives or dies. It's the hawk."

There was a long silence. Then Jenna smiled a little. "It's late for deep theology."

He sat forward. "Will you come to Gortin with me some day?"

Surprise made her pause before she replied. "OK. If you and Dianne are going some day, I'll tag along."

"That's not what I meant."

"Then no, I won't. I told you."

He sat back again. "Oh, what a good girl am I!" he rhymed, mocking.

There were shadows beneath his cheekbones. She put her feet to the floor and leaned her elbows on her knees, chin on her knuckles.

"Paul, what's wrong?"

He rummaged in his pocket and pulled out the razor shell. "I rescued that from the bin."

"Why was it in the bin?"

"Dianne came back from London today. I forgot to pick her up at the airport."

"Clever of you."

"She found this in our bedroom. She said it was putting sand all over the dressing table."

"It probably was."

"So she threw it in the bin." That would have hurt. Jenna didn't reply. "And she found Jack asleep in the sink."

She clapped a hand to her mouth. "Hadn't you told her about him?"

"No."

"In the sink?"

"Yes."

She couldn't help the tickle of laughter at her throat. She began to chuckle. Then she was laughing aloud at the picture in her mind. Paul watched her, the shell still in his hand. Then a smile tugged at his own mouth. As her laughter subsided, Jenna said, "I'll take him back."

"No. He's a buddy now. Dianne'll have to get used to him."

The apple with the bite out of it was on top of a book she had left on the floor. He picked it up and began to eat it. She remembered his hand on the wall as he stood at her door. She looked again at the hollows on his cheeks.

"When did you last eat?" she asked sharply.

He stopped crunching and cocked his head to think. "Some toast this morning." He began to chew again.

"This morning!" She sat for a minute, considering. Dianne was just back. It was obvious they had had a row. She remembered their meal on New Year's Day and how much he could eat when he was hungry. Was that the last proper meal he had had? She stood up. "I've got some beef burgers and microwave chips. I'm going to cook you some calories before you keel over."

"Sounds good," he said, his mouth full of her apple. "Got any Coke?"

"No, but I'll make you tea."

He wrinkled his nose derisively as she left the room. It took her nearly fifteen minutes. She didn't like cooking at any time of the day. Cooking when she would normally be going to bed was very strange. She turned the burgers under the grill. Around Paul, nothing ever seemed to be predictable. She set the plate of steaming food on a tray and carried it through to the sitting room, pushing the door with her foot.

He wasn't in the chair. His coat was thrown over it and he was lying on his side on the sofa. His head was against the end nearest the window, resting on the red and black cushion. He had taken his shoes off; they were tossed askew on the floor. His legs were drawn up to fit his length to the other end. He was sound asleep.

Very quietly, she backed out again. She threw the chips in the bin and covered the burgers with a plate. She came back and stood looking down at him. Then she lowered herself to the floor so that she sat by his sleeping head. She tilted her own head to view his face. His lashes swept his cheeks, black on almost white, lashes which she would have loved to have on her own lids. His forehead was broad, his eyes widely spaced. His mouth was relaxed, slightly open, his teeth just visible behind the red curve of his lips. Hair twined on the pale patch of skin behind his ear and there was a slight shade of darkness dusting his chin. One hand was open beside his cheek, palm up, the long fingers curling a little, the wedding ring neat in its place. His breath was even and deep. She noticed a small patch of something at the corner of his nose. She looked closer. It seemed like blood. He must have scratched himself on his rambles.

It was late, that time of night when the imagination is loose and strong, when restraints are weakened by the need to let go of the day and dream along the path to rest. Silently, Jenna rose and switched out the light. Then she sat on the floor beside him again and, very gently, put her hand on his body, near the hollow of his waist. Beneath her hand, his side rose and fell evenly. He must be exhausted.

She wouldn't fall for a married man. She would protect herself from that. It had happened to a friend at university, who had spent her days yearning for her lover to have time for her, to evade his wife. In the end he had dumped her, the girl had failed all her exams and her heart was still broken. Everything in Jenna rose up to protect herself from such a fate. Besides, it was wrong.

And yet. He had come to her tonight; he had left his wife and fled to her. She felt a small triumph in that, and was ashamed. He did not accept self-denial as a virtue, and therein lay his danger. Small patches of thought spilled from the shadows and laid themselves around her. His voice, challenging: "You're afraid of what's in you, Jenna. You're afraid of what you could be and what you could do."

Yes, I am afraid. Afraid that there will be a struggle and that you will win, and that I will lose and win and be lost and found, all on one battlefield. When even the hollow of your upturned hand captivates me, what is goodness, badness? Where is the bastion that has guarded me all my life?

In the colourless room, she watched the slight tremble of his mouth in sleep. Her midnight thoughts took hold and she travelled to places she would never go in daylight. His eyes moved behind his lids. He was dreaming. Of squirrels, maybe. And hawks.

~

Something woke Jenna in the early morning. She stirred in the bed and raised her head from her pillow. The front door. The front door had just slammed. She sat up and felt something in her hair, behind her ear. She touched it and heard the rustle of leaves. She pulled it out. It was a sprig of ivy. She recognised it as being from the rampant climber which crawled over the wall of her tiny back yard.

She pulled her knees up under the bedclothes and dropped her head onto them.

He has been here, in my room. He has bent over me. We have watched each other sleeping. Those dreams, those midnight dreams, they must not stay with me in the day. They must not.

Like a small boat fleeing to harbour, Jenna went home that day, back to the village, the manse, where everything was ordered and sure, where the smell of baking was the same as it had been when she was a little girl, where her father's study was still a refuge of tranquillity and wisdom.

In the kitchen, Cora stood back and looked at her daughter with approval. "When you described your hair on the phone, I couldn't quite imagine it. But it suits you."

She turned back to the scales and weighed some flour. Jenna was beating eggs. A missionary was home on furlough from Zambia and he was speaking in the church the following night. There was going to be a special supper for the congregation afterwards. Cora's contribution was four dozen tray bakes. She nodded at a tub of cherries.

"Chop those cherries for me, would you?" She sifted the flour into a bowl and conversation stopped briefly while the mixer roared. She glanced at Jenna. "We don't normally see you on a weekday. You look well. Considering what's happened."

The cherries were sticky and Jenna tried to stop herself licking her fingers. "It was for the best, Mum."

Cora turned and put a floury hand on her hip. "I thought you got on well. Your Dad liked him."

"Dad didn't really know him."

"Yes, he did. We all did."

The back door was flung open and suddenly the kitchen was full of Luke. A streak of tortoiseshell fur sped in past him, waiting rewarded. Luke held his bag hefted over his shoulder with one hand. Without breaking his stride he lifted two chocolate cakes from the cooling rack on the ledge.

"Hey, Jay! what are you doing here?"

"I just felt like coming home for a bit."

Luke and bag made a bulky exit into the hall. "No accounting for some," he mumbled, his mouth full of cake.

Luke spent much of the evening revising. His mock exams were coming up soon. Jenna brought him coffee and a sandwich in his room at supper time. He was sprawled on his side on the bed, his head propped on one hand. A bulging ring binder of notes was open in front of him. Jenna stepped over his CD player on the floor. Rock music came from it. At least Luke never played his music too loud. She didn't think her mother and father had any idea how lucky they were.

"By the way," said Luke turning a page without looking up, "Paul wants to do a city shoot soon. He says he's been commissioned to get some new Belfast pics and I can help him."

"I didn't know you and Paul were still in touch."

Luke felt around till his hand found the sandwich. He took a bite. Then his eyes swivelled up beneath his brows. "You weren't the only one who got his number." He looked back at his notes, crumbs scattering over the ink. "He's more fun than Adam the aardvark anyway."

Jenna grinned at the top of his head. Luke knew she had said goodbye to Adam. That comment meant he approved. He ripped another bit of sandwich with his teeth.

"He says he'll pick me up at your house."

"Does he indeed? Can you afford the time?"

He looked up. "I can't work all the time. There's a party at Beezer's on Friday week. I can walk to your place from there and stay over. We could do the shoot next day."

We? Jenna felt a pang of jealousy. She turned to leave. "OK. Just come in quietly. I'll probably be asleep for hours by the time you get in."

Luke waved the sandwich airily. "I'll not disturb your beauty sleep. Are you going to have a nose job now you've got the hair fixed?"

Jenna reached for a jumper which lay in a heap on the floor. "Watch your mouth, brat, or *you'll* need a nose job!" she growled. Luke rolled backwards laughing as it landed on him.

She found her father in his study.

"Hi, Dad. Getting ready for tomorrow night?"

Donald sat back and put an arm out to propel her to the low soft chair which occupied the corner on the far side of his cluttered desk.

"I won't have too much to do tomorrow thankfully. Someone else will do the talking. I can just listen for once. And drink the tea and eat the buns afterwards."

And talk to all the people who will surround you, Jenna added silently. He had helped, advised and comforted so many people and they loved him for it. Some had brought their troubles to this room, sat in this chair and held up their broken hearts to him. Even when he was tired and sometimes even when he was ill himself, he never turned anyone away.

"Dad?"

His head tilted in curiosity. "What's on your mind?"

She hesitated, trying to feel her way to what she wanted to say. "Don't you ever ..." she waved a hand round the room "... get tired of all this? Being who everyone expects you to be?"

"Yes, indeed I do."

"So why do you do it?"

"Because people need me. Because I know I'm doing what I was meant to do."

Jenna frowned a little. "But how can you be sure you're doing what you were meant to do? That you're doing the right thing?"

Her father leaned an elbow on his desk. "Is this about Adam?"

She shrugged. "In a way, I suppose."

Donald looked down and moved some papers about. "If sticking with Adam didn't feel right, then you've done the right thing."

"Oh, I've no doubts about that."

"Then what is it?"

Jenna reached for a pen on the desk. She fiddled with it, twisting it in her fingers absently. Suddenly she said in a rush, "Have you ever felt in your heart that something is very, very right, but your head tells you it's very, very wrong?"

Her father gave her a long steady look. "Are you going to tell me any more?" She shook her head, half smiling. He sighed. "Follow your head. The heart knows no boundaries and that leads to all sorts of trouble."

She stopped fiddling, went very still. "Boundaries? But maybe the boundaries which we set for ourselves stop us finding wonders elsewhere."

He laughed. "I wish you'd tell me what's on your mind, Missy."

She moved in the chair, restless. "I'm talking just ... generally."

"No, you're not. If I didn't know what a sensible girl you are, I'd be worried. Outside those boundaries are ..." he leaned towards her and pulled a fierce face "... dragons!"

She was silent for a moment and then she stood up. "Well. Maybe I'll go and sharpen my spear!" she said, her voice light. She leaned down to put her arms round his neck and plant a kiss on his warm cheek. "I love you, Dad."

He smiled up at her. "I love you too, Missy."

She went to the door, hesitated, and then turned. "Do you think you could stop calling me Missy? Please?"

He was already picking up his pen, but his eyebrows rose as he looked at her. "But you'll always be Missy to me."

"Please."

"I'll try. If you promise to stay my little girl?"

She gripped the door handle. "No promises, Dad."

She had almost closed the door behind her when he called her again. She put her head back into the room, inquiring. Her father had sat back again, put his pen down.

"There are many new, attractive things – and people – beyond this village, Jenna. They're not all worth having."

"Maybe not all of them," she said.

The hall was in semi-darkness, lit by one lamp on the table below the portrait which Paul had taken. Jenna stopped to look up at it. She put her hand up and stretched to touch her own face with the tips of her fingers. That's the girl who's no trouble at all, the girl that Paul didn't need to bother about that day, the one in the group he could ignore. She pulled her hand back and touched the side of her head where he had tucked the ivy into her hair while she slept. *You're not ignoring me now, are you?*

The sitting room door was closed. Her mother was watching television and, probably, doing embroidery. She was a talented needlewoman, her fingers never still, always working, always aiming to make money for some good cause. Jenna went through to the kitchen where everything was neat and clean again, all the spoons and bowls put away, the cakes ready in their tins. She turned on the outside light and unlocked the back door.

With her arms folded against the cold, she crossed the lawn and paced the length of the back fence. The light from above the back door splashed across the grass and lit the wire and posts for half its length. Then the line marched away into darkness. The lights of the village pricked the sky in the distance, blocked by the jagged silhouettes of the old huts crouched in the field. The lights from the sitting room were muted by heavy curtains, but above, half way along the upper storey, the lights of Luke's room were a bright patch on the dark house.

Jenna wandered past the gable of the house, the broad sweep of lawn damp under her feet, not a sound from any wild thing. She stood still under the stars. In front of her, the bare branches of a cherry tree spindled up towards a sickle of moon.

Suddenly she whirled round and ran. A hand on a fence post, feet flung high, knees bent to take the fall on the other side. She collapsed onto the lumpy field, exhilaration firing through every bone in her body. She ripped at a clump of grass and threw it high into the night. As it drifted down to fall on her hair and shoulders, she laughed aloud. *Clap, clap, clap for me now!*

CHAPTER TWENTY-ONE

IT WAS AN awkward evening. Was it his birthday or the first anniversary of Christopher Shepherd's death? They sat round the remnants of the meal which Dianne had cooked, drinking coffee from tiny cups and eating birthday cake. Adam was peeling the marzipan off his piece; Dianne looked cool and self-possessed in a green top and skirt; Hazel was quiet. Irritation was gnawing at Paul. Dianne had shut Jack in the garden shed.

Hazel looked round the table. "It's a pity Jenna's not here. I like her." She turned to Adam. "Is it really over between you?"

Adam lifted his cup. "Afraid so, Mum. It wasn't going anywhere. Better making a clean break."

Paul sat back and looked at the ceiling. "I thought she dumped you."

"How would you know?" said Adam scornfully.

"Oh, just going by your track record."

"Paul!" said his mother. "That's not nice."

"But true," Paul shrugged.

Dianne broke in smoothly. "I still see Jenna sometimes. In fact, I was going to see if she'd take that cat back."

"I'm sure she would," said Adam.

Hazel brushed some crumbs into a heap and dropped them onto her plate. "The poor little thing. I'll take him if you like. Widget might be grumpy for a while, but he'd get used to him."

"Well, there you are!" said Dianne. "Two homes on offer. He'll be spoiled."

Paul spoke very quietly. "Jack's going nowhere." He looked up, straight at his wife. "He's staying here."

Dianne folded her arms on the table. "We'll see."

There was a silence. Adam swallowed the marzipan and changed the subject. "I've something to tell you." His mother and Dianne looked at him expectantly.

Paul's eyebrows rose. "Rachel's under the table. Metaphorically speaking, of course." He flicked a piece of cake in the air and caught it in his coffee cup.

Dianne put her head in her hands. A flush spread over Adam's fair skin.

"I'm going to England," he said.

Hazel's eyes rounded. "Another sales trip, you mean?"

"More than that. To stay. The boss wants me to set up an office just outside London so that English business can be dealt with more effectively." He moved the salt and pepper together neatly. "It's promotion. Good promotion."

Dianne sat upright in delight. "Wonderful, Adam! You'll be near us. I mean," she corrected quickly, "near my father's house. I'm sure he can help you some way."

"That would be great. I can do with all the contacts I can get."

When his mother spoke again, there was a small quaver in her voice. "When do you go?"

"In a fortnight. The office is already leased. I just have to set up the procedures and ... staff it."

Paul stood up suddenly and pushed in his chair. He leaned on the back of it to stare at Adam. "Let me guess. You'll be bringing some staff with you. Maybe just one."

Adam looked down at the table, moved the salt again, lined up the pepper beside it. Then he looked up defiantly. "Maybe."

Paul leaned across the table, picked up the salt and moved it to the other end of the table. He picked up the pepper. "I'm going out for some fresh air." He put the pepper on the window ledge as he left the room.

He went through the kitchen and out into the back garden. Bad temper was sparking through him like static. He knew he was leaving silence behind him, but the only one he felt guilty about was his mother. He would talk to her later.

The stars were hidden by rumpled black clouds which skidded along in the fresh wind. As Paul picked his way along the dark path to the garden shed, he heard a faint mewing and a scuffling at the door. Jack was much too small to make an impression on that door, even in its dilapidated state.

He called softly and the mewing increased in volume and hope. He slid the bolt and bent to put his hand to the crack in the door. His fingers closed gently but firmly on the little body which wriggled through. Jack settled on his shoulder, small rump in the palm of his hand, as he stepped into the shed and wedged the warped door behind him. Only the faintest hint of light filtered from the cold night through the pane of glass in one wall.

There was nowhere to sit. In fact, Paul hardly knew what was in here. It smelled of rust and earth and old wood. There was an ancient pair of shears hanging on a nail on the wall opposite the window. In one corner there was a collection of tools: a hoe, a fork, a spade. Well, he did remember using those. Once. When Adam had helped him with the front garden last autumn.

The kitten was licking his ear, whiskers tickling and purrs escalating to heights of delight, deafening him. Paul hunkered and dropped cross-legged to the floor. It wasn't too clean but he didn't care. He set the kitten down beside him and it rolled onto its side and started to wrestle with his fingers, its teeth nibbling harmlessly and claws half sheathed.

"Hey!" he teased, "behave yourself. You're a manse cat. Love thine owner." He ruffled the soft fur of its tummy .

The shed was lit suddenly by a slash of light from the back door as it opened again. Footsteps paced away and back, approached, hesitated. Then the shed door was tugged open. The kitten jumped in surprise and hid under Paul's knee. Paul looked up into the face of his brother.

"Come back in, idiot. Mum's upset."

"I wonder why."

"Because you walked out. Remember what day it is."

Paul stood up slowly, hooking Jack into his hand as he rose. "Thanks for the birthday card," he said.

"What birthday card?"

"Ah. Silly me. There wasn't one."

"Don't be so selfish."

Idly rubbing Jack's chin, Paul walked towards him. "Of course. It's also the anniversary of the day your dad died."

Adam's hair tugged in the night breeze as he stood with his hand on the shed door, stopping it from banging backwards. Impatiently he swept his other hand across his hair. "Yes. The day your mother's husband died."

"Did you have to choose today to tell her you were leaving? And so suddenly?"

Adam shrugged. "Well, we were all together. Seemed like a good opportunity. You're back now. She's just swopping one son for the other. Anyway, you were always her favourite."

"And you were always his. Are you really going to England to open an office?"

"I am."

"Is Rachel going with you?"

"What is this? The Spanish Inquisition?"

"Is she?"

Adam looked away. "She is."

Paul held Jack up and tickled his ear. "You'll live together over there. Won't you? This is all part of a plan. Isn't it?"

Adam turned suddenly and moved away towards the light of the back door. "It'd freeze the balls off a monkey out here. Get back inside. Mum wants you."

Paul stepped out of the shed and, gripping a delighted Jack in one hand, he wriggled the bolt on the twisted door until it gripped.

"Were you and Rachel planning this while you were still seeing Jenna?"

Adam spun round. His foot kicked a pebble which rolled away in the dark. "What's that to you?"

Paul came up to him and they stood face to face, Adam's in shadow and in turn shadowing Paul's. "She's not the kind of girl you do that to."

Adam snapped his fingers. "She's a girl like any other."

"Did you ever really know her at all?"

Faintly, Paul saw Adam's eyes narrow. "What's this about?"

"Maybe it's about you being a bloody bastard." Paul's voice was calm.

Adam took a step forward and thrust a finger into Paul's chest. His voice was low and vicious. "Oh no. You're the bloody bastard. My father said so. And he was right."

Jack bit his finger.

~

Later Adam left the room briefly. Dianne was in the kitchen. Jack raced across the room, a ping pong ball springing from his flying paws, pinging off chair legs, spinning under the table. He skidded after it, twisting and turning, ears perked and eyes darting. The ball flew past Paul's foot and he kicked it across the room. Hazel laughed as Jack leapt in the air and turned after it before his paws hit the ground.

"He's a lovely kitten," she said. "You must be feeding him well. His coat's shining like glass."

Paul sat on the sofa beside her and she linked her arm though his. "Happy birthday, Paul, and many more of them."

His smile flashed briefly. "There'll be many more anniversaries like this one for you too."

"I'm not really one for anniversaries. Christopher was dead yesterday, he's dead today and he will be tomorrow too. What's special about a date? Besides ..." she stopped and fiddled with his sleeve, – "there's been an anniversary every December for twenty-nine years and no-one mentions it."

"I think of him. Often." He heard Dianne in the kitchen. She would be back any minute. "How do you feel about Adam going to England?"

She was quiet for a moment. "Not happy." She turned her face to him. "But I've got you back now." Adam's steps sounded down the stairs. Quickly Hazel pecked Paul on the cheek. "And you're my firstborn. It's back to the way it was twenty-nine years ago. Just you and me."

Adam flung the door open. Jack was just behind it and there was a soft thump. The kitten picked itself up and shook its head vigorously. Adam glanced down. "Toughen up, scrap," he said. "It's a big bad world. OK, Mum. Better get you home." He rocked on the balls of his feet and smiled broadly. "I've a lot of things to see to."

Paul went down the drive with his mother, steering her by the light from the front door past his own car and the edge of the lawn. It was a crisp night, with a frost not far away. He opened the car door, but before she got in, she put her arms round his waist and hugged him. Surprised, he kissed her brow. She reached up to tousle his hair.

"You're so like your father, Paul," she said, soft, meant only for him. "He wouldn't have been easy to live with either."

"I'm not hard to live with!"

Her voice stayed low and serious. "I can see the strain in

Dianne. She's not settled and she's not happy. All evening, the air between you two could be cut with a knife. Work at it while she still loves you."

He shook his head. "Apart from you, no-one ever has."

Adam revved the engine impatiently. Hazel turned and put one foot into the car. She looked up at Paul again. "Don't be silly, son." She lifted her finger in a gesture he remembered well. "And anyway, apart from me, how many people have you bothered to love?"

Paul slammed the door.

~

When he came back into the house Dianne was rattling plates as she cleared the table. "We'll have to do these ourselves," she said. He watched her. "Aren't you going to help?"

"Sure, seeing it's the butler's day off."

"Oh give it a rest!" she snapped.

"I will if you will," he shot back.

There was dangerous tension in the air. Paul's irritation was making his head ache. Jack was beginning to tire and abandoned the ping pong ball to sit on the arm of the sofa. Paul gave the kitten a quick pat and began to lift dishes. He filled the basin in the sink while Dianne dealt with the remnants of the meal. After a long silence she said, "I want that cat to go."

"He's staying."

"You had no right to take him without asking me."

"I don't need your permission to do anything."

She flung round. "You do because I live here too!" The silence stretched out again between them. Paul continued carefully placing wet dishes in the drainer. Then she said it. "There's a solution to that, of course."

He looked round. "Luther wants you back." It was a fact.

Dianne raised her hands and dropped them again in frustration. "Paul, you are twenty-nine years old. You have talent to burn. You had a great career, a reputation most society photographers would die for." She raised her voice. "What are you doing here? I'm no use to you here."

Paul turned and leaned back against the sink. "More to the point, I'm no use to you any more, am I?"

She tossed her head. "No, you're not. I deserve better."

He crossed his ankles. "Why do you think Luther wanted to marry you? He needed all the help he could get. Marrying you would have opened doors again for him and his wretched family."

"I was doing that for you!"

His mouth curled in distaste. "You never do anything that isn't for yourself."

"You are horrid! I hate you!" Dianne swung into the sitting room. Paul followed her, trying to get his prickling annoyance under control. She sat down on the sofa and knocked Jack onto the floor with a sweep of her arm. It made it easier for Paul to say what he wanted to say.

"I'm going to move into the spare room. Tonight."

She looked up, her mouth a thin line. "Very well. Perhaps that would be a good idea."

He made an effort. "Dianne, it's not just you. I don't make anyone happy ..."

Dianne let out a sudden squeal of rage. She was looking down the side of the sofa. She plunged her hand down and pulled out a handbag. One of the shoelace straps had been bitten in two; the chewed ends dangled bizarrely from each side. Dianne thrust it towards Paul.

"Look what that cat has done!" she yelled. "I bought that today. It's a Fendi."

Before Paul could move, she reached down the side of the sofa again and swept Jack into the air by the scruff of his neck. Dangling from her fingers, he wriggled in distress as, swinging him high, she stormed into the kitchen. Paul strode after her.

"Careful with him!"

Dianne opened the back door and hurled the kitten across the back path. There was a thump and a high pitched cry. Paul reached Dianne in a fury.

"What the hell have you done to him? If you've injured him I'll ..."

She turned round and spat, "You'll what?"

With all the force of her arm she flung the door shut.

"Stop!" Paul had seen what Dianne did not. Jack had rolled quickly to his feet and was running back through the door. There was a silent resistance as the door stopped before it latched. Jack was so small there wasn't even the sound of a snap to account for the strange angle of the kitten's head as it lay caught in the sharp edge of the door.

Paul swore and pushed Dianne roughly out of the way. Her hand was over her mouth, her eyes huge and all her rage vanished. "I didn't mean to do that. Paul? Paul? I swear. I didn't mean to do that."

Paul opened the door gently and, as he lifted him, a night breeze rippled the fur on Jack's motionless back.

"He's dead." Paul's voice was hoarse as he examined the little body. "His neck's broken."

The look he turned on his wife was one that made her back away in fear. His hand itched to hit her. He was giddy with the desire to lash out, blinded by a broken dam of annoyance and frustration. Control came slowly. He would not hit her. He would despise himself. Instead he filled his lungs and roared.

"Go to hell! Go back to England where you belong! One or the other. Get out of my sight!" Dianne was trembling, her arms crossed in front of her in defence against his rage. "Now!" he roared again.

Dianne turned and fled.

CHAPTER TWENTY-TWO

PAUL STRODE DOWN the central corridor of the university. He had taken many graduation photographs when he had a studio in England, but he had never been in a university before. He had no idea there would be so many cars and so many people. He had driven round the entire campus once. Finally, he had bounced the car onto a patch of grass and abandoned it impatiently.

Inside, there were people everywhere: students, older people who might have been lecturers, mature students, catering staff, cleaners. Paul's eyes swivelled and searched, stabbed into corners, scanned above heads. Notice boards, shiny notices, tatty notices, notices in Chinese. He passed a clattering snack bar and went in, searched, swung out again. People laughing, arguing, poring over notes. Sitting, standing, squatting, thumbing mobiles.

Paul went on and on and on. He passed the chaplain's room. He spun back and veered into it. A man, there on his own, looked up and smiled. "Hi ..."

"Jenna Warwick. I'm looking for Jenna."

The man's smile widened. "Yeah, she's about. Why don't you ring her mob..."

"It's switched off."

"Ah. Well, she doesn't have much on a Wednesday so she's usually in the library. That would explain ..."

"Where's the library?"

The man came to the door and pointed. "It's back that ..."

Paul didn't hear the rest.

This library was big. Not like the one Christopher used to take him to every Saturday. Adam liked books on cars and aeroplanes, with lots of pictures. Paul went for stories. He would creep into a corner and sit alone. He didn't need pictures, they were all in his head: shooting rapids; leaping across the rooves of skyscrapers. The trembled thrill at his core was physical. He still felt it sometimes: the curl of the squirrel's tail; the slash of a shooting star; a nugget of snow cupped in the twist of a holly leaf.

And now. Knowing she was here somewhere – he might be about to see her, to find her. He put his hand on the end of a book stack. Round this shelf? Maybe over at that table? Round this corner? He wished and searched. Hunted and wished. It had worked before. In that study booth? Maybe down these steps, reaching her hand up to fetch down a book? His rapid steps, his darting eyes, the swing of his coat, were pulling looks his way.

Momentarily he lost his sense of where he was. He turned too fast. Dizzy, he dropped into a chair and covered his face. How many damn shelves were in this place? He squeezed his eyes shut within the blackness of his palms and wished again, urgently, furiously. She was a studybug. She had to be here. Had to be.

Jenna trudged up the main drive from the shore. She had meant to be in the library by now, but a prickly restlessness kept her on the move, sent her down to look over Belfast Lough from the patch of grass and rock near the bus stop. She hitched her bag up on her shoulder as she wandered to the main steps, up and into the long corridor. She slowed. Maybe she should give it a miss today. Head back into town and window shop. Maybe drop in and see Dianne. She could ask about Paul, casually. "So how's that husband of yours? Set up his studio yet?" She turned back.

Slowed again. The less she knew of Paul the better. She frowned, working it out. It was eight days since he had slept on her sofa and vanished in the early morning. Eight days and still he lived in her mind like an inset in a picture. Yesterday was his birthday. She shook her head. No, she really had to work today. She turned back and headed for the library.

~

When Paul lifted his head from his hands he saw the rows of computers at the other side of the room. He stood up and scanned them. She wasn't there. He slumped against the bookstack and felt the familiar rush of the tide of loneliness threatening him again. It lapped at his feet and began to rise.

Then he saw her. She was wearing her cream coat, her canvas bag slung from her shoulder and bumped against her hip. She walked towards the lines of computers, edged her way past chairs, stopped to lean over and chat to a male student across a divider. They exchanged a laugh. She found an empty seat and shrugged off her coat. Another student waved across at her. She waved back as she sat, dumped her books on the table and bag on the floor. Her hair skimmed her ear and she tucked it back out of the way as she bent to her bag and pulled out a file.

Now that he'd seen her, he stayed where he was, a smile hovering. She inserted a disk and tapped keys, watching the screen. Then she opened her file and flipped a few pages. She set it down and began typing. She looked back at the page, her fingers paused over the keyboard. Then she typed a bit more. She stopped, sat back and flexed her fingers on the edge of the table, frowning at the screen. Paul's smile widened. He was watching her in her world, a place he had never been. There was intimacy in this. He was close, seeing her as she was when he was nowhere in her universe, far from her thoughts. Her fingers rattled on the keys again, slowed, stopped. She leaned forward and put her chin in her hand.

~

She'd bought him a birthday present. How pathetic can you be? *Hi, I bought you a book. Oh, no reason. I just saw it and knew you'd like it. It's nothing, really. Of course, maybe I got your birthday wrong? Couldn't quite remember what you'd said.* Liar.

She lifted her chin from her hand and shook her head to clear it, to concentrate.

~

She'd moved her head and her hair had fallen from its niche behind her ear to feather round her jawline. He began to move towards her. Enough of this.

~

At last she was beginning to get somewhere. This paragraph actually made sense. Hmm. She began to type again, rapidly now.

~

She was four seats along in the row. He called her name.

~

She looked round at the first sound. The inset flared and became the picture.

"Come with me, Jenna."

She felt a flush creeping from her neck and into her cheeks. Heads bobbed up around her.

"I'm working," she said in a loud whisper.

"Come with me," he said again, clearly. More heads turned. He glanced round, then back. "If you don't come with me, I'll sing 'Hound Dog' again. Loud."

She stood up, scarlet, and began to edge past the three chairs between herself and Paul.

"Bring your stuff."

"Paul, I've just arrived," she hissed.

He mimed playing his guitar and took a deep breath. "You ain't ..."

"All right!" Furious, she gathered up her things. The student she had spoken to earlier had tipped his chair back, arms crossed and a grin on his face.

~

The first giggle tickled Jenna's throat when they were passing the security gate on the drive down to the shore. Paul slowed for the junction with the main road as the giggles became laughter. He eased the car into a rare gap in the traffic, moved up a gear and glanced round.

"What's so funny?"

"You are!"

His face relaxed into a smile. If she lifted her hand she could touch the crease of his coat at his elbow. Her laughter died and she didn't speak again until, a few hundred yards further on, he pulled into the park at the Lough Shore.

Silence flooded the car. He turned in his seat, towards her. It was happening again. Rossnowlagh; when he stopped the car and told her he wasn't twenty-nine. He was now. She tilted her head slightly in question.

"What is it?"

He pulled the door handle. "I've something to show you."

She opened her own door. "Right now? That whole exhibition was just because you want to show me something?"

As they slammed the doors, he looked at her over the roof, slight puzzlement between his brows. "Yes. So?"

He went to the boot and opened it. She followed. Inside she saw two tripods, a camera lying loose and a bag, the zip partly open to show the dark cap of a lens.

There was also a shovel and a green towel, folded into a ball, wrapping something.

Paul picked the towel up carefully, held it in his palm. Jenna watched his long fingers pull the folds apart, drop the corners to hang below his hand. Shock knocked her speechless. Jack was curled in a ball as if asleep by a fire. Paul's finger stroked over the ear, gently down the shoulder, followed the line of the curved leg and touched the curled white paw. But there was no purr, no yawn, no flexing of the toes in pleasure, no pink tongue flicking across the nose.

Jenna put her hand on the fur and felt the stiff coldness of him. "What happened?"

"He chewed a Fendi handbag."

She looked up, her hand still on the black fur. "That was a death sentence?"

"It turned out that way." He began to fold the towel over the kitten's body again. "His neck was broken."

"But not by you."

"Not by me."

She turned and walked across the car park towards the sea. A short path ran beside the stone wall of a raised flower bed. There was a long bench running the length of the curved wall on the side that faced the sea. She sat in the middle of it. She heard him lock the car and follow her.

When he sat beside her, she saw he had brought the bundle and the spade.

"I'm sorry," she said. "He was cute little guy."

"The best."

"Luke will be sorry too."

"Yeah."

He had left space between them. "Why did you tell me now? You could have told me some time, phoned even." She shrugged. "He's only a cat, after all."

His head swung round. "Yes, he was. But everything ..." he swept his hand round, encompassing the sea, the land, herself "... everything is also what you make it."

"And what did you make of Jack?"

He pulled one knee across the seat to face her. "Company. Fun. Something that loved me." His elbow was on the back of the seat, hand on his chin, one finger crooked at his lips as he thought. "Something connected to you."

She looked away quickly, across the stones and the short beach ridged with seaweed. There weren't many birds about, or people. It felt cold and barren. She couldn't decide what to say, except that he shouldn't say things like that.

He stood. "So I want you with me when I bury him."

She looked down at the concrete slabs under their feet. "Where are you going to bury him?"

He put his foot on the seat beside her and in one leap was on the top of the wall, standing on the scrub of the winter flower bed. "Reach me up the spade."

Jenna took a quick look up and down the path. The only person about was jumping across stones further along the beach. She lifted the spade and pushed it up onto the wall. She lifted the folded towel up also. Then she held out her hand to him. "Help me up."

Swiftly his hand reached down and clasped her wrist. She wrapped her own hand round his and stepped up. Her palm slid into his as she got her balance beside him. Then she let go. Paul scraped clear a patch beneath the brown leaves and bark which crusted the soil. It was good soil with only fine and dormant roots and he was able to dig deep. When he stood back, Jenna placed the small bundle in the hole. Then she took the spade from Paul and filled in the hole herself. Paul bent and pulled the bark and leaves across the fresh soil. When they stood back, no one would have been able to tell that Jack lay beneath.

They sat on the edge of the wall, their feet hanging over the seat below. Across the rumpled surface of the grey lough, a cargo ship nosed its way towards the open sea. A dog trotted by on the rough beach, the stem of a frond of seaweed gripped proudly in its teeth.

Jenna watched the ship, the scent of the sea strong in her head, her hair blown across her face. "Had to be a door." she said.

Paul looked back towards the city, where two huge yellow cranes stapled the shipyard to the city. "Yep."

"Dianne?"

"Yep."

"Having a row?"

"Yep."

Neither spoke for a minute.

Then Jenna said, "I'm sure she didn't mean it."

"She didn't."

"So don't be too hard on her."

He didn't reply to that. They sat for another while in silence. Then Paul jumped down and held up his hand for hers. She pushed it away.

"I jumped the fence at home. This is a doddle."

She jumped down, turned and pirouetted proudly in front of him, ending in a mock bow. He put his hands in his pockets and grinned.

"The circus for you!" Abruptly, he stopped talking, his eyes still on her face. His hand came up and pushed her hair out of her eyes. Tucked it behind her ear. "I want to photograph you," he said.

She twisted her head away from him. "Don't be daft!"

"It's not daft." He looked up at the sky, checked the clouds. "The light's OK and you look brilliant." He took a few steps backwards and then turned to sprint back to the car park. "Stay there!" he called over his shoulder. When he came back, he had a camera slung around his neck and a tripod tipped over his shoulder.

Jenna was standing with her arms folded. "You didn't ask me if I wanted to be photographed."

He bowed low, twirling a graceful arc with his free hand. "My lady, may I have the honour of photographing you?"

"No."

"Too bad." He straightened and checked the sky again. He looked around. "Here won't do. Come along the path a bit. Down here." He walked away, where the path led along a ridge above the stony shore.

She didn't move. "What happened to 'Sorry I disturbed you. Go back to the library now and finish your work.'?" she called.

He came back. The edges of his coat swung around his walk. The image imprinted on Jenna's brain. *He is perfect.* He stopped in front of her.

"Yes, I left that bit out, didn't I? Do you want to go back to the library and finish your work?"

She looked down at the ground, scuffed a scrawny weed between the paving stones. She couldn't stop the curve of her lips as she looked up again. "No."

He raised his hands in a shrug and dropped them. "I knew that. That's why I didn't ask. Now come on. There's a bench on this grass round the corner. It's perfect."

She tossed her scarf over her shoulder and followed him.

~

At first she was stilted and huffy and he used the tripod. She sat with her knees together and her hands in her lap. He chatted constantly, asking about her day, about her mother and father. He told jokes, stupid ones. He made a face and pressed the shutter as her smile broadened in response.

She began to relax, barely noticed when he freed himself from the rigid tripod and began to move round her. She forgot the constant slide of the shutter in the pleasure of listening to his voice, watching his easy crouch, the top of his head, the spring of his step, the balance of his feet, the quick flash of his eyes as he checked her again.

She turned round and leaned on the back of the bench as he moved behind her.

"Let's see that scarf."

She lifted an end of it and spun it round her head, laughing. Fun was trickling through her, tingling in her fingers, brightening her perceptions – of him, of the day, of the sea, of the wind. She lifted the scarf to cover her mouth and nose and wiggled her eyebrows at him. Behind the camera, she saw his delight. Something deep within her flowered. She pulled her knees up and knelt on the seat, arms along the back of it, grinning. She put her chin in her hand; she waved at him; she posed like a pouting model. Always he circled her, the tension in his body betraying his concentration now that she was relaxed and with him in this.

He crawled full length under the bench and lay on his back, his head and camera emerging from the front. She didn't need to be told. She lay above him, along the seat and looked down into the lens. His fingers made rapid adjustments; the shutter slid again and again and again.

She sat cross-legged on the grass. "You look like a frog," he said.

She pulled some grass and threw it at him. "Called Fred!" she cried, happy.

~

"Thanks for the sandwiches." He was sitting on the bench again, leaning back with his hands in the pockets of his coat.

Jenna was sitting sideways facing him, her knees pulled up,

her arms wrapped round them. "Well, I didn't want my cushion eaten when you woke up."

"The red bit looked specially tasty. The duvet was good too."

"Luke's."

"I raided your cornflakes."

"I noticed. Why did you go out into my back yard?"

White tops broke on the creases of the sea. The cargo ship was a grey ghost on the horizon.

"I like being outside. I like seeing what outside looks like in different places."

She hugged her knees and nodded. "Outside feels different in different places as well."

"And smells different."

They were silent for a while, contented. Jenna dropped her chin onto her bent knees, thoughtful. "My back yard isn't exactly the Glens of Antrim though."

He laughed. "But the ivy's great!" He caught her eyes and all the merriment left his face. "Jenna?"

"What?"

"You look lovely when you're asleep."

There was enough mischief in her still to retort, "So do you!"

He paused to digest that, enough time for her to regret the words and to feel the blush heating across her cheeks. Then he said, "I like your room. And I like where you put my hat."

She hid her face in her crossed arms. "Teddy bears need warm heads too," she said, muffled. She moved a little so that she could peek at his face. He grinned, put out his hand and placed it on her head. She felt him lace his fingers through her hair.

"But they don't have to sleep in the bed with mummy bear."

She lifted her head then, looked across to where the tide was creeping up the stones and shingle. With the movement, his hand slid down and nestled at her neck. She bit her lip, fighting the turmoil, the almost-defeat. She pressed her cheek against his hand, trapping his fingers.

"Dianne," she said, low. "You're married. You swore ..."

He stood suddenly, pulling his hand away. She turned and lowered her feet to the ground. He faced her, held up his left hand. For a second time in front of her, he pulled the gold ring from his finger. He held it between his finger and thumb and brought it close to her face.

"Watch me," he ordered.

He walked down the grass and jumped over the tussocks at the edge of the shingle. His coat streamed behind him as he strode down a tongue of beach between the stones. To Jenna, it seemed as if her breath had frozen in her lungs. She was supposed to be in the library, working, forgetting, moving on. Not watching this. How do you fight the irresistible? How do you stop the inexorable?

How do you make yourself want to?

The sea was lapping at his feet when he stopped. He lifted his hand, pulled his arm back and threw the ring in a long arc across the lough. Invisible at this distance, nevertheless a slant of sun caught it just above the water and Jenna saw the faintest spark against the grey before it vanished without a ripple. She gasped. When she heard him beside her again, she was bent forward, her face hidden in her hands.

His palm touched high on her back. Fright and fury came to her rescue. She leapt up and sprang to the far side of the path.

"You won't lay this on me, Paul! You won't blame me. Your marriage is your problem. Don't drag me into it." She was breathless with the enormity of it.

He leaned forward towards her. "Listen to me, Jenna. I have left her. She will leave me. The deed only remains to be done."

"Why? Why have you left her?"

He raised his hands and let them drop again. "We're not in the same place any more. If we ever were. You can take the girl out of

Knightsbridge but you can't take Knightsbridge out of the girl."

She came back and stood in front of him. He looked up into her eyes, his coolness making her want to shake him.

"Listen to yourself!" she said. "Have you any idea how little you understand Dianne?"

He frowned. "What's to understand?"

Jenna took a deep breath at that, let it out and sank to the bench beside him. "She has needs and wants, just as you have. She had friends that you took her away from, places, her father, her whole way of life. How much have you stopped to think about that?"

"She knew what she was doing."

"I don't think she did. And look at you. You went away, but you came back to where you felt you belonged. You can take the man out of Ireland, but you can't take Ireland out of the man."

He smiled a little. "Touché!"

"You both want to be where you belong. But it's not the same place."

His eyes seemed very blue in the winter sun, his cheeks pale and his mouth slightly parted as he regarded her. "No. And it's not the same things."

Her hand was along the back of the seat. She picked at the weathered green paint behind his shoulder, looked at a fleck that stuck to her finger. Her voice was hesitant. "I know ... she doesn't want children."

He turned his head away from her, a gust of wind from the sea almost taking his words. "I don't want to talk about it any more."

She hit his shoulder making him whip round in surprise. "It's not always about what you want!" she cried.

His hand came up to grip hers, the one which had hit him. "Yes it is! It's about wanting and looking and searching and not finding." She held her breath. He was so close, so intent on her face, on her eyes and then her mouth. "Then it's about finding and wanting ..." he extended a finger to stroke her nose gently "... and not having."

They sat like that, suspended in limbo. Jenna knew it was another moment to be remembered, nestled in the deepest parts of her. She didn't know how long it was until she tried her voice. It was a whisper.

"But we're friends."

"No, we're not. You and I could never be friends. And you know it as well as I do."

She tried to speak to those soft, intense eyes; cleared her throat and tried again.

"Why did you go away? Why did you go to England?"

He set her hand down gently and the moment was gone. "To get away from failure."

"Failure? You!"

He leaned forward and examined the ground between his feet. His glance flicked to her and away again to the sea. He was about to tell her something. She could read him so well. Why was that?

"I could never please Christopher – my step-father. He wasn't a bad man. In many ways he was a good man. And he really loved my mother." He sat upright again. "But Adam was his son. He took me on because my mother and I came as a package. I believe he tried. But he never accepted me, never loved me as a father would." He glanced at her again and she didn't move, afraid of making the door shut. This was another quiet step on the long corridor within the palace. "I would do things, maybe mow the lawn to surprise him when he came in from work. But he would just say something like 'Glad to see you working for your keep, lad!' " His fists clenched. "He never, ever, called me 'son'. I used to wait for it every day. Maybe this would be the day. He would introduce us as 'my son Adam. Oh, and this is Paul.' "

"But you have his name."

"He adopted me." He turned and gave a small laugh. "I told you he tried. He was a church-goer. My mother still is. I threw myself into that." He gave a genuine smile. "I used to play the guitar at church – leader of the gospel band! Can you see it?"

The image delighted her. "Yes, I can!"

"When I was twenty-one, I was working in a studio in Belfast and borrowed his car for a shoot in Fermanagh. I took a corner too sharply and cut a gash right down the side of it on a wonky fence post." He paused. "Christopher was furious. He shouted that I was half English and why didn't I go to England and get out of his life?"

"So you did."

"I did. I decided that I'd stop trying. I'd stop even remembering."

She touched his shoulder. "You're still doing that, aren't you? Forgetting. Just blocking things that don't please you."

He wasn't finished. "I would have liked the chance to be everything he wasn't." He looked at her with that rare open gaze when he had betrayed part of his heart to her. "I would have liked that."

A thought struck her. "In a way, you were practising on Jack."

The look he gave her was bland. "Who's Jack?" he said.

Jenna waited for the quirk of his mouth that would show he was teasing. It didn't come. She wouldn't mention Jack again. "Maybe you will some day. Have the chance to do it right, I mean. And there's your mum. I like your mum."

His smile was instant. "My mother's a star. She always stood up for me. Me and her against the world!"

They were quiet while a middle-aged couple strolled by, hand in hand. They gave the brief nod of strangers as they passed.

"Now I know why you know so many choruses and church music. My Dad could give you a job."

"No thanks. When I gave up on Christopher, I left small gods behind as well."

"So what about the big one?"

He made an impatient movement. "They're all too small."

She chewed her scarf, thinking. "Maybe that's because we're too far away. They must be massive up close."

His sudden burst of laughter made her jump. He threw up his hands to the sky. "Oh, I love female logic!" he cried.

She watched him with pleasure. When he was laughing in real delight, his eyes narrowed, his cheeks dimpled and the bridge of his nose crinkled a little. He jumped to his feet and pulled her up after him. Then her face was pressed against the wool of his jumper, his arms tight around her. She was too stunned to move. His voice was at her ear.

"My God, Jenna, I need you."

The first thought that tumbled across her scrambled brain was that she had power. Power to hurt. She had never really experienced that before, not as consciously as now. She took a deep breath and brought her hands up to his chest, pressing herself away from him.

"Don't do this to me, Paul." She felt his grip tightening against her again. She brought her arms down hard and angry against his, breaking his grip. "No! If you want to betray your wife, leave me out of it. Sort out your own mistakes." She bent to pick up her canvas bag. "I wouldn't be Adam's Plan B and I certainly won't be yours."

He stood back, furious now himself. "Run away then! Climb back into your little cage. Go and tremble behind your beloved bars!" He walked away a few steps and swung back again. "You still don't know who you are, do you? Good, bad? Or just still scared?"

She hooked her bag over her shoulder and, shaken, gazed at his sudden fury. "There's a difference between needing and wanting," she said. There was a mist drifting in across the sea, making the far shore float in a haze. "You said you need me." She looked at her feet, tears very close. Would she say this? Should she say this? She flicked her hair from her eyes and said it. "I'd like somebody to want me, not just need me." She swallowed. "Because that's what I'm feeling now. Wanting."

He stepped towards her. She fled onto the grass towards the road. Her steps slowed until she stopped and turned round. Paul had sat on the bench facing the sea. His hands were between his knees, his head dropped, his hair ruffling in the wind.

"Paul," she said, just loud enough. She knew he'd heard her by the slightest movement of his head. "I am still scared. Because Adam hurt me. But you would break my heart."

Slowly his head turned to her. His face was closed and shuttered. "Go away," he said, clear as ice.

She stood for a moment, then turned and left him there.

CHAPTER TWENTY-THREE

LUKE PHONED HER that night. "Hey, Jay."

"Hey, LW."

"Message from Paul Shepherd." Curiosity peeped through his words.

"Oh?"

"He says he'll give me your bag of notes and stuff when we meet up on Saturday."

Thank goodness. She wasn't going to ask for them. He would have found them on the back seat later.

"OK. I'll get them off you then. Are you staying over in my house on Friday night?"

"Probably Saturday night as well. Paul wants to go up the north coast." He paused. "Two questions, Jay."

"What?"

"Why has Paul just rung me to say he can't meet me at your house on Saturday morning and that I have to catch him at the City Hall instead? And why does he have your stuff?"

"You'll have to ask him the first one. The second one's my business."

"OK, keep your hair on ... Are you going home this weekend?"

"No, I'm going to stay up and do stuff."

"Mum won't be pleased. She was hoping you'd help her with shopping on Saturday."

She couldn't face going home to the manse and the village. The desires and doubts that she had now were too big for the old harbour. She would ride this out on the open sea, alone. "Pity about Jack, wasn't it?"

"What about Jack?" Luke asked, surprised.

"Paul didn't tell you?"

"Tell me what?'

"Jack got caught in a door. Broke his neck and killed him."

"Bloody hell! Shit. Poor furball. How'd it happen?"

"Oh, just an accident. You know kittens. As soon as they find their feet they're walking suicides."

"I bet Paul's not happy." After a moment, he asked, "How did you know? And he didn't tell me?"

It didn't surprise Jenna. She was the only one he would tell. "Don't mention it to him, Luke."

His voice sharpened. "You seem to know him pretty well."

"So see you Friday night then."

"Shit, no. You'll be asleep when I get in."

~

It was late that evening when Paul dropped his keys on the hall table and listened to the sounds of his house. Footsteps stopped at the top of the stairs. He looked up at his wife, cool and elegant, one manicured hand on the bannister. Her voice was frost-crisp.

"Why are you not answering your mobile?"

"There's no-one I want to speak to." He turned towards the sitting room. Dianne came halfway down the stairs.

"Even Toby?"

Paul swung round, frowning. "Toby?"

"He tried here when he couldn't get you."

"How'd he get this number?"

"I don't know. I'm sure it's not hard – Bella maybe. He wants you to ring him back." She laughed scornfully. "Don't tell me he fancies you!"

"OK, I won't."

Paul walked into the room and, despite himself, looked round the floor. Through the door into the kitchen he saw that the shoe box lined with an old grey jumper in the corner by the back door had gone. She'd probably tipped it into the bin. He flung himself down on the sofa. Dianne stood in the doorway.

"By the way, Daddy rang also."

Paul tipped his head back against the soft cushion and forced his eyes to stay open. "Oh? What did Daddy want?"

For the first time, Dianne's voice became hesitant. "He suggested that I go over and stay with him for a bit." She bit her lip and looked at him sideways. "He's been lonely since Christmas ... and he's had a cold ... he's a bit under the weather. And it's what you want me to do."

"Don't tell me. You've already booked your flight. Tomorrow. You're going to slum it on a bargain airline. You've been upstairs packing."

Her chin came up. "Quite the mystic, aren't you? Full marks."

Paul raised his head and looked her in the eye. "I hope you've booked a taxi."

"Of course. I wouldn't depend on my dear husband. Not after the last time."

She turned away. He spoke to her back, making her freeze momentarily.

"Give Luther my regards. You deserve each other."

~

He was dreaming about being lost, lost in snow. He was running around, small and cold, stumbling in the drifts. Suddenly, there were clocks rearing out of the snow all around him, Grandfather clocks, huge and brown and menacing. Pendulums swung fast. Faster. Too fast. He lurched from one to the other, crying to be let in, pleading with the clocks to stop their frenzied ticking and let him in. His feet mangled the snow into lumps and hollows. He looked down at his footprints. New snow was filling them up. Erasing them. Erasing him. The maker of footprints. The maker of nothing.

The crashing tide of loneliness woke him. He sat on the edge of the bed and dropped his head into his hands to steady himself, to banish the dizziness and nausea of the dream. Then he stood, naked, and pulled the thick duvet from the bed. Downstairs, he opened the back door. It wasn't bolted. Neither he nor Dianne had given it a thought. The minutiae of life together was disintegrating.

Stepping outside, he felt instantly clean and free. By the light of the half-moon he found his way to the shed and crouched, propping his back against the wood. He had no idea what time it was. It didn't matter. He shrugged himself deeper into the duvet, using his hands as hooks across his body, his feet holding the edge beneath his toes. It was cold, but there was enough cloud cover to keep the frost from biting.

This was better. Brushed by moonlight falling through dark and drifting clouds, Paul was lulled by the murmur of grass and the softly swaying winter branches in the gardens around him. He savoured it all, every star, every twig, every pinch of the cold. Before he returned to bed he would banish the need, the image of sugar-brown hair, the wind-pink nose above the edge of red scarf. All of her had to go. If he had to do this alone, so be it.

~

From the window of the spare bedroom, Dianne looked down at him. She had heard him go and knew where he was going. Bloody fool! This time she would not go after him and pull him to her to warm him. He would be all right – very cold but that duvet was thick.

Without saying it, they both knew it was over. He had changed beyond all recognition from the stunning charismatic man she had met. Then, he had just secured his first big commission for a major glossy fashion magazine. She was to be such an asset to his society career and she would enjoy his money and his fame. She hugged her shoulders. So many friends had envied her when she married him. Then so many of them had raised their eyebrows when she had come to Belfast with him. They never expected that. Neither did she. Belfast was where soldiers went. It hadn't worked. Luther was right. She was going back to where she belonged, the only play she knew.

She turned away from the window briskly and felt for the door to return to the warmth of her own bed. That reminded her. The proofs for the catalogue of Luther's new exhibition would have arrived today. She stepped round the dark shape of her full suitcase, climbed into bed and opened a jar on the bedside table. As she smoothed cream onto her hands she made a mental note to ring Luther in the morning and tell him to bring the proofs when he met her at the airport. She adjusted her pillow. And if he had let them use that ghastly purple on the cover, she would send them all back again to be redesigned. She settled her head. Luther had an awful eye for colour.

Many streets away, Jenna lay sleepless. She watched the dim black mound of the teddy bear on the pillow beside her, wearing the black woollen hat, as if it might turn and speak.

She curled her legs up, trying to find comfort and sleep. She remembered when Paul had given her that hat, how it had felt as though his hands were upon her head. The head is a lonely place, but the heart is a dangerous one. She put a hand out to touch the dried sprig of ivy leaves which lay on her bedside table, beside her radio. She had done the right thing today, but she didn't feel any better. *Why don't I feel good, Dad? Why do wI want to go out to fight the dragons of the dangerous places?*

She curled her body tighter under the quilt. *If I've been good, why do I feel so bad?*

CHAPTER TWENTY-FOUR

THE GALLERY WAS doing well. Luther found it hard to say so, but Dianne's family name and connections were helping enormously. Mingling with the guests at this invitation-only viewing, Dianne pulled in her stomach. She was wearing a black satin pencil skirt and she was putting on weight. Luther was a man of few words, but he regarded her with triumph and ownership. She understood that. It was what life was about – alliances and money. When affection came into it as well, it was a bonus.

Across the room, Luther caught her eye and winked. She lifted her chin. Luther was being successful after all. Her thoughts flitted briefly to Paul, back in Belfast. God, that seemed so far away now. What the hell had got into him? He had been part of this. A year ago, he would have been here working the room, making contacts, turning down commissions just because he didn't like them. He could afford to.

She had made one brief phone call to tell him she was staying on to help with the gallery for a bit. All he had said was, "You didn't need to tell me."

At least he had answered the phone.

Luther threaded his way towards her. He was looking smooth and confident in a dark gray suit and white shirt. The tint of his hair was echoed in the gold stripe of his elegant tie. He stood beside her and his hand rested impudently low on her back.

"This should be worth a bit," he said, low into her ear.

"And half of it's mine," she responded through lips that kept smiling at the guests nearby.

"We'll see." Luther patted her bottom. "You're getting tubby," he murmured. His fingers pinched. "Not a good image, my love."

She put the steel point of her heel on his foot and leaned on it. A small man with a doughnut of gray hair wandered by. She beamed at him. "Hello, Ambrose. Giving the House a miss tonight?"

Luther looked down at his foot where her heel was making a severe dent in the toe. "I don't mind about my toes, but have you any idea how much these shoes cost?"

"I know exactly how much they cost," she whispered, twisting her heel and making a definite tear in the leather. "I know the cost of everything. I know how much your belt was. The belt you had to let out a notch when you were dressing tonight."

Luther shook hands with a couple who had just arrived, then turned back. Through gritted teeth he muttered, "Do you want a replay of your fifteenth birthday?"

Dianne waved cheerily at Arabella who had just given up trying to understand a piece of metal on a spotlit plinth. She put her hand on Luther's shoulder affectionately and mouthed, "Dumped in your pool again?" She removed her heel. "Maybe when you get rid of the green gooey stuff. Not to mention the frogspawn." She swung away from him. "Harry, darling! How's the vineyard? Let me show you this amazing piece over here. It would look incredibly wonderful in your villa. I thought of you as soon as I saw it."

~

This time it was Bella who was sitting on the chair by the log fire in the study. Dianne was lying curled in a ball in one corner of the red leather sofa, her arms tight around her knees, the look in her eyes provoking unusual concern in Bella's. She didn't feel cosy; she didn't feel warm; she didn't feel anything except an appalling fear.

"That's two months," Bella said.

"I've been stressed."

"My ass," said Bella.

Silence fell again. Bella examined her nails. Then she twirled her ankle and admired the leatherwork on her Gucci boots. Dianne was going to buy a more expensive pair tomorrow. She hadn't told Bella she would, but then Bella didn't need to be told. However, Dianne wasn't thinking about that now. Bella was making her think of something else; forcing her.

Now Bella reached into her bag and held out a packet. "Go do it, darling. I'll wait." When Dianne didn't uncurl, she shook the small box impatiently. "You have to. You know you do."

Slowly, Dianne sat up. It was as if she were wading through a treacle of dread. The tingling in her breasts had been telling her for some time but that and every other sign had been explained away. Stress, not eating properly, late nights. Even leaving Paul. Bella had laughed aloud at that one. "Don't be daft, Di! You've been happier than a pig in muck since you came back." With a tilt of a slim eyebrow she had added, "Probably Paul has too." Then she had sighed a nostalgic sigh. "Now why didn't he pick me instead?"

Dianne stood suddenly and snatched the box. "You'll wait?"

Bella sat back and lifted a copy of *Vogue* from a mahogany rack. "Wild horses, darling, ..." she flipped the pages "... wild horses."

Twenty-four hours later, Dianne was toying with her fork in an intimate booth for two. Luther was getting better tables now. He had been going over Dianne's plans for the renovation of the foyer of the gallery. Her ideas were good, her instinct and style immaculate. After a few minutes, he stopped talking and covered her hand, stilled her fingers.

"What's up? Is it about your divorce? We'll get it started soon. When we're less busy."

Dianne looked at him, at his round cheeks, his pale lashes, his look of well-being, the possessiveness of his hand on hers. She had to tell him; he had to help; he mustn't be angry. She took a deep breath.

"I'm pregnant."

Luther's hand tightened as hers began to shake on the white cloth of the table. It was the first time she had said the words and the very saying of it punched a stake of fear through her stomach. There was an alien in there, a parasite, something growing inside her which she didn't want, which she hated with all of her being. Luther lifted his hand from hers.

A waiter hovered. Luther waved him away and fell back in his chair. "You stupid girl," he said. There was no request for a repeat of the information, no request for proof, no question about whether she was sure.

"You knew, didn't you?"

"I know women and I know you exceptionally well. I know when you're lying. A few things haven't been adding up these last few weeks."

She put her elbows on the table and covered her face. "Oh Luther, what am I going to do? I'm so scared."

His voice came low, confident, stating facts. "It isn't mine. We're too careful."

She lowered her hands but her voice would not come.

"It can't be mine," he repeated.

Still she didn't answer, because he was right. Luther would never, ever, lose control. Even in the middle of passion his mind would be working, calculating, never ever making a mistake like that. His voice hardened.

"So it's his." She bit her lip and his hand shot across to take her chin. "Say it!"

The dam broke and she hit the table, rattled knives and forks, sent a spoon to the floor. "It must be!"

Her chin jerked from his grasp and he clenched his fist beside his wine glass. A waiter looked and left quickly.

"Christmas," Luther muttered. "Christmas. Parties and carelessness. And you with him after, before you came back to me ..."

He stopped talking, his cheeks flooded with colour. He folded his arms on the table and bent his head. She looked at the swirl of blond where it parted slightly at his brow. Now she was beginning to feel annoyed. That was good. It elbowed at the fear.

"He was – is – my husband, for God's sake!" She paused, then added, "But he didn't touch me after Christmas. Not once. We were busy." She stopped there. Paul had not wanted her at all, but she wasn't going to tell Luther that.

Luther raised his head. "Are you going to tell him?"

"Good God, no!"

He sat back again, his hands dropping to his knees. "This isn't good. Not good at all."

"Well, full marks for deduction," she hissed. "Didn't you hear what I said? I said I was scared. I'm petrified. I don't want to be pregnant. Not now, not ever. Gallery or no gallery. You know that."

"I know that." He took her hand and fiddled with her fingers. "But I'll talk you round some time." The flush faded a little and she saw his mind working, calculating. Then he looked her in the eye. "Then there's only one thing to do." He paused and she told him with her eyes that she knew what he meant. "Have you told Bella?" She nodded. "She'll go with you. Your father need never know." He lifted her hand and kissed it. "I love you, you idiot.

Enough to take you back again." His face stilled above her fingers and his words were clipped and clear. "But not anything from him. Kill it."

She recoiled a little at his blunt instruction, but she had her father's money. Relief rose like a fever. It would be all right. It would be as if it had never happened. She would get rid of the parasite and she would never, ever, let this happen again. A thought struck her. She had to be sure of one thing. "Paul must never know about this, Luther. Never."

He threw a cold glance at her and clicked his fingers for the waiter, wordless.

~

Paul did not appear at Jenna's door again and she didn't expect him to. He had betrayed himself to her and she had rejected him. That was the last of it. She had lost him, every part of him. But then, she reminded herself, she had never had him.

But, in truth, she had. Resisting him had become a habit and she had walked away from the most alive, the most intoxicating, the most dynamic man ever to have streamed across her sky. His last words to her were a banishment. He wouldn't try to persuade her; he wouldn't give her the opportunity to change her mind. The door was slammed and the key was thrown away, just as surely as his wedding ring.

Even so, she would turn off her laptop in the lengthening evenings and linger over closing the curtains onto the street – just in case he should be standing in a pool of light, waiting to stride into her house and throw himself down in her chair.

Four times, Luke stayed over on a Friday night and spent Saturday on location with Paul. Always, he met him in town and always he loved it.

"Paul's brill, you know, J. He's got the patience of Job when he wants to get a shot."

"Paul says you have to take hundreds of shots just to get one gem."

"Paul says the only reflectors he wants to work with are the moon and the earth."

"We stayed in Belfast today. Paul got me to look for shapes and patterns in buildings. Paul says I have a good eye for composition."

"Paul says photography's not about taking pictures. It's about seeing."

Paul says. Paul says. Sometimes Jenna wanted to put her hands over her ears. Never once, apparently, did Paul say, "Say hi to your sister." Every time she saw her brother, she thought of him having been with Paul, spoken to Paul, been in Paul's car, and jealousy shot an arrow through her.

That last day had been delightful – until it ended. Paul was light and funny; he made her laugh until she ached; he made her feel so good that she could have been a model all her life. Indeed, there was more in her than she knew and that day Paul had drawn from her unknown parts of herself by the magic he made simply by being with her.

He came into her mind at any time. He never truly left it. Walking into the university she would remember how he had started to sing 'Hound Dog' in the middle of the library. He had stormed into the university, walked through hundreds of students just to find her. Only Paul would do it and only Paul would succeed.

Where was Dianne? Jenna had got used to the odd petulant phone call from her when she was bored, or when she wanted company on a shopping trip. Jenna had become quite an authority on handbags. But there had been no contact for some weeks. Was Paul's prophesy right? And if so, had she left him yet? And if she had ... Jenna chewed her thumb ... if she had, Paul didn't think it worth telling her.

And then there was Max. Max who had been so amused when Paul came for her in the library; Max who told her that he had watched her walk away with Paul and thought what a great figure she had. He was a post-graduate student also and Jenna could talk to him about dissertations and word length, bibliographies and library books. His hair was brown and long and curly, his body chunky, his jumpers baggy, his jeans faded and ripped at the knees. She blew her bank balance on some trendy clothes and hung out with him in the coffee bars. When he had come into her house for the first time, he sauntered round her sitting room.

"Hey, nice print. Like birds, do you, Jen?"

"It's not a print. It's an original." She set down two coffee mugs and tossed some books and CDs from the sofa. "It was taken by a friend of mine."

"Cool." He moved on. The razor shell was on the window ledge. Max stood looking out at the street, absently tapping the shell against his palm.

"Careful with that. It's fragile."

Max looked down at it, surprised, then dropped it back on the window ledge. "OK. Plenty more where that came from."

Jenna opened her mouth but shut it again. It was enough that Max had stopped touching it. Still, when he sat in the chair – her chair? Paul's chair? – she raised her chin and smiled at him.

Life goes on.

On a damp day at the beginning of March she brought Max with her on one of her increasingly rare visits home. He shook her father's hand.

"Hi, sir. I've never been in a rectory before."

Donald smiled. "You still haven't. This is a manse."

"Oh. Right. I thought they were all the same."

Cora bustled in. "You'll have a drink, Max. What will it be?"

Max opened his mouth and Jenna said quickly, "Coffee, Mum. Max is a great coffee drinker. Aren't you, Max?"

"Yeah. Yeah, sure. Coffee'd be great."

Luke emerged and checked him out for five minutes. After

an effort at conversation, he wandered off again. They had absolutely nothing in common, not even the same A levels.

After lunch, Jenna took Max for a walk round the garden. They stood at the stone pillars and iron gates and she told him about the village up the road, beyond the bridge; about how her father loved the people here.

Max made a face and a curl escaped from behind his ear and blew across his nose. "Yeah, well. I suppose you'd have to, to put up with some of the weirdos about."

The grass was damp and mossy underfoot as they walked round the side of the house to the back. The remaining kitten, bigger now but still as playful, came with them, pouncing on leaves, wrestling grass, and murdering twigs. It galloped across the lawn and hurled itself onto the back fence, running along the top rail and falling off on the other side in a twirl of tail and paws.

Max looked across the field, one hand in his pocket and the other round Jenna's waist. The trailing hems of his frayed jeans were wet.

"What're those?"

"Old buildings from the war."

Max swung her round and made for the back door. "I'm surprised they haven't knocked them down and built houses. It's a good site."

Next time Jenna talked to her mother on the phone, Cora said absolutely nothing about Max. They didn't approve. She was sure that her father had told Cora not to say so, so Cora said nothing instead. It was just as eloquent.

Next time Luke stayed over at Jenna's house in Belfast, he threw himself down on the sofa with a take-away. He ripped a chunk of batttered fish with his alabaster teeth and said between bulging cheeks, " So are you still seeing Max?"

"I am. This place is going to reek of chips for days. And don't drip mayo on my cushion."

Luke checked round his knees, scooped up a drip and licked

his finger. "He's not your type."

"Nobody's my type, according to you."

"Well, the choice so far hasn't been massive. Adam the aardvark or Max the moron."

"Max is not a moron."

Luke swallowed and burped. "Speaking of the aardvark, he's gone to England, apparently. Did you know that?"

"Gone for good?"

"Seems so. Work or something."

Jenna turned this over for a minute. She found she didn't mind. In fact, try as she might, she found she didn't care at all. Then a thought jabbed sharply. "Paul's not going back, is he?"

Luke nibbled a chip into his mouth like a rabbit with a blade of grass. "Not that he's told me." He looked at his sister from under his brows. "But then, he doesn't tell me much. He only told me about Adam because I asked." After a pause, he said, "You haven't seen Paul lately then?"

She gave a careless shake of the head. "Not for weeks."

Luke chewed noisily and thought. It seemed to lead him back to Max. "Seriously, why are you with Max? Are you on the rebound from ..." he waved a chip in the air "... oh, Adam, I suppose?"

"No, I'm not. Max is just a normal guy. He's easy to get on with. He's ..." she shrugged "... normal."

"The aardvark was normal. It's another word for boring. You don't 'do' normal, Jay."

"So you do, I suppose?"

He emptied the last chip into his palm. "Shit, no. I'm as odd as a bunion on a bee's bum."

Luke always ended up making her smile, even when she could throttle him.

"So where are you two going tomorrow?"

"Don't know yet." He picked delicately at a piece of lettuce that had caught on his pullover and examined it. "I don't think

Paul's looking after himself right."

"Oh? Why?"

He made a face. "Dunno. He looks a bit ..." he searched for the right word "... stressed."

"He has a wife to notice things like that."

Luke held out a hand and rocked it from side to side. "Hm. Well. I'm not sure about that."

All Jenna's attention was on him now. "What do you mean?"

"Just some things he does. Like he says he's run out of bread and stops at a shop. Or last time we were a bit late back. He didn't ring home to say he'd be late or anything." He stretched out his legs and leaned back. "And he keeps taking naps. He mustn't be sleeping well at night."

"Naps?"

"Yeah. We'll stop to eat some sandwiches or something and next thing you know ..." he clicked his fingers "... he's asleep. Head against the car window." He sagged sideways, demonstrating.

"So long as he doesn't fall asleep when he's driving!"

Luke stood up and crumpled the wrapper into a ball. He lifted one knee and flicked the wrapper neatly under it, straight into the wastebasket. "Shit no. I talk too much for that. I'll be back tonight, by the way. I've someone to see tomorrow." He turned to the door. "Is there water for a shower? Ta."

"Leave some toothpaste in the tube this time!" she called as he sprinted up the stairs three at a time, humming 'Glory, glory, hallelujah'. The smell of chips swirled round the hall in his wake.

In the small hours of the morning she woke, unsettled. She sat up and switched on her bedside light. Paul wasn't looking after himself. Dianne had probably gone. Was he not eating properly? Was he not sleeping? She hugged the teddy bear and rubbed her cheek on the black wool of the hat. The missing of him descended heavy on her like a shroud. She was hurting more inside her cage than if she had flown free and risked a storm of bullets. *I care about him*, she whispered to the bear. *I really do. My God, it even hurts if I think he's hungry.*

She rocked a little. Faintly, the sound of a snore came from Luke's room across the landing.

CHAPTER TWENTY-FIVE

NEXT MORNING, JENNA found Luke's cereal bowl and mug dropped in the sink as usual. She ladled marmalade onto a piece of toast and thought about going home to see her mother and father. Max had gone home to see his folks this weekend. Or maybe she should head up to the university to see if there was anyone about to have lunch with.

It was no use; she had the concentration of a gnat. She pulled out the ironing board and rammed the iron across a few t-shirts and tops. Now she was feeling cross. Lack of sufficient sleep was fouling her mood. Luke was with Paul. Again. She slammed the iron across a white shirt and ironed a razor sharp crease right across the back. She rumpled it into a ball and threw it back in the basket. Not once, not *once* had he asked for her. Luke would tell her if he had. She put her hands on her hips and addressed the iron: "This cannot go on!"

Outside. She had to get outside. She shrugged into her cream coat as she slammed the door behind her. It was a crisp morning and March was going to go out like a lamb. The road at the top of her street was loud with Saturday morning traffic as she turned the corner past the church. Piles of apples and oranges and lettuce were arranged on sloping pallets outside the greengrocers. Smells from the home bakery made her turn her head briefly.

She loved the florists. She could never afford to buy anything, but lingered if there was time before the bus came in the mornings. This morning, restless discontent drove her on and on and on, hardly knowing where she was going. Coming down on her hard was disgust at herself and all that she was allowing to suffocate her. For that's what it was doing. What was it Paul had said? Want more for yourself. Reach for the moon and the stars and the sun. Well then, Mr Shepherd, point taken. I will do just that. And I'll do it without you. If you can shut me out, forget me so completely, then I'll erase you from my memory. I have to. *I have to.*

She walked on again, considering her options. She didn't want to be at university still. She had never wanted to stay on for another year. She ducked round two elderly women, obviously sisters, strolling along in the middle of the pavement, shopping bags hung from their bent elbows. Her parents were going to sell the house. She couldn't keep it herself without a job. They expected her to go back to the manse to live if she hadn't got a job by the time she graduated. She clenched her fist. Damned if I'm going to do that!

It came to her as she stood at the edge of the street, waiting for a gap in the traffic. A simple course was open to her. By the time she had dodged across to the other side, she had made up her mind.

Luke was going to university in Scotland. She would go to Scotland too.

What was there here? There were very few jobs. Her head was up as she pushed her hands into her pockets and strode on. That was it. She would go to Scotland and make a fresh start. Adam and then weeks of Max had shown her that she did not crave company like theirs. Max was OK. He was well-meaning and easy to be with. But ... Luke was right. She didn't do normal. Not any more. If that made her odd, then the world would have to cope.

It was time to wash Paul Shepherd from her brain. He wasn't

safe. There was something so intense about him he was fright and delight all in one. Despite all he had said that last day, despite putting his arms round her and telling her he needed her, he had taken himself out of her life completely. She stopped at a furniture shop, her thoughts taking over and stopping her feet. How could he do that, specially if Dianne had left him? Fleetingly she considered ringing his phone. She would hear the lovely golds and silvers of that voice again. Her hand came up to the shop window, fingers splayed. She had never known anyone like him in all her life and with certainty she knew she never would again. Her fingers left their imprint on the glass. He had told her to go away and had vanished from her. She hadn't meant it to be like that. But hell would freeze before she asked him why.

She spun away, bumping into a huge man with a tiny terrier on a lead. The decision was made. She would leave for Scotland when her course was finished. Inside her was a need to be busy, to feel that she was using her life, not just living it. If nothing else, the vanished Paul Shepherd had given her the confidence to do something about it. Her lip curled. Thank you for that, Mr Smart-guy. But for nothing else. As of now, you've gone, out of my head, out of my sleep. All of you has to go. I'll do this alone. So be it.

She was on her way back, nearly at the church on the corner of her street, when real rebellion kicked in. Why wait till the summer? Why don't I chuck it all in and leave as soon as I can? I need to go away. Far, far away from here. Her head was light with excitement as she hopped up the two steps to her door and held out her key. She would talk to Luke before he left in the morning.

~

She was in a grand house, looking for something, but every time she thought she had found it, there was a tiny puff of smoke and it had gone again. In the dream it didn't seem strange that she didn't know what she was looking for. She knew it was there, if only ... There was a ringing sound. Surely there was someone in this mansion who would answer the phone. The sound grew louder and she shouted for someone to pick it up. The ringing became so insistent that she was going to have to answer it herself. Her feet hit the sheepskin mat before she realised she was dreaming and the phone was her own, shrilling at the bottom of the stairs. She peered at the clock. Six o'clock! Who the hell was ringing at this hour? No doubt Luke was sound asleep. When he was a small child, he had slept through a three hundred pound bomb exploding in the village. A phone wouldn't even make him scratch his nose. She hadn't heard him come in last night, but then she rarely did when he was staying over. She turned on the light and made for the stairs.

It was her father. Alarm spread to her toes, colder than the cold floor. "What is it, Dad? What's wrong?"

His voice was strained. "I've some bad news. It's Luke."

Jenna's mouth went dry. "Luke? But he's here. He's staying over ..."

"I'm at the hospital, Jenna." He stopped and she heard him take a deep breath. "Luke was attacked last night. He was found in an alley. He's not too good."

Tears started to her eyes and she pushed her knuckles into her mouth. "Oh Dad!"

Donald seemed to gain strength at the sound of her sob. Later Jenna would remember and think it was so like him. His own distress lessened when he had to deal with the distress of another. "Can you be ready in a few minutes? I think you should come. I'll call for you. Your mum'll stay here." He swallowed. "Luke's in theatre."

Jenna stumbled up the stairs. Pointlessly she pushed open the door of Luke's room. The quilt on the bed was awry because he never straightened it, but this night he had never arrived. She dressed, shaking from head to foot. "I think you should come," her father had said. It was bad.

~

She was never, ever going to forget this car journey. Never, ever. The streets in the early morning were waking with the milkmen, the first buses, the newspaper vans. Workmen walked the footpaths with their lunches in tins under their arms. It was all so normal and yet her father was explaining to her that Luke was critically injured. The hospital contacted them by looking for the entry for 'Home' on his mobile phone. His parents had seen him only briefly when they arrived because a rib had punctured one of his lungs and he was rushed to theatre.

A security man on his way home had seen Luke's leg protruding from an alley only three streets from Jenna's house. He must have lain there for hours. Donald glanced at Jenna as he drove in the gates of the hospital. "I'm sorry, love. I have to tell you. You need to know, so you won't be ... shocked when you see him."

Jenna's elbow rested on the car door, her head dropped onto her hand and her eyes closed. "Then tell me ..." she looked up "... is he ... in danger?"

Donald swung the car into a space near the A & E entrance. He pulled the brake and switched off the engine. His keys dropped into his hand and his fingers closed tightly over them. Jenna had never heard her father's voice break before. "I believe so," he said, hoarse.

Her head went back, her eyes tight with tears and her skin crawling with shock and fear. "Oh, poor Mum!"

Cora was sitting on a black metal chair in the corridor. All colour was gone from her face and she looked cold, as if it were icy in here instead of stuffy and antiseptic. She clutched her handbag on her knee and her feet were planted flat in front of her. Her tan raincoat was strained a little round her full figure.

She had put on a little weight recently. Jenna bent to kiss her and Cora's lip trembled but she did not cry.

"No word yet," she said, her voice clipped and high. They sat in a row, silent, and waited. Then they were in a room with a doctor, an older man with a kind face and receding grey hair. He wasn't wearing a white coat. He was saying that they had successfully released air from Luke's chest cavity, leaking from his punctured lung. However, he was still sedated and probably would not regain consciousness for some time. They would have to wait and see. He had probably been the victim of a random attack, and there had been more than one attacker. They could tell. And they had probably used iron bars. They could tell that too. They had seen it before.

But Luke's not a statistic, Jenna wanted to cry. This is Luke! This has never happened before, not in the history of the world. Not to Luke; not to us!

She didn't like the way the doctor was talking. He was too sombre, too considerate, too gentle with them. This was the way people talked to relatives when things were really, really bad.

She licked her dry lips and reached for her mother's hand. "Exactly what has happened to him?" she asked.

The doctor folded his hands and spoke the list for her. "He has had one leg broken – the tibia; the knee is also fractured. Three ribs are broken and his lung is punctured." Jenna held on to her mother's hand more tightly. "Two of his fingers are broken. He has multiple contusions all over his body. His nose is broken and there are injuries to the mouth area." The doctor paused and shuffled a notepad on the desk before continuing. "He was beaten badly around the head. His fingers were probably broken as he tried to protect his head." The doctor slumped back and Jenna realised he was upset himself. In a perverse way, this gave her hope. He will do his best for Luke. "We have done a brain scan. We may need to do more. The next twenty-four hours are critical."

Her father spoke, his voice steady, surprisingly normal. "You think he may have injury to his brain?"

"We have to wait and see, I'm afraid." He stood up. He had more patients. "The nurse will come and take you to him when he's settled."

Later, much later, they sat round a bed and in it, they were told, was Luke. There seemed to be wires and drips everywhere. The quiet noise of the respirator and the constant beep of the heart monitor became the underlay of a nightmare. His head had been shaved and there were staples in a long curved line above his left ear. His nose was swollen and black beneath the oxygen mask. His left leg was bandaged and had large metal bolts fixed onto it. His chest was strapped. A nurse was constantly reading dials, checking drips, making notes. She left the room only rarely.

Jenna glanced at her father. His eyes were closed and she knew he was praying. Her mother had her eyes fixed on Luke's face. Every muscle in her body seemed to be rigid. Her eyes were too bright for the pallor of her skin.

"Mum?"

"What?"

At least she responded. "Would you like some tea? There's a machine down the corridor."

Cora just shook her head and continued to watch her son as if to move her gaze were to take away his life. Then she said slowly, "His teeth, Jenna. I think he's lost some of his lovely teeth."

Jenna had already taken that in somewhere amongst the jumble of dread. That her mother could reach into the tangle of bandages and broken bones, bruises and pain and pull out the fact that Luke had lost some teeth, was frightening in its simplicity. Lots of people broke bones. People broke ribs. People got beaten up. But Luke, Luke had lovely teeth and they had been smashed. "Leave some toothpaste in the tube this time!" Jenna had called up the stairs after him. They were the last words she had said to him.

The nurse checked the monitor and then gently patted his hand. "He's a strong lad," she said softly.

"Will he be all right?"

The nurse looked at Jenna and then back at Luke. "It'll take time. We'll have to wait and see."

Wait and see. Wait and see. This phrase was going to be spoken many times, like a chorus in a play.

Donald stood and put his hand on Cora's shoulder. "I'll be back in a minute," he said gently and kissed her on the gray cheek. New lines were chiselled on her face.

Jenna looked at her father, alarmed, as if it was somehow not right to leave the room. "Where are you going?"

He looked back from the doorway. "It's Sunday. I'll have to get someone to cover the services for me."

It pulled Jenna back into reality. It was Sunday. There was a name for today. She pushed herself up from the black vinyl seat of the hospital stool. "I'll do it, Dad. You stay here. Will I ring Ian?" Ian was the senior steward in the church.

Her father pulled out a pocket book and gave it to her. "Yes, please. His number's in here." He waved a hand vaguely. "Tell him ... ah ... tell him what's happened and ..."

"And you'll be in touch. Yes, Dad."

Jenna found a corner by the public phones and felt herself becoming the minister's daughter again. She slipped effortlessly into the role while she contacted not only the church steward but her mother's closest friend in the women's group as well. She heard herself calmly repeating the words: "Yes, a shock, yes. We'll have to wait and see. Wait and see."

It occurred to her that there were others who should know what had happened to Luke. His friend Beezer. What was his real name? She had never heard Luke call him anything else. She went back to the room where Luke was and the nurse looked in the bedside table and found his phone, the same one on which the nurses had found his home number earlier as they cut his blood-soaked clothes from his body. Jenna went out again and thumbed through to the phone book. Thank God, there was a number for Beezer.

The call was answered on the second ring. "Hiya, muppet!" said a young and lively voice. Jenna realised she had phoned him on Luke's phone.

"No, it's Jenna, Luke's sister." There was total silence at the other end while Jenna told him. She talked again about waiting and seeing, about promising to contact him as soon as he could come to see Luke. Beezer's voice broke on curses and threats to disembowel the thugs who had done this. "You and me both, Beezer," she said. In truth, they would probably never be caught. They would sleep off an alcoholic haze and have a laugh about it tomorrow. If they even remembered what they'd done.

Then she rang Max. "God, that's terrible, Jen. I'm really sorry. Probably not see you this week then?"

"Probably not, no." She wasn't even angry.

She went back and sat on the black vinyl stool again, and watched her brother, her gawky, daft, adorable brother fighting for his life with every sigh of the machine by the bed. Her father was closer to her mother now, his hand on hers where it lay motionless on her lap. He glanced up and gave a quick smile of thanks to Jenna.

"All sorted," she said. Her mother was too quiet. She was always talking, always organising, always knowing what to do and who should do it. Now she was in a shell, remote and frozen, rigid in her focus on her son.

A bleakness built in Jenna, layer on layer, as time lumbered on. This was a turning point for all of them; one of those hairpin bends of life. Everything was in the shadow of 'wait and see'. Luke wasn't moving. He lay, odd, Luke but not Luke. Curiously his brow was untouched, crossed only by a thin white bandage at one side above his right eye where there was a small but deep cut. She leaned forward. "Hey, LW. Hang in there. Outer Mongolia's waiting."

Suddenly she had to leave. She fled out the door and down the corridor. In the hospital foyer no-one paid any attention to her. A man was asking where the lifts were. An orderly pushed an old wizened woman in a wheelchair in the direction of the X-Ray department. A cleaner in a pink apron pushed a floor-polisher, flicking the lead behind her. Two young women stood hugging clipboards with their crossed arms as they chatted and broke into laughter.

Jenna looked around. None of these people know. It's just Sunday. It's just another Sunday. Don't they know this day has never happened before? Not in the history of the whole world. She went through the double doors and out into the open air. The car park was full and visitors were weaving across, carrying flowers and fruit and bottles of Lucozade. It was afternoon and it was raining gently. The cold had lifted and a damp warmth was edging into the day.

Jenna felt old. She thought of her mother, frozen in shock. Her father, torn between duty to others and love for his son. She didn't think he had ever faced such a choice before. She sat on a low wall and looked back at the jumble of hospital buildings. Just a few bricks, just a few small spaces separate tragedy from normality, just as only moments separate now from then. From what seemed like long, long ago, she heard Paul's voice. "The problem is often the key," he had said.

She could not do this alone; not this. She would turn the key. She drew her phone from her pocket and dialled his number.

He wasn't going to answer it – he really wasn't going to answer it! In disbelief, she heard a polite female voice asking her to please leave a message. Reason circled just in time. Maybe he was in the middle of an important assignment. Her voice was calm as she described what had happened. Yet it was a strain, wanting to hear him and not hearing him; feeling the niggling wonder if he saw who was ringing and chose not to answer. Her voice rose. "Where did you leave him, Paul? Where did you leave him last night? Why could you not drop him off at my door? Is that too difficult? Can you not even drive down my *street*?" She choked, crying and shouting at the same time, careless of the startled faces turning towards her. "And now he might *die!* Luke might *die!*"

She ended the call and doubled over, her arms crossed tight on her stomach and her eyes squeezed shut on a lake of tears.

CHAPTER TWENTY-SIX

HE CAME, SILENT, in the middle of the night.

Exhaustion had driven Jenna to the dim and empty patients' day room. She had curled herself into a low brown chair and lay back awkwardly, hunched between the wooden arms. She came out of a fitful doze and raised her head, grimacing at the pain in her neck. Then the physical pain from cramped muscles was sucked away by the crippling knowledge of where she was and why. She was rubbing the back of her neck when she saw him. He was seated opposite her, his black coat in the half-light defining his dark shape. His hands rested on the arms of the chair and his eyes were steady on her.

Slowly she lowered her feet to the ground. He didn't move a muscle. Was it really him or was she still dreaming? The strain of fear and fatigue crackled through her body like forked lightening. As if calling to a chimera she reached out and poured all her fear into a cry. "I need you, Paul!"

He gripped the arms of the chair and pulled himself forwards. "That was always enough for me," he whispered. He held out his arms. "Come here."

She went to him like a child and he cradled her across his lap and into himself and she was sinking, falling, spiralling into a haven of consolation. Her arms round his neck, his hand holding her head cuddled firm against his shoulder told her he was no chimera; he had really come to her when she needed him. She was beyond tears and he seemed to know that, just letting her clamp onto him and be still. The outdoor misty scent of him was filling her nostrils; the feel of him, solid around her, was like a drink in the desert. Her voice was muffled against his coat.

"Were you in a forest somewhere?"

"Up a mountain. I'd left my phone in the car." She did not know how long it was until he spoke again. "I left him at his girlfriend's house, Jenna. About five o'clock. He asked me to."

She didn't want to move as she pondered this new information.

"There was a girl here earlier. Small girl. Dad spoke to her. She was upset that they wouldn't let her see Luke. I think she was called Naomi."

His jaw brushed her hair as he nodded. "That's the name."

"Luke must have been walking back to my house when ..."

Paul tensed and withdrew from her a little. "How is he now?"

Jenna detached herself and let reality flood back, but it came with less force, as if now there was a defence against its power. She felt calmer, more able to think clearly. Since the moment Paul had banished her with harsh words there had been desolation at her core. She had invited those words. But then she discovered that life was just a silly scramble of days without this man, a landscape without a map, a journey without a destination.

When she let go of him, he stood also, not touching her now, and that was all right. He was here and there was still much to deal with.

"The same. There was a scare earlier when they took him away for another brain scan. They're afraid of bleeding on the brain." Her voice was steady, communicating facts.

"Your parents?"

"What do you think? Distraught. Mum's a bit of a worry. She's not saying much."

"I want to see him."

Only Paul would put it like that. Someone else would ask if it would be possible to see him.

"I think it's very restricted ..."

His hand flicked impatiently. "I want to see him."

Jenna went into the room where Luke lay and bent to her parents in turn, planting a small kiss on each of their taut cheeks. Luke's face was still, so still behind the tubes and the bandages and the bruises, a motionless shell, devoid of the light brightness which made him Luke, a body dependant on sighing and beeping machines and on the invisible will of those who loved him.

"Mum, Dad, you remember Paul? The photographer? The one who was teaching Luke? He was with him yesterday?" Her father nodded. Her mother looked round at her but said nothing. "He's here and he'd like to see Luke."

Her father frowned. "I'm not sure ..."

Jenna looked up and saw Paul already in the doorway. What obstacles could he not find a way past? One hand gripped the edge of the door; his gaze was fixed on Luke. Then he walked into the room without hesitation, stopping at the opposite side of the bed. With the most gentle of touches, he reached out his hand and, with the back of his curled fingers, touched Luke's forehead. He held his fingers there. Jenna saw his lips move and even in the extremity that was in the night, she thrilled to see him there.

Paul looked across at her parents and his eyes lingered on her mother. To Jenna's surprise, he came round the end of the bed and put a hand on each of their shoulders.

"You're giving him all you can," he said.

Cora put a hand to her eyes and her shoulders jerked as a sob tore through her throat. Paul would never cease to surprise Jenna. He bent down and his voice was so gentle as he spoke in her mother's ear. "Cora. It's bad and it's OK to cry."

Not only did he call her by her name, but the touch of his hand on her arm brought her to her feet and then she was weeping on his shoulder in a storm of agony. He held her while her whole body shook with pain and wept out the last day of rigid fear until she was drained and empty. Over her head, Paul spoke to Jenna.

"Go and get her some tea." He ducked his head to look at Cora's face. "And some tissues," he added.

Donald, watching, smiled weakly. "You're a loss to the ministry, Paul. You have a sure touch."

~

Alone in a corridor somewhere in the hospital, Paul stopped walking. His knees felt weak and he put his hands flat against the wall below two huge murals of red poppies. He dropped his head so that his brow rested against the wall between his hands.

"Me for him," he whispered. Wishing didn't cut it this time. His words were more desperate, deeper, hacked out from a childhood long gone when he believed in more than wishing. He pressed his head harder against the wall. "Me for Luke," he whispered again. "Let him live and I'll stop fighting." He balled his hands into fists and brought them to his temples. "Let him live and let her forget me..." He hit the wall, his mind white hot. "... even if I can't forget her."

~

They were days lifted out of time after that. Early on Monday morning, thirty-six hours after the attack, Luke was out of immediate danger and Paul drove Donald and Cora home. It was a great relief to Jenna for she was worried about either of them driving when they were so tired. They left their car at the hospital. There were plenty of friends who could drive them back later.

Jenna waited at Luke's side although she was almost incoherent with tiredness. Carefully she put her head down on the pillow beside his. His scalp was bruised and swollen, naked without its spikes of brown hair.

"Come on, LW," she whispered in his ear. "I'm the one supposed to get the nose job, not you." She touched his arm and the strangeness of his immobility frightened her. "I suppose you can choose what nose you'd like now. They could give you a Roman nose." Her mouth wobbled into a weak smile. "How about that?"

She started to cry and in an extremity of fatigue, between one sob and the next, she fell asleep slumped on the side of the bed. Then she was being gathered up, and Paul was saying he was going to take her home. Something about the taxi service being free for its next passenger. Her tears began again as if she had not slept between them.

She was in his car, her nose stuffed, her eyes swollen, her head a globe of throbbing pain and her neck hardly capable of holding it. She must have given Paul her key because she was climbing into bed – how had she got there? And wasn't it still daytime? – and Paul was pulling the clothes over her and she was drowning in sleep. On the edge of oblivion, she heard him say he would be back in the evening. She pulled her arm from under the clothes and held it out, pleading. "Don't go."

His answer didn't come at once and then she felt his hand grip hers, firm and warm. "OK. I'll go and say hi to your sofa again." Her arm was tucked back under the cover. She thought she felt a hand on her head, and then she was dreaming, dreaming that lips touched her temple and lingered there.

Luke stayed with them. The week became a choreography of worry and hope. People came and went: the headmaster of his school, Naomi, Beezer. Beezer was pale and furious. His fists were clenched as he spoke to Luke above the ceaseless beeping of the monitor. "Listen muppet, you come round. Exams soon and you've a hell of a lot of catching up to do." He rubbed his nose with the back of his hand. "We'll find those guys. We'll find them and they'll be pouring them into buckets when we've finished with them."

His voice broke and he gave Luke's shoulder a little shake. The nurse put her hand on his arm in warning. "Easy, easy! He's a bit fragile, remember!"

Luke lids stayed shut above the bruise that was the centre of his face and his chest rose and fell to the rhythm of the ventilator.

After that first awful time, Paul did not stay at Jenna's house again. Nevertheless, he was often with her. She never had to find her own way to the hospital for he called for her every day and every evening he left her at her door. They shared a great anxiety about Luke. Plainly Paul had grown fond of him, but his concern was quite different to Jenna's in its manifestation. He rarely spoke of it whereas Jenna talked incessantly – about the treatment, the signs for good or bad, pulling apart every word the doctors said. Sometimes, Jenna would catch Paul looking away at something only he could see and his expression was drawn, his eyes pained.

Cora brought her embroidery to the bedside and her needle flew through the canvas stretched across its frame. It was a release for her energy. Paul asked to see it one day and she handed it to him. He ran his fingers over the bright colours of a bird of paradise. He handed it back. "It's beautiful."

"Thank you, Patrick. It's a cushion cover," she said. "Does your wife sew or anything?"

"No, she doesn't."

On Thursday afternoon, Jenna found herself in the hospital canteen with Paul's mother. She was surprised to discover that Hazel had met Luke.

"Yes, once. Paul had been giving him lessons in taking pictures of birds. I don't know all the technicalities of it, but they talked about water reflections and panning and shutter speeds and focal length and things like that. So they were in the park near me and

Paul popped in to see me before they left the town." She smiled. "He's good like that."

They were sitting at a long table by a window which gave a view of more walls and windows and wards. The room was filled with noise and clatter, off duty staff and waiting relatives. Paul had dropped his mother at the door of the hospital and disappeared again. Jenna had no idea where he was. Maybe up another mountain. After Hazel saw Luke and spoke to Cora and Donald, Jenna brought her to find a cup of tea. It was difficult to know what to say for they had not met since Adam and she had parted. But Hazel was direct and guileless.

"Paul enjoyed Luke's company. Odd because he's such a loner usually."

"Luke can be great company when he's in the mood. He wants to be a photographer himself now."

"Well, he could be. According to Paul, he has real talent. And Paul's quite a perfectionist. He told me Luke had a natural flair for composition, for spotting the great shot."

A glow of warmth spread in Jenna just to talk about Luke. "Luke never said much, but I know he loved it."

"I think Paul thinks of Luke almost as a son, you know."

Surprised, Jenna's eyebrows rose. "A son?"

"Almost. He doesn't say very much, but it's as if he wants to pass on his craft to Luke. He's found an apprentice." She laughed. "Imagine – Paul the patient teacher! How odd!"

Odd indeed. 'Patient' was not a word Jenna would have attached to Paul, not to that restless bundle of fizzing energy.

Hazel propped her elbows on the table and cradled her cup at her chin.

"You've changed your hair. It's a pity it didn't work out with Adam. Did you know he's gone to England?"

"Yes, I did."

Hazel put her cup down carefully. "Do you mind?"

"No. Although I'm sure you miss him."

"Yes, I do. But I've got Paul back and, between you and me ..." she leaned over the table and lowered her voice "... he's my favourite."

Jenna decided to be just as direct. "They're very different. But then they're not full brothers."

Hazel had turned to look at two junior nurses who were pulling out chairs at the table next to them. Her head swung round, her eyes wide. "Who told you that?"

"Paul did."

Had she made a mistake in saying that? Hazel was quiet for a minute, puzzlement between her brows.

"Paul told you that?"

"Yes."

Hazel sat back and gazed at Jenna. "Paul knew Luke very well. I didn't know he knew you even better." Heat began to creep across Jenna's cheeks. She could think of nothing to say. Finally, Hazel spoke again. "Yes, Paul's father was ..." she waved a hand "...I suppose they call it 'the love of my life'. He was in a dangerous occupation. Any day, he could be blown to pieces. So we didn't wait for legal niceties, I conceived Paul, and then I lost his father. There wasn't much of him left to bury."

Jenna looked down at her carton of juice and squeezed it. "I'm sorry," was all she could think of to say.

"At that time, there were people who thought I'd been a slut. Including my father! But I was so glad we'd taken what we could while we could. People don't always, and they lose what they might have had." She stopped, and Jenna stilled as the words cut deep because they came from someone who knew and because they came from Paul's mother. "People's opinion could go to hell! And Paul is so like his father."

Jenna gave a quick smile. "Then I can understand why you fell for him. And I think Paul's a bit like you as well."

Hazel studied her thoughtfully. "Funny. He never mentions you."

"Why would he?"

"Did you know Dianne has gone back to London? Weeks ago."

"No."

"I don't think she'll be back. They were never suited." She sighed. "You probably wouldn't notice, but he's not wearing his wedding ring any more."

"Really?"

"I asked him about it once but he just said it had fallen into the sea!" She laughed at the silliness of it. "It's too bad, but I don't think anyone could live with Paul for very long, least of all a Sloanie from London." She stood and reached for her coat on the back of her chair. "No, don't get up. Stay and take some time to yourself. You're worn out."

Jenna smiled up at her. "Thanks for coming. They're going to try reducing the sedation to see if Luke comes round."

Hazel leaned down and put her hand on Jenna's. "I'll be praying." She turned to go and then paused to look back. "I wish Paul could have found someone like you instead. You're a nice girl."

After she had gone, Jenna sat and looked down at the table, the drink carton crumpled between her fingers. *Yeah. A nice girl called Missy.*

~

A week after Luke was attacked, he moved his fingers. Then he moved his leg – the one that wasn't broken. The tubes were removed and he began to cough. Jenna and Cora were at his side when the dark lines of his lashes flickered and rose. His eyes were unfocused at first and then they moved round the room until they snagged on his mother. Cora leaned over him, the lines on her face furrowed deeper as the week had passed by.

Luke coughed again and then his voice came, weak and gravel hoarse. "Shit, Mum." His body shook as his words seared through his throat. "What the bloody hell happened?"

Cora's hand flew to her mouth, her eyes filling with tears. "Hello, my darling. You're in hospital. You were attacked in the street." She caressed his head. "But you're OK now."

All Jenna's bones felt like jelly. She gasped for air, relief flattening her lungs. Leaning over him, opposite her mother, she breathed, "Hey LW. Welcome back."

Luke's eyes swivelled to her and he winced as more pain breached his defences. "Throat," he forced out, and then coughed again.

"You've had a tube down your throat for a while. It'll get better." Telling him what else had happened to him could wait.

"Where's Dad?"

Cora answered. "It's Sunday. He's taking the services today."

Slowly, Luke drifted away from them again, but this time his sleep was deep and natural. A doctor came and checked him, looked at his notes, pulled back his lids and shone a light into his eyes. Then he turned to Jenna and her mother and smiled broadly. "I think he's made it," he said.

When she could think straight again, Jenna looked at her watch. It was lunchtime. Her father would have a service in an old people's home this afternoon and then the evening service in his own church. He was probably at home now. She went out to the car park and phoned him.

"Great news, Dad! Luke came round and he seems OK."

Donald gave one shuddering breath before he spoke. "Thank God!"

"I think you should come to see him now."

"I'd like to, but I can't ..."

Jenna felt anger gathering in her. She had never been angry at her father before. "Why can't you?"

"Because I've commitments ..."

Jenna kept her voice level. "You've no greater commitment right now, Dad. Luke asked for you; he needs you and Mum needs you."

"Jenna, I'll go straight there from the church ..."

The tautness in her snapped. "Bloody hell, Dad! Stop being a minister and be a father for once!"

She snapped the phone shut and flopped down onto the wall round the car park. A voice behind her made her jump.

"Shouting into phones is a bad habit."

Her head swung round. "Will you stop sneaking up on me!" Paul sat down on the wall beside her and the news took over and bubbled out of her. "Luke's come round, Paul! He's come round! He spoke to us. He said 'shit'. He's going to be OK!"

Paul's eyes widened momentarily. Then his body folded over his knees and he dropped his brow onto his crossed arms. Jenna watched him, surprised at the strength of his relief. When he didn't straighten, she put an arm tentatively across his back. She felt the ridge of his spine, the taut muscles beneath his coat. Her hand strayed to his head, bowed still, motionless. Gently she placed her palm on his hair. As if stung, he jerked upright suddenly and she snatched her hand away.

He let out a long breath. "That's great," he said. "That's just great. Go, Luke!" He ran his hand down the back of his head and closed his eyes again. "The world's too poor to lose people like Luke."

She got to her feet. "Come on. I'll buy you a Coke to celebrate."

He didn't reply at once, looking up at her with an expression she couldn't interpret.

"Come on," she urged.

Finally he stood up. "OK. A last one then."

She didn't know what he meant but was too happy to puzzle over it. For a change they left the hospital complex and found a coffee shop some distance down the road outside. They sat in a corner, where Paul lifted a can of Coke to his mouth and drank deeply. Jenna felt light and happy. She watched his Adam's apple working and laughed.

"You do realise the gas is going to come down your nose very painfully in a minute."

He slammed the can onto the table with satisfaction. "That's the best bit!"

Jenna stirred her milkshake with the straw. The fur edges of the cuffs of her coat brushed the table as she took a long sip. Mouth pursed round the straw, she looked up to find him watching her. A smile was just slipping from his lips as if he hadn't meant to smile. The beautiful curves of his mouth never ceased to fascinate her. For a full minute, she examined every feature of his face – his lashes, the blue of his eyes, the tousled line of his hair. Always, her gaze slipped back to his mouth, to the corner that nudged slightly higher and made a dimple in his cheek. Then he hiccuped and screwed up his face, his nose creasing.

She sat back and laughed aloud. "Told you it would hurt!" She became serious again, almost shy. "You've been great this week. Thanks."

"You don't need me any more now, if Luke's going to be OK."

Alarm filled her. "Yes, I do!"

He seemed to change the subject. "When I saw you on the phone, you were saying that Luke and your mother needed your dad. Don't *you* need him?"

She thought about that. "No." She spoke slowly. "I suppose I don't."

"But you love him."

"Of course."

"Yes," he said. "Those are the people you can leave. The people that you love *and* need are the ones who really screw up your life."

Her eyes widened at the bitterness in his voice. She bit her lip and looked down at the table. "Why didn't you tell me Dianne had left you?"

His lip curled. "Because I'm still a married man, Saint Jenna."

He was hurting her, unexpectedly hurting her as if, now that the strain of the past week was lifting, he was reverting to the stranger that he had become before. It was unbearable.

"But you'll get a divorce?"

He shrugged. "I don't know. I don't care."

"You don't care?"

He pushed his chair back abruptly. "As I said once before, you're a big girl now. You can find your own way home."

Stunned by his sudden change of mood, she watched in disbelief as he walked past the tables and out the door. Then heads turned as she scrambled to her feet and ran after him. He was nearly at the next corner, his hands deep in his pockets and his stride long and quick.

When she was close enough she called, "Paul! Come back." She ignored the passers-by who turned, amused at this girl in a furry coat running after a man in the street. She caught up and pulled his arm. Unlike that day on Rossnowlagh beach, he didn't stop but almost dragged her along. "Stop, Paul. I do still need you!"

She stumbled as he whirled round. "It's too late, Jenna! It was always going to be too late!"

She was crying now. "It's not, it's not!"

He gripped her shoulder and bit out the words. "You walked away from me. Well, this is what it feels like."

Then he was gone, out of her life again. If he had slapped her she would not have recoiled more. Tears streamed down her face.

The shapeshifter had taken many forms but none as ugly as this. A woman with a baby in a pushchair stopped and asked her if she was all right. She nodded and turned away. She searched for a tissue to blow her nose and then ran all the way back to the hospital.

CHAPTER TWENTY-SEVEN

EVERYTHING ABOUT HIM felt heavy.

The gear stick was moving though treacle, the steering wheel was fighting his grip, the pedals were stiff under his feet.

But guilt was like granite inside him. With great care Paul nosed the car through a gap in the Sunday afternoon traffic and into his own street. No point in having a wrestle with insurance companies now. His mouth twisted at the thought. Cars were parked along one side of the street, narrowing it. A dog trotted across in front of him; a man came out of a gateway, two children skipping round him like puppies.

His temper was getting worse. He was going to have to watch that. The week had cut canyons in his resolve deeper than he had foreseen; his mind had become more fragile, his tongue unleashed was a stinging whip. Jenna had been right to leave him, to walk away. She just didn't know how right she was. She also didn't know just what miracles she had worked in him.

As he approached his own gateway Paul gathered strength into his left arm and ripped down the gears, his movements jerky. Dianne had often called him selfish. She wasn't the only one to call him that. But Jenna was the first person who had made him care that it was true. She was the first person ever to have made him vulnerable as a man. The day his step-father had yelled at him to go to England was the day he had resolved to give up, to harden any soft centre which still remained, to want nothing from anyone and to live entirely within his own skin. Dianne had been an arrogant self-indulgence, a hostage to his self-interest and pride. If he was still the person he was then, still the golden boy of London society, the ambitious young peacock, then it might have worked. He snorted as he turned into his gateway. Dianne was never going to settle here. He'd known it, and he hadn't cared.

Jenna had sneaked under his defences, gentle and innocent, and made him open a door long closed and rusted shut. She made him want to take someone else into his life and heart and mind.

That was the first miracle. And it was a big mistake.

But what really annoyed him – he slammed the car door with force – *really* annoyed him, was the total disarming of his powers of self-deceit. Things shouldn't stay in his memory when he didn't want them there. People certainly shouldn't. When Jenna had walked away from him that day by the sea, he had invoked that power. Never before had it failed him as it did now.

But that wasn't the second miracle. What really sent angry fear shivering through him was that Jenna had made him realise that everything that had happened to him, everything that was going to happen to him, was not folded away into some neat place of invisibility. It was all there still, all of it. Memory and knowledge are locked in the brain, not erased from it. Somebody had found the key and panic brushed the back of his neck.

That was the second miracle. A bad, bad one.

Thank God Luke would recover and he did not regret answering Jenna's cry. Paul jabbed his key into the front door lock. But after this week, he had miracles to fight. But not for long. Not for long.

The small hallway still held the smell of toast from this morning. Keys in his raised hand, he paused, nostrils flaring. There was the aroma of coffee, which he had not brewed that morning. He threw his keys onto the hall table where a small swirl of dust lifted and settled again. His coat landed over the bannister and he walked into the sitting room.

Luther Chevalier was lounging on his sofa.

Paul stopped dead.

Luther raised the mug in his hand, his tone hectoring. "Really, Paul. Is this stuff the best you can do now Dianne's left you?"

Paul pushed the shock down deep inside him and sat in the chair near the door into the kitchen. His guitar was propped against one arm of it.

"Obviously Dianne took all the good taste with her," he replied evenly.

Luther looked round the room slowly. "Obviously." He took another sip of coffee and leaned back, stretching his arm along the back of the sofa. "This place is quite ..." he waved a hand vaguely ... "bijou, I suppose you could call it. If you were being polite."

Paul watched him calmly. "So Dianne still has her key."

"Well guessed." Luther reached into his pocket and held up a key from which dangled a gold fob with an inset of Belgian lace. Paul recognised it; he had bought it for her in Bruges on their honeymoon. She had called it "a funny little trinket". He looked round quickly.

"Is she with you?"

"Not bloody likely!"

Paul sat forward, tired of this. "What do you want, Luther?"

Luther set the mug on the table in the window and stood up, all sarcasm gone. Instead his manner changed to one of ruthless business, a manner Paul remembered in him. It was unpleasant and forceful.

"I came for the rest of Dianne's things. Even you have probably gathered that she isn't coming back to you."

"She belongs with you. She always did."

Luther walked past the chair and peered into the kitchen, hands in his pockets. Suddenly he veered back and leaned over Paul, his face close and angry, a pale spray of straw coloured hair trembling over his reddening brow. "I've got her back, you bastard. You were just a bit of fun on the way."

Paul raised one hand to Luther's shoulder and pushed him away, slowly but firmly. He rose and faced him.

"Well, she was a bit of fun for me too."

Luther raised his fist. Paul blocked the swinging blow with his forearm. "Don't hit me, Luther. That would be a very bad idea."

Luther calmed himself with an effort. "Dianne wants to know when you're filing for divorce."

Paul laughed in surprise. "I've no bloody idea! I don't even know how to do it. I've never been divorced before." He walked to the fireplace and stood still. When he turned back, Luther was still by the kitchen door, his hands fisted at his sides. Paul strolled to the window. "Where's your car?"

"Parked up the street, already packed." Luther's lip curled in a sneer. "You'll find things a bit emptier upstairs."

"Why didn't you park in the drive? It would have made lugging all that stuff a lot easier."

"But then you'd have been warned and I wouldn't have had the wonderful sight of your face when you came in and saw me."

Paul nodded in understanding. "Ah. Of course." He strolled back and pulled his guitar upright, twirling it on its base. "I don't think I'll bother with a divorce. What does it matter to you two anyway?" He held up his left hand. "I'd just give you my ring if I could, but I seem to have lost it somewhere."

Luther's hand shot out and grabbed a fistful of shirt at his neck. The guitar thudded to the floor with a discordant jangle as Paul reacted instantly, wrenching Luther's hand away and propelling him backwards till his legs buckled on the edge of the sofa and he sat heavily. Paul put his face close to his and hissed, "Touching me is a very bad idea too." He straightened. "Let's try and be civilised, shall we?"

Over his head, Paul noticed that a framed picture of Charles Burke was gone from the wall. Everything has its blessings. "Why can't she come over for her own stuff anyway? Why can't she ask about a divorce for herself?"

"Because she's not well."

Paul frowned. "How not well?"

"She's getting over a small operation."

Paul's eyebrows knitted further. "Women's stuff?"

Luther got to his feet slowly and put his hands in his pockets, his smile thin and bitter. "Yes, in fact I'm glad you reminded me. She told me to tell you. Only fair, she said."

"Tell me what?"

"She's had an abortion. It didn't go well and she haemorrhaged."

The shock swelled in Paul again, burst into slow fragments, pierced his body from the inside.

"An abortion?"

A ghastly relish bloomed over Luther's features. He took a slow spin round the room and stopped in front of Paul again. "Well, you didn't think I'd pay for your brat, did you?" He leaned forwards. "A bog-Irish half-caste!"

The room was beginning to fade, to retreat into a mist of irrelevance. "Mine?" Paul whispered.

Luther's laugh was triumphant. "Oh yes. Yours. Think I'd make a mistake like that? Dianne said it was yours. She said she knew it was yours."

Paul gripped the back of the chair. "You're lying."

"I'm not lying." He jabbed Paul's chest and this time Paul did not react. "I don't care if she's sick now. I don't care because she'll get better, and she's flushed the very last bit of you out of her. The very last bit." He snapped his fingers. "Down the toilet."

Darkness closed slowly round the edge of Paul's vision, like someone softening the lights. Dimly he saw Luther bend down and pick up something from the floor beyond the sofa. He saw him hold open an album of photographs, an album he kept upstairs. He heard Luther say something about having fun when the wife's away.

"Put some make-up on the bitch and she'll make a better whore!"

Luther hurled the album at him. It flew over his head and smashed against the corner of the ceiling. Pages loosened and exploded from their mounting. Paul felt the floor tilt and he dropped onto the chair. Finally, Luther had felled him with a blow that left not a single fingerprint behind.

The front door slammed as Paul slumped forward and covered his face with his hands. Pictures of a laughing girl, a scarf, a wooden bench, settled round him like the charred aftermath of a bonfire in the wind.

The brightness of daffodils burnished the library as the afternoon wore on. The red leather sofa had been pushed back and Dianne lay on a chaise longue by the window. She set her mobile down beside a bowl of black grapes on a low table. Across the sweep of lawn Luther's house stood more proudly, its gates newly painted and the work of a gardener evident in the neat flowerbeds and the stripes of the first cut of the lawns. She wished he was back. He had just phoned to say that he had spotted an exhibition of American artists and wanted to stay in Belfast until the next day, to visit it. There might be contacts to be made. He would catch the ferry just twenty-four hours later than planned.

Dianne dropped her head back on the soft cushion. Her brain worked slowly. What had he been doing all day? He was to go to the house in the morning and take no more than an hour; less surely? He could have visited the exhibition and still made the ferry. She picked at the grapes. Bella had brought them.

"Grapes, Bella? I'm not in an old people's home yet."

"Eat those and stay out of it a while longer, darling. Toby says you must be incredibly good and get better."

Dianne had looked anxiously at Bella. "Toby won't tell Daddy, will he?"

Bella plucked a grape and bit it. "Of course not," she lisped round the juice. "Toby's top of the range. Patient confidentiality and all that." She licked her fingers. "A terrible miscarriage. It happens."

Now, Dianne looked out at a cloud of starlings swooping and swirling across the sky above the trees at the back of Luther's garden. She ran her hand across her stomach. The bleeding had lessened and the ache in her belly had diminished a little. God, what a messy, ghastly business! She bit her lip. She had expected to feel happy. She didn't expect to feel hollow, but she did.

You have killed a child.

She shook her head like a cat shaking off rain. Her hormones were all over the place. They would settle down. At least Luther had not run into Paul. "No, no sign of him," he had said when she asked. Her father would come in soon, bringing tea on a tray for them to share. She decided to doze until then.

Her phone rang again. Probably Bella. She reached for it and answered, her voice dull. In seconds her eyes widened and she jolted upright as a familiar, and yet unfamiliar, voice rasped in her ear.

"Is it true?"

"Paul!" Shock whitened her knuckles.

"Is it true, you bitch? I want to hear it from you."

"Is what true?" Her voice seemed to be trapped deep in her throat, struggling to make a sound.

"Have you killed my baby?"

Days ago she would have been fit for this. She would have

hurled abuse back at him and felt nothing of his pain. Now the same pain seemed closer to herself than she ever suspected it could be. Something reached down the wire and made her crumple into guilt and emptiness. She could say she had an abortion. She could say she had a miscarriage. She could say it wasn't a baby. They had called it a foetus. She could simply deny it all. "What the hell are you talking about?" She could shout again about his selfishness. "It was my baby too!" but that thought was too new, too shocking, too unexpected, to put into words. It echoed round her head like the eerie howl of a wolf in mountains.

"Have you?" Paul was trembling. She could hear it.

"Yes," she whispered.

The line went dead.

For half an hour her father, puzzled and alarmed, tried to console her. She wept in paroxysms which hurt her womb and made clots of blood ooze from her body with every gasp. Her father must have called Bella because suddenly she was there, her arms round her, her voice devoid of its usual world-weary drawl.

"Come on, Di. What happened? What's wrong?" Bella pulled another tissue from a box on the floor and wiped Dianne's nose. "You have to tell me, you know. This isn't just hormones."

On a sudden thought she reached for Dianne's phone and flicked to the record of recent calls.

"Paul called you." She gave Dianne a little shake and bent her head to look into her face. "What did he say?"

"He told him!" Dianne cried, a wail of distress.

"Who told who what?"

"Luther told Paul about ... about ..."

Bella stiffened. "The abortion?"

Dianne nodded, her sobs shuddering into the misery of exhaustion. Her eyes felt as if they would never be normal again. Her hair needed washed and it straggled in pallid strings round her blazing cheeks. Bella pulled aside a strand which hovered close to the corner of Dianne's mouth and tucked it behind her ear.

"He would have been born in September," Dianne whispered, her voice hoarse.

"Don't think like that, Di. You didn't want it, remember."

Dianne turned huge and flooded eyes to her. "He might have looked like his father."

"You don't know it would have been a boy. Stop thinking about it."

"My mind's taking me over, Bella. I'll never forgive Luther for this."

"You might have a point there, darling."

Dianne pounded a fist on her knee. "He's a liar, he's a horrid liar!"

Bella rubbed her shoulders, back and forth, back and forth. "But you knew that, Di. You shouldn't be so terribly surprised. You're not a saint either. That's why you suit each other so well." She let go of Dianne gently and stood. "Now hush. I'm going to get Toby to come and give you something."

Dianne grabbed her hand as she turned. "Oh, Bella! He would have been magnificent if he'd looked like his father."

Bella bent and kissed her brow. "I'm going to phone Toby. I'll be back in a minute."

With the familiarity of a best friend, Bella went up the curved stairs and across the landing, past the armchairs, the table and the punctilious ticking of the grandfather clock. The semi-circular table held a lustred vase of daffodils today. Along the passageway, past the Chinese urn, she turned the handle on a bedroom door. She was not going to risk Charles Burke overhearing her. The room had the odour of emptiness, the bed smooth and cold. At the window she pulled out her phone, just as Dianne's father appeared on the lawn below, to walked distractedly amongst the shrubs and flowerbeds.

Bella called Toby first. He said he would come as soon as he could.

"I told her this might happen," he said. "I didn't want her to do it. Feelings can turn somersaults after an abortion. She may need something for depression, specially after how it went with her."

"Give her whatever she'll take." Bella paused. "Paul knows."

Toby drew in his breath sharply. "My God! How?"

"Luther told him. I think that's what's set her off."

Toby cursed in words that made Bella move the phone from her ear momentarily and stare at it, eyebrows raised. "Luther Chevalier should come with a health warning. He's a twisted mongrel."

"Yes, well. She says she'll never forgive him."

Toby gave a sharp laugh. "She will."

Bella checked her nails. "Yes," she said, "she will. Eventually."

She phoned Luther next. She could hear the hum and bustle of a hotel bar. It faded slightly as he moved to a quieter spot. "I've just heard you called a twisted mongrel."

He bristled. "Who by?"

She buffed her nails on her lapel and leaned against the window frame. "By someone who was right."

There was a silence. Then he said quickly, "Dianne? Is Dianne all right?"

"Not really. No."

Alarm surged into his voice. "What's wrong?"

Charles Burke was turning and walking slowly back to the house, head bent and shoulders slumped. Bella ducked back from the window. "Some would say you are."

"Bloody hell, Bella! Tell me!"

Finally her rare temper flashed, her voice jagged as a saw. "How many steps ahead can that brain of yours imagine, Luther? You can see round the globe if it's anything to do with money but you can't see consequences an inch from your nose!"

"Bella!" he shouted, angry now himself. "What's this about?"

She drew herself up, feet planted as if he stood in front of her. "While you were getting your revenge on Paul, didn't it even occur to you that Dianne might get caught in the crossfire? Didn't you even think that Paul might contact Dianne?"

There was a long silence, and then a groan. "Oh, my God."

Bella sat on the edge of the bed, calm again, and twirled a toe. "Back tomorrow, aren't you? Twenty-four hours to think of a way out of this one. You should manage it. You always do."

She had Paul's number and tried it next. There was no reply and the answer phone kicked in. She snapped her phone shut. What message could she possibly leave?

CHAPTER TWENTY-EIGHT

LUKE WAS AGITATING to get home but he was still getting dizzy sometimes when he tried out his new crutches, so the doctors were being cautious. Jenna reached from her perch on a stool beside the bed and placed a hand of cards on the table which was wheeled across Luke's knees. He sat on the chair in the narrow space between the bed and the window. His leg, encased in plaster, protruded from beneath the table. He threw down his cards. "Shit!"

"You're hopeless!" She gathered up the cards triumphantly. Luke's had slid to the floor under the bed.

He eased himself up in the chair, taking care of his splinted fingers and wincing from the pain in his ribs.

Jenna shuffled the cards. "You OK?"

"Yeah. Just a bit fed up."

"I'm not surprised." The line of staples arched across his shaven head. "But your hair's starting to grow again. What colour will you make it this time?"

He just smiled a little and tilted his head up to look over the sill of his high window at the view over the city. The gap in his mouth where his teeth were missing still gave Jenna a sting of shock. She gave up on the cards. "Want me to get you a paper at the shop downstairs?"

"No, it's OK."

She sat forward. "What is it, LW?"

His words lisped from his still-bruised mouth. "Oh, just remembering lying on the ground and the sight of a boot heading for my face. It ... still scares me. I really thought I was going to die. Well, I knew I might."

"We thought you might too. You weren't the only one scared."

He grinned. "Sorry."

"Don't apologise. Just don't do it again."

He was solemn again. "I've nightmares sometimes. I see a flash of white jumper, a flash of red something, and then boots. Boots. All aiming at my head. And I put my hands up and I'm panicking ..."

"Have you told Mum or Dad?"

"I told Paul."

"Why him?"

He shrugged and then winced a little as his ribs jagged him. "He listens as if he understands." He turned questioning eyes on her. "Know what I mean?"

"What did he say?"

"He said that, with him, it was clocks, grandfather clocks. He doesn't know why." He looked out the window again and was quiet for a moment. "He told me to enjoy every minute I'd been given back." He turned back to his sister. "I remember exactly what he said. He said, 'Milk each moment dry because you don't know which one will be the one that takes you away.'" He frowned. "Wasn't that odd? I memorised it because it was so odd."

Jenna put her arm on the sill and rested her chin on it. "He's an odd guy."

"But he's good. I mean, he really loves ... things. He stood at this window and looked out for ages. He seemed to look at the view in bits, concentrating as if he was memorising it. And he really loves natural stuff. Like birds and trees and stuff." He stopped, thinking. "As if he's part of it."

"You think he's good? I think he's a prick."

"Jay! Language!"

"Hah! Pots and kettles come to mind!"

Luke felt his head gingerly, tracing the line of staples down behind his ear. "It doesn't suit you, though."

She made a face. "Because I'm a good girl. And don't pull at those."

"I'm not pulling. Dunno what Paul thinks of you."

"Why should he think anything?"

Luke narrowed his eyes. "Before I landed in here, he never mentioned your name. Not once on any shoot we were on."

She spread her hands. "So he doesn't think of me at all then. Why would he?"

His eyes were still narrowed. "Yeah. Why would he? Where is he anyway? He hasn't dropped in in days."

She stood up and reached for her coat. "Oh, goodness knows. Probably underwater, photographing mussels in Strangford or something."

He remembered something. "Oh yeah, Dad said the Aardvark phoned."

She hunted for the sleeves. "He never told me that."

"Probably won't either. News had travelled apparently and the Aardvark wanted to know if I was dead yet."

"I know you didn't like him but be fair!"

The fur hood was caught inside out down the back of her neck and she hooked it out. Luke shoved the table sideways against the bed and reached for his crutches. As Jenna reached to get them for him he waved her away angrily.

"I can do it. I'm going to the toilet, not running a marathon."

"OK, OK, keep your hair on!"

She caught his eye and he started to grin gummily. She was round the bed and at the door before either of them stopped laughing.

"Hey," he called as she opened it. "What about the Moron? Max thingy?"

She turned back. "Seen him once since you were mugged. I don't think he knows how to handle it."

Luke manoeuvred the crutches under his elbows and started to lean forward onto them. "I'm good with that. You don't have much luck with men, do you?"

"I'm good with that," she replied. "Who needs them?"

Small quick footsteps sounded in the corridor outside, pausing as the soft squeak and roll of a bed being moved, passed the door. There was a knock and Naomi's head peered round, the school tie loose around the open neck of her shirt. Luke's face lit up and he smiled a gappy smile.

"Hi, Naomi. I'm just going," Jenna greeted her. Naomi stood grinning, her bag still on her back. Jenna pointed a warning finger at Luke. "Remember I'm getting the bus home to Mum and Dad's tonight. Be good. You're not up to being Heartbreak Hunk just yet." She took a step towards the corridor then looked back at Naomi. "Oh, by the way. Go and get a coffee. He's going to the bathroom all by himself. He should be back in about an hour."

She ducked out again before Luke could launch a crutch in her direction.

~

Jenna knocked gently on the door of her father's study and pushed it open. The scents of her childhood enveloped her: the smell of old books mingled with the sharper scent of new books; the rattle of the drawers of his desk, the slight rasp of his chair as he swivelled. All this was joined now by the clicking of the keys on his new computer. He was like a child with a new toy.

"Hello, Missy. Look. Look at this." He angled the screen

towards her and pointed. She bent to look. "I can work out the whole preaching plan on this and print it out." A small printer nestled on a new table beside the desk, next the door. "And look." He searched, his fingers moving the mouse swiftly, and double-clicked an icon. "This is a database of all the church members." He looked up, his eyes bright. "I can enter all the family names and even have columns for when I last visited them. Isn't it great? And I can even ..." another double click, a calendar appeared "... have my appointments computerised and it'll give me reminders. Isn't it amazing?"

She was reminded of Luke. Her father was once young like Luke, and he still showed flashes of a vibrancy that Luke had inherited from him. He turned his attention from the computer and studied his daughter as she sank into the deep, worn chair in the corner.

"You look as if you could do with a good sleep. Are you still worried about Luke?"

She smiled briefly. "No. He's made terrific progress. I beat him at whist today."

Donald grinned. "I wish he wouldn't tell the congregation I taught him how to play it."

"Well, you did. And me too. A dentist's already called to see him. I think they'll bridge the gap very well." She gave a small laugh. "He's more annoyed about his teeth than his leg – or his head."

"Typical!"

Jenna fiddled with her fingers and then looked up at her father. "Dad, I know keeping the house in Belfast has been a strain on you and Mum." Donald gave a dismissive gesture but she ploughed on. "Specially this year, after the others moved out and you had to pay it all yourselves. I really appreciate it."

"You know we do it happily. You have a bit of privacy and comfort and we know where you are."

Jenna studied her feet then began again. "I know you were going to sell it when I finished this year." She looked up, meeting his eye. "But you can sell it now. You'll get a very good price for it. I'm moving on."

Donald's brows drew together. "Moving on? What do you mean?"

Nerves began to ripple in her stomach but she had to say this; to tell him. "Dad, I dropped out of university on Wednesday ..." At his sharp intake of breath she raised a hand to make him wait. "I've thought about this very hard and I want you to respect my decision." She opened her palms. "Please Dad. I know you and Mum have sacrificed a lot for me and when I get a job, I'll pay you back for what I've cost you this year."

He had been relaxed; now he sat forward, searching her face. "Why, Jenna? Why are you giving it all up at this stage?"

She shrugged. "I don't want to spend any more of my life like this. Actually ... I didn't want to last summer. One degree's enough."

"But your potential, Jenna! You could go so much further with your ability. A doctorate even."

"But don't you see, Dad? Everyone ..." She struggled for the right words. "I ... have the potential to be and to do many things. I can't fulfil them all. I have to fulfil the potential that ..." she smiled weakly, a little embarrassed ... "is closest to my heart."

"And what is that?"

She breathed a little easier. He was listening and it made her words more fluent. "I'm thinking of going overseas for a year. Volunteering. There are organisations which badly need volunteers. They build houses and schools in places which have suffered hurricanes and floods and even civil war. Central America maybe."

Donald's eyebrows had been slowly rising. "I know of them. And how do you intend to support yourself?"

"Luke can do his exams – the doctors are sure of it, and he might get a little extra time to sit them, considering."

"What's that got ..."

"He'll probably do well and get his first choice of university in Scotland. I'm going to go over there to find a job and a flat. He's going to join me in October." She made a face. "He'll carve his own patch and won't want to live with his sister for ever. I don't want him under my feet for ever either. When I've saved enough – and I won't need a lot – I'll go abroad."

Donald's voice rose, incredulous. "You mean you've talked this over with Luke already?" She nodded. "And you've already told your tutor you're dropping out?" Another nod.

Her father swung his chair round to his desk, propped his elbows beside the keyboard and covered his face. The light from the desk lamp threw dark shadows from his fingers across his lined cheeks. He sat like that for so long Jenna reached across and touched his arm. "Dad?"

He dropped his hands. "This is a shock, Jenna."

They sat in silence until Jenna broke it, her voice strong. "You told me once that your mother was upset when you decided to candidate for the ministry. She wanted you to continue in business because you had a talent for it; she wanted you to be rich. Isn't that right?"

He nodded. "But she forgave me later, before she died. She saw I was following my ..." He stopped and dropped his eyes. He rubbed his hands together slowly. "You'll have to tell Mum. First Luke and Outer Mongolia. Now you. She blamed Adam's brother for Luke's plans. Now she thinks Paul's not so bad after all. So do I. He's been a real tower of strength to all of us through this. At least Mum can't blame him for you dropping out. But she'll go up the walls. "

Jenna slumped back in the chair, silent. The very mention of Paul's name was an arrow twisted in her side.

"Remember last week?" she asked. "When Luke came round and you weren't there and I phoned you?"

"Very well."

"You had to learn to put your family first. Maybe I'm learning to put it ... not last, never last. But down the list a bit." She looked at him anxiously. "Do you know what I mean?"

Donald reached forward and took both her hands in his. "I do. I know exactly what you mean. You're my daughter after all, and I'm proud of you." He squeezed her hands. "Whatever you do." He paused. "But answer me one thing. I know Adam hurt you very badly and I don't want you to do anything impulsive. Are you still hurt? Has this anything to do with him?"

She met his eyes. "No, Dad. This has absolutely nothing to do with Adam Shepherd."

She hoped he would leave it there, but still he held her hands.

"You talked to me before about doing the right thing or the wrong thing. About rules. I've often puzzled over what was in your mind then." He looked away at the untidy lines of books on the shelves under the window and asked again. "Are you sure?"

"I'm sure. This has nothing to do with Adam."

Leave it there, Dad. I can lie to you and I will.

To her relief, he released her hands and sat back. "OK. Now go and tell your mother. I'll hide in here."

She stood and put her arms round his shoulders from behind his chair. "Where you always hide!" She kissed the top of his head.

~

When she heard what Jenna had done and planned to do, Cora reacted with shock, as Donald had done. She set her embroidery frame down on the arm of her chair and switched off the television. The bird of paradise was nearly finished. She put her hand over her eyes for a moment and sat still. When she looked up again Jenna noted the lines from her nose to the corners of her mouth, lines which had been there before but not carved so deeply as they were now. She spoke slowly, remembering something.

"When Luke was still in a coma, I was sitting with him one morning. On my own. Paul came in. I think he was surprised to see me. I was in the chair and he sat on the stool. We didn't have much to say, but I told him how much we appreciated how he was helping us."

Her mother had got his name right. She hadn't called him Peter or Patrick this time.

She went on. "I think I said something about it being difficult being a mother, a parent. I tried to keep my children safe, and I failed this time. I wasn't with him when he needed me." Her voice broke and her chin tightened.

"You couldn't have been, Mum. How could you?"

Cora took a deep, steadying breath and went on as if she hadn't spoken. "Paul leaned back against the wall and put his two feet up on the end of the bed. On the covers! He said I'd reminded him of a rare butterfly he'd seen once in a park. He'd held out his hand close to it and after a while the butterfly landed on his fingers. He said he'd had to keep his hand open or he would have hurt it; that when you close your fingers too tight on something, it struggles to get away. You might even kill it."

Jenna waited but her mother picked up her needle again. "And then what?" she prompted.

"He said people have wings too. They just don't know they have. But Luke would probably have found his after what happened. I told him he'd make a great dad. But he just got up, touched Luke's hand and left." She waved her needle at Jenna. "He'd left a mark on the covers too."

"Do you know what he meant?"

Cora drew a long green thread through her needle and bit it

with her teeth. "I think I do. Strange man," she mused. "So do what you must, love. What's Luke's phrase? 'Chill, Mum.' " She leaned back and pushed her needle through the cloth. "What's Outer Mongolia compared to losing Luke altogether? Scotland's a day trip. I think you should do what you feel is right."

"I thought you'd be upset. I'm glad you're not."

Cora stopped her needle and looked up over her glasses. "Oh, I'm upset all right. But I'll deal with it. The world's taken a tumble round us this past while. I'd rather it did all its tumbles at once and then calmed down again." She pursed her lips, thinking. Then she sat up straighter, business brightening her eye. "There'll be a lot to sort out. You won't go before Luke's a bit better, I'm sure. And then you'll need to look for a place to stay. Dundee, I suppose? Well, I'll go over with you ..."

As Cora talked on, she abandoned her sewing and reached for a bit of paper to make a list. Amused, Jenna realised she had provided her mother with a perfect distraction, a channel for her bruised emotions. She yawned and said she was going to bed.

Cora's pen paused over the unfinished list. "OK love. Stick on the kettle on your way up, would you? Dad'll be looking for his supper soon."

~

Jenna's torch picked a lonely path across the field, but she craved solitude and quiet after leaving her mother. The scent of an early spring night rolled through the holes and crevices of the old hut. Some beams of moonlight helped guided her round the end of the broken bench. The dry leaves of last autumn rustled under her feet as she switched off the torch and picked her way to the clouds and stars set in the gap of the old window. She leaned her head against the carved initials in the loose wood and imbibed through her skin the world of trees and dew, owls and bats, and rustlings in the grass.

The ease with which she was turning her life upside down was unsettling. She'd expected a struggle, to have to argue and persuade and finally to leave, heroic in her determination. She put a hand on the cold smooth wood of the ledge and leaned out to follow the dart of a bat above the silvered grasses. This was the spot where Paul had stood, looking sad and thoughtful. The wind ruffled his hair and the rain speckled his shoulders as he told her that it wasn't all right not to know. It was here that he had first started to get under her skin, to dissect her, to make himself memorable in her heart.

Now, Paul invaded every aspect of her life, even gently brushed the lives of her family. Everywhere she turned, he had been there before her, or his mind came alongside hers as if his fingers lay upon her head again.

She folded her arms tight against the cold and looked up at the stars, at the moon edging the clouds with silver braid. Everything was in place for her to leave. She filled her lungs with the damp green air of night, felt the ghosts of dead men stand beside her. Was she making a new start or was she running away? Maybe it was both.

She bit her lip. The decision she had to make now was inescapable. Would she leave, silent, along the new road that was rolling so smooth before her feet? Or, before she went, would she go to Paul and tell him how he complicated her heart and mind and soul?

She had to make a choice and she did not know which one would hurt her more.

CHAPTER TWENTY-NINE

THE NEXT DAY, Jenna began to pack. She wouldn't leave until Luke was further on the way to physical recovery and his tentative attempts to resume work for his exams had become firm evidence of his fitness to sit them. Nevertheless, a restless discontent nipped at her.

She put all her books and files into a box in the hall. She phoned Max and asked him to put a notice up in the university saying they were for sale. When he heard what she was planning to do he told her he thought she was an idiot.

"Maybe I am. But while I'm finding out, could you ask around for some cartons and boxes for me?"

"Sure. How's your brother, by the way?"

"He's on the road to recovery. Thanks for asking."

"Good ... Um, Jen?"

"What?"

"We haven't seen each other for a while ..."

"I have been otherwise engaged, Max. And you knew where I was."

"I, well, I met this girl ..."

She rolled her eyes. She could write the script. "Look, I know what you're going to say. We didn't exactly click, did we? But thanks for some fun. Have a good time. Maybe I'll drop you a postcard. And good luck with the dissertation."

"Yeah, cool." His tone relaxed. "If I get some boxes I'll leave them round."

And that was that. Later in the morning, there were two calls from surprised and concerned friends. Jenna tried to stop the hope from rising each time she heard the phone ring. That way the crushing disappointment was easier to bear. That was the theory anyway. Word had spread that she had dropped out. She was polite but determined, sorry to say goodbye but promising to meet up again before she left.

In the afternoon she visited Luke again. He was sitting out in the chair, crutches lying on the floor under the bed beside him. He was leafing through a huge red file of notes. As soon as she came in he raised his eyebrows.

"Did you tell them?"

"I did."

"And?"

"They're not happy but they won't make waves. In fact Mum wants to go over with me to help find a flat." When Luke groaned, she pointed out, "It's a small price to pay for no big waves. And don't scratch that scar."

"I'm not scratching it. I'm just feeling it. Stop nagging."

Jenna shoved the tissue box and a bottle of raspberry squash out of the way and dumped her bag on the table. "Has Paul been in yet?"

He shook his head. "Nope. Haven't seen him in a week now." He slammed the file shut and hoisted it towards her with his good hand. "Ask me some questions from that. I've been revising all morning."

~

That evening, Jenna got a takeaway, curled in her chair and watched a film. She didn't hear a word of it. When she finished and cleared up, which involved crumpling the wrappers into the bin, she lifted the razor shell from the window ledge and ran her fingers along the roughness of the mottled halves, feeling the sharpness of the edges, tilting the inside towards the light to see the luminescence of the pearly surface. She closed her eyes and touched the cool shell to her cheek. She felt the tightness of longing in her throat. Surely he couldn't vanish again? Surely he could not leave her like this? For the first time, a tear for Paul and all she knew she had probably lost, traced a path over her fingers and ran down the mottled shell. The trauma of Luke; the decision to leave home; the strange man who would not leave her mind and heart, – in the dusk of her sitting room it all hit her suddenly with a force of tonnes. She gave in to the tears. Just this once and then never again over Paul.

She stretched out on the sofa on her stomach and thought of the night he lay there sleeping and how, in her mind, she had gone past the barriers of wisdom and flown free with him beyond the cages of convention. She buried her face in the red and black cushion and remembered how he once threatened to eat it.

One other time she had wept, in a cold car park. Paul had told her to find things that are worth tears. She had found that. He had also asked her a question – is it your heart or your pride that is hurt? Then, she didn't entirely understand him. Now she did, all too well. She pushed her hands under the cushion and pressed it to her salty cheeks.

The tears were cleansing and when she sat up and blew her nose, she was thinking more clearly than she had in days. There were too many puzzles about his behaviour. She could not leave without talking to him again, without asking, telling, searching, explaining, making him explain. The decision was made. She tucked the cushion into her stomach and doubled over it. Just to see his smile and hear his voice and know herself alive to the ends of her nerves ...

The phone rang.

It was Hazel. Crushed, and unsteady from her weeping, Jenna

stood in the hall with a foot on each side of her box of books. She wiped her nose on the back of her hand.

"No, I've just got a bit of a cold, that's all," she laughed shakily.

"A lemon drink and a good sleep will work wonders."

The magic solution to everything. But why was Paul's mother ringing her? Her voice seemed brittle, as if she were making an effort to be casual.

"I just wondered if you'd seen Paul lately?"

Jenna frowned. "No. Why?"

"Well, I'm sure I'm worrying unnecessarily, but he seems to have disappeared."

"He does that sometimes, doesn't he?"

"Yes, but he usually keeps in touch with me. He drops in or rings every few days. And now he's not even answering my phone calls." Her voice was tight with worry now. "That's very peculiar."

"But he often doesn't answer his phone."

"He always answers if it's me," she said firmly. "Or gets back to me if I leave a message."

"Maybe he's gone over to stay with Adam. Or see Dianne."

"I've tried both of them. Adam says he hasn't heard from him in a month. Dianne hasn't been well – I didn't know that – and seemed very upset when I told her I couldn't find him." Her voice dropped. "I think I'll ring round the hospitals."

Alarm was rising through Jenna. She shoved the box out of the way to concentrate more easily. "Have you been at his house?"

"No ..."

"I could check it in the morning."

"I haven't a key. He has a key to my house but he never gave me one of his."

"I'll go anyway."

Sleep was far away that night. Jenna hugged the teddy bear

with the black hat but it gave her no clues although she wished very hard that it would. Wishing worked for Paul; why could it not work for her? After some hours of drifting consciousness, Jenna rose and dressed. A taxi left her outside Paul's house as dawn rose over the rooftops.

Paul's car was gone. A wagtail scuttled up the drive in front of her as she examined the house. Droplets of morning dew sparkled on the untidy grass and shrubs and on a pile of stones in one corner of the front garden. Knots of daffodils were in bloom; purple and yellow crocuses carpeted a patch near the gate pillar, a triumph over neglect. Upstairs, the blackout blinds were drawn on the window of the darkroom.

Jenna tried the doorbell first. As she expected, there was no answer. Cupping her hands round her eyes, she peered through the glass into the sitting room. The reflections made seeing detail difficult. There seemed to be bits of paper strewn on the floor at the far end, near the door into the kitchen.

Frowning, she went down the side of the house to the back. Inanimate over winter, the garden was letting spring creep up on it. The grass was greening through the dew and tight buds of new growth tipped the branches of the bush where the robin had perched last Christmas. The unkempt flower beds were stirring into life. A flurry of blackbirds and sparrows clattered into the air. From the neighbouring garden, over the straggling hedge, the laden branches of a cherry tree in full and glorious bloom, swayed in the light breeze. Jenna reached for a branch, pulled it down and marvelled at the beauty and complexity of the heavy pink blossoms. She let it bounce back upwards. Unlike many men, Paul would appreciate those.

The door of the garden shed was warped and stuck. With a hard tug, it opened. Inside were only old rusty garden tools and in the corner a small litter tray. Jack must have been kept in here sometimes. Against the back wall of the shed there were faint footprints in the dusting of soil and grit of the floor. Jenna hunkered in front of them. Paul's. They must be Paul's. She felt a little throb of the heart just looking at them. She remembered his footprints on Rossnowlagh beach. Was that all he was going to leave – his footprints, so easily erased? She put her palms gently over them, closed her eyes and wished that the maker of these would come back to her.

Over all this, the house sat solid and silent. Jenna peered over the higher sill of the kitchen window. She could see mugs and washing up liquid. There was a loaf of bread sitting out on the ledge above the fridge.

She had to get inside. She stood back and looked up at the back of the house. There were no windows open anywhere. There was a pane of glass in the back door. A good crack with a stone might do it. She gave the door handle a shake – and was amazed to find it unlocked. She smiled wryly. Such a thing as remembering to lock the back door was probably a detail too far for Paul.

Inside the wrapping, the bread was dotted with blue patches of mould. In the fridge there was a carton of milk. Jenna unscrewed the top and wrinkled her nose. She poured the curdled contents down the sink and washed it away. At the door into the sitting room she called his name, then stopped. They were photographs. The floor was strewn with black and white photographs. Behind the chair was a damaged and torn photograph album. She picked it up. It was a plain traditional album with leaves that used photo corners, not plastic sleeves. Some leaves still hung, bent and torn, from the ripped spine. Her fingers lingered on the name written on the scuffed cover. It was her own, written in a graceful, cursive hand.

Shocked, she sank into the chair and began to pick up the scattered pictures. They were all of herself. One by one, the pile grew on her lap. Here was the one taken last Christmas, by the sofa in this room. Paul had surprised her when she looked round, the gold cross for her mother hanging from her fingers. Her hair was longer then, tossed from her shopping trip with Dianne. She was wearing the denim jacket and the scarf lay in a heap on the floor beside her. Heat flooded her face as she remembered touching his bare foot and the intimacy of kneeling beside him as he sang 'Hark the Herald Angels Sing' for her.

Here were the ones he had taken the day he had searched for her at the university. She was laughing, mouth wide and eyes sparkling as she twirled the scarf above her head. Something like a sob escaped her as she lifted the next one. She was sitting on the grass, cross-legged. She could hear him now. "You look like a frog!"

She slumped back and covered her face with her hands. He could put together a collection like this and then walk out of her life. Something wasn't adding up. Urgency surged through her. Carefully, she folded the covers over the pile of photographs and set them on the sofa. She had to find him, *had* to. Then she saw the guitar. It was lying beside the chair, caught awkwardly against the side of the sofa, as if it had fallen. She picked it up by the neck and set it carefully against the wall where she knew Paul usually kept it.

Paul would never let his guitar fall like that. He would certainly never leave it there. Something was wrong. Very wrong.

A mug was on the low table at the window. It was half full of cold coffee, with a skin of milk. In the hall, she called his name again, high and frightened. His phone was on the hall table. Little wonder his mother couldn't get an answer. It was ringing here until the battery went dead.

On the stairs she felt the full force of the emptiness, the abandonment around her. The soul of him was gone from here. The bedroom at the front of the house, where she should have sensed him most, was cold and stale. The dressing table was bare of brushes and creams. Dianne might never have been here. Even the wardrobe was empty. She looked at the bed, and felt heat throb within her. He would have made love to Dianne here. Slowly, she swept her hand across the cover. It was snow white with a small border of green leaves and pink flowers.

What would it be like?

When finally she turned to the door again, her eyes caught on a silver handle on the floor, protruding between the wall and the dressing table. She picked it up and turned it over. It was a brush; an expensive brush with an engraved back. Entwined in the bristles were blonde hairs. Jenna set it on the dressing table and shut the door tight behind her.

The single bed in the smaller room had been slept in. The quilt was thrown back and there was still a depression in the pillow. This is where he slept. A bottle of water was on the window sill with a packet of strong headache tablets beside it. Jenna's mouth was dry and fear for him was rippling over her skin. She knelt beside the bed and pulled the pillow towards her. With her head laid gently in the hollow that his head had made, she pushed her hands beneath the quilt to spread her fingers in the place where his body would have spread its warmth.

Where are you, Paul? What has happened here?

By the light from the red bulb in the darkroom, the beetle still peeped from beneath the leaves in the photograph on the wall. Trays and bottles, equipment and paper littered the ledge. She switched off the light and closed the door again. She didn't want to find any more photographs.

As she came down the stairs she saw the post in a heap beneath the letter box. It was mostly junk, a few bills and a postcard from Austria. After the usual 'having a great time' message, the sender had scrawled, "So when are you coming back to the big smoke, Skipper? The aristos and eds miss you."

Skipper? The signature was illegible.

She found a pen in the kitchen. On the back of one of the

junk mail envelopes she wrote, "Paul, phone me as soon as you get back. Jenna." She looked at it. It said nothing of how she was feeling, alone in the echoes of his house, in the deserted, musty kitchen. Nothing of the fright, the conviction that something was very wrong. Even if he would treat her like this, he would never go away without reassuring his mother. She took the pen again and scribbled, "I want to talk to you." She chewed the pen. That's stupid. But she didn't want to cross it out. That would look even more stupid.

The bolt on the back door was stiff as she worked it shut. When she slammed the front door behind her, she stood in the driveway and looked back. Now she wished she had brought something away with her, something to link her to this house which had been so full of him. The very air had tasted of his vigour and enthusiasm. Now it was diminished, forsaken, just bricks on a common street. On an impulse, she picked a bunch of daffodils from amongst the shrubbery and grass.

Buses were running but traffic was sparse this Sunday morning. As she walked down the street to her own house, the bells on the church at the top of the road started to ring. It was the beginning of a new Sunday and yet she felt as if a long day had passed since she had left at dawn. Her footsteps slowed, her head lowered in thought as she inhaled the scent of the daffodils in her arms. Then she turned and went back up to the church. The flowers would last. Small gods or big ones, there was no-one else to ask.

CHAPTER THIRTY

HAZEL HAD GLEANED nothing from her phone calls to the hospitals. Now, she was even more concerned. So was Jenna.

"No sign at his house either. It's deserted and it looks as if he hasn't been there for quite a while. Although the back door was open and I was able to check inside."

"The back door was open?" Hazel sighed in exasperation at her son. "That's just typical! Was everything in order? Did you see anything unusual?"

"Everything was fine."

"Did you lift his post?"

"Yes, I did." Jenna hesitated. Don't hide everything. It won't sound right. "There was just some junk mail and stuff and a postcard from a friend in Austria. I threw out some sour milk as well. And ... his phone was still in the house. No point in keeping trying to ring him."

There was a silence. Jenna didn't know what to say next. Then Hazel spoke, her voice tense with worry.

"What do we do now, Jenna?"

"I think ... wait. It's all we can do."

Jenna arranged the daffodils on the mantelpiece below the picture of the robin. Then she put the razor shell beside the daffodils.

Upstairs, she took the black woollen hat from her teddy bear and brought it down to her chair. She pulled her legs up and curled into a ball with the hat on her knees.

A week ago, they had been together. He had been so good, so kind, so gentle. He had pulled her through a trauma as no other could have done. He had held up her family effortlessly, with an unerring instinct for what to say and when to say nothing. He had answered her cry with a generosity of spirit that was a revelation. Then he had walked away. She buried her face in the soft wool and cried out again, silent and pitched far, calling on the strength of the thread that she knew bound them together, for she had felt it do so.

You kept the photos of me. You put them in an album. You wrote my name on it.

Exhausted from her restless night and dawn rising, she fell asleep. Several hours later she woke, stiff and sore. Slowly she raised her head. Nothing had changed except that the room was dimming into evening; the shell still sat beside the daffodils, the hat was fisted tight in her fingers. She pressed the back of her hand to her mouth to quell the choking loneliness and fear.

I've buried my halo, Paul. Come and see.

This was the world without him, and now she knew she couldn't bear it.

Later, showered and in her towelling robe and pink slippers, she sipped a mug of coffee and tried to watch the news. A small sound outside her window made her look up. She turned off the television and listened again. Another noise, like a soft bump against her front door. Not a knock. Just a soft bump. She lifted a corner of the curtain and peeped out. There was a figure sitting on her steps, leaning forward, head hanging. The figure was wearing a black coat.

She flew to the door.

Paul raised his head and looked up over his shoulder at her. His face took away any words she might have spoken. His hair was unkempt and a week's growth of beard made him strange, different to her eyes. And yet … and yet …

In the light from her hallway, his eyes looked full of pain, the pupils large, a furrow of desolation marked on his brow. He opened his mouth to speak and it was a hoarse whisper.

"Are you drunk?" asked Jenna. *Why did I ask him that?*

He put a hand on the wall and pushed himself to his feet, turning to face her, two steps above him.

"My dear Jenna … " he coughed and cleared his throat. " … I don't drink. Not a drop. Hadn't you noticed?"

She came down the steps, her slippers soft on the cold ground. "I'm sorry, I …"

He leaned close and opened his mouth. She felt a puff of his breath on her cheek. He looked at her seriously.

"Smell anything?"

"No."

"Not even bad breath?"

She shook her head.

Suddenly he swung round in the street, arms flung wide.

"Maybe I *am* drunk!" He raised his arms high and looked up. "I'm drunk on the night, on the stars, on God, on life …"

He spun back towards Jenna and stopped. His hands stretched out towards her and his voice tripped on a sob.

"Save me, Jenna."

She stood motionless, eyes fixed on his pleading figure. His hands dropped helplessly to his sides. Slowly he turned from her and began to walk away. Without knowing she formed the word, his name came from her lips, feather-soft. It reached him. As if no dogs barked, no babies cried, no traffic passed, it reached him. He stopped, his back still to her. She said it again, stronger.

"Paul."

He swivelled on one foot, saw her lift her arm and hold out an open hand to him. Everything paused; nothing breathed. Then in four strides he reached her, ignored the open hand and went straight into her arms, allowing himself to be enfolded, caressed. This is what it must be like to be a mother, Jenna thought, stroking the back of his head, crooning, comforting, instinctively finding the universal sounds that wrap around the hurt and fear of a child.

He buried his head in her shoulder and his arms came round to hold her so tight that he almost stopped her breath.

She made him tea and a cheese sandwich. He sat in her chair and devoured it. She made him another. When she came back with this one, he had stopped chewing and was staring at her mantelpiece, at the daffodils and the shell and the robin. She sat on the sofa and watched him.

"The daffodils are from your garden. I put them there and tried to make you hear me calling you."

"What time?"

"About three."

He nodded. "You were at my house?"

"This morning."

The shadows under his eyes blended into the darkness of stubble on his skin. Normally he was a mixture of dark and pale, with sea-blue eyes dancing behind the long fringes of his lashes. She had never seen him like this. He was defeated, distressed and achingly vulnerable.

"Where have you been, Paul?"

He dropped his head back in a gesture of exhaustion and didn't reply. Instead, eyes closed, he extended his arm towards her, palm open.

"I need you, Jenna."

This time she made no mistake. She took his hand and knelt beside him. "I'm here. I'm here now," she said gently.

His eyes opened and he turned his head to her. For a moment

their gaze locked. Then he put his hand behind her head and twined his fingers in her hair. His other hand came round and found the warm skin of her shoulder beneath the collar of her robe. She felt a sensation totally new. Waves of something she couldn't identify rolled through her body making her throat constrict and her legs tremble beneath her. Despite his fatigue and the dusting of beard that darkened his face, he was Paul, he was back, and he had come to her first. She drew in a breath that was pure power. Power over him and over herself. It helped her to draw away.

She pulled him to his feet and took off his coat. He let her, passive, even submissive, as if all his energy to think for himself had gone from him.

"You've still got the pink slippers," he said suddenly, surprising her.

She steered him to the door, certain in her movements.

"Never mind my slippers. You need a shower and a good sleep. Come on. You know where the bathroom is. We can talk tomorrow." He did as he was told, allowing her to take over, to direct him. Halfway up the stairs, she spoke to his back. "I'll sleep on the couch this time. You need a bed."

He stopped momentarily and put a hand to the bannister to turn round. She gave him a little push. "Go on."

She found him a towel. Before he closed the bathroom door, he called her name, his voice stronger than before. She paused.

"You're not sleeping on the couch tonight. And neither am I."

She looked back. His eyes were brittle-bright. She felt as if her voice was coming from very deep in her throat. "I've only a single bed." But it was a faint whisper and the last word was almost inaudible.

Jenna couldn't sleep. She lay on the couch in her bathrobe and waited. There was an inevitability about this night. A certainty. It filled the house, from the badly fitting back door to the fraying mat on the street step; from the hallway to the roof tiles. Longing pulsed in the air and Jenna could feel the rhythm in her own body.

She waited. Merely a breath would tilt the scales on which she stood.

She waited. Her life was about to change beyond redemption. How could fear and joy be melded into the one coin, struck from the one die? And how could that coin spin on its edge for such achingly long minutes?

When she saw the faint glimmer of his body in the doorway, she thought that only he could descend those stairs without making a noise. He was naked. Then she remembered. Paul Shepherd always gets what he wants. Maybe, this time, so would she.

Silently he came to her side and dropped onto his heels. His hair was wet and tossed. As he looked up into her face in the dim light, she could see the longing open and free, pooling from the dark planes of his cheekbones into the deeper shadows of his eyes, tense in the muscles of his shoulders.

If she moved now, there would be no going back. His gaze was like a blue magnet. Slowly, she put out her hand and her fingers gently touched that amazing mouth beneath the new dark hairs. He closed his eyes. With her index finger, she traced his upper lip, from one corner, up over the first curve of the bow; down into the dip; up again over the swell of the other curve until her finger came to rest lightly at the other corner. His mouth opened and he captured her fingertip gently. She felt the moisture of his tongue as his eyes opened again. He took hold of her hand and separated the fingers with great care. He kissed each one slowly, absorbed as if they were the most important things in the world at that moment. Then his mouth moved down into the hollow of her palm.

Jenna swung her feet to the floor and sat forward a little, concentrating. Her hands moved over his shoulders, reached over to explore a little way down his back, traced the edges of his shoulder blades.

He was truly beautiful.

She turned her attention to his mouth once again, her head tilted slightly to one side. She feasted on the sight, never before so softly attainable. Only one word slipped from her, a whisper on the edge of breath, "Yes". His lips were soft and beautiful and moist and yielding. Then like a thunderbolt everything changed and she was being devoured, consumed, scorched. The gentle waves in her body grew into a raging storm.

He broke away and stood quickly. He bent over her and slid one arm round her back, the other under her knees and lifted her.

It was the beginning. The beginning of the end.

As he turned at the top of the stairs, she clutched his neck more tightly, hiding her face. "Paul, I've never ... I ..."

He pulled back. "I know." He kissed her full on the mouth, long and soft. "What do you feel?" he whispered then.

She smiled into his eyes and shook her head. "I haven't the words."

"Do you trust me?"

"Yes."

He laid her down on top of the quilt on her narrow bed. "There's room for two. Cuddled up. But I think your teddy bear will have to sleep on the floor."

"He'll cope."

She rolled onto her side, aware and careless of the robe which parted over her legs. There was languor in her voice and body. Since the brief fire downstairs, Paul's actions had slowed, as if he knew he must take care, take time. He lay beside her and pulled her to him gently, wrapping her in his warm body, folding her into the length of himself. It was like coming home. She felt a sigh escape him and drift through her hair. "Oh, Jenna," he breathed. He moved slightly to kiss the top of her head and his arms tightened further. "Jenna, Jenna, Jenna."

He was a new country, a man far beyond the borders of her hopes and dreams. This time she would keep him. If this is the only way to have him, then this is the way it shall be. While he lay contented, for the moment at peace, it was she who began to move. Tentatively she ran her hand down his side, feeling the curves and hollows of his body. Her fingers seemed twice alive, to his reactions and to her own pleasure in this cocoon of time and space. There was no other world.

She smiled against his chest as she felt her power again. He stirred and his own hands began to explore, gently at first, sensitive to her innocence. His arms slid beneath her robe and it became a barrier not to be borne. He tugged it from her shoulders and she arched her back to help him slide it from her and push it to the floor. In one smooth movement he rose on one elbow and folded his palm round her newly bare breast. His touch was light and sure. She covered his fingers with her own, smiling into his eyes, her lids heavy. His breath brushed her cheek as he lowered his head to kiss her. Into her ear he whispered, "I think you're a scarlet woman after all."

There was no part of her that he did not want to know. She offered herself with a freedom which she had not known she possessed, because this was Paul, the other part of her mind and soul. She knew enough to know he was skilful. Beneath his hands and lips, her skin became a conflagration of sensation. Once, he lingered as his mouth slid down along the silk of her stomach and towards the core of her, where a heaviness had grown so strong and thrumming and insistent she could not bear his hesitation. As his eyes flicked to her face, she wound her fingers through his hair and pushed him lower. His lips curved against her skin and he travelled on, the tiny dark hairs on his face only heightening the fire, covering her in the maleness of him. She felt his breath, heard words, murmured and warm. It was something about flying. Then she stopped thinking any more.

He paused only once more. When the muscles of her legs had become liquid and the longing unbearable, she moved beneath him of her own accord, knowing only that she was not yet satisfied. She wanted him closer, closer still. He took his weight on his arms, stilled, searched her face, silently asked a question. She pulled his head down and thrust her body towards his. Answered, he moved rapidly and then she was flying indeed, beyond any boundary she had ever known. Her legs gripped him, helping, urging, wanting, beyond any fleeting pain, for this was Paul, only Paul, for ever Paul, only ever, ever, ever ...

He held her while she slept. With her he could forget for a time; be blissful, and absent from his griefs. Her hair and body smelled of almonds. His smile became a gentle kiss above her brow. He was the one who was supposed to turn over and go to sleep!

Everything he had ever wanted was in his arms. Did it matter that there was need as well? So many women had taken from him. They said "Give me," and for a time he was happy to oblige. But he had been faithful to Dianne, despite temptation. Then it had all died. All his desire, all his senses, were consumed in imbibing the world in which he still lived.

Jenna had woven herself into the fabric of his mind so intricately that he was unable to unravel her from it. He traced the edge of her ear through a veil of fine hair. She was part of this, part of him and desire – no, much more than that – flared again. Jenna was as generous with her body as she was with her gentle, quiet mind. For the first time, this had been perfect, a communion of pleasure. Her breasts were perfect because they were her breasts. Her waist was perfect because it was her waist. The most intimate parts of her were perfect – he shifted slightly and she smiled in her sleep and gripped him closer – and he exulted in the knowledge that he was the first man to have touched her this way. She would always be first his. Eternity could not take that away.

What would she do in life? Where would she go? Would she marry? With a sting of loss and jealousy, he knew that she probably would. It was too much. Unconsciousness was stealing over him like a strong drug and he welcomed it. Just as blackness began to drop its curtain, he felt blood trickle onto his upper lip and drop slowly onto Jenna's hair. It triggered a guilt that thundered through him with a force that made him shake.

I should not have done this. I should not have done this to her.

And then the curtain fell.

CHAPTER THIRTY-ONE

JENNA WOKE IN the dark and had no idea how long she had slept. She was lying in her own bed, close to the side against the wall, looking at her own ceiling, seeing the familiar strip of street light above the curtains. The light just filtered to the edge of the dressing table and touched the chain of a pendant she had dropped there earlier.

But everything had changed. She squirmed onto her side in the tiny sliver of space which Paul had left her. He was on his stomach with his face turned towards her, his arm across her waist. He was very still as she leaned over to kiss him lightly. She put her hand on his shoulder and tilted her head to watch him. Sometimes dreams do become real. He was here, in her bed, almost filling it. His warm body and steady breathing transformed this room forever in her mind.

Now it was cold. Carefully she wriggled down to the end of the bed and stood. Her feet landed on her discarded robe and she put it on, grateful now of its heat. Her slippers could be anywhere. She felt her way round the bed to the door and tripped over the teddy bear on the rug. In the bathroom, she examined her face by the light above the mirror. Did she look any different? She felt slight pain but nothing that would stop her welcoming him again if he woke. She smiled into the mirror and brushed her hair back. Maybe she should wake him. Something sticky clung to her fingers as they threaded through her hair. She held her fingers up to the light. It was blood.

In the weak light, she turned her head and combed her fingers through her hair again, feeling slight dampness above her left ear. It was definitely blood. Frowning, she rinsed her fingers and held the strand of hair under the running tap to clean it. There was no sign of a cut on her temple. She towelled the patch of wet hair.

Paul was still asleep on his stomach. There was a small torch in the bedside table. She felt for it and knocked a book to the floor with a thud. Still he did not stir. The small beam of light showed two dark patches on the pillow under his head. She looked closer. He had had a nosebleed! Jenna giggled. *So that's what I did to his blood pressure!*

When she had hauled the quilt from Luke's bed and spread it over Paul, she dropped her robe again, then crawled up beside him from the foot of the bed and quietly slipped under the cover. With some tissues, she mopped at the dark patches then spread tissue over them. His body was so still as she wound herself round him again. She wanted him to wake. She wanted him to love her again. She began to ache with the thought and her hands roamed across his skin, learning the map of his being, the frame of the soul inside him.

~

She woke again to his movements in the dark. He was raised on one elbow, looking down into her face. Delighted, she reached for him, then stopped as he spoke. Hoarse and urgent, he whispered, "Save me, Jenna."

She pulled him to her and hugged him. "You're dreaming."

His breath brushed her neck. "I'm not."

She chuckled. "If you're awake, let's not waste time talking."

He moved so swiftly he left her breathless. Exultant, she matched him in swift passion. *I've got you, I've got you, I've got you!* He spared her nothing this time, no gentleness, no slow stirring of the fire. Impatient with the narrow bed, he threw the quilt to the floor and pulled her down with him. She drowned in luxurious, sensuous delight. At one point, joined together, they sat face to face, her legs wound round him. Her eyes were closed, her lips swollen, her head thrown back, her breasts thrust against him. Supporting her back, he cupped her head with one palm and tilted her face to his. He kissed her deeply and moved within her. His voice was the only thing she heard in the night. It stood out as if spread on silence, for nothing else mattered enough to hear.

"I'm sorry, Jenna. I'm sorry."

She tried to reply but couldn't. She couldn't even wonder. Not yet.

~

The phone was ringing. Jenna raised her head and realised she was on the floor, between the bed and the dressing table, almost on top of Paul. His leg was twined round hers and his head was pillowed in a fold of the quilt. A darkened trace of blood stained his cheek at the corner of his nose. Despite the strident ringing, she watched him stirring, almost fragile in sleep, eyes flickering beneath his lids. Her lips curved. He was beautiful. He would hate the description but she could think of no better one – the dark-and-pale face, the smooth stomach ... She struggled from the tangle of clothes and limbs. The clock on her bedside table said five past ten. The light diffused from the curtain's edge was now daylight. She dragged her robe behind her, feeling the cold of morning slipping across her skin as she skipped down the stairs.

It was Dianne.

She sounded bright, but behind her words of greeting there was tension. Jenna draped the robe round her shoulders as her mind raced. Dianne's husband was lying naked on her floor upstairs.

"Silly really," said Dianne, "but Paul's mother told me he hadn't been in touch for a while. Adam says he hasn't heard from him either. So I just thought I'd check with you."

Jenna played for time. "You're in touch with Adam?"

"Yes. He called here to see Daddy. I thought he was coming to see me because I wasn't well, but Daddy and he talked business for absolutely boring ages." Momentarily side-tracked, her voice became conspiratorial. "By the way, I think he's single again. Rachel's gone off with someone else. They were only over here a few weeks. Bizarre. Poor old Adam looked a bit moochy. So you might get him back again. If you wanted to, of course," she added as an afterthought.

"Sorry you haven't been well."

"No." There was a pause. "A bit horrid actually. I had a miscarriage. Ghastly business, but I'm getting over it now."

Jenna gripped the edge of the cupboard. "A miscarriage? I'm so sorry."

"These things happen and all that."

"But you didn't want children." Jenna squeezed her eyes shut. What a crass thing to say!

"No, I didn't. Hated the thought. But it's funny. I think ... Knowing he was there ..." Her voice trailed off. "Anyway, how's your brother? Adam said he'd had an accident or something."

"He's getting better."

"Oh jolly good. Anyway, if you run into Paul will you let me know?"

"Sure."

On the way up the stairs, Jenna yanked the belt of her robe tight. She stopped in the doorway, leaned against the wall. Paul was sitting on the floor with his back propped against the bed. His head was turned to the door as she came in.

"You heard?" Jenna said.

"Yes." The quilt was wrapped round his legs. He looked wary.

"Why didn't you tell me Dianne was pregnant?"

"I didn't know until last weekend."

She nodded slowly, putting pieces together. "When you went AWOL. Because she lost it?"

He rose so quickly he startled her. "She didn't lose it – she threw it away!"

Jenna took a step back from his suddenly angry face. "What do you mean?"

"I mean she's a bitch and a liar."

He was changing again, changing from the magical lover of only hours before. Just as suddenly, his fury died and he sat heavily on the bed. He propped his elbows on his knees and knotted his fingers in his hair. Before he dropped his head, Jenna saw the bleakness of the night before swimming back into his eyes. He dropped his hands and looked up at her.

"She had an abortion. She killed my child."

Oh, God! Jenna's mind reeled from shock. She couldn't go to him, but neither could she leave him. Caught, she sank cross-legged to the floor. There was a long silence while so many feelings swirled inside her. Paul stayed silent, waiting. When she began to speak she thought he probably knew what her first question was going to be.

"When ...?"

He leaned forward and reached for her hand. She snatched it away.

"Jenna, I haven't touched her since Christmas. I told you. It was over then. It was finished before then." He spread his hands, pleading. "I threw my ring away in front of you."

While she digested this, he stood and made for the door. He stopped for a moment, seemed disorientated. He put both his hands over his face, his eyes tight shut. Jenna was about to speak when he touched the top of her head briefly.

"I'm going to make a phone call. I'll have to use your phone."

His voice came up the stairs. He was ringing his mother. "Oh, you know me. I always turn up again. Yes ... sure ... Yes, I'll call in soon ... We'll catch up then ... I know. Sorry."

The conversation was short and Jenna could imagine Hazel's relief which would manifest itself as a scolding. She was the only person from whom Paul Shepherd would take a scolding.

"Well?" she asked when he returned, staying crouched with her back to him.

"Well what?" he said.

"Aren't you going to ring Dianne too?"

"No."

"But what do *I* say to her?" She twisted to look up at him, upset and puzzled. "She asked me to let her know. Do you want me to lie to her?"

He dropped to his heels behind her. Her senses skipped and danced all over again at his nearness. "If you like. I don't care." His hands came round under her arms, under her breasts, pulling her to her feet. He held her back against his body for a moment. Her bones became like liquid as he bent his lips to her ear, his hands still cupping her breasts. "Let's not lose this, Jenna. Let's not spoil it. I don't want to go back out there yet. I want to stay here, with you. For ever and ever." There was almost a sob in his last words. Then he turned her around. That was it. That was all he had to do.

With the passion and amazement of a new convert she welcomed him. He raised himself on his arms and she held his head, his hair gripped in her fingers. There was moisture on his lashes. She felt his weight again as he moved both hands under her, down, down, to pull her closer. As his movements became stronger, thought dissolved into sensation and she discarded guilt and goodness as chaff from another world.

~

He was restless again. The passion and the peace had both dissolved. She found him standing in the sitting room, half-dressed now, arms folded across his bare chest, looking out at the street. Jenna came up behind him.

"What will the neighbours think? A bare-chested man standing at my window. You realise my reputation is in tatters?"

He turned round and she raised her arms, made a noose round his neck and leaned against him. The hollows between his ribs were a little deeper than they should be.

"Just as well the sitting room is all they can see." His answer was automatic, humourless. He unhooked her arms and held her away from him, both her hands held in his. "Rachel has left Adam again."

"Dianne told me. I'm not surprised."

"Neither am I. Rachel likes the chase, not the capture. She's like a cat tossing a mouse." Paul gazed at her for a moment, his head cocked. Then, "He's been asking about you. How you are. If you're seeing anyone."

Jenna's eyebrows rose. "Really? What did you say?"

"He asked my mother. She said she didn't think you were. She says he's talking about trying to get transferred back here. I think he's raised her hopes that you and Adam might get together again."

She shrugged. "So?"

"Don't go back to him."

She was so shocked she was speechless. She dropped to the sofa. "I could be offended at that, Paul." She spread her hands. "What was last night? A one night stand?"

He sat beside her and pulled her into his arms. She stiffened, not mollified. "No, no no!" It was a fierce cry and he gripped her so tightly she had to relax or be hurt. "You don't understand."

She pushed at his chest, tried to pull away to look at his face. "No, I don't understand! Make me understand! What had happened at your house? Why was there an album of photographs of me torn on the floor? Why did you disappear? Why are you saying all these odd things?"

He pulled her back to his shoulder and dropped his chin onto the top of her head, stroking, stroking, stroking her hair. "Ssssh. All in good time. You and I have a lot still to say to each other."

"Lots and lots and lots."

"Shouldn't you be in a library or something?"

"I've dropped out. I'm not going back."

The stroking stopped abruptly. "What! Why?"

"Because of you. I didn't want to stay here without you. So I decided to move to Scotland and start again; try to forget you." She looked up, mischief in her eyes. "You've made that impossible now! You could always come with me."

He shook his head slowly. "No, I can't."

She snuggled closer. "Well, I don't mind now anyway. Wherever you go, I'm coming with you."

His fingers were still playing with her hair. "No, you can't, Jenna."

She drew away and put space between them. "Will you stop talking in riddles? You're annoying me."

"Think in riddles," he flashed, suddenly impatient.

She was so sensitive to him her soul must have been visible in her eyes for he moved swiftly to bring her to her feet and hug her. "I'm sorry. I'm a grumpy old bastard."

"No wonder Dianne left you." The words fell like a dropped boulder. *Oh, God, why did I bring that name up again?* She backed away, gave a short laugh. The thought of Dianne and what she had done wasn't going to spoil this. "Now I'm sorry."

"Like you said. There's a lot to talk about." He turned his back and walked to the hall. She followed him and was alarmed to see him slipping his coat round his bare shoulders.

"Where are you going?"

"I need to go out. I have to go. I *have* to." It was as if he were convincing himself.

She made herself stay at the door of the room. "But you'll be back? We haven't eaten yet. It's brunchtime."

The buttons of his coat were still open as he scooped her into his body like a lost child just found. His voice trembled through his skin as her cheek pressed against him. "Never doubt me, Jenna." Almost fumbling, he pulled her head up urgently and kissed her until her breath was gone. "I'll be back and then you'll have to trust me ..." he kissed her again "... and stay with me ..." and again "... and never leave me alone ..." and again "... but most of all, you'll have to forgive me."

Puzzled and breathless she said, "You couldn't have done anything I won't forgive you for."

"I'll be back by teatime."

He released her and in an instant was gone.

Then the silence began.

Back in the bedroom, the debris of the night before was still strewn across the room. But it was cold now, a shambles merely, not the accompaniment of loving passion. A yellow leg from the teddy bear poked out from under the quilt on the floor. She picked him up and shook him straight again. When she lifted the quilt, her slippers fell from a fold.

With the borrowed quilt back on the spare bed, Jenna stood in the middle of her bedroom and felt the bitter tang of desertion in the air. There was not one sign that Paul had ever been here; not one. Trying to shake off the heaviness in the room, she lay down on her bed again as if Paul had just placed her there. She stretched, pointing her toes and arching her arms above her head. Little aftershocks still quivered within her as she ran her hands across her waist, down along her belly, and remembered. Also vivid was the memory of his anguish and anger when he told her of Dianne and the abortion. Jenna's face creased into disgust. It was a dreadful thing to do to a man, to reject his child from the womb. And then to lie, to say it was a miscarriage! In irritation, she tossed onto her side and something caught her eye.

Two patches of blood dried on the pillow.

He had left something after all. She traced the edges of the stains, brownish now, and wished that, just once, he had told her that he loved her.

In the bathroom, she raised her face to the water streaming over her. Part of her was basking in the glory of consummation. Part of her was trembling, nervous of the way things were, the obstacles to come. She wanted Paul here now and yet he would never be in anyone's cage. How could she want that for him? She would rather fly free with him and take the chances that came, the storms that buffeted, the havens they found on the wing.

There was so much yet to know of him. What did he mean by the things he said? Of one thing she was certain. They had broken the barriers and were now standing on common ground. He would not walk away again, and neither would she.

She wound a towel round her hair, wiped the condensation from the mirror and smiled at her reflection. At this moment, the glory was all she would recognise.

CHAPTER THIRTY-TWO

CHARLES BUTLER'S LARGE walled garden was green and brown and yellow and red under a spring sun. Dianne tightened her grip on her father's arm as Toby, walking with them, stopped speaking and let his words fall into the lush air, settle over them like clinging, crushing ivy. Charles covered his daughter's hand with his own and spoke to Toby.

"Are you absolutely sure?"

Toby dipped his head in a familiar mannerism. His neat grey beard brushed his silk tie. "There can be exceptions. Miracles even. But in Dianne's case I doubt that there will be any reversal. I'm sorry."

A fan of sunshine unfurled over the garden as a cloud passed away from it. A magnificent magnolia tree was in full flower. When Paul had first seen that tree in its rich abundance, he had crouched on the grass for a long time, just looking. He had moved to another angle, crouched and studied it again. When he had completely circled it he lay under it, looking up, enchanted by the waxen chalices, cream with their blush of pink. Then, inevitably, he photographed it. She remembered standing just there, holding a branch down as he instructed her to keep it still while he focused on one flower. She'd got bored helping and he told her to go away.

But the pictures were good. One appeared on the cover of a national gardening magazine. She told everyone it was the picture she had helped him to get. She suspected in fact that it wasn't, but Paul never contradicted her.

As Toby's words finally grounded in her resisting brain, the rows of tulips and crocuses along the edge of the path dissolved into a grey mist, mixing crazily with magnolia blossom. Toby gripped her waist. There was a summer house close by and the edge of the ornate metal chair pressed the back of her knees as she was lowered into it.

"Deep breaths," Toby ordered in his clipped medical tones.

The world steadied again. The irony of what she had just been told cut like the lash of a whip. Her haemorrhage had been followed by a severe infection. It seemed that she had inherited her mother's fragility in reproduction. She had never wanted children and now she had been told that she could never have any by natural means. She had been rendered infertile.

Charles felt her brow and spoke across her as if she wasn't there. "Why would a miscarriage result in sterility? I know there were complications, but even so ..."

A robin hopped up onto the wooden step, cocked its head at them and flew away to a currant bush. A bluebottle buzzed and banged against the wooden roof.

Toby spoke without hesitation. "You have to understand that each person is an individual, Charles. No-one can predict every outcome."

"But I can pay for the best ..."

Toby raised an impatient hand. "Your money will not buy this, Charles."

Charles' heavy frame slumped forward onto his elbows on the wrought iron table. The wind carried the scent of new growth, freshly turned earth, an exuberant fecundity.

"It's just ... after her mother ..." He stopped on a shuddering, broken breath. With one hand he covered his face, pressed his fingers into his eyes. "We have lost my grandchild! My only hope of a grandchild."

With wrenching, gulping, ugly sobs, Charles Butler began to cry.

Toby crossed his legs, folded his hands on his lap and studied his knuckles.

"Oh, stop it, Daddy," Dianne snapped. Toby's eyes swivelled to her, reproach in them that only she could see. "I want to go in. And I want Luther."

Toby had set his phone on the table when he sat down. It began to ring. Dianne glanced at it and her eyes widened. Toby lifted it, rose gracefully and adjusted his cuffs. "I must get to the hospital. I've a clinic. Call me any time."

As he walked across the grass, he flipped the phone open, glanced quickly back at Dianne and then walked further away before speaking.

~

Luther was in casual clothes, his collar open and faded jeans just beginning to dig into spreading flesh at his waist. One exhibition had just finished at the gallery and Luther was completely redesigning it before the next one. It was Dianne's idea and now she wasn't there to help. Instead, she was lying on the chaise longue in the window of the library. Luther had come at a summons from Charles.

Now, when Dianne finished speaking through dry lips, he sat forward in the leather armchair and dropped his head into his hands, fair hair feathering through his fingers.

"My God!" he groaned. "How could that happen?" He looked up, his eyes glittering in the light reflected from the glass fronts of the bookcases opposite. "I'll sue! I'll destroy them."

"You can't, remember? Nobody knows about it. And it would be bad publicity," she added.

He sprang to his feet and paced up and down in front of the

fireplace. An embroidered fire screen stood on the fender, the vase of spills beside it. Finally he jabbed his fist downwards violently and spoke through gritted teeth.

"None of this would have happened if it hadn't been for Paul Shepherd." His fist jabbed again. "Curse him. Curse him!"

"Luther, you told me to do it! Don't blame him."

Luther swung round on her. "Why not? Nothing has gone right since the day you set eyes on him." He thrust a finger at her. "You're defending him! Why are you defending him?"

"I'm not defending him ..."

"Yes, you are!" He stood over her. "I suppose you want to go crying back to him now."

"No! I ..."

"You know what's wrong with you, Dianne? You always got what you asked for, and when you got it you didn't want it any more. You wanted him, you wanted me; you didn't want a baby, now you're upset because you can't have one!"

"Don't shout at me, Luther! Don't you dare! And you were horrid to Paul and no-one's seen him in days. I'm not well yet and you're supposed to be comforting me."

"So who comforts me, then? I'm rescuing the Chevalier family name by blood and sweat, and now I'm told there'll be no family. As for that man, I hope he's driven over a cliff." He thumped a fist into his palm. "I hope he's dead!"

"You told me to do it!" There was only one thing to do when Luther was like this. It never worked with Paul, but it usually worked with Luther. She burst into tears.

It did work. He squeezed onto the edge of the chaise longue and put his arms round her. She sobbed into his jumper.

"I'm sorry, Di. I'm sorry. It's just such a shock."

"Well, how do you think I feel?" she wailed. "I can never have children!"

With a tone of exasperation, he said, "But you didn't want any,

Di. I did, but you didn't."

"I do now." She sniffed and he handed her a tissue from a box on the table.

"I do love you, you know."

She blew her nose noisily and tossed her hair. "It doesn't sound like it."

"You can be enormously trying sometimes."

She lay back. "Shouldn't you get back to the gallery? Those workmen will make a dreadful hash of things if you're not there."

"Yes, they will." He bent over her and touched his mouth to her brow. "You must be nearly better now." He put his hand on her waist and his pupils dilated. "I miss you."

His meaning was clear. She put the back of her hand to her forehead. "Yes, well. We'll see."

He took her chin and turned her face to look at him. "Don't get upset when I let off steam. It's just me. We need each other, and I'm keeping you now. Having children doesn't matter as much as having you."

When he released her chin, his fingers left marks.

~

Much later, Bella perched on the arm of the chair and ate a bowl of ice-cream which she had somehow acquired on the way through the house. She looked elegantly casual in an expensive trouser suit. At Dianne's words, the spoon stopped momentarily between her lips and then she scooped the ice-cream into her mouth. Her cheeks hollowed as it melted.

"Paul phoned Toby?"

"Right under my nose. Toby left pretty quickly."

"Well then, Paul's about, isn't he? He hasn't vanished. Stop worrying."

"I even tried Jenna this morning. You know – that student I

told you about? The one that was ditched by Paul's brother?"

Bella mopped delicately at a drop of ice-cream on the arm of the chair. "What would *she* know? Not exactly Paul's type, I should think."

"God, no!" Dianne's brow puckered with worry. "But why would he want to talk to Toby? And what will Toby say to him?"

"What could he say that Paul doesn't know already? Anyway, didn't we think Toby fancied him?" When Dianne said nothing, Bella scraped the bowl clean and set it down on the fender. "Look on the bright side, Di. You'll not have to go back on those blasted pills. Or no more thinking for the two of you just at the critical moment. Honestly, men lose their brains as soon as they lose their trousers."

Bella giggled her wonderful giggle and Dianne began to feel her self-control creeping back. There was a ruthless act of will to be performed. Babies were smelly, noisy, creatures who turned your mind to mulch and your house into a rubbish tip. People would sympathise and be nice to her. And then they would forget. So would Luther. She'd make sure he did.

The image of a tiny face, the child she could have had, the child who might have been formed by the lines of a striking father, was receding at last, fading into the vault of unhappy memories, a foetus, a thing, not human, merely an embarrassment.

She swung her legs to the floor. "I need to get back to the gallery. It's a busy time. Fancy shopping tomorrow? I'll need some new clothes. Just a short trip?"

Bella grinned. "Welcome back, Di."

~

The River Lagan was dimpled dark and light, the burnished gold from the lamps lifting and folding on the surface like rippled silk. The walls of the huge Arena had absorbed the clubbers and only lovers and the lonely walked along the paved path by the river.

Jenna leaned on the railings and looked down at the meandering water. They had both wanted to be outside tonight because no walls could contain the storm of feelings which buffeted them. Paul had not spoken for some time, a replica of herself in stance, arms on the railings, wrists crossed, but bigger, darker, less at ease.

It didn't matter. There was time to say everything. There would be years to say everything. She stole a glance at his still profile, the long feathers of his lashes, his lips closed and solemn. He had shaved and changed and was more like the man who had disturbed her dreams for so long. She was so happy. The fence was jumped, the cage door broken. She couldn't imagine why she thought it was impassible, or why she feared to test it. No, that was wrong. She did know. It was because never before had she desired something so badly that everything that stood in the way became blurred, irrelevant, and finally invisible. It's like birth, she thought. Birth is difficult, painful, traumatic, but the baby emerges into a new, infinitely bigger world of possibilities. The problems are still there but with new air comes new strength.

"I don't know what I'm going to tell Mum and Dad."

He just nodded once, slow and remote, not really hearing her.

"Will you come with me to see Luke tomorrow? I think he might get home any day. He's asked about you." When he still didn't reply, she sidled a little, touching her arm to his.

The contact stirred him and he straightened, turned and focused on her. He put his arm round her shoulders and she leaned into him. Together they looked across, beyond the empty dock where the SeaCat moored, to the fragmented segments of light still burning randomly in the office blocks on the opposite bank. A small freighter rocked gently, the very faintest lapping of water audible from its hull. After a moment Jenna twisted to look up at his face. It was irresistible in the dusky shadows and she put a hand to his cheek. He kissed her palm as he had done so exquisitely the night before.

"Paul, stop talking in riddles. Where were you and why do you say some of the things you say? What does 'save me' mean?"

He drew a long breath and exhaled slowly, a long soft sound. He drew her to sit on the low wall behind them, between the lamps among the palm trees which bordered the Arena. Wooden slats had been fitted to the top of the wall to make a seat. Further along, a teenage boy and girl were giggling together. Paul took Jenna's hands and she turned to face him, her knees touching his.

The reticence had gone. On his face was only determination and, strangely, sadness. Why? He should be feeling as happy as she was. Then she remembered Dianne and what she had done. There was no point in leaving things unsaid. There was much that would have to be faced without reticence or fear.

"I'm sorry about what Dianne did."

"Even Dianne has no idea what she did."

Sudden irritation made her frown. She didn't want to be dragging Dianne's legacy round like a ball and chain. Impulsively she began, "I hope your divorce ..."

"Stop it, Jenna!" Her eyes widened in surprise at his sharp tone. He tightened his grip on her fingers. "I'm not divorced, remember."

She shrugged. "No, but you will ..."

He put a finger over her lips. "Stop."

She pushed her hands playfully between the open edges of his coat and placed her palms on each side of his body. "Stop what? This?" She kneaded gently. His ribs seemed to have protruded even more since yesterday. "You've been starving yourself. I'll have to get you fattened up. By the time you're forty, you'll have a midriff!"

He closed his eyes then for a long time and she fell quiet. When he opened them again, they seemed to be burning, to have all the pain of the world in them. It was those burning eyes that lit the first tiny flame of fear in her.

"Paul?"

He dropped his brow to hers and slanted his eyes up to meet hers. "I want you to swear that you won't leave me."

She pulled back in surprise. "Of course I won't leave you. Don't be silly. I've just got you!"

He chuckled, short and low. "You got me a long time ago, Jenna." A cool breeze blew off the river and he pulled her hood up, tucked her hair inside. Then he lifted her face and kissed her. Against her mouth he whispered, "Swear."

"I don't need to. I mean what I say. How could I leave you now? Could you leave me?"

He backed away a little, trailing her hands with him. He turned his cheek to press her joined fingers to his face. The flame of fear jumped again, blue and yellow and burning.

"Jenna, I'm going to hurt you very much."

Her voice became small, almost lost in the dark. "You're frightening me. Is this something to do with forgiving you? About riddles?" Desperately, she leaned towards him. "I'll forgive you anything. Just stop frightening me."

The girl who had been giggling with her boyfriend further down the wall gave a squeal and jumped up, laughing. The pair ran past Paul and Jenna, the boy wearing a baseball cap, snatched playfully for the girl as she ran. Paul watched them scamper out of sight, then turned his burning eyes back to Jenna. There was no restlessness, no fidgeting, no flicking glances here and away again. He was going to tell her something, perhaps open the last door on the long corridor to the centre of his soul.

"I had a car accident before I came back here. On my way home from covering a country wedding in Kent...."

"I remember Dianne saying something ...."

He put his fingers to her lips again. "Don't stop me. Just listen.

If I stop, I mightn't start again."

Her eyes were huge and fixed on his mouth as if his words were physical beings, entities falling from him, circling, crowding, crawling into the crevices of her fear.

"I was very shaken up and my head hit a metal strut, hard. I was taken to A & E and then straight in for a brain scan." He stopped, swallowed, spoke shakily. "I've never told anyone this."

There was a cocoon weaving around them both, a withdrawing from the river, the lamps, the clustered buildings, the smell of water, the beat of the young at play.

She touched his arm. "Go on."

Resolution possessed him again. He took her hand where it lay in her lap. At first she thought he was changing the subject.

"Remember I told you about the hawk I saw at Gortin, just after I saw the red squirrel?"

"I remember."

"I was afraid for the squirrel. And I knew that only the hawk would decide whether the squirrel lived or died." She nodded. He took a deep breath and locked his eyes on hers. "Jenna, there's a hawk in my head."

She frowned. "What do you mean?"

"The scan showed up something in my brain which shouldn't be there. Deep in my brain. Something bad."

He was watching her intently, pain etched in every shadowed line. He was still beautiful to her. She shook her head a little and opened her hand.

"So ... they fixed whatever it was?"

Now his words became gentle, his hand soft on her cheek, all his caring for her. "No, Jenna, they didn't. They couldn't."

Bewilderment, disbelief, worry, an inane impulse to laugh, all tangled into a knot and must have shown on her face for Paul slide closer and folded her into his arms. Her cheek was against his chest, her arms round him, her eyes wide open on the lights of the buildings across the river, his hand on her head; she was the child now and this was the way she would forever remember hearing his next words.

"I'm going to leave you." He dropped a kiss on top of her head and rocked her a little. "I won't have another birthday and I won't have another Christmas. This is as old as I get." His arms tightened. "I didn't feel ill for quite a while. But it's starting. I'm starting to feel ill now." He paused only for a breath. "Jenna, I'm dying."

Now there was no water, no light, no buildings. Jenna became a rotating cut-out, twirling in a vacuum from a spindle of shock. *But I can feel his heart beating beneath my cheek! It cannot stop!* Then she was gasping for air, gripping the railings, away from him, away from the treacherous blackness that had wiped out all joy.

With her back to him she asked, "This is for real?"

"Yes," he answered simply. She covered her face. It was like being hit by a demolition ball. Even so, daggers of lightening lit her memory. He fell so deeply asleep; he was losing weight; he hadn't time to rattle bars.

Even Dianne doesn't know what she did.

Save me, Jenna!

She stayed there for several minutes until she heard him stand and his hand rested at her waist.

"Tell me what you'll do, Jenna."

There was such tension in him that his hand trembled where it touched her.

Swear you won't leave me.

There were many questions to ask but just now, at this moment, there was only one thing to be said, one thing that he needed to hear, one thing that came to her as a simple fact. Slowly, deliberately, she drew close to him and took his pale face between her palms.

"I will not leave you, Paul. What is the shock to me compared to the reality for you? I'll hold you, and if I have to hold the hawk as well, then I'll do that too."

In one movement he smothered her against him like a man clutching at a rock in turbulent seas. His voice was muffled by his arms around her and by the emotion in his throat.

"I don't deserve you." He held her in an iron band as if he would engrave her body onto his. "I thought such a person as you did not exist." Then he held her out from him, a hand on each shoulder. A twinkle of light snagged on his eyes; the shadows from his cheekbones were longer than she had noticed before. "Jenna Warwick, I love you." He sounded almost amazed.

She smiled faintly. She had heard what she longed to hear. Why did she feel so old? Her hood had blown away from her face again and a strand of hair tickled her nose. "Then everything else is just detail, isn't it?"

The journey home was a voyage of silence. Jenna glanced sidelong at Paul but he was concentrating on the late-night traffic, and did not look at her or touch her. Or perhaps he was thinking. She leaned her head on the side window and her eyes jumped from street light to street light as they passed. The tail lights of cars stretched ahead, taxis veered off to their different destinations. She looked up at the sky, through the ragged frames of clouds to tiny stars, dimmed by the lights of the city. She hadn't taken this in; not really. Questions were stirring now; something that might be anger was scratching its way to the surface.

Like hitting your thumb with a hammer, the crescendo of pain begins only after the blow.

CHAPTER THIRTY-THREE

PAUL'S SHOES LAY just inside the sitting room door, one askew across the toe of the other. Jenna tripped over them and spilled coffee on the sofa. She mopped up the spill with a tissue. "Why didn't you put them an inch or two to the left? I'd have spilled the lot then."

He was prowling. She knew this mood. They had still said very little to each other. He pulled back a curtain and stared out, dropped it again and circled the room, tapping the razor shell against his fingers. He set it down again on the mantelpiece and pulled a daffodil from the vase, snapped the stem. He took a mug from Jenna and left it on the floor.

"Don't leave that ..."

He silenced her with a brief kiss and then pushed her hair back to tuck the daffodil behind her ear.

"I'm going to sleep on the sofa tonight," he said, adjusting the daffodil.

She gave a little laugh of surprise. "Why? Tired of me already?"

Restlessness was back again; his foot missed the coffee mug by an centimetre. "I would never get tired of you, Jenna, even if ..." He drummed the back of the chair. "I've been waiting for you to get angry. You're going to get so mad with me, my darling. It's taking longer than I expected."

"That's the first time you've called me that."

" 'My darling'? " She nodded and he smiled. "There are many first times this week."

Her composure broke like crashing surf. "And how long till the last times, Paul? How long till then? How many sentences are we not going to finish? How many weeks do we have of catching up – 'How's the dying going today, darling? By the way, what'll we have for supper?' " Her voice was louder than she thought it would be. "You *knew* this. You knew this all along and you made me love you!"

He spread his hands in a helpless gesture. "I didn't make you do anything."

The injustice of that made her gasp. "You pursued me; you tormented me; you told me you needed me. What the *hell* did you expect would happen?"

He raised his eyebrows. "I can't help it if I'm irresistible."

Her bag, empty of books, lay limply beside the sofa. She kicked it, sending it flying towards him, the fringe splaying in the air. He caught it easily, dropped it on the floor.

"Now we're getting somewhere." He sat in the chair again and pulled one ankle across his knee. "I've seen you really angry once before. It was a wonderful sight. Remember? The night at the Christmas party and Adam had just snogged Rachel in front of you. I followed you to the car park. I knew then you were a passionate woman." His eyes darkened and his mouth twitched. "You just didn't know it yet."

Jenna slumped to the sofa and hugged herself, misery prickling her skin. "Why did you do this to me? If you hadn't come back last night, I would still be getting ready to leave, to go to Scotland and this would never have ..."

She couldn't help it. Furious with herself and him, she slid from the cushion to the floor, drew up her knees, buried her face in her arms and wept. Shock, devastation, and sorrow shook her from head to foot. Swiftly he dropped to the floor beside her. She pushed him away violently.

"You think I'm a saint! 'Saint Jenna' you called me. The good girl who'll do anything for anybody, the girl with the delicate conscience!" She raised her voice, hoarse. "Well, I'm not a saint. I'm not even good."

He was silent, leaning back against the edge of the sofa. Then he took her hand and gripped it tighter, trapping it when she tried to pull away.

"You said you loved me."

She threw her head back, her eyes feeling like swollen sponges. "I do. It's just ... I don't like you very much just now."

He drew up a knee to turn towards her, took her chin and she didn't resist. "I have never liked me at all. That's one of the things you have brought to me. A sense that maybe I wasn't so totally unlovable."

She pulled away and stared at him in disbelief. "Don't be so daft!"

"Can I tell you something?"

She sniffed. "You've never asked permission before."

"When Christopher was near death, I flew over to see him for the last time. My mother needed me and I hadn't been there as much as I should have been. I stood beside the bed of this skeleton of a man, a man who had tried and failed to accept me." He paused, his eyes unfocused. Jenna stayed very still, her sobs suspended. "He was almost deformed with pain, even morphine wasn't helping much by then. I leaned over him. I told him I was there ... " he took a shaky breath "... I called him 'Dad'. He opened his eyes, looked at me, looked round the room, then in a weak but clear voice he asked for Adam. He said 'I want to see my son'."

She put her hand on his arm. "Oh, Paul."

"I left the room, got the next flight back to London. I hated him. Next time I saw him he was a corpse. I came back for the funeral but that was only for my mother's sake." His hands balled into fists. "All through the day, while they were saying prayers over him, I hoped he was in hell."

"He didn't deserve that, Paul."

His eyes were bright with fierce remembered fury. "Neither did I." He gave a short bitter laugh. "I swore I'd be more successful that Christopher could ever have imagined. I was already well known but when I met Dianne I decided she was my next stepping stone to the rich and famous. And so she was. Until everything changed and ..."

"And you found you didn't need stepping stones. You needed an anchor."

His eyes widened and he hooked her to him. "Jenna, you're connected to my mind some way. I don't understand it, but you ... know me."

She played with his fingers where they hung over her shoulder. "I remember saying to my mother one night when I was quite small, that I couldn't imagine being married. I couldn't imagine somebody loving me when they didn't have to. I knew my mum and dad and Luke loved me, but they had to – they were family."

He lifted his hand from her shoulder and stroked her hair back. "That's it. That's it exactly."

The phone in the hall shrilled. Paul groaned. "Don't answer it."

Jenna blew her nose and got to her feet. "It might be to do with Luke."

It was her mother. "Got you at last. I was trying earlier. Where were you?"

It was cold in the hall. Jenna gave the box of books a shove nearer the wall. "Is Luke OK?"

"That's why I'm ringing. He's getting home tomorrow!"

"Oh, great news!"

"He gets out after the doctor sees him and he'll be home by teatime. We can collect you at your house on the way. I was saying to Dad that if you've left university, you don't need to stay in Belfast any more anyway."

Jenna bit her lip. It was truly great news but she was not going back home, not yet. And she wasn't going to tell any more lies.

"Sorry, Mum. I'll give Luke a ring tomorrow, but I'm staying here for the moment."

"But Jenna, I sent for a brochure of Dundee ... "

"Something very important has come up and I have to stay here. I'll see you when I can. How's Dad?"

Cora's voice rose, incredulous. "What's more important than Luke getting home?"

"A man."

Now interest was piqued. "Oh? Who is it? Is Adam back? He can come too ... "

"No, it's not Adam. Sorry, I must go. I'll ring tomorrow."

She hung up, sorry and not sorry. Her family seemed so far from her mind at the moment, even Luke. She began to speak as she pushed open the door.

"Luke's getting home ..... Paul!"

Blood was on his hands and on the scarlet tissues strewn on the sofa round him. The tissue box that had been on top of the television was almost empty. He held one palm cupped beneath his nostrils.

"It's OK. I think it's stopped."

She sat beside him, put an arm across his back, alarm vibrating through her. She took the last tissue and carefully wiped the trickles of blood from his lip.

He sat back. "I'm fine. This happens a bit more often now."

She looked down at his blood, some of it streaking her fingers. "The red sweet wine of youth. Remember?"

He touched her finger with the blood-reddened tip of his own.

"I remember."

"I don't want to be alone tonight, Paul."

He kissed her brow. "Neither do I."

Upstairs, Jenna snuggled into him as he pulled her close. His breathing became deeper, more even. Then, just as sleep crept up on her, she jolted awake again, raised herself on one elbow.

"It's not true," she said with certainty. "It's just not true, Paul. Paul? Can you hear me? We'll go to a doctor here and he'll tell us all that can be done and everything will be all right. This is the twenty-first century, for God's sake."

He didn't move in reply and she thought he had gone into one of his deep, almost unconscious, sleeps. She had nearly fallen asleep again when she felt him stir slightly. His throat moved against her temple as he spoke, low and determined.

"Christopher died by an inch a day. I'm not going to be like that. I'm going to go with my boots on."

He eased her body against him a little and she twined her legs through his. "And how are you going to manage that?"

"I've wished for it. And Toby thinks I will."

"Who's Toby?"

"Shut up and go to sleep."

"I still don't like you, you know."

He cuddled her. "You've a great way of showing it."

Two mallards were fighting on the water, causing other ducks to bob on the ruptured surface and thrash hastily away. The dark green heads of the mallards darted and pecked each other. Squawking and splashing, one dragged the other underwater by the wing. Suddenly the fight broke up and they pelted, side by side, across the lake towards a female who turned tail and paddled furiously away.

"Keep going, girl!" called Jenna. "They're not worth it!"

"Hey! You're supposed to be supporting my suffering ego."

She turned and grinned at Paul who was lying flat on his back on the grass. "Your ego doesn't need supported. It needs pruned with a machete."

She came and lay beside him and they looked up at a beautiful spring sky. He pointed at a cloud. "Look, there's a dog with a bone."

She squinted. "It's a cat with a mouse."

"No way. Jack didn't have a tail like that. Neither does Widget. It's a dog."

Not by the flicker of a muscle did Jenna let him know that she had noticed his idle mention of Jack. His mind was easing out of its cramped space, opening the gates and creeping out into the reality of his entire life. If she had helped him unfold fully into the light of his day, then maybe his twilight would be easier to bear. She turned her head away. No, it wouldn't; no, it wouldn't.

A mother and two children came close to the edge of the pond. There was a boy of about four and a little girl of two. The girl held a whole slice of bread in one plump hand and a large purple soft toy under the pink sleeve of her other arm. She teetered and her mother gripped her shoulder, bending to her. Anxiously she asked, "Would you like mummy to hold your heffalump?"

As one, Jenna and Paul turned and buried their faces in each other's shoulders to muffle their simultaneous snorts of laughter. Jenna didn't know how it happened, but her tears of laughter became tears of anguish as she gripped him, felt the warmth of him in the spring sun, heard the deep loveliness of his laugh, smelled the grass beneath him. He pulled back, still laughing, and saw the wet tracks on her cheeks and the crumpled chin. He sat up abruptly.

"Stop crying, Jenna! I don't need this."

The mother glanced round and ushered her children further away. The honking of ducks and geese, the splash of feathers and the cries of children in the playground, did not disguise the annoyance in his voice. Jenna sprang to her feet.

"Well, I do! I do need it! Have you really thought about how I feel? Have you really?" She swiped a hand angrily across her eyes. "This is a wonderful day in the sun, enjoying ourselves, feeding ducks. And I keep ... " she gestured helplessly "... thinking about the big black abyss ahead. About coming back here without you and seeing you everywhere." She dropped to her heels on the grass in front of him. He was sitting with his arms hanging over his drawn up knees, fiddling with pieces of grass. "Why did you come back, Paul? You would have hurt me less if you hadn't come back. I wish I'd kept resisting you."

He looked up, past her, where a seagull circled low, swooped down with its legs thrust out and plopped on the water in the middle a flock of ducks. There was a cacophony of squawks and a flurry of flapped wings. At first she thought he wasn't going to reply. Finally he looked back and held her gaze.

"Do you mean that? Because I can go away again. If I do, you'll never see me again. Because I do care about how you feel." He reached out to her. "Oh Jenna, I have thought so much about how you feel. I was going to leave you alone. I tried, after Luke came round, remember? And I discovered ..." he gave a dry laugh "... that you were dropping your defences, just as I was raising mine." His voice dropped, his shoulders slumped. "Maybe this is too much. I'll go away again, if you want," he repeated.

"I didn't say that. And why wouldn't I see you again?"

He didn't blink as he replied. "Because I'd be dead, instead of waiting to die."

"Why?"

A small white dog appeared from behind him and snuffled past, trotting between them. Paul watched it go, thinking. Then he stood and held out a hand to pull Jenna to her feet. He put his arms round her waist and held her loosely in front of him.

"Let's both be selfish, shall we? You tell me exactly what you feel – like you just did – and I'll tell you how I feel."

"That'll be a first."

He bit her nose lightly. "Yes, another one." He turned round and started walking along the side of the lake, keeping his arm round her. Their feet crunched over the empty husks of beech-nuts.

"When Luther left that night, I decided to kill myself."

"That's not funny."

He raised a finger to silence her. "I went up to the Giant's Causeway and found a cliff. I sat on that cliff-top watching the breakers crashing over the rocks below. It was so high there were gulls below me the size of my thumbnail. I stayed there all night. I knew it could all be over very quickly. The scariest bit would be falling. Once I hit the rocks I wouldn't feel anything more."

He stopped talking, waiting for her to say something. A flotilla of brown speckled ducks was following them, close to the bank. Small wakes fanned out on the water from their tails and overlapped. Their honking was surprisingly deep for such small birds.

"Why didn't you do it?"

"I thought about it for days. I washed in streams and cafes. I was put out of the last one because I was looking like a tramp. I went to Gortin and lost myself in the forest."

They reached the end of the lake where there was a small bridge and stopped in the centre of it. The island in the centre of the lake was dense with trees and bushes. Birds preened and slept and foraged along the fringes by the water.

"Did you go to Rossnowlagh again?"

He gave her waist a little squeeze. "No. I don't want to go there again without you."

She looked up at him. "Then we'll go."

"Yes. Soon."

She was frightened to think what he meant by that. On an impulse she said, "How about staying in the hotel?"

His nose crinkled as he smiled. "So you *don't* want me to go away again then?" He dropped a kiss on her cheek. "Finally I decided to commit one last huge selfish act. A prize-winning selfish act. If it didn't work, then I'd go back up north and jump."

She turned round to face him. "Did it work?"

He took her face between his hands and tilted her head up. His eyes were almost black against the white of his skin, piercing her own with deep intensity. "Oh yes," he breathed. "Oh yes."

There on the little bridge he kissed her long and deeply. The new feelings stirred easily inside her and she reached up to pull him closer, moulding into his body with an instinct now loosened from its hiding place.

When he broke away he kept her face close to his. "Luke was going to recover and I had made a bargain with some god or other. I said I'd trade my life for his. I'd accept what was going to happen to me if Luke recovered. I'd stop fighting."

"Oh, Paul ..."

"So when I met you in the car park at the hospital and you told me that Luke was going to be OK, it was like my death sentence all over again. And from your mouth." She remembered that well, how he had reacted to the news. "And when Luther told me that Dianne had destroyed my baby, there was nothing left. He had taken the last of me. The very last of me. "

She shook her head. "There was me."

"I knew that. But I didn't want to do this to you. To do what I'm doing now; making you cry." He hugged her and rested his chin on her head. "I went away to be noble and came back just as selfish as I've always been. I didn't want your pity. I couldn't stand that, Jenna."

She chuckled into his neck. "Don't worry. I'm pitying myself more than you."

"So I decided to see if you loved me for who I was and not because of what will happen to me." He pulled away and touched his forehead to hers. "You didn't let me down. You don't have to love me, but you do. I've made it as a human being."

She smiled gently, all her previous anger dissipated. "I've always known you weren't an easy person to know. But I didn't realise how complicated you are."

He pulled her close again. "Right now I'm not complicated at all." His hand strayed down her back to stroke the curve of her thigh. He brought his lips close to her ear. "Let's go home."

~

Outside the bay window, the street was dark now. Cars lined the kerb and light from the street lamps glinted on chrome and metal. On the other side of the road, a door opened and a woman was silhouetted as she stooped to put an empty milk bottle on her step. The small chink of the glass was loud in the empty dark. Several doors further up, a cat was sniffing at a car tyre. A gust of wind rattled a crisp wrapper along the footpath to trap it in a drain.

Jenna was sitting on the floor of her sitting room, her back against the wall at one side of the bay window, her eyes above the level of the sill. In her hand was the wilted head of the daffodil. She had found it lying on the sofa. One petal had dipped in blood.

She had left Paul asleep, sprawled over the whole of the bed. Fitting in around him was physically wonderful but not the best way to sound sleep.

She flicked the limp flower in her fingers. Making love in the afternoon was rather different from drinking coffee in the coffee bar or studying in the library. Her world had moved; moved into a different plane, a new orbit. Every tree, every building, her home, her family, her friends, would always and forever be seen across the great gushing river of these days. Two nights ago she had stepped out from tradition, hesitation, principle. She had entered a new reality, a swirling vortex of freedom in which she had to find a new rudder, a new compass to navigate to a landfall which she did not wish to find.

It was too late to retreat. Much too late.

She dropped her head back and watched the cat stroll past the window. It sniffed a dandelion beside the lamp post and sneezed. It glanced round and saw Jenna at the window. For a moment its yellow stare fixed on her before it turned and padded across the street, tail flicking low.

In sleep, Paul looked fragile and vulnerable. Had he always had this air of transience? It was hard to tell, hard to remember without the bias of new knowledge. But was it ever possible to imagine Paul as an old man? He burned a trail through life, unconstrained and pulsating with vitality. Such a desire for life could not be sustained. It had to burn out.

In her imagination, the rain beat again on the roof of the old hut behind the manse as Paul looked bleakly through the dilapidated window at the rain sheeting across the field. It's not all right not to know, he had said. Not all right at all.

The door opened quietly and Paul came to her side. He had pulled on his black jeans. Above them his body was pale and smooth in the dusky light. Briefly he touched her head and then sat on the floor opposite her, back to the wall. He pulled up his knees and touched his bare feet to hers. She wriggled her toes against his and he smiled.

"Hungry?"

She patted her stomach. "Starving. But it's too late to go out. I'll raid the kitchen."

"What's that?" He nodded at her fingers.

She held up the daffodil. "A memory of last night. It's got your blood on it."

"Keep it. It'll be worth thousands when I'm dead."

She was silent for a moment, stroking the flower. "You said once it wasn't all right not to know. When did you know for certain?"

He rubbed his shoulder and left arm. "Christmas. I knew I would meet the doctor at the Butler's house and I didn't want to go. But you said I should go, so I did."

A car started up across the street and headlights lit up the columns of parked vehicles. The car swung out and swept light and shadow across the room before it straightened to roar crazily away.

"Don't you have a doctor here?"

"No."

"But how can you still be on the books of a doctor in London?"

He opened and closed the fingers of his left hand. "He's a friend."

"Is that who Toby is?"

He nodded. "He's a good guy." He stopped fiddling with his hand and picked at the wall beneath the window sill. "I refused to see him after they got the results of my tests back. He tried to talk to me but I didn't ..." he took a deep breath "... I didn't want to know. He wouldn't tell anyone else. He's an honourable doctor."

"But he told you at Christmas?"

He kneaded his upper arm again and tangled his toes with hers, watching but not really seeing them. "Do you remember when you were going to school? How hard it was to get up in the morning?" She nodded. " I remember it so well. I would think: I know I have to get up, but right now, I'm still in bed, warm and snug. Right now, in this instant of time, I'm not running for the bus, I'm not realising I forgot to do my Maths homework. I'd close my eyes tight and think: one more minute, even for one more minute, it's not happening. And it was worth it." He lifted his eyes to hers. "When Toby told me I wouldn't see thirty, I froze. Then I closed my eyes tight and I said: one more month, two more months. Right now, I'm alive. I'm not in pain. Right now, it's not happening." Swiftly his legs curled under him and he was beside her, hugging her to him desperately. "Jenna, Jenna. Now I'm all grown up and I want to stay awake, not go back to sleep."

Both his arms were round her and his face was buried in her hair. He murmured, "I can't do this alone. I can't." He kissed her hair. "And the worst of it is, I've found the best reason in the world for wanting to grow old. I want to grow old with you."

Locked together with him, Jenna realised that tonight he had opened all the doors; tonight she was at the centre, the very centre of his heart.

CHAPTER THIRTY-FOUR

THE SILVER AND emerald of the long drapes formed a graceful frame to the high, narrow windows. Seated behind the desk, Toby's neat figure was outlined against the light; he was leaning slightly forward, arms resting on the rich mahogany, hands clasped, and his gaze calm and neutral. Dianne slid into the leather armchair opposite him, one of two angled in front of the desk. She had known this room, this tall elegant building, for many years. As a child, she had marvelled at the high reaches of the ceiling and the curling, wandering flower mouldings round the lights and cornices. It was a room that, just like Toby himself, radiated wealth and care, ease and knowledge. Bad news and good news also. She held her bag across her knees and placed her feet together.

Toby inclined his head slightly. "Thank you for coming."

Dianne's chin rose a fraction. "Why didn't you call at the house? I would have seen you there."

"I would have been honoured. But alas, I have other people to see today also."

She caught his tone. "You're cross with me, aren't you?"

"That's irrelevant. I'm your doctor."

"So have you the results?"

Toby placed a hand flat on a folder beside him on the desk. "I have."

Her heart, already beating harder than usual, began to thunder.

"And?"

Toby clasped his hands again and regarded her levelly. "I was very surprised you asked for this. I thought you were sure."

"I was. I am. It's just ... routine. Isn't it?"

"No, it's not routine at all. Are you sure you want this, Dianne? Have you thought it though?"

"I asked for the test, didn't I?" Then she faltered. "I need to know. It's ..." She looked down and fingered the strap of her bag. "It's more that ..." she looked up "... I couldn't live with not knowing for the rest of my life."

Still holding her gaze, Toby reached across and slid the folder to him, flicked it open.

"Very well." He would know the contents of the file very well, but ran his fingers across lines which she could not read upside down. Two pigeons bickered on the window sill behind him. He kept his eyes downcast as he read. "The child – the foetus – was female. And the father was the man from whom the samples of hair were taken." His eyes swivelled up to her. "Luther Chevalier."

Almost white. One of the pigeons was almost white. It must be something to do with – genes. Toby's fingers were now folded beneath his chin, thumbs stroking his beard at the jaw line. She could not read his expression. She realised she was staring at him, gathered herself and stood.

"Thank you, Toby. I don't think there's anything else." The room seemed smaller, stuffier. She turned towards the door, her head light.

"Will you tell him?"

Without turning back, she asked, "Who?"

"Paul thinks you robbed him of his child. A much wanted child."

"He'll get over it."

She took a further step and was reaching for the door handle when Toby's hand gripped her shoulder and swung her round. "Tell him!"

Shocked at his sudden nearness and the change in his tone from clinical neutrality to a harsh insistence, she reacted angrily. "That's my decision! Maybe I'll tell him some day. When it doesn't matter any more."

Toby took a deep breath and visibly controlled his features. "It matters now. Speaking as a friend, I ask you to tell him."

"And what about Luther?" Dianne's eyes narrowed. "Why are you so worried about Paul?" Toby's eyes flickered momentarily. Dianne gave a sudden hoot of realisation. "You've still got a crush on him, haven't you?" She wagged a finger. "He wouldn't have you, would he? He told you to go to hell. But yes, he's a hard man to forget." She patted his cheek. He recoiled, his brows knitting into a silver line as she continued. "Lots of *women* have discovered that."

Toby walked back behind his desk and rested on his knuckles. "The decision is yours alone. I regret my lapse." His chin dipped. "Good day, Mrs Shepherd."

Dianne swung on her heel to leave. Just as she closed the door behind her, Toby's words slithered through the gap: "But now you have to live with knowing, all your life."

~

Jenna was in her dressing gown, rinsing breakfast dishes when the door bell rang. On the step was a stack of cartons with a pair of legs in ripped jeans beneath them. The legs walked in and all the cartons fell in an untidy heap to cover the floor of the hall.

"Max!"

He swept his hair from his eyes. "You wanted boxes? Found these in a skip at the back of the shop near me."

She didn't need them now, but she couldn't deflate his obvious pleasure in having found them. "Thanks. That's great. Did you carry them all the way here?"

"Yeah. Lucky it's not windy." He swung one tattered trainer over the other and leaned casually against the wall. "So how've you been? How's your brother?"

"OK ..."

Max glanced up to fix on something beyond her right shoulder. He pushed himself upright, mouth hanging open. Paul was standing at the bottom of the stairs, beaming at Max. He was dressed only in a towel which hung loosely on his hips, his hair wet and drops of water glistening on his naked chest. He waved a hand at Max brightly.

"Hi! Max, I believe? I'm Ignatius O'Malley." He dropped down the last stair in bare feet and delicately picked a path through the boxes to Max, arm out to shake his hand. "Pleased to meet you."

To Max's credit, he took the hand offered. "Ig ...?"

"...natius," beamed Paul. He turned to Jenna who was holding her breath. He wouldn't! He did. He whipped the towel from his waist and began to dry his hair as he strolled to the sitting room and paused in the doorway. "Hope there's plenty of water, old girl. Cormac's in the shower now. Knowing him, there'll be none left for Alexander." He faced the front door again and flung the towel round his neck cheerfully. Jenna couldn't look at Max. "But then," Paul went on, "Alex's still asleep. I don't blame him." One eye crinkled into a deep wink at Jenna. "Quite a night, eh?"

With that he swivelled his slim hips and shimmied into the sitting room.

Max retrieved his eyebrows. "Who ... what...?"

Jenna opened the street door wide, keeping her face straight with difficulty. "Ignatius O'Malley. Anyway, thanks for the boxes; they'll be most useful. Sorry I can't ask you in."

Max hopped down the steps. "Yeah. I can see you're busy." He bestowed a glance of admiration on her. "Does your Dad know about this?"

"Heavens no! It's a big secret."

Max nodded knowingly and scuffed slowly away.

Jenna leapt over the boxes and flung herself after Paul. "You menace!" she yelled.

He held up the towel by one edge, knuckles shaking, and pretended to cower behind it. She snatched at it wildly. He made a bolt past her for the door, his laughter deep and throaty as he wrapped the towel round himself on the run. There was the sound of empty cartons being kicked out of the way as he fled through the hall and a sudden yell as his bare foot hit the box full of books by the wall.

"Serves you right!" Jenna raced after him. His steps halted suddenly.

He was falling, folding, sinking, almost gracefully, slumped sideways against the wall. His legs crumpled and Jenna thrust out her arms in alarm. She was in time to ease him down amongst the tangle of cartons and save his head from the full force of the floor.

"Paul!" It was a call more than a scream, a cry from a depth of fright which had been hollowed in her silently, unknown, but awash with dread. His eyes were closed. She tossed boxes out of the way to lay him more comfortably. She grabbed his coat from the hooks on the wall and wrapped it round him. She put her own coat, with its fur trimming, gently under his head.

When his eyes flicked open, relief made her head light. "What the hell happened?" His voice was stronger than she expected.

"You fell. Or fainted or something. Don't move for a minute." He moved to push himself upright, but she held him back. "Stay still." The darkness of his hair against the cream fur was somehow memorable, a nugget of this moment preserved in textured colour.

He lay obediently, a puzzled frown between his brows. "I missed the bannister!" he said suddenly. He looked at her, amazed. "I missed the bannister. I reached for it and then ..." He frowned again. Jenna bent to thumb away the lines creased above his wide blue eyes. Beneath the coat he gripped his left arm, his eyes unfocused as his fingers traced the flesh. His gaze flew up to her again and she waited, still stroking his head, silent, watching the first drops of blood creep from his nostrils.

"My arm didn't go where I told it to."

Minutes later he stood up carefully and Jenna slipped the coat onto him. "OK now?" Her throat felt rusty, unused. In the pockets of the coat she found several tissues to soak up the blood which trickled from him. It stopped quickly this time. She wound her arms round him and tried not to feel the weakness in his arm as he gathered her in.

There was everything to say, and nothing.

It was just an accident. Maybe you tripped.

Yes, maybe.

You must have a bruised behind!

Wait till I try sitting down!

You were awful to Max.

Now I won't have the fun of letting you catch me.

There was the unspoken to speak.

It can't be yet. It can't be. We've had no time.

Frantic kisses: eyebrows, lips, ears; a tight, tight embrace as if there were one body and not two.

We're going to find a doctor today.

No!

Rocking, rocking, rocking.

I'll have to do more of the driving. But that's OK.

I'm a bad passenger.

We'll fall out.

Making up'll be fun.

We're going to find a doctor today.

No!

Yes!

Then the last, dragged out from its deep, long-bolted dungeon.

Will you be with me when I tell my mother?

CHAPTER THIRTY-FIVE

UP IN A lift, along a grey corridor, past wide lobbies with wheelchairs and patients' trolleys, past notices telling everyone to wash their hands and how to phone the Samaritans, in a small consultant's room with a washbasin, boxes of latex gloves on the wall and a couch covered with paper from a roll at one end, Jenna heard with her own ears confirmation of what Paul had told her.

To please her ("That's another first," said Jenna), Paul submitted to further tests. She heard words like 'ataxia' and 'dysmetria'; heard of remission and aggression. Then there were the words 'prognosis' and 'grave' and Paul shaking his head at every suggestion of treatment. When risks and limited benefits were explained, Jenna could only agree with him.

In the warm sunshine of an afternoon in May, they left the hospital gates and took a bus to the centre of the city. On a bench in the grounds of the City Hall, they ate some sandwiches and watched the buses snaking their way round to their forest of stops. People queued, or jogged after them, or tapped their feet and looked at their watches. The noise of traffic was incessant and the newspaper seller at the corner was already shouting, a bundle of the early edition of the *Belfast Telegraph* under his arm.

Several pigeons bobbed round the bench and Paul threw down a crust. A fight broke out and the pigeon with the crust was chased by three others who gave up when the crust was airborne in a clatter of wings over the statue of Queen Victoria.

Paul was being moody. This afternoon's appointment wasn't one to be happy after.

"Buses," he said.

"Cars," she replied. She was used to this.

He looked out across the crowds and up along Donegall Square.

"Shops."

"Children."

"School children."

"Homework."

His mouth twitched a little. "Maths!"

She groaned. "French!"

He looked round at the magnificent facade of the City Hall, the white stone, the pillars, the green dome. "Beautiful."

"Photograph."

"Luke."

"Luke photographed the City Hall?"

He nodded. "Many times. I gave him several projects to do on it."

"He's very cross about you."

"I know. He waved his crutch at me and said ..." he rumpled his hair to mimicked Luke "... 'Shit, Paul, that's not fair! Why aren't you mad?' "

"What did you say?"

"I said I *was* mad. It's just that it makes my head hurt and it hurts enough already."

An ambulance raced past, was held up by a white van, squeezed round it and blared through the traffic lights. Jenna thrust her hands into her pockets and frowned. "What's it all for, Paul? You and me."

He looked surprised. "What do you mean?"

"We've fallen in love big time, and now ..." she shrugged her shoulders.

"Am I supposed to know the answer to that?"

"Send me an e-mail from the after-life when you find out."

"Straight to your Dad's computer! His should be able to receive it."

How could they be funny? How could they make jokes and feed pigeons and look in shop windows and go home and decide what to have for tea? Knowledge lumped on her shoulders like a bag full of stones. The fact that his mother refused to believe it added to the burden. Nonsense, she had said. You always suffered from headaches. Take some aspirin.

Paul had been quiet for a long time after they had visited Hazel and come home with an apple tart and a chocolate cake. Then he told Jenna, "I think we should let my mother believe what she wants. In the end it'll be easier for her. We're alike and I understand her. She's reacting just the way I did. Leave her alone for now."

It was the middle of the night when he spoke. They did a lot of talking in the dark hours. The daytime was for living, seeing, doing, filling as much time as they could together, pulling back on time, straining against the passage of days and the weakness of flesh. But at night, lying wrapped up together, the soul was thin-skinned. There was a lifetime of sharing to be parcelled into those nights, those dwindling nights.

When she scolded him for not telling her of his illness because, if she had known, she would have given in to him earlier, he had snorted with derision.

"No, you wouldn't! You would have run away a lot further." He stroked his hand along her side. "Anyway, once I accepted it myself, I tried to put you out of my mind. It didn't work."

There were times when he went away on his own for there were thoughts that even she could not help him with – or rather, thoughts that he spared her. Then she worried as he became more unsteady and could not drive any more. Yet she knew that it was good and necessary for him to be alone. Despite their love and closeness, Paul Shepherd was a man owned by no-one.

At times also, she had to be alone herself, to take deep ragged breaths of fury, to rage, to walk and walk and walk and wonder how she would get through this. *It's all right for him, the bastard! I'm going to be still here with a whole life to live round the gaping void of his absence.* And then the roaring anger would fade as she realised that that was how her life would have been anyway, barren and cold, if he had not come to her that night. It was better, inexpressibly better, to have known him and loved him, to have become soft and vulnerable because of him. To have delighted in a conjunction of physical, mental and emotional joy was to hold forever a strength in the heart.

Donald and Cora's inevitable disapproval was overlaid by shock and distress at what awaited Paul. Jenna talked to her father for a whole afternoon, holding nothing back, dissecting goodness and badness, trying to put into words that made sense how she was torn apart by joy and grief, made ragged by the twin claws of love and fear.

Now he knew what had tormented her mind when she sat in his study before, when they had talked about boundaries and dragons and when she had refused to promise that she would remain his little girl. He gave her no answers and she respected him more for that than if he had uttered trite phrases and glib assurances. In the end, there was a trace of salt on his own cheek when he hugged her.

"Life's not fair, young lady. Life's not fair. And it's not black and white either." He sighed. "Some people think it is, but they're the people who haven't lived."

Jenna rested her head on his shoulder and absorbed the scent of her father, a scent which had been so familiar to her all her life. "They've stayed in the cage," she replied.

"Yes, they're safe ..."

"But bored!" She raised her head to smile.

Cora was more forthright. She whisked a feather duster round the living room. "What do you mean – he won't take treatment? Of course he'll take treatment. Lasers or surgery or something."

"It's dangerous, Mum, and wouldn't help much ..."

Cora lifted a wooden elephant, a present from a missionary on furlough from Zambia, and swatted it with the duster. "So a brain tumour isn't dangerous? What's the man thinking of? He needs to think of you, Jenna." She pummelled a cushion and then sat down abruptly, the feather duster dangling from her hand. "Really! My son has been nearly killed, my daughter has given up university in the middle of her course. She's living with a married man, and ..." she waved the feather duster "... she's not making him get himself cured." Jenna took a breath to speak, but Cora's breath was quicker. "You know what Mrs McCormick said to me the other day? She said it must be lovely living in a manse. You're all so good; it must be so calm." She rolled her eyes.

"Nobody makes Paul do anything. And I think you're losing your duster,"

Cora lifted it. Half of it was missing and Jenna's cat was shaking feathers from her whiskers.

Luke had an exam in the afternoon and Donald went to collect him. Luke was still finding his leg stiff and he tired easily. He was pleased to see Paul. After tea, Donald and Paul went for a walk alone. Jenna didn't know which of them had suggested it; it just seemed to happen. She never knew what they talked about. All Paul would ever say later was, "I like your Dad."

Then he and Luke began to talk photography and Paul's cameras were retrieved from the car. Heads together, they sat on the floor of the lounge and discussed portrait photography. Paul explained soft boxes and umbrellas and how to disguise the subject's double chin, or big nose.

"But the very best light to use is natural light," he said. "If you can, place your subject outside, or in light from a window."

Luke put a table lamp on the floor and crawled round Paul, looked through the viewfinder, moved the lamp, looked again, shuffled further, his long legs hitting the television stand. Only Jenna noticed Paul's slightly slower movements, his constant checking of his left arm, flexing of his fingers.

Luke rocked back on his heels and set the camera down. "Yeah, I see what you mean." He pulled at the carpet, mussing it, quiet. His Adam's apple worked in his throat.

Paul punched him on the shoulder nearly overbalancing him. "Cheer up! Did I tell you I'm leaving you all my cameras and stuff?"

Luke scrambled to his feet, his hands clenched by his sides. "Shit, Paul! Won't you even try?"

Then he fled from the room. Cora was appalled. "I'm so sorry, Paul ..."

Paul raised a finger and silenced her. I wish that worked for everyone, thought Jenna. How does he do it? Supporting himself on a chair, he pulled himself to his feet. "He needs an explanation."

He touched Jenna on the shoulder as he passed her to follow Luke. It was a habit she loved. He touched her at every opportunity, lightly, fleetingly, a tactile symbol of his passionate allegiance.

They stayed the night. Sleeping arrangements were never discussed. What her parents did not mention, they did not have to confront. Jenna was the last to bed and she stood in the hall in the soft light from the lamp above the family portrait. It seemed like a lifetime ago. She barely recognised herself now. That was a different girl. Her long untrimmed hair spilled across her shoulders. Her hand rested casually on her father's shoulder where Paul had asked her to put it, her nails pink with the varnish which Dianne had applied. That was a portrait of Missy. This afternoon her father had called her 'young lady'. She doubted that his old name for her would ever cross his lips again.

Just at that moment, she felt a strange sensation. There was a settling inside her, a faint feeling that something had subtly, minutely changed. She felt a tingling in her nipples, a new sensitivity. Her hands cupped her breasts and her lips curved into a woman's smile. She had wondered; now she knew. There was still time to wait, just to be sure, before she told Paul.

~

The middle-aged man who strode through baggage reclaim was ruler-straight and distinguished. His small leather case was of the highest quality as, it was obvious, was he. In no doubt that this was Toby, Jenna moved to greet him. He shook her hand formally and his glance slipped to her still-flat stomach before returning to her face.

"You are as lovely as he said you were. You are well?"

"Paul told you?"

His beard dipped. "Indeed, my dear. With great excitement. How is he?"

"It's ... things are moving a bit faster now." She swallowed and Toby put his arm round her back as they crossed to the car park. "He wanted to come, but he was so sound asleep I couldn't bear to try to bring him round. I left him a note in case he wakes."

"Has he pain?"

"Not as much as we feared. And he has something for it if he needs it. He's mostly sleepy and a bit unsteady."

Toby nodded and did not speak again as Jenna slipped Paul's car into the rush hour traffic. Having to do all the driving now was just one of many things that made life stressful. When they arrived, Paul was in the hallway leaning on the door frame. He was irritated.

"I wanted to *go*, damn it, Jenna!" He hurled something that landed behind the telephone on its shelf. It was the note she had left on the table beside him as he slept on the sofa, his head pillowed on the black and red cushion.

"Charming as ever, I see." Toby appeared behind Jenna, his voice calm and tinged with humour. He held out his hand and Paul took it, still grumpy. Jenna was hanging her coat on a peg when Toby let Paul's hand slip and pulled him into a bear hug, slapping his back. When he released him, Toby's eyes were moist.

Jenna made a snack while the two men talked. Toby wanted to know everything that had been said at his most recent hospital visits. Paul told him sporadically, sometimes searching for words as if he couldn't quite pick the correct ones. Jenna wasn't hungry and was content to sit in a corner of the sofa listening, putting in her own comments now and then. Paul occupied 'her' chair and Toby seemed relaxed at the other end of the sofa. *What does Toby see, I wonder?* Paul was thinner, the beautiful planes of his face attenuated and angular, his natural pallor now an unrelieved white. But his eyes were still so blue, so very blue. They still danced with life and love when he was awake, as they sparkled now, his irritation easing away in the pleasure of seeing an old friend.

Finally there was no more to tell. Toby, legs neatly crossed, became quieter, thinking, distracted. Jenna filled the silence by offering sandwiches, another drink. Paul's eyes had closed again and his face was still in the light of the early summer evening outside.

"You are very brave, Jenna."

She shook her head. "No I'm not. I love him. That's all."

He nodded. "That is indeed all." He lifted his bag from the floor and snapped it open. "I would like to do a few checks myself, if he will allow it. Just minor, you understand."

"Do you even go on holiday with your stethoscope, you old

quack?" Paul's voice made them both swing round. His eyes were open again. "Come on then. You can't do me any more harm."

Later, when he snapped his bag shut again and sat, Toby seemed uneasy.

"If you want to say something, say it," said Paul, irritation creeping into his voice again.

"You haven't asked about Dianne."

Paul's eyebrows rose. "Why should I?"

Toby sat forward and spread his hands. "Why indeed?" His stance was uncharacteristically tense. Jenna watched him, alert. There was something going to be said. "She is well again. But ..." Toby stood up suddenly and spoke quickly, firmly. "I have decided to tell you something which I should not tell you because it is not my position to do so."

Paul frowned. "About Dianne?"

"About the abortion." Jenna's eyes flew to Paul. *Don't upset him please!* His fingers tensed on the arms of the chair. Toby continued, resolute. "Despite all her outward confidence, she wasn't a hundred per cent sure of the father of the baby. She was fairly sure but not totally. Unknown to anyone, she asked for tests to be performed on the foetus." He pointed to Jenna. "Paul, this young lady is the mother of your first child. Dianne's was not yours."

Jenna's hand flew to her mouth in shock. Then she dropped to the floor and slid to Paul's side. His head had gone back, loose against the chair, his eyes shut tight, his breathing fast. Jenna gripped his hand and dropped her forehead to his arm. Toby sat down again quietly, leaving them in their silence. When Paul pulled himself forwards, Jenna looked up into his eyes. There was nothing more to say. Except one thing.

"Luther's?"

Toby shook his head. "Already I have spoken where I should not. And only for your sake. I can say no more. Dianne said she hadn't told you and I could not live with that." He coughed. "As a friend."

It was past eleven o'clock that night when Jenna pulled the car into the pavement in a leafy avenue in south Belfast. All the way across the city, Toby had spoken of the beautiful buildings, the new developments, the flurry of night life. Not by one word did he refer to having said goodbye to Paul. Jenna had left them alone. She had sensed that she should give them that.

This was the home of an old friend with whom Toby had trained many years ago and where he was staying the night. The street lighting rippled in the swaying shadows of cherry trees, in full leaf now, their flowers long shed. Across the road, a woman patiently held a slack lead as her poodle lifted its leg against a tree.

Toby made no move to open the door. Jenna turned off the engine.

"Thanks for coming. It means a lot to Paul."

Toby gave a thin smile. "Believe me, my dear, it means a lot more to me than it does to him." He shrugged. "But that was always the way." He looked through the gate at the villa set in large grounds and began to talk quietly as if to himself. Wrought iron lamps flanked the front door and tendrils of trailing plants hung from baskets on the wall. "And now I have to go in there and be polite and happy and make conversation. Even though I have just ..." He stopped suddenly and Jenna heard the soft smother of a sob.

She put a hand on his arm. "Thank you for what you told us tonight. It was a big decision for you."

Toby put his hand on hers where it lay, and faced her, controlled again. "Jenna, I must tell you. I said you were brave and you must continue to be." He squeezed her fingers. "Paul will not see the baby."

Jenna didn't flinch. "I know."

"I don't know how this ... will end. It's impossible to know."

He met her eyes deliberately. "It could be sudden." This time she said nothing and he went on, relentless. "If there is anything you both would like to do, anywhere you would like to go together, then ..." he squeezed her fingers again "... I think you should do it soon."

"OK." Her voice was a hoarse whisper.

Toby flung open the car door and stepped out. She got out herself to say goodbye. They stood on the footpath facing each other awkwardly. She held out her hand. "Thank you," she said again.

He ignored the hand and hugged her. "Take care of yourself, my dear. That's important. Keep in touch with me." He coughed. "You know?"

She pulled away and nodded. A fresh breeze blew a strand of hair across her mouth. "Of course."

He looked down at his feet. A soft summer rain was beginning to glitter on his hair. "I would like to see the baby, if I may?"

She smiled a reassurance. This was not a man who was used to making requests. "I hope you won't mind being called 'uncle'."

His beard dipped. "That would give me the greatest pleasure." He turned to the gate. "Now I mustn't keep you. This rain is getting heavier." He walked through the gate and his feet crunched on gravel. He slowed, stopped. The gravel slewed under his heel as he pivoted. The lamps by the front door cast a nimbus of light round his head and left his face in deep shadow. His bag hung from one hand and his spine was straight, shoulders square. His words came out of darkness.

"I love him too, you see."

CHAPTER THIRTY-SIX

PAUL TURNED HIS head and pressed his ear to Jenna's bare stomach. She stood in the bedroom and Paul knelt on the floor in front of her, arms round her and eyes closed. Jenna bent over his black head and ruffled his hair, smiling gently. Her hand dropped to rest lightly on his shoulder.

"It's too soon to feel anything, you idiot."

"Your tired, my darling. Why couldn't the old fraud have taken a taxi?"

"That wouldn't have been hospitable! The man flew over just to see you."

He turned his head again to kiss her skin, run his lips across from hip to hip. "Your skin's so soft." He put his hand on her, below her navel. "I think there's a slight bump. There is! Put your hand there."

She chuckled. "It's my body. I know there's a slight bump."

"Toby flew over to see an old friend from way back. He just came here to see me on the way."

Gently she detached herself and sat on the bed. "If you say so." She took his hand to help him up beside her. "How are you feeling?"

He leaned on her mischievously until she fell over sideways and he fell in a heap, half on top of her. "Not too bad." He growled in her ear and bit it. "Good enough anyway."

She giggled, delighted, and stretched in delicious anticipation.

In the darkness, she cuddled close within his arm. "You asked me once if it was my heart or my pride that was hurt." She raised her head from his chest to look down at him. "Remember?"

"Very well. You were in the pink dress that tore on a thorn."

"It was my pride then." She settled her head on him again and reached across his body to find his hand and pull it to her lips. "This time, my heart hurts. You knew the difference then. I know it now."

He turned over and lay face to face with her. "You mustn't be unhappy. You must move on. We've talked about this so often. I can't bear you to be unhappy. You must get over me, for yourself and for the baby."

She extended a finger from under the covers and brushed his nose. "Don't be daft, Paul. Tell a dog not to bark; tell a fish not to swim."

He fondled her hair, twining it round his fingers. "I told you something else that night. Reach for the moon and the stars and the sun. I want you to do that still. Do it for both of you."

She raised herself on one elbow. "But you *are* the moon and the stars and the sun for me. I've grasped them all already."

He rolled onto his back and took her face between his hands. "And you are my first and last, the one I have needed and wanted and loved. The one who gave me such a passion for life that I hunted you down and I want more than anything to stay with you."

There were tears tracing her cheeks now, funnelling down along his fingers. He pulled her down so that she lay on top of him, warmed by the mounds and hollows of his body. His arms round her gave her a little shake.

"Listen to me, Jenna. There are more moons and stars in the universe than we have known. You'll find more. I know you will."

She rolled to lie beside him again. In the dark she felt her teddy bear fall sideways against the wall where he had been propped.

His voice thickened. "You'll tell him – or her – about me, won't you? Don't forget me."

"As long as I'm alive, and your child is alive, and his children after him."

They were quiet then for some time and Jenna thought he slept. Indeed he might have, for he slipped in and out of sleep at random now. Eventually he stirred and his hand smoothed across her waist.

"Remember what you told me about moments? When we were in the old hut. The time you jumped the fence."

"I do. You were so odd."

"You told me time is only a succession of moments. Jenna, are you really listening to me?"

"Yes."

"I'll always be only moments from you. Do you hear me?" She nodded against his neck, unable to speak. "I will always be only moments from you," he repeated firmly. He settled her more comfortably against him and his chest rose and fell beneath her fingers.

Then he spoke again softly, gently. "I think it's time to go to Rossnowlagh again."

~

The beach was a vibrating rainbow of colour set on sand of summer gold. Where they had walked in solitude seven months before was, this early evening, a bright canvas of squealing children, bouncing beach balls, sprinting young people and precarious sandcastles. The roar of the surf was muted behind the motor of the ice-cream van; the tide had receded to the furthest extent of its ebb and the silver lines of the breakers were far away.

Jenna threaded her arm through Paul's and they walked slowly down the path to the sand. The salty tang of the wide shore filled their nostrils again and permeated the folds of their clothes. Today there was no need for coats. They threaded with care between the wind breaks and beach towels, the piles of clothes, picnic baskets and yellow and green striped folding chairs. One mother peeled a wet swimsuit off her little daughter and rubbed her vigorously. The child chattered and danced. A short-legged white terrier with a black spot over one eye hurtled past, paws cutting deep and tossing crumbs of sand.

The ice-cream van was leaving and the last person in the queue was walking away licking his ice-cream. Paul and Jenna sat on one of the huge boulders.

"I don't think this is the place we sat on New Year's Day," said Jenna, looking further along the beach.

He shook his head. "No, that's along there a bit."

There was something about the way he was holding himself, the way his eyes moved.

"Are you feeling dizzy?"

"Just a bit." He turned his head to her. "Thank you, Jenna."

She took his hand. "What for?"

"Being with me all this time. Putting up with me. Forgiving me for what I've done to you."

She laughed gently and patted her stomach. "Specially this."

He bent to lick her nose playfully. "We both had fun doing that. You taste salty."

The beach was emptying gradually and they sat together watching the families packing up and heading home. A breath of salt wind brushed their skin as the evening wore on. Paul seemed lost in thought. Then he moved slightly and spoke.

"I'd like to feel the sand again. On my feet."

His fingers didn't work as well as they once had so Jenna helped him remove his shoes. When his feet were bare he dug his toes into the sand and scuffed it about in pleasure. He had had to put down his cameras for good some time ago but Jenna had her small digital camera with her. She backed away from him, raising it.

"Smile!"

He broke into such a smile that her heart lifted as she took the picture. It was one of his broad, lopsided smiles that crinkled his nose and lifted his beautiful mouth into a curve that raised the sparse flesh on his cheekbones. Feeling relieved, she gazed along the yellow beach and breathed in deeply.

"I'd like to go for a run," she said. "Would you mind?"

"Go for it, baby! I'll enjoy the sight. Leave your camera with me."

With a bounce of delight she sprinted away, running, running, running, leaping over sandcastles abandoned to the sea. Running, running, running over clumps of seaweed, patches of shells, three jellyfish. On and on she ran until, panting, she slowed to long, loping strides and turned in a long arc. She stopped to get her breath and saw that she had run farther than she realised. Her breasts tingled and she spoke to the tiny baby inside her.

"I had to do that before you turn me into a whale!"

She searched the edge of the line of boulders for Paul. When she spotted him he was a tiny figure far away, so far away from her. Terror hit her with the suddenness of a boxer's punch. Last time they had come here he had made her confess to being scared, to being a maker of footprints, a maker of nothing. She dropped to her heels and covered her face with her hands. *Will I go back to that? I am so besotted with him will I crumble when he leaves me? Can I face this? Can I?* How many times had that question been asked already? She dropped her hands and sought him out again. *I have to. I must.* She crouched until the pit of her stomach was calm again.

As she trotted close to him she could see he was still pressing his feet into the sand which he had loosened with his toes. He looked up to smile. His eyes were still so bright she could see the blue of them even at this distance. They were still moving slightly oddly; there was just something about his gaze which she could not quite identify.

"That was Olympian!" he declared. "Feel good?"

She fingered her hair to straighten it. "Wonderful. Soon I won't be able to do that." She looked at the sky. "It's getting cooler. Maybe we should go in."

He held out a hand and she took it, drew into his side as he spoke. "Jenna, have we said all we need to say to each other?"

"What do you mean?"

"I don't want you to find that there are things you wished you'd said. And I don't want to leave anything out that I want to say to you."

She thought. Finally she shook her head. "We've done a lot of talking. I can't answer for you, but I think you've endured everything I have to say."

He drew her into an embrace. "Good. For it will be a long time apart, but still it will be only moments."

Her chin wobbled as she tried to smile for him. "I think that must be the stupidest thing I've ever said."

He tilted his head and mused for a moment. "Nope. I don't think it's the stupidest. There are a few other candidates for that."

She punched him gently. "You always were a charmer!"

When she helped him up to walk slowly to the hotel she looked back at the place where they had been sitting and saw the two firm prints he had left in the sand.

Their room was large, mulberry and green on the bedspread and curtains. There was a bay window which overlooked the sea. The beach was close below them, just beyond a short apron of grass. Paul stood propped against the edge of the window and Jenna leaned against him as he circled her with his arms and pulled her back against his body. Together they looked out at the tide swirling closer through the closing dusk, but still some distance away.

"I don't want to get any worse, Jenna," he whispered. "It's not fair on you."

She gave a little snort. "Me? It's not too great for you either." She turned in his arms to face him. "We'll manage. A day at a time. That's the pact we made, remember. Besides, I love you."

She always remembered the intensity with which he gazed at her then. His eyes picked up a shimmer of light as his mouth came down on hers. In that window alcove above the sea, Jenna abandoned herself to an abundance, an overflowing of love and care which streamed from him in a tide which was as ceaseless as that beyond the window. His arms strained to find their old strength and to mould her to him; his mouth and fingers traced the contours of her face as if he had not already imprinted them on his mind. She responded with all her heart and yet this was love, not passion. They were burning a brand on time and space, saying we are here, together, now; whatever has passed, whatever is to come, we are here, together, now. It was a declaration of all that they meant to each other, all that they had found in each other, and a lament for all that they would lose.

Paul woke in the middle of the night, feeling drugged. His head hurt as he raised himself to look down at Jenna who was sleeping on her back beside him. She was getting more beautiful every day. Her skin glowed, her hair shone and her face was filling out a little, giving her the contours of a new maturity. Her night gown was rumpled round her and he moved it aside across her stomach. Despite the pain in his head he bent slowly to kiss the soft skin above the slight swell of her womb.

"I love you, my son," he whispered, his voice hoarse and fading. "Be good. Make up for your bad old Dad."

He did not know how he knew it was a boy. The knowledge was simply there. Jenna stirred and turned onto her side. A tiny smile flitted across her lips and vanished. She must be dreaming. He tried to whisper something to her too but his voice would not work again. He had said his last words.

Carefully he swung round and dropped his feet to the floor. He waited with his eyes closed while the pulse of nausea stopped beating. Something was draining from him; he could feel it on his skin, seeping silently from deep inside, a falling away.

He held his robe round him, unable to put his arms into the sleeves. By leaning along the end of the bed, he made his way through the near dark to the bay window. He was so tired, so tired. He sank into the soft chair which faced out to sea and propped his head against the wing of it. He could see the stars. That was good. He wanted to see the stars. Below them the sea was very near the top of the shore. He could not hear the roar of the breakers but he could see them, line after line, crashing into tossed braids of white foam which cut across the night.

Swirl after swirl of lace edged across the beach, closer and closer, creeping inexorably towards the footprints he had planted firmly and deliberately in the sand. Calmly he watched the sea coming to erase them until sight faded from his eyes.

A softness of peace fell in feathered folds across him, a peace more certain than his loneliness or fear had ever been. All pain had gone and he felt light, so light ...

It's all right, Jenna.

It's going to be OK.

You're going to be OK.

I love you.

EPILOGUE

JENNA WALKED BAREFOOT along the sand. They were not staying in the hotel overlooking the sea. Even after two years that would have been too much.

Ahead of her, glimpsed through the crowd of chairs and children, dogs and rugs and buckets and spades, was the mixture of people that she called family. Luke was home for the university holidays and walked with a slight limp which he would never lose. Outer Mongolia would wait for a year or two. Donald bent to take a ball from a passing labrador and throw it. The dog bounced after it, tail whipped aloft in excitement.

Jenna smiled to see her father so relaxed. He was taking more time to himself now, slowing up and enjoying his family. She wished he might consider retirement soon, although that was perhaps too much to hope.

Cora was sitting in a deck chair patterned with bright orange flowers, holding the pages of a magazine against the ruffling of the sea breeze. Jenna knew that magazine. It was the one which had carried pictures of the London wedding of Miss Dianne Butler and Mr Luther Chevalier. The pictures had been taken in the opulent surroundings of their exclusive art gallery. It was such a happy occasion for Miss Butler, after the tragic and untimely death of her first husband.

Jenna was passing the hotel now, high on the shoreline. She sought out the window of the room where dawn light had silvered Paul's body. She had stumbled to her knees to hold his still-warm hand and to realise that the moments, the long march of moments, had begun while she was unaware.

She had been furious with him for that. Her grief had been fierce, as strong as the instant love for their son which had filled her like a wind thundering from a deep valley the moment he was put into her exhausted arms. She had traced his tiny puckered lip, from one corner, up over the first curve of the bow, down into the dip, up again over the swell of the other curve until her finger came to rest lightly at the other corner where it tucked into the swell of his plump little cheek. His father had bequeathed his own beautiful mouth to his son and the sight of it was a tug at his mother's heart every day.

Hazel was helping to build a huge sandcastle some distance beyond Cora. Hazel had grown old; the sum of grief and years had creased her skin at last. Her journey had mirrored Paul's. From denial she had travelled through anger and fear and then an acceptance which had drained her energy and left her weak. Because of this, Jenna formed a bond with her. The two women, united by an inexpressible loss, found expression in the silent communion of mutual pain.

The only one missing was Adam; Uncle Adam, who could not get the day off. He was still single, older and wiser. Jenna had made her peace with him and hoped that he would be a good uncle.

The excited chatter of a small child was loud as she approached. Toddling from behind the sandcastle came a small body, shimmering with clinging sand. He was holding out something in his hand and was bursting to explain in the new wonder of words. "Mummy, Mummy! Daddy shell! Daddy shell!"

He reached up sandy fingers and she took the shell. It was a razor shell, just like the one he had known all his short life.

"We'll take this one home, shall we? We can put it beside

Daddy's shell."

The razor shell sat on the mantelpiece beside the photograph of Paul which she had taken at this spot, when he was only hours from death. Paul must have known that and had deliberately made sure that the last picture she would have of him was a happy one.

She lifted her son and smoothed his hair. It was very fair, although already it was beginning to darken. He would probably grow to be as dark as his father.

But where are you now, Paul? How could you just leave me like this? Without a sign, without anything? I'm cross with you!

And then he was there. Her eyes widened at the chimera by the edge of the sea, feet apart and hands on hips, just out of reach of the nearest wave, teasing her. His long coat was battered by the wind, his face was alive and dancing in the light of the sea, the foam of the breakers crashing behind him.

Her little boy went still, looking where she was looking. Then it was over, gone. The memory that had nestled in her brain for so long had welled up to comfort her; that was all. Then she became aware of the child's face close to hers as he leaned back in her arms to look at her. His eyes were puzzled, a little frown between them.

With a sudden jerk he swung round and pointed to the sea. "Daddy?" he asked.

Her breath caught. "Did you see Daddy?"

He turned back to her and nodded, a slow movement of certainty. Then he was wriggling again. "Down! Down!"

She set him on his feet and he scampered to his granny squealing that he wanted to knock down the castle now. Jenna sat on the boulder and bent her head. A tiny sand beetle struggled across a shred of seaweed.

Sunshine swelled across her and warmed her like the touch of hands upon her head. In the sand at her feet there was a scuffling of small footprints where her child had jumped around, excited, in the place where Paul had left his own last mark.

Her spirit surged into life. She stretched her arms like wings unfurling from a chrysalis. She had known the love that puts strength in the heart. That would never leave her, but it was a flare to light the years ahead, not a candle to throw shadows in a cage. He had been right, so right. He was gone now, but she was ready for the future, a mature woman who had much to give, worlds to find and boundaries to leap.

Did she wish none of it had happened? That she had turned this way instead of that way?

No. A hundred times No.

Her son danced round the sandcastle squealing in glee: dancing, running, jumping, until the sand was a chaos of small footprints, this way and that, pointed right and left, deep and shallow, more and more and more of them until they were countless beneath his feet.

Author's note

Very many of the places which are described in *Maker of Footprints* are real places which I know well. There are some pictures of these locations on the book's page on the publisher's web site – www.ploverfiction.com.

I am particularly fond of Rossnowlagh, which is a beautiful strand on the west coast of Donegal, facing Donegal Bay and the Atlantic Ocean. I spent many happy days there as a child and have revisited often in adulthood. It has changed over the years and one of the most significant developments has been the growth of the local hotel, The Sand House (www.sandhousedonegal.com), the hotel of the narrative. I cannot recommend it highly enough. Most of the rooms, like Paul and Jenna's, have a wonderful view over Donegal Bay; its staff are friendly and the food is delicious.

The bench where Paul and Jenna sat to have one of their most significant exchanges is at the Loughshore Park near the University of Ulster at Jordanstown. I can even show you a picture of the raised flowerbed which has some feline significance in the story.

The park with the ducks is Ward Park in Bangor, Co Down. It is wonderful for a relaxing walk on a summer day.

Gortin Glen, one of Paul Shepherd's favourite places, is near the village of Gortin, not far from Omagh in Co Tyrone.

The City Hall in Belfast is a most impressive building, completed in 1906, and constructed with Portland stone. At the time of writing, the building is closed for renovation, but tours of the interior will resume in 2009. The grounds remain open.

For Jenna's family home, I have drawn on my memories of the house I lived in as a teenager in Co Antrim, not far from an airport which was used during the war. Over the back fence, there were the remains of huts, much as I have described, though not exactly.

Do visit the web site to look at the photographs. There are others which I have not mentioned here and perhaps it will bring alive for you yet again the lives and loves of these people who have been, and still are, so very real to me.

Sheila Johnston, May 2008